The VILLAGE MIDWIFE

BOOKS BY TILLY TENNANT

THE VILLAGE NURSE SERIES
A Helping Hand for the Village Nurse
New Dreams for the Village Nurse
A Family Surprise for the Village Nurse

THE LIFEBOAT SISTERS SERIES
The Lifeboat Sisters
Second Chances for the Lifeboat Sisters
A Secret for the Lifeboat Sisters

AN UNFORGETTABLE CHRISTMAS SERIES
A Very Vintage Christmas
A Cosy Candlelit Christmas

FROM ITALY WITH LOVE SERIES
Rome is Where the Heart is
A Wedding in Italy

HONEYBOURNE SERIES
The Little Village Bakery
Christmas at the Little Village Bakery

STANDALONES
The Summer of Secrets
The Summer Getaway
The Christmas Wish

The Mill on Magnolia Lane
Hattie's Home for Broken Hearts
The Garden on Sparrow Street
The Break Up
The Waffle House on the Pier
Worth Waiting For
Cathy's Christmas Kitchen
Once Upon a Winter
The Spring of Second Chances
The Time of My Life
The Little Orchard on the Lane
The Hotel at Honeymoon Station
My Best Friend's Wedding
The Cafe at Marigold Marina
A Home at Cornflower Cottage
Christmas in Paris
Eden's Comfort Kitchen
The Little Island Flower Stall

TILLY TENNANT

The
VILLAGE
MIDWIFE

bookouture

Published by Bookouture in 2025

An imprint of Storyfire Ltd.
Carmelite House
50 Victoria Embankment
London EC4Y 0DZ

www.bookouture.com

The authorised representative in the EEA is Hachette Ireland
8 Castlecourt Centre
Dublin 15 D15 XTP3
Ireland
(email: info@hbgi.ie)

Copyright © Tilly Tennant, 2025

Tilly Tennant has asserted her right to be identified as the author of this work.

All rights reserved. No part of this publication may be reproduced, stored in any retrieval system, or transmitted, in any form or by any means, electronic, mechanical, photocopying, recording or otherwise, without the prior written permission of the publishers.

ISBN: 978-1-83618-621-2
eBook ISBN: 978-1-83618-620-5

This book is a work of fiction. Names, characters, businesses, organizations, places and events other than those clearly in the public domain, are either the product of the author's imagination or are used fictitiously. Any resemblance to actual persons, living or dead, events or locales is entirely coincidental.

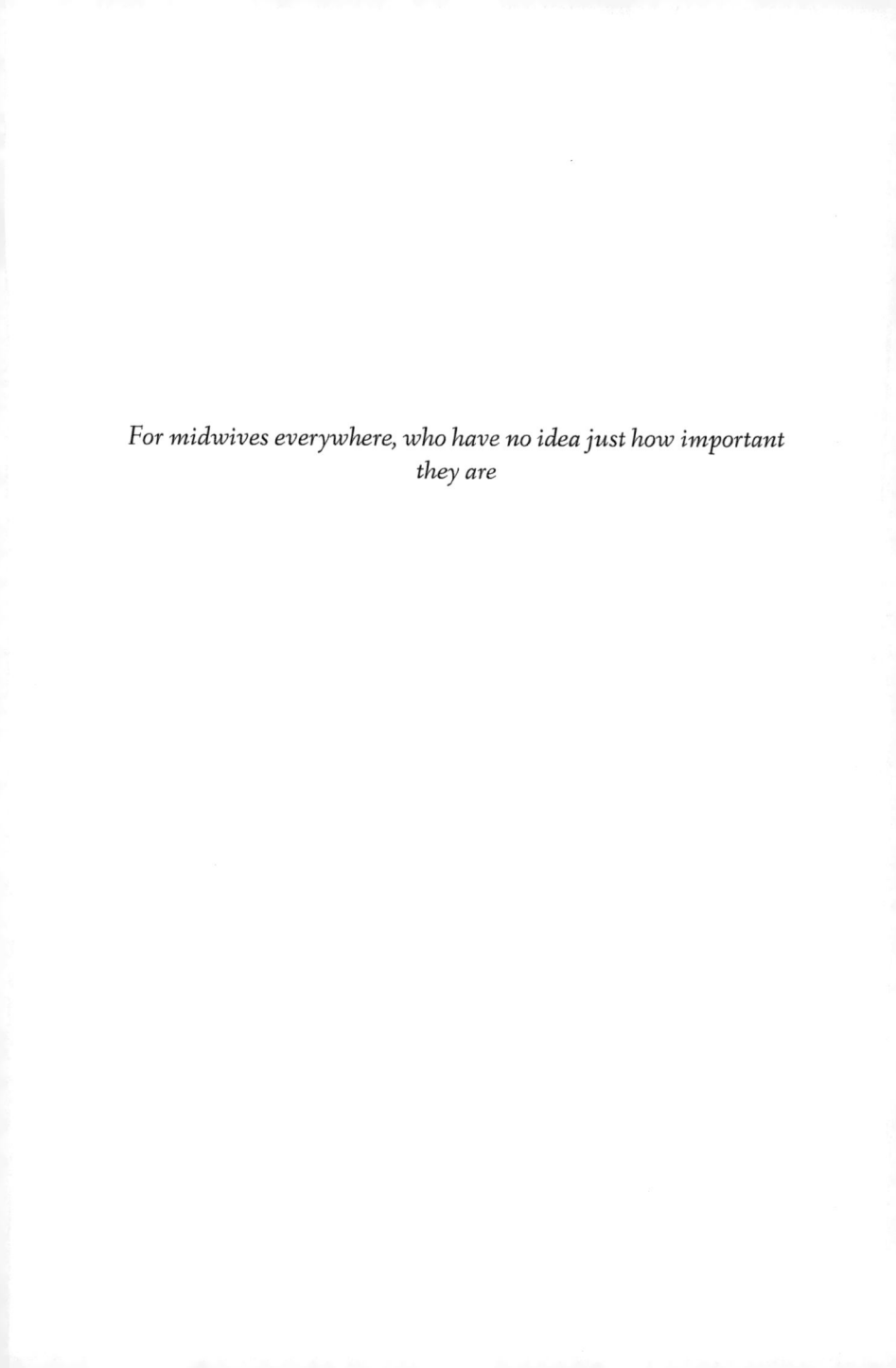

For midwives everywhere, who have no idea just how important they are

1

No day as a midwife was the same as any other. That was one of the reasons Zoe loved her job so much. That and the joyful reward of helping to bring new life into the world. Even when things didn't have a happy ending, she felt a deep sense of purpose from the comfort and advice she was able to give.

This damp, gloomy Manchester day started at 5 a.m., when one of the mums in her care, Molly, went into labour two weeks early. It was Molly's first, and she'd been nervous all along, repeatedly asking Zoe to be at the birth. Zoe couldn't always make it for various reasons to do with shift patterns and schedules, but she'd promised that she would be there if she could.

It was lucky that Zoe had already been awake when the text had come through, watching from her window as the neighbour's cat danced along a garden fence and then chased something into the hedge, as the rest of the street slept and the sky began to lighten.

Ritchie was dead to the world, mouth open as he drew in a noisy breath which made her smile, but then Zoe's husband had never struggled with sleeping. It had been a constant source of amusement and sometimes contention over the years of their marriage, but now she was glad. It was bad enough that she faced a working day running on coffee and adrenaline, but it didn't seem fair that he'd have to as well. They'd joked about inventing some kind of mega alarm to wake him when their baby arrived and it was his turn to do a night feed, and he'd agreed in all seriousness that she'd probably have to get him up, but she'd decided that made no sense. If she had to rouse him, then that meant she was already awake and so she might as well feed the baby anyway.

Since she'd become pregnant herself, the need to pee had started to disturb her far too often. And then, as soon as she was up, the morning sickness might set in, or if not that, something else would have her wide awake and struggling to drop back off.

It was Zoe's first pregnancy, and it was funny to think that even though she cared for other pregnant women every day as a career, her own experiences often took her by surprise. She knew very well how debilitating morning sickness could be, but to experience it first-hand had made her realise that even the mildest cases could be seriously disruptive for everyday life. She was well aware that being pregnant could affect everything from hair and skin to how often someone needed the toilet, but she still hadn't quite been prepared to see the changes in her own body. She knew about mood swings but had reflected with shock on her own reaction when husband Ritchie had forgotten to stack the dishwasher one evening earlier that week. It was all at once territory so familiar to her and yet a strange new world. Exciting, yes, but she felt she was on a learning curve as big as the expectant mothers she cared for, despite her training.

Now, the vast, glossy-walled corridors of the hospital were quiet as Zoe marched towards the labour suites. It was tiring, of course, even more so in her current state, but she still loved the building during the early hours. It was far more peaceful than during the day, with only the most crucial functions going on, barely any visitors, less noise from the city outside the windows, and many of the patients sleeping. Still, she could hear some commotion already coming from the room where Molly was being attended by a colleague. It was clear Molly was struggling.

'I didn't expect to see you here so soon,' Linda, the other on-call midwife said as Zoe stepped into the room.

'Yeah, I was already awake.'

'Ah...' Linda gave a knowing smile. 'And how are you feeling? Apart from not sleeping?'

'Not too bad. Knackered, of course,' Zoe replied briskly as she washed her hands at the sink. 'I just keep thinking, if I'm like this now, what am I going to be like in six months?' Without waiting for a reply, she took herself over to Molly and rubbed her hand with an encouraging smile. 'How are you doing?'

'I don't know,' Molly said weakly. 'Is it normal for it to hurt this much? I thought that was only when you're pushing.'

'There's no two labours the same,' Zoe said. 'I wish I could tell you it will get easier, but nobody can say that for sure. But keep thinking about how wonderful it will be in the end. And once it's all over, we quickly forget how bad it was.'

'Is that a big fat lie to make me feel better?' Molly grimaced.

'No,' Zoe replied gently. 'That much I can tell you with confidence. This time next week, all this pain will be a distant memory.'

Linda shot her a sceptical look.

'All right,' Zoe added with a slight smile. 'Maybe it will take a bit longer than a week. But I absolutely promise it'll be worth it.'

Linda gave her another look, and Zoe recognised this one too. Perhaps she shouldn't always be tempted to make promises like that, but when she was with a woman so obviously in need of encouragement and reassurance, she tended to resort to whatever promise would get her through. It didn't always end well, and she knew that. But she wasn't about to issue a caveat like that to a young woman who was going to struggle to make it through the next few hours as it was. If it helped to tell Molly that everything would be fine and that there would be a happy ending, then she was going to, no matter how much her colleague might disapprove.

By ten that evening, Molly had barely progressed. Zoe had called for consultant assistance an hour earlier than that, but even the midwifery team's combined efforts coupled with the doctor's considerable expertise hadn't managed to get the birth back on track.

'Heart rate's dropping,' Zoe said, glancing at the monitor. There was no reason to panic – she'd dealt with situations like this many times before. But later, when she thought back to that day, that moment stuck in her mind. Something pricked at her senses, some presentiment, something that told her the day wasn't going to end well. If she'd known then what she'd later discover, would she have done anything differently?

The consultant nodded. 'Right, let's get theatre prepped.' She turned to Molly, who was barely able to see straight after the barrage of different painkilling drugs she'd received. 'We want to make sure you and baby are safe, and things are getting difficult, so we're going to get you ready for a caesarean. OK?'

Molly gave a weak nod. Zoe reached to smooth her hair away from her face. She'd never given birth herself, but she'd seen enough of them to know that at this stage Molly would likely have agreed to anything. She'd want it over, to finally hold her baby in her arms and forget the ordeal that had been necessary to get them there.

In the back of her mind, even though Zoe felt sympathy for Molly, even though she'd seen first-hand how tough it could be, there was still a kick of excitement as she thought about the baby growing in her own belly – how, in a little over five months she'd be looking forward to holding her own child in her arms.

'Nearly there,' she said with an encouraging smile. 'The worst is over.'

'But I want to do it myself...' Molly whimpered and then started to sob with such obvious exhaustion there was hardly a sound in it. 'I feel like I've failed...'

'You've done all you can do,' Zoe said. 'You've been through more than any person ought to go through today – remember that. You've been amazing, but now it's time for us to do what we get paid for. It's only a little help to get you to the end.'

'Will it hurt?'

'Not a bit. It can't possibly hurt any more than anything else has today, right?'

Molly let her head fall back onto the pillow and closed her eyes. She'd been in and out of lucidity like this since they'd upped her painkillers. Zoe mopped her brow and then looked up to see a pair of porters race in to assist the team into theatre.

They rushed with a quiet, controlled sense of urgency down a set of corridors into a sterile space, and Zoe hurried to start the playlist Molly had wanted on when the baby was born. It was likely Molly wouldn't know if her request had been granted either way because she was far too woozy at this point, but Zoe had always felt it important that she did her best to fulfil the patient's wishes anyway.

It was Taylor Swift. Zoe only recognised the more famous songs, but she hummed along to those under her breath as the consultant directed her and she did her best to assist.

A short half hour later it was all over. There was a second of heavy silence, filled only by the sounds of Molly's birth tape playing at a low volume, and then a loud cry split the air.

Zoe went over to Molly and smiled. 'A girl. I'll weigh her and do a few quick checks, and then you can hold her while they fix you back up.'

Zoe took the baby gently to the scales. Naked, crying out and red raw, they always seemed so vulnerable at this point – as vulnerable as they'd ever be in their lives. They weren't cute and bonny, as they would become in a few days, but there was a fierce, primal sort of beauty that couldn't exactly be considered conventional. Some were instantly prettier than others, but as Zoe's colleague Helen always said, they needed time to cook before they had the sort of face a mother could love. It was such a funny way of putting it, it always made Zoe laugh, but she could see Helen's point, especially now as she laid Molly's newborn down to weigh her.

'Eight pounds on the nose,' she called over as she did a quick examination for any immediately obvious problems before taking her back over and laying her onto Molly's chest. 'There you go. Do you have a name yet?'

'Tarryn,' Molly said.

'That's lovely. We don't get many of those.'

'Can I have my phone?' Molly asked. 'I want to phone my boyfriend to tell him.'

'I'll be able to get it for you when we're back on the ward. Where is it he's working again?'

'Dubai. He has a flight home booked for next week. We thought that would be enough time for him to be here when I went into labour.'

'But baby Tarryn had other ideas, eh? That's how it goes. Will he be able to bring it forward?'

'Not sure, but my mum is coming to stay so I'll have help. It's just that I wanted him to be here.'

Zoe gave her a smile full of sympathy. More often than anyone realised, expectant mums didn't get what they wanted for their births, but most forgot all that sooner than they'd imagine.

'All done here.' The consultant smiled briskly at Molly. 'You can go and get some rest now. Congratulations.'

Zoe made Molly and her baby warm and comfortable for the trip back to the ward.

'Thank you so much,' Molly said. 'You're the best.'

Zoe beamed. 'I don't know about that. Just doing my job. The porters will take you down, and I'll be along shortly. Do you want a cup of tea? Something to eat, maybe? I can get the kitchens to do you some toast.'

'I'd love that, thanks.'

Zoe busied herself tying up loose ends and completing her notes while Molly was taken to the ward to rest.

'That was a sticky one,' the consultant said as she did the same. 'Good call to come and get me.'

'Thanks for coming down so fast.'

The consultant went on her way, and a few minutes later Zoe was done too. She'd come in early for Molly's sake, but her official shift wasn't due to finish for another hour. She knew she wouldn't leave on time, even then. Her husband complained about that all the time, but she'd got so used to it, she shrugged it off now. She'd arrive home and climb into bed, and Ritchie would wake and moan about how cold she was, but then he'd grab her feet and warm them before they both went to sleep.

She smiled and ran a hand over her belly as she walked down the corridor towards the ward to check on Molly. What kind of dad would Ritchie be? One of those silly ones, she always thought, that had no practical common sense to offer but would be great at taking their kid to the park and watching cartoons on the sofa with them. He'd be the fun parent and she'd be the caregiver, but she didn't mind that. As long as it worked and they gave their child the best start they could, that was all she could ask for.

2

As a row of distant hills rose up ahead, sunlight like a halo cresting the ridge, Zoe paused mid-sentence and stared. Lining either side of the narrow road were trees heavy with late summer greenery. A low mist swirled in the hollows of a distant field, sparkling in the morning light.

'It's quite a sight, isn't it?'

She turned to see a quiet smile on the face of her old friend, Ottilie, who was feeding the steering wheel through her hands as she navigated the tight turns of the road they were travelling.

'It's gorgeous!' Zoe breathed.

'I don't think I could ever get tired of a view like this. Whenever I have to leave Thimblebury and then I come back, the minute I see these hills, I know I'm home. And I don't just mean home as in this is where my house is. Oh no, it goes way deeper than that.' Ottilie threw the briefest glance Zoe's way before turning her attention back to the road. 'Want to know a secret?'

'What?'

'I came this way deliberately, hoping it would help to sway you. Is it working?'

'You mean there are less windy roads into the village?'

'Yes. But none as beautiful as this one.'

'If the only factor I had to consider was whether the view is amazing, I'd have already made up my mind.' Zoe turned to her again, tucking chin-length hair behind one ear, cheeks dimpling as she offered a smile. Not sombre, exactly, but not quite as joyous as the smiles she'd once felt able to wear with ease. It was a smile nonetheless, and they'd been in short supply since... in truth, she couldn't remember the last time she'd felt real happiness. Certainly not since she'd lost her baby. 'But it isn't.'

'Good place for a new start, though,' Ottilie said, her smile brighter and more certain. The smile of a woman who had already travelled the road Zoe was about to embark on and had reached the end of it changed for the better.

'I mean, it's lovely...'

'Wait until you see the village. It's small but perfect. Quiet, friendly... you might not know it when you first arrive, but trust me, it'll be exactly what you need.'

'You're certainly a good advert for life there.'

'That's what I was hoping for.'

Zoe pushed that smile across her face again as she turned her attention back to the road ahead. A silver thread trailed a section of a distant hill.

'Up there...' Ottilie took a moment to point to where Zoe was looking. 'A waterfall.'

'Wow! I didn't think you got those around here.'

'There are a few if you know where to look. Places where underground springs break through, I think, or so Heath tells me. There's one that feeds the most gorgeous swimming hole. I'm not sure we'll have time today otherwise I'd take you for a dip. When you're here next summer...'

'*If* I'm here, I'll look forward to it.'

'*If*. Of course. If you're here...'

Zoe glanced to see Ottilie grin, her freckled nose scrunching up. She wore her caramel hair longer now than Zoe remembered. She seemed easier, more comfortable in her own skin than Zoe recalled too. And while Zoe was grateful for her quiet, supportive optimism, she wasn't sure the move her old friend was trying to persuade her to take was the right one at all. On paper it seemed perfect, but paper wasn't real life, with real dilemmas and real complicating factors and real unknown variables. On paper was a simple cut-and-dried fix for her circumstances, but it would take a lot more than that to mend her broken heart.

It was a strange situation to find herself in, emotionally. Zoe hadn't seen much of Ottilie since her move to the Lake District, but back when they'd shared a flat as students, Ottilie had been the cautious one, and Zoe had been the life and soul of any party, the one who lived with abandon and never worried about what her future might hold. She'd almost needed Ottilie to ground her. Now, Ottilie was the optimistic one, living her best life, overcoming the pain of the tragedies that had marked it in recent years, and Zoe was filled with trepidation for what hers might throw at her next. Zoe's tragedy wasn't the same, and she couldn't imagine what Ottilie had gone through, but her own felt real and painful enough to her. She wasn't convinced that the move Ottilie was proposing was the right one, but Zoe could hardly argue with the evidence of a happy, settled and now visibly pregnant Ottilie sitting in the driver seat beside her.

'How are you feeling?' Zoe asked.

'Fine.'

'Not too tired? Managing OK?'

'You're not on duty now,' Ottilie said with a smile. 'There's no need to fuss; I'm doing well.'

'I'm asking as a friend, not as a midwife.'

'But I'm sure you must be thinking professionally, somewhere in the back of your mind. I know you – you can't help it. And I know I'm an ancient mum according to the received

'Early twenties. He has complex needs – learning difficulties, diabetes... I could go on. I suspect there are things that haven't been officially diagnosed too. He's a great kid, though, once you get past those issues and get to know him. You'll definitely have to meet Geoff and Magnus at the shop. They're our local power couple.'

Zoe smiled. 'I think you might have mentioned them once or twice. I'm looking forward to meeting them. Heath's grandma too.'

'God, be careful what you wish for!' Ottilie said with a laugh. 'Flo is an acquired taste!'

'I'm still looking forward to meeting her, if only to see if she lives up to her reputation.'

'I'm sure she will. I'm sure we'll barely get out of the car before she's upon us, like one of those cloaked things out of Harry Potter.'

'Cloaked thing? Like a wizard?'

'No... You know, the big flying hooded things that suck the joy out of everyone they touch.'

Zoe had to laugh properly this time. 'Dementors? God, this is so nice. It's good to have a normal silly conversation that doesn't involve soul-searching, or blame, or reminders of what I've lost.'

As Ottilie continued filling Zoe in on the residents of Thimblebury, the tiny village nestled between the hills of the Lake District that she now called home, Zoe watched the horizon, noticing as rooftops began to appear, a haphazard cluster of stone cottages soon following.

'Here we are,' Ottilie said, nodding to a sign that said: *Welcome to Thimblebury. Please drive carefully through our village.*

Zoe was at once captivated by the tranquillity of narrow roads, so clean and ordered there had to be an army of elves patrolling when everyone was asleep, keeping it tidy. Back in wisdom, but honestly I feel healthy and strong and not knackered by my old age at all.'

Zoe's light laugh was easier and more genuine now. 'I'm sorry I asked.'

'Thanks for asking, though. I'm being looked after by everyone – better than I'd like, sometimes. Heath follows me round the house with pillows and foot massages, and everyone at the surgery watches me like a hawk, even if they pretend not to.'

'I'm looking forward to meeting your team properly. I've spoken to Dr Cheadle, of course, and she was...'

'I think the polite phrase you want is *a character*.'

'That's the one. But they all sound interesting.'

'They're that all right.'

'And fun.'

'That too. We're like a little family. Not in a cliquey way. We're close, but they're very welcoming to newcomers to the team. I think you'll slot right in.'

'*If* I decide to work there.'

Ottilie grinned again. 'Yes, of course, *if* you come to work with us.'

The road ahead forked, and their route took them down an even narrower one than they'd previously driven. It twisted and turned in unexpected ways, overhanging trees now creating a dappled tunnel, daylight breaking through in bursts where the branches thinned. After a few minutes of amenable silence, Ottilie spoke again, pointing to some roadside fencing.

'Daffodil Farm is up there, where the alpaca herd are kept. That's Victor and Corrine's place. They're lovely. I hope we get time to pop up there and meet them before you have to go back. I'll take you along to Hilltop too. Ann is a sweetie. She's got her work cut out with her son, Darryl, but she still manages to make a big fuss of you when you go up there.'

'How old is her son?'

Manchester, there was good and bad, but rarely anywhere as pin-neat and charming as this. And yet, for all the neatness, there was something bohemian about it too, an air of secret, hidden chaos and fun that only added to the charm. She noticed a garden full of household oddments being used as planters: ancient tin baths, chimney pots and shoe racks, amongst many other things.

'That's Flo's,' Ottilie said.

'There's an interesting look going on in the garden.'

'I call it junk rather than interesting, but, weirdly, I think it suits her. I don't hate it – at least, not at her place, though I'd hate it at mine. Wordsworth Cottage is just up ahead.'

'I can't wait to see it. I'm still having a hard time imagining you as a country bumpkin.'

'Believe me, if Ottilie five years ago could see me now, she would have a hard time too. I never imagined myself somewhere like this, but now I'm here I can't see myself anywhere else.'

'You almost left though, didn't you? You said so.'

'Twice, actually. Only because I thought I would have to.'

'But you're glad things worked out?'

'Very.' Ottilie slowed the car and then pulled to a gentle stop outside a charming double-fronted cottage, with a gated, meandering path leading to a front door shaded by trees. 'Here we are – my little house.'

Zoe gazed up at the house as she got out of the car, and for a startling moment she saw for herself a life that, like Ottilie, she'd never imagined she'd want. 'It's so pretty! Have you done much to it?'

'After the flood the first year I was here, there were a lot of repairs, and I've modernised it a bit, but not much apart from that. It's funny, when I first got here, I wanted to change everything, but that's because I still had my city head on. Now that I'm settled, I don't mind that it's a bit...'

'I think they call it cottage core.'

Ottilie pushed open the gate and led the way up the path. 'You'd know better than me. I've hardly got my finger on the pulse these days. I'm reliably informed by my friend's daughter that I'm like a boomer. And I don't think she means that as a compliment.'

Zoe grinned. 'Oh dear. Are we already at the age where people under twenty think we're ancient?'

Ottilie twisted a key into the front door and pushed it open. 'Probably, although don't forget I'm a few years older. Compared to me, staring my fortieth birthday in the face, you're a spring chicken.'

Zoe laughed lightly. 'I don't feel like one! And it's only two years' difference, and you're not that close to forty!'

'Oh well, then welcome to the club. Keeping up with trends is exhausting anyway – who needs it?'

'I'm with you there.' Zoe wrinkled her nose. 'Oh God, we really are old now!'

'I think we might be getting there!'

Zoe followed Ottilie into the hallway and took in the polished wooden stairs with brass rods and the strip of floral carpet running up them. The walls were a delicate pink, and there were flowers standing in a vase on a display table, and Zoe was warmed by the instant homeliness. 'This is lovely!'

'Thanks,' Ottilie said. 'I like it. Come on – we'll make a pit stop to refresh and refuel, and then I'll give you the guided tour. Is it tomorrow you're scheduled to go and chat to Fliss?'

'Yes, she said to go at lunch.'

'Don't have your dinner then; I expect she wants to feed you.'

Zoe shrugged off her jacket. 'That'll be a first. I've never been to a job interview where I've been fed.'

'It's hardly going to be an interview at all. Between you and me, I think she's already decided she wants you working at the surgery. The ball is in your court, really – it's whether you want us that's the million-dollar question.'

'She's never met me.'

'Her exact words were: "If Ottilie thinks she's all right, then I'm sure she'll be all right. I've got better things to do than read from an approved list of questions and listen to answers I couldn't give a fig about." And that pretty much sums her up.'

'I don't know whether to be flattered or worried.'

'I wouldn't be either. Fliss is just that practical. She's got no time for what she sees as pointless protocols. She wants to know if you're personable and you're able to do the job, not where you see yourself in five years and what your worst and best traits are. I told her you were lovely and more than capable of doing the job. You can thank me on your first day.'

'*If* I join the team.'

'Yes.' Ottilie grinned as she took her own coat off. 'I keep forgetting about that little word.'

'But I do appreciate you having my back.'

'I'd say that's what friends are for, et cetera, but I do have an ulterior motive. If I can have you look after me during my pregnancy, that would make me very happy. I think a lot of the other local mums-to-be will feel the same when they meet you.'

'You're not going to parade me around the village for every pregnant woman to inspect, are you?'

'It had crossed my mind.'

3

There was a knock at the front door as Zoe got settled at the kitchen table. Ottilie raised her eyebrows. 'That'll be Flo.'

'I don't mind if you want to ask her in.'

'I know you don't, but I ought to warn you to brace yourself anyway.'

Zoe watched Ottilie leave the room. Next, she heard voices at the door, and then Ottilie returned a minute later. The woman who followed her in was short and slender but with surprisingly dark hair for a woman in her eighties, and she looked far from the stereotypical frail old lady. And when she turned her attention to Zoe, she gave the impression that if Zoe chose to tangle with her, she'd always come out worst off.

'Oh,' Flo said, giving her a quick once-over. She looked at Ottilie. 'She's young to be bringing bairns into the world, isn't she? Barely out of the cot herself.'

'I'm older than I look,' Zoe said. 'But I'll take it as a compliment.'

'How old are you then?' the woman asked.

Ottilie stepped between them and gestured for her to take a seat, then offered introductions, even though it was clear nobody needed them. 'Flo, this is Zoe, an old friend of mine from nurse training. And Zoe, this is Flo – my soon to be grandma-in-law.'

'I've heard all about you,' Zoe said. 'It's lovely to meet you.'

'I've heard about you too,' Flo said, eyeing her with what felt like suspicion. 'You're moving to Thimblebury? At this rate, half of Manchester will be here.'

'I don't know about any of that,' Zoe said, catching Ottilie's wry grin. 'But as far as I'm concerned, I'm only visiting to see what I think.'

'What's wrong with it?' Flo asked, shuffling to get comfortable while Ottilie put the kettle on to boil.

'Nothing,' Zoe said. 'I mean it looks very nice. I just haven't seen much of it yet to make up my mind whether I'd like to live here.'

'Better than Manchester,' Flo sniffed, leaving Zoe unable to decide whether Heath's cantankerous grandma approved of people wanting to relocate to her village or not. 'I'll never understand why everyone's falling over themselves to live there.'

'Zoe *isn't*,' Ottilie said. 'That's why she's come to look around here.'

'Before you know it, there'll be housebuilding all over the place and I won't recognise a soul,' Flo continued.

'Of course you will,' Ottilie said patiently. 'Zoe's only one more person from outside.'

'Yes, but just you wait until the sale goes through on Hilltop Farm. Then we'll see.'

Ottilie spun round from the cupboard where she'd been looking for mugs. 'Hilltop? Ann's place? She's selling? She never said!'

'And you go up there all the time. I did wonder why you hadn't said anything,' Flo replied with the merest hint of triumph that suggested she was pleased to have information that hadn't yet reached Ottilie.

'I go up there all the time in my professional capacity,' Ottilie said in a tone that took Zoe a little by surprise. It was sharper than she'd heard her friend use before, but then, knowing the history between her and Flo, perhaps she oughtn't to have been shocked. There was a strange sort of grudging friendship between the women, cemented into place by Ottilie being engaged to Flo's grandson. Ottilie liked Flo well enough but didn't always agree with her opinions or her attitude.

'I thought Darryl was the patient?' Zoe said.

'He is,' Ottilie replied, 'but I do try to keep an eye on Ann too, under the radar. She's... fragile. If you know what I mean. She has a lot to deal with, and her resilience has been tested over the last few years. So I call in every morning on a workday before I head to the surgery and see how they are.' She turned to Flo. 'Who told you she was selling up?'

'Magnus.'

'Of course...' Ottilie poured water into the teapot and brought it to the table. 'That's so sad! Why is she selling?'

'Money I expect,' Flo said in a practical tone. 'Isn't it always about money?'

'I suppose she's been struggling for a while,' Ottilie said thoughtfully. 'But I didn't think it would come to this. I'll have to go and see her as soon as I can. I'll miss her and Darryl so much.'

'I'd have thought you'd be glad,' Flo said. 'One less job for you to do every morning.'

Ottilie frowned slightly at the suggestion and looked as if she was searching for the correct response when Zoe cut in.

'Magnus – remind me... that's the shop owner?'

'Someone's been schooled well,' Flo said, giving her another one of those silent appraisals that Zoe was already beginning to recognise.

'Ottilie gave me a quick rundown as we drove here.'

'Forewarned is forearmed, right?' Ottilie said, throwing Flo a significant look. Flo didn't seem to notice. Instead, she turned back to Zoe.

'Married?'

'Who?' Zoe asked.

'You.'

'I'm...'

'You don't have to answer,' Ottilie said.

Zoe shook her head. 'I know, but I have nothing to hide. I'm going through a divorce.'

Flo folded her hands over one another on her lap and regarded Zoe shrewdly. 'He was a bad 'un? Knocked you about?'

'No!' Zoe recovered herself and lowered her voice. 'Nothing like that! We just... drifted apart.'

'In my experience,' Flo replied tightly, 'nobody *just drifts apart*. There's always a reason.'

'I lost our baby,' Zoe said tersely, and for the first time since she arrived, Flo had the decency to look ashamed.

'I'm sorry to hear that,' she said.

'And,' Zoe continued with a brief nod to acknowledge Flo's sympathy, 'we struggled after that.'

'That's a real shame.' Flo looked up as Ottilie placed a mug in front of her. 'But we shouldn't dwell on it. All this talk of losing babies... tempting fate to say it out loud.'

'Oh, for heaven's sake!' Ottilie began, but then she checked herself too. 'We should stop talking about it, but only because that's not what we're here for. Zoe's come to see what she thinks about Thimblebury, and we're hardly selling it to her so far, are we?'

'You're coming to be the new midwife?' Flo asked Zoe. 'Seems a bit... well, I wouldn't have thought that was the job for you, given your circumstances.'

'Flo,' Ottilie warned, but Zoe put a hand up to stop her.

'You're right,' she said. 'It seems difficult for some to grasp why I'd carry on looking after other expectant women when I've lost my own.' She shrugged. 'I thought about giving it up, but I don't know what else I would do. It's more than a job... it's like it's part of me. I know it sounds daft when people say something's a calling, but I suppose that's the nearest thing I can compare it to. I can't see myself doing anything else.'

'What do you want to do it here for?' Flo asked. 'We're hardly overrun with expectant mums.'

'That's where you're wrong,' Ottilie cut in, looking pointedly at her own belly. 'Or have you forgotten?'

'You, and Stacey's girl...' Flo looked confused. 'Who else?'

'Yes, there's Stacey's daughter Chloe, Maisie Jenkins and Tegan Forester. Not to mention a couple of the mums at the parent and toddler group. And if Zoe did come to take on the role, she'd be responsible for neighbouring villages too, so there'd be plenty to keep her busy.'

Flo gave the vaguest shrug, as if mentally she'd already moved on from that particular topic. 'I wonder what will happen to Hilltop Farm now that Ann and Darryl are leaving.'

'Whatever happens, it's none of our business, is it?' Ottilie said mildly.

'I dread to think who's coming to take it on.'

'Surely it'll be a good thing. Ann would be the first to admit the place is run-down. It needs some money spending on it, and presumably someone who's gone to the trouble of buying it will do that.'

'And then there's Melanie leaving that house Victor built for her.'

'Actually...' Ottilie glanced at Zoe. 'I've spoken to Victor and Corrine about that. He's willing to rent it out at a very reasonable rate if someone should need it.'

So that was why Ottilie had been keen for Zoe to go and meet them. She tried not to be irritated. It seemed Ottilie really wanted her to take the job at the surgery and had gone out of her way to make the move as easy as possible should she want to make it. And while Zoe appreciated her friend's enthusiasm, she was beginning to feel harassed. She wanted to make up her own mind, but it was hard not to feel the weight of Ottilie's hope. 'I'll bear it in mind,' she said shortly.

'I wouldn't want to climb that hill every day,' Flo said. 'Is that kettle done yet? I'm parched.'

'Daffodil Farm is in a lovely spot,' Ottilie said, going to stand by the kettle, presumably so Flo could see it had her full attention, and that the tea would be made the instant it boiled. 'And accessible enough with a decent car.'

'Cold in the winter,' Flo continued. 'All exposed on top of that hill.'

'I've never heard Corrine or Victor complain. And the alpaca seem happy enough.'

'Well, they're hardly going to write out cards for the suggestion box, are they?' Flo huffed.

Zoe bit back a grin. She was beginning to see what Ottilie had meant when she'd warned her about Flo, but she was also finding her more entertaining than she'd expected. 'Is the cottage close to the main farmhouse?'

'No, a couple of fields away,' Ottilie said. 'It's close to Penny's – that's Corrine and Victor's other daughter. They gifted both girls a bit of land to build on. It'd be peaceful enough if you wanted it, but the good thing is, there are nice people not too far away if you needed anything.'

'Penny's dogs howling day and night...' Flo continued. 'I wouldn't thank you for it.'

'Lucky for you then,' Ottilie said as she poured boiling water into the teapot, 'nobody's asking you to move up there.'

'Still, I suppose beggars can't be choosers.' Flo turned to Zoe. 'I expect you'll be falling over yourself for the new doctor like everyone else is.'

Zoe held back a frown while Ottilie sighed. '*Simon* has been with us... well, about a year give or take. However long it is exactly, he's hardly new. And he's also with Stacey now.'

'Stacey,' Zoe said, 'now let me think... that's Magnus's husband's sister, right? Runs the parent and baby group and has the pregnant daughter?'

Ottilie nodded. 'Got it. And there was me thinking you weren't listening.'

Flo got up and began to search the cupboard. 'Doesn't stop people looking.'

'What are you after?' Ottilie asked.

'Some decent biscuits.'

'Here...' Ottilie pulled out a pack and handed them to her. 'That's the best I can do, I'm afraid.'

Flo took them back to the table.

'So Simon is the other partner at the surgery?' Zoe asked.

'Right again,' Ottilie said. 'He's lovely, easy to get along with and very good at his job.'

'Too charming,' Flo said. 'You can't trust the charmers.'

'You can when there's nothing more to it than being nice. Remember that?' Ottilie arched an eyebrow at Flo. 'Remember what it used to be like to think the best of people?'

Flo ripped open the biscuit pack and fished one out. 'I call a spade a spade.'

'Call it a spade when it *is* a spade, not when it's a... I don't know... when it's a...'

'Pitchfork?' Zoe offered.

Ottilie grinned at her. 'See, you're already tuning in to our weird village wavelength. Couldn't have put it better myself.'

Flo huffed and rolled her eyes before shoving a biscuit into her mouth. 'Where's Heath?' she asked, spraying crumbs across the table as she did.

'Gone to help Simon put up some shelves.'

'Friendly with him all of a sudden.' Flo reached for another biscuit.

'They've always been friendly,' Ottilie said. 'We'll go over there,' she continued to Zoe. 'When you've finished your tea and we've settled you into the spare room. Fliss says she'll come over to us to say hello. Lavender might pop in too, if she has time. That'll be the whole team in one fell swoop, right there for you to meet.'

'That sounds good,' Zoe said, reaching for her cup.

'Tomorrow I'll take you on a little tour around the area.'

Flo sat up. 'Are you going into Kendal?'

'We might,' Ottilie said. 'It depends on what Zoe wants to do.'

'Can I come? We haven't been to that café in ages.'

Ottilie looked awkward. 'That's not really the reason… We're going so that Zoe can get a feel for the area to see if she likes it.'

Flo folded her arms and huffed.

'I don't mind,' Zoe said, and Flo's sulk turned into a smile of triumph.

'See!' she told Ottilie. 'Zoe doesn't mind. What time will you be picking me up?'

Ottilie let out a sigh, her face such a picture of exasperation that Zoe felt the immediate urge to apologise. 'We'll see,' was all she said, but it was clear from Flo's smug gulp of her tea that the old lady saw it as a done deal.

4

Kestrel Cottage was a new build, rendered in painted hardwood panelling and topped with a neat slate roof. It was compact, the grounds contained by a low drystone wall and a row of young trees bravely defending it from the winds that swept over the hills. If Zoe was very still and quiet, she could hear the bleating of distant sheep.

There was a meeting with Corrine and Victor, the owners of Daffodil Farm, to settle the final arrangements. It was three hours in which Zoe had been offered at least four different types of cake and so much tea she was now sloshing wherever she went, and then Victor had taken her across to the house that was to be hers for the next six months in his old Land Rover. She'd agreed on six months because she still wasn't sure Thimblebury was the place for her.

That was also the reason she hadn't yet given her ex, Ritchie, the go-ahead to buy her share of the house they'd shared in Manchester. At least, that was what she told herself, though, in her heart, she knew there was more to it than that, reasons she didn't want to acknowledge, even in the privacy of her own thoughts. What she'd told Flo was true – they'd drifted apart – but that didn't mean she no longer loved him. There was love, of a sort – she knew that much. What she couldn't decide was whether it was the right kind of love, the kind of love that kept couples together. Her feelings had been confused, even as they'd started their divorce, and they were hardly any clearer now the deed was close to being done.

She could admit that she cared for him still, but beyond that she really didn't know. It was exactly the same kind of doubt that clouded her mind about the move to Thimblebury. Ottilie had persuaded her in the end by showing her a snapshot of a life so wonderful and cosy it couldn't possibly be real, and Zoe had been seduced by it. But now she was here, the newest resident of a tiny village in the Lake District, alone in an admittedly cute but also isolated cottage, she wondered whether she'd made a terrible mistake.

The living room was furnished in another couple's belongings, and that hardly helped her to feel at home. It was all perfectly nice, perfectly good and modern, but so obviously someone else's taste, every item speaking of a marriage built brick by brick, only to have been toppled, that it made Zoe sad. Sad for them and sad for herself.

She ran a hand across the back of the cornflower-blue sofa and gazed at the whitewashed floorboards and walls, shelves in the alcoves at either side of the log burner stripped bare of the personal trinkets they would once have housed. With a sigh, she made her way through to the kitchen, furnished in glossy units and granite worktops, empty in the same way, staring back at her like a body without a soul.

'Melanie and Damien were ever so happy here,' Victor had said cheerfully as he'd handed Zoe the keys at the front door. 'If not for the divorce, neither of them would ever have left it. I hope you love this little house as much as they did.'

Right now, Zoe didn't feel happy at all. She felt like running back to Victor and Corrine's warm kitchen and handing the keys back. She sat at the breakfast bar and took a deep breath.

'Stupid cow,' she told herself. 'It's only a house. A nice house. Like Ottilie says, a house you're bloody lucky to get around here, where there are hardly any for rent or sale.'

She'd arranged for her own belongings to follow in a removal van. The furniture left behind by Victor's daughter and son-in-law on their separation would do her just fine, and it would feel far more like her home once her own odds and ends were in.

As she poked around, opening and closing cupboards and inspecting the stove, from the corner of her eye she noticed movement beyond the boundary wall that was overlooked by the kitchen window. She looked up to see a man striding across the fields. It was difficult to see what he looked like from this distance, but the confidence and agility of his movements suggested strength and purpose. She wondered vaguely if it was Victor's son-in-law, Leon, who lived close by. Then she noticed the dog. She couldn't tell what breed it might be, but it was about the size of a Labrador, shaggy shades of grey and full of energy. It looked a lot like a dog she'd had as a girl, and she smiled as it chased to and fro, racing in circles around him as he walked.

A sudden gust of wind lifted the lid from the recycling bin in the back yard, sending it skittering across the ground. It took a second to locate the right key on her bunch to open the back door, and then she hurried out to secure it, giving the man a cursory glance through the gaps of the wooden gate as she did. Ordinarily, she'd have said hello, but she was preoccupied with rescuing her bin lid. She managed to grab it and then plonked it back on the box, securing it with a stone from the garden. A moment later, the dog was bounding towards her. It leapt up at the gate, tail wagging furiously.

'Hello!' Zoe leaned over to fuss it. 'You're a big hairy thing, aren't you? What's your name?'

'Griz!' The man strode in their direction. 'Griz, come here! I'm so sorry,' he said as he caught the dog by the collar and reattached the leash. 'He's gone a bit crazy with all this open air today.'

'That's all right; he's lovely. What's his name? Griz?'

'Grizzle.'

'That's cute.' Zoe rubbed a hand over the dog's head, and he licked it. 'Hello, Grizzle.'

'He seems to like you,' the man said. Zoe was struck by how handsome he was close up. 'Then again, he's as soft as they come – he likes everyone. Got him from the rescue home a couple of months ago.'

'That's nice. That you gave him a second chance, I mean.'

'They said he had a nice owner before, but it was an older man who had a stroke and couldn't cope with him after that. He's still young – needs a lot of exercise.'

'Lucky you live out here then where there's plenty of space.'

'I don't. Not yet. Maybe. What do you think? Do you like it here?'

'I've not long moved in, actually.'

'Right... so how are you finding it? I mean, have you been here long enough to decide what you think?'

Zoe tucked a stray lock of hair behind her ear and folded her arms against a wind that was colder than she'd anticipated. She held up her keys to show him. 'Just got these keys, literally half an hour ago. Maybe if you come back to me in a month I'll be able to answer your question... So you're thinking of moving to Thimblebury too?'

'I don't want to jinx anything, but...you never know, we might well end up neighbours.'

As she took in his thick, dark hair and soft eyes the colour of chocolate, and the way his voice rasped over certain vowels in the most attractive way, Zoe was struck by how much she'd like that, and it took her quite by surprise. There was an accent she couldn't place, but it wasn't from the north of England like her own. It was from somewhere around the home counties, perhaps.

He paused, his lips formed in the shape of the first syllable of a new question, but then he frowned. 'You're cold? I'm sorry; I didn't mean to keep you.'

'It's all right. I dashed out without a jacket, and that's hardly your fault.'

'I won't make things worse. It was nice to meet you... Sorry, I didn't ask your name.'

'It's Zoe.'

'Zoe. Hi. I'm Alex. Maybe I'll see you around.'

Grizzle was straining to get at something he'd seen in the distance. And then he pulled free, his lead trailing behind him as he began to gallop across the fields.

'Griz!' Alex yelled. 'Grizzle! Come back!' He turned to Zoe. 'Sorry, got to... Hope to see you again.'

She watched him for a moment, marching over the fields, shouting for his dog and getting nowhere. There was something oddly adorable about it, funny and a little bit sexy, like he didn't care that his dog was making an idiot of him, and she had to smile as his shouts became ever more exasperated.

By the time he'd caught up with Grizzle, they were so far away Zoe could no longer hear them. She figured he wasn't coming back to continue their conversation as she watched him carry on in the opposite direction, which left her strangely disappointed. But now she had quite visible goosebumps from the chill, and decided it was probably a good idea for her to head back inside anyway.

As she opened the back door, her phone began to ring. She pulled it from her dungaree pocket to see Ottilie's name on the screen.

'Are you in?' Ottilie asked as Zoe swiped to take the call.

'Just about.'

'Can I come and visit?'

Zoe grinned. 'Could I stop you, even if I wanted to?'

'I doubt it. I've made a casserole – thought you might not feel like cooking on your first night.'

'Even if I did, I hardly have any food in yet. Casserole sounds lovely.'

'Perfect! I'm on my way!'

Zoe tucked the phone back into her pocket and scanned the horizon. The figure had gone, perhaps hidden in a hollow or already on his way down the hill. Alex... that was his name, wasn't it? Zoe rolled it around her mouth. *Alex.*

Her mind wandered back to those brief moments, looking up into those soft brown eyes, and she couldn't help but hope that wasn't the first and last time.

Zoe pushed her plate away. 'Your cooking's improved since we were in halls.'

Ottilie laughed. 'It couldn't have got worse. In those days, I thought a Pot Noodle sandwich was a delicacy.'

'I remember telling my dad about your Pot Noodle sandwiches,' Zoe said. 'He was horrified.'

'I'm not surprised. When I think back, our diet was pretty horrific, wasn't it?'

'We were poor students; I suppose we could be excused.'

Zoe collected their plates and put them into the dishwasher. 'I'll have to figure out how this works later,' she said, taking a moment to study the control panel. 'When I've managed to fill it up. Though, living alone, I'll probably only have to start it once a week.'

'How are you feeling about it all?' Ottilie asked as she

returned to the table. 'Still wondering if you've done the right thing?'

'How did you...? I didn't say—'

'You didn't have to. I've been in your shoes – remember? I can't tell you how many times I asked myself that question when I first came to Thimblebury. I know you've been doing the same. It's a big step – it's only human to have doubts.'

'It doesn't help that this house – lovely as it is – feels like it's in the middle of nowhere. I mean, I know there was nothing else in the village and I was lucky to drop on, plus I have Daffodil Farm not too far away...'

'Leon and Penny too, don't forget. Have you met them yet?'

Zoe laughed. 'Not yet... I thought I had met Leon, but it turned out I was being an idiot.'

'Oh, you've always been an idiot. What did you do?'

'Oh, it was just some guy walking a dog. Thank goodness I didn't call him Leon or anything.'

Ottilie frowned. 'Walking a dog up here? There's no walking route up here. It's either Victor's land or Hilltop Farm's. Are you sure it wasn't Leon? Did he have a black-and-white collie with him?'

'No, it was grey and shaggy, sort of a Heinz. He said his name was Alex. Come to think of it, he did tell me he was thinking of buying around here. Hilltop Farm is for sale, right?'

'Yes. Perhaps he's thinking of buying Ann's place then. What was he like?'

'Pleasant enough,' Zoe said, wanting to say so much more than that. She could have waxed lyrical about his eyes, and his voice, and the way he smiled at her, but she'd have sounded ridiculous. She'd barely spoken two words to him, after all. It *was* ridiculous. Besides, there was every possibility she would never see him again.

'I'll have to ask Ann when I go to see her tomorrow,' Ottilie said. 'I'm so used to going there every morning to look in on her and Darryl and make sure they're OK, it's going to be strange when I don't have to. I feel so sorry for her. Things must be really rough for her to uproot Darryl like that. She'd never do it unless she absolutely had no other choice. I wish there was something I could do to help.'

'Is she moving far away?'

'A little bungalow a few miles down the road. Once they get settled in, I'm sure it will be better for them. She's been struggling with Hilltop ever since her husband died. It's a big place to take care of, and then there's the fact that her son needs so much care and attention, and not being able to do much actual farming meant that money was always tight too. She couldn't afford to hire help, and I think she felt a bit stuck in the end. I don't blame her for moving on. I'm only surprised she managed to hold on for this long.'

'So if she's got a place to go to, she presumably wants a quick sale?'

'I would imagine so.'

'I wonder if he's already bought it?'

'The man you met today?'

'I mean, if Hilltop is what he meant, but it seems that way, doesn't it?'

'Well, I expect we'll find out soon enough.' Ottilie went to the shopping bag she'd left on Zoe's kitchen worktop and pulled out a covered dish. 'Tiramisu?'

'You made pudding as well? I love tiramisu!'

'I know you do – that's why I made it.'

'Can you marry me instead of Heath, please?'

'Sorry, I am quite excited to marry him. We could adopt you. How's that sound?'

'Whatever it takes to get casserole and tiramisu every week, I'm in!'

Ottilie chuckled as she opened a drawer. 'Where are your spoons?'

'Along one... that's it.'

Ottilie grabbed a pair of spoons while Zoe looked for the bowls that she knew Melanie had left behind. 'Where are they...?' she murmured. 'Oh, sod it!' she exclaimed, coming back to the table. 'I vote we eat it from your dish. Who needs bowls?'

Ottilie laughed. 'Heathen.'

'It'll save on washing up too.'

'You have a dishwasher!'

'Yeah, but I did say I only wanted to run it once a week, so...'

Still laughing, Ottilie uncovered the dish, and they both dug their spoons into it.

'That's amazing!' Zoe said, letting the flavours of coffee and cream flood her mouth. 'So good!'

'I thought I could keep the leftovers for lunch at the surgery on Monday. I told you we do the communal lunch thing, didn't I? It's my turn to take pudding on Monday.'

Zoe grinned as she dug for another spoonful. 'Bold of you to assume there'll be leftovers!'

Having seen Ottilie off later than either of them had planned after laughing and talking like they'd never left their student days, Zoe was tired but happier than she had been when she'd first taken possession of the cottage. Still, she went round the house more than once to check the doors were all locked before going to shower and change into her pyjamas, and the silence outside her windows was so absolute and profound compared to what she'd been used to living in Manchester that she almost shot through the bedroom ceiling when her phone began to ring. She'd plugged it in to charge at her bedside but retrieved it with some trepidation when she saw the caller ID.

'Hey... anything the matter?'

'I can't just call to see if you're OK?'

Ritchie's voice was all at once jarring, yet comforting and familiar.

'Of course, it's ... well, I hadn't expected it.'

'It's late, I know. Sorry about that. I can ring off if you don't—'

'Don't do that. It's not late, but it's been a long day.'

'I hear you moved into your new house today.'

'Who told you?'

'I saw your brother. He told me.'

'Ah.'

'Don't shout at him – I asked. I know you've moved away now, but that doesn't mean I can't ask how you are, does it?'

'I wasn't going to shout at him – it doesn't matter who knows. Yes, I'm all moved in. More or less. I've got some boxes to come, but I'm here.'

'It's nice? It's the Lake District, right?'

'Yes. It's lovely. Seems lovely, but it will take time to get used to it. I start my new job on Monday. That's going to take some getting used to too.'

'You didn't have to leave Manchester, you know. How will you cope?'

'I'm not sure whether to be thankful for your concern or annoyed that you don't think I can cope.'

'You know what I mean.'

'I know, sorry... like I said, long day. There's plenty of support around here. I'm sure I'll be fine.'

'You don't know anyone.'

'Not properly, not yet, but I will. Ottilie made it work.'

'Ott— oh yeah, *her*.'

Zoe's forehead creased at the change in his tone. 'What does that mean?'

'If not for her, you'd still be in Manchester.'

'What if I was? It doesn't make any difference to you.'

'I know, but—'

'Ritchie, don't do this. We agreed it was for the best, and we can't keep going back and forth on it. I don't know about you, but I haven't come this far to undo everything. And we can't go back to the way we were – it wasn't healthy for either of us.'

'So you keep saying.'

'We agreed,' Zoe repeated. She rubbed at her temple. 'Not that I don't appreciate you calling, but it's late and—'

'Of course. Sorry, I shouldn't have called.'

'Don't make me feel guilty.'

'I'm not trying to.'

'But you are.'

'Will you message me? Later in the week – to let me know how things are.'

Zoe nodded, forgetting for a moment that he couldn't see her reply. She didn't see the point, and yet, knowing that he wanted to be sure she was OK pulled at her resolve.

'Zoe...?'

'Sorry, yes. I'll text you.'

'If it's a problem, then...'

'It's not. But don't worry too much if it's not for a few days. I'll be busy.'

There was a pause too long for Zoe's liking until he relented. 'Right then. Don't forget to text me. If you don't—'

'I will. Bye, Ritchie.'

She ended the call without waiting for his response. If he had anything else to add, it would have to wait.

After plugging the phone back in, she dropped to the bed and sat staring out of the window. Dusk had claimed the world beyond it, turning the hills into black shadows with only a handful of yellow lights to mark out where there were houses clinging to their sides. Above them, the sky was indigo, becoming ink blue, the first stars blinking. Why did this have to be so hard?

Her hand went to her belly, an instinctive move that only

saddened her whenever it happened. Six months after she'd lost her baby, she still did it. Her life would have looked so different now if only she'd managed to take better care of her child, if only there had been some way to prevent the loss that haunted her. She blamed herself, even though she'd told so many other women who'd suffered the exact same tragedy that it wasn't their fault. Her professional mind knew she wasn't to blame, but that didn't stop her feeling it. She'd lost her baby, and then she'd lost so much more. Things had to get better soon, didn't they?

5

Zoe's first day as the new midwife for the village of Thimblebury and its neighbours featured no actual expectant mothers. Instead, she found herself numbed into frustrating boredom by systems that needed to be set up, software that she needed to be registered on and lists of patient details.

Her colleagues at the surgery were every bit as welcoming as Ottilie had promised they would be. The senior partner, Dr Fliss Cheadle, was cheerful but brisk, putting her head around the door for a quick good morning, asking if Zoe needed anything and not waiting for the answer, only shooting back a 'jolly good, I'll let you get on; you know where I am if you change your mind'. Dr Stokes – Simon – was charming and sincere, and spent a few more minutes putting her at ease, but explained that his schedule was full and shortly after made his excuses to leave. Ottilie said the same thing, and it was down to Lavender, the receptionist and – as she termed it – surgery mum to sit alongside Zoe whenever she could and help her get to grips with all her initial admin.

'Tegan Forester...' Lavender tapped at the screen of the monitor. 'Be prepared – when you see her, the appointment is likely to run over. Not likely, guaranteed is more like. Born worrier, that one.'

'Older mum too,' Zoe murmured as she clicked to read the background notes.

'Caught out,' Lavender said with a tone of authority.

Zoe glanced across. 'You know her? Personally, I mean?'

'Only as much as everyone knows everyone else personally around here. It's common knowledge she wasn't planning a baby.'

'Two previous pregnancies...' Zoe read out loud.

'Yep. Youngest of those is now seventeen, so...' Lavender gave a careless shrug. 'I don't think she's filled with enthusiasm for starting all that baby business again, but it's her choice to carry on, so what can you do? I expect she'll come round – that's usually the case, isn't it?'

Zoe went back to the main screen, Lavender still reading alongside her. 'Maisie will be all right,' she said, pointing at another name. 'A bit wet behind the ears, but she's a little sweetheart who won't give you any trouble at all. Her family, on the other hand...'

Zoe nodded silently but was beginning to wish Lavender would find something else to do. Much as she appreciated the input, Lavender's running commentary was becoming distracting. And the fact was, she wanted to meet these women without preconceptions. She wanted to get to know them herself, to form her own opinions and forge a bond of trust with them, and she wasn't sure a load of gossip beforehand was going to help her to do that.

'Who's that?' Lavender peered more closely at the screen. 'Don't know that one... Ah, new referral... strange, though – where's she been referred from? She doesn't live in Thimblebury... what's the address...?' She took the mouse from Zoe and began to look for further information, but Zoe, doing her best to look less hassled than she was beginning to feel, took it gently back.

'I'm sure you've got lots to do, and I can manage from here. Thank you so much for your help.'

'Oh...' Lavender stood up with a brisk smile. 'Of course... you're right, probably should get back to reception. You'll get used to me,' she added cheerfully. 'Tend to get involved in things that don't need me. Can't help it – I'm a natural sniffer-outer. Love problem-solving and little challenges. My dad always said I should have become a detective.'

'Ottilie says you're worth your weight in gold. I expect I'll be coming to you with a lot over the next few weeks, but I don't want to use up your goodwill on the first day.'

Lavender made her way to the door. 'Don't worry about that. New systems and whatnot – it's always a bit daunting. Ask me anything, whenever you need to. I'm only a holler away, and it's what I get paid for.'

'Thanks, Lavender. I'll be sure to take you up on that offer soon enough.'

Zoe let out a light breath as the door closed, leaving her alone, and then turned her attention to the screen. Her eye was drawn back to the name that had puzzled Lavender. Billie Fitzgerald. Hilltop Farm...

Zoe frowned. Hilltop Farm. Wasn't that Ann's house? She delved into what notes were on the system and saw that the referral was from another health authority based out of the area and that there was a previous Essex address, still on record and still being used for correspondence. So this was a pre-emptive referral? Billie Fitzgerald was planning to move into the area but hadn't yet?

Deciding that fact put her into the *worry about later category*, Zoe continued down the list, smiling as she came across Ottilie's name. There wouldn't be much midwifery going on there if she knew Ottilie at all. Her friend would be self-sufficient for as long as she could; though she'd always report in for her checks, she'd doubtless solve any other minor problems she might have using her own medical knowledge. Zoe had looked after some expectant mothers who had phoned her night and day over every tiny niggle, but Ottilie would not be one of those.

There was a light tap at the door. Zoe's colleague and friend poked her head around it. 'Everything going OK?'

'Fine,' Zoe said. 'I was just thinking about you. Or rather, reading about you.'

'I'm sure it's riveting,' Ottilie said with a wry grin. 'I'm doing the tea rounds – want one?'

'I'd love one!' Zoe said.

'I thought you'd say that.'

Ottilie let the door close again, her footsteps echoing down the passageway until Zoe could no longer hear them.

She glanced out of the window as she stretched, noting the pleasing patchwork of blue sky freckled by threadbare smears of white cloud, smiling over the stone walls and slate roofs of her new home. Beyond the village lay the Lake District itself, majestic hills and valleys and vast silver-grey lakes, waiting to be discovered. Allowing herself a moment, she got up and went to lean on the windowsill, drinking in the view and thinking about all that discovery, right there for her to experience. Despite her doubts over whether the move to Thimblebury had been the right decision, she already had a feeling she was going to like it here.

The sound of engines roaring across the tranquil fields around Zoe's home woke her early on Saturday morning. Far too early. With a frown, she poked her feet into some slippers and went to the window to look. She couldn't see where the commotion was coming from, but she could still hear it. Perhaps it was something going on at the neighbouring farm, Hilltop, which was out of view from this vantage point. Daffodil Farm, on whose land her house stood, seemed quiet enough when she went round to the other side of the house and looked out, so it seemed a safe bet.

The sun was newly risen, and the light skimming the fields was pale and fresh as Zoe made her way across them. She'd downed a quick coffee, puzzling over the commotion that she could still hear in sporadic bursts, which sounded all at once miles away and yet close enough to disturb her inside her little house. It was a cold morning but pleasant enough, and her decision to walk over to Hilltop to confirm her suspicions had been an easy enough one to make.

As the neighbouring farm came into view, she could hear good-natured calls echoing across the yard, accompanied by bursts of tuneless singing and whistling, and then saw that there was a removal van parked outside, Victor's battered Land Rover and one other car that she didn't recognise alongside it.

'Hello, my love!' Corrine's arms were taken up by a box as she noticed Zoe's arrival. 'Come to help?'

'Um... what am I helping with?' Zoe rushed over to offer Corrine assistance with her load.

Corrine gave her a grateful smile as she grabbed the other end, and they took the box to the removal van between them.

'Ann's moving out...' Corrine gestured for Zoe to help lift the box into the back of the van. 'Didn't we tell you?'

'Well, I knew she might be, but I didn't realise it would be so soon. I thought she was still selling the house.'

'Ah, I expect she was last time we mentioned it. But then everything went through very sudden and here we are. Offer made and accepted and cash in the bank.'

'When's the new owner due to arrive?'

'Not sure. I wouldn't imagine we'll have to wait too long to meet them.'

As she walked back to the house with Corrine, Victor came out with a box of his own marked 'kitchen'.

'Morning!' He gave Zoe a familiar nod. 'Come to muck in, have you?'

Everyone seemed to assume Zoe had come to help, and as she didn't have much else to do, she decided she might as well. 'Are there more boxes to be brought out? Or is there something else you want me to do?'

'Ask Ann. She's inside, panicking about everything.'

'She's never moved house before,' Corrine said, wagging a finger at her husband. 'And this is a big undertaking for someone on her own. Don't be impatient with her.'

'Not on her own, is she? We're here,' Victor said airily before going on his way with his own contribution to the day's work.

Corrine clicked her tongue on the roof of her mouth as she watched him for a second, and then cleared the vexation from her face as she turned back to Zoe. 'I haven't seen your bits and pieces arrive yet? When are they due?'

'To be honest, I don't have a lot to bring over. Haven't bothered with my old furniture because there's perfectly nice furniture in the house already. There's a few personal bits, crockery and bedding and that sort of thing still to come. My parents are planning to bring it over when they can, but I'm OK to manage until then.'

'Oh, well if you need anything in the meantime, remember you can always ask us. I think Ann might have a few things she's no more use for – we could ask her. You might find they suit your needs.'

'Ann!' Corrine called as they crossed from bright sunlight to the gloomy interior of Ann's low-ceilinged kitchen. The soon to be ex-owner of Hilltop Farm, however, was nowhere to be seen. 'We've another pair of hands if you want them? Ann?'

Then she appeared from a side door, her eyes red and puffy,

sniffing hard. Corrine shook her head and dashed across the floor with open arms.

'Love!' she said, folding Ann into an embrace. 'Don't cry! It's going to be fine.'

'I-I know,' Ann stuttered through fresh tears. 'It's just... it's all going to change. And I feel so guilty leaving Hilltop behind when it's all I have left of—'

'Of course you do!' Corrine soothed. 'It's only natural. You're bound to be nervous and a bit afraid right now, but it's going to be a good change, you wait and see. You'll have more time for Darryl without this big old place to worry about. You've been saying for a long time what a burden it is, and you shouldn't feel guilty about wanting an easier life, not one bit. You don't think your Jim would begrudge you that much, do you?'

'Of course not, but he worked so hard on this farm, and I'm giving it up, just like that.'

'Not just like that. After trying very hard to make it work on your own. You've done all you can do – everyone says so. You've got a lovely new house to go to, and all your friends will be nearby, same as they are now.'

Ann pulled free of Corrine's arms and gave a pleading look. 'What about Darryl? Do you think he'll hate me for taking him away from here? He loves this place so much, and he feels so safe, and I—'

'You didn't think it would be easy, you said as much, but you wouldn't be doing this if you didn't feel, deep down, that it would eventually be the best thing for him, even if he doesn't see it that way at the moment. Anyone who knows you knows that you always put him first, and this is no different. Come on – dry those eyes and crack on. Look' – she gestured at Zoe, who was watching awkwardly, not acquainted with Ann well enough to offer her own words of comfort but desperate to hug her, as Corrine was doing – 'we've got another pair of willing hands too. Before you know it, you'll be sitting in your new house with your feet up, watching Darryl settle in.'

'Oh...' Ann offered a bemused smile to Zoe. 'I'm sorry, I didn't—'

'Don't worry about it,' Zoe said. 'I don't know how much use I'll be, but I'm at a loose end today so happy to help if you need me. Has it all got to be out by today?'

'I was hoping it would be. I can't really afford to hire the van for a second day.'

'It will be,' Corrine said. 'You're all packed and that's the worst of it done – all we have to do now is load it all onto the van.'

Corrine watched her go. 'Poor thing,' she said.

'Has she been here a long time?' Zoe asked.

'She has that,' Victor said. 'Since she got married, and she were only a slip of a girl then. She's looked after this place through thick and thin, and it hasn't been easy.'

'Nobody blames her for finally having had enough,' Corrine added. 'Most of us are surprised she lasted this long after her husband died.'

'Have you met the new owners yet?' Zoe asked.

Corrine shook her head. 'All we know is it's a cash buyer who made up his mind pretty quick after he'd seen it. But Ann said she'd had it on the market on the quiet, didn't want a big fuss until it was sold.'

'I think *some* people knew,' Zoe said, remembering that Flo, Ottilie's almost grandmother-in-law had told them the first time Zoe had come to visit. She also recalled the recent referral to her for Billie Fitzgerald, who'd been registered at this address.

'I expect they did, but only those who know her well. We knew,' Corrine added, glancing at Victor, 'but only because we'd be affected by Hilltop changing hands.'

'So it's another farmer taking it on?' Zoe glanced between the couple and noted immediately the uncertainty.

'We don't know,' Victor said. 'But I expect we'll find out soon enough.'

'All we know is he's a family man,' Corrine chipped in. 'At least one adult daughter because Ann said she came with him one of the times he came to look around.' Corrine took in the kitchen, as if she approved of the idea, and then continued. 'This house needs a big, happy family in it. Ann and Darryl have had some terrible luck, and you can feel it in the walls. The old place deserves a new start as much as they do. A lick of paint and some new blood – it's exactly what Hilltop needs.'

'Ah, a bit of work on the land wouldn't go amiss either,' Victor agreed.

'Yes, but...' Corrine began, but then stopped whatever she'd been about to say as Ann came back in.

'I'll get the kettle on,' she said, visibly cheerier than when Zoe had first arrived. 'We all want tea, I'm sure?'

'That sounds lovely,' Corrine said.

'Is there something I can be doing to help in the meantime?' Zoe cast her gaze over a wall of boxes stacked in one corner of the room. 'Perhaps I can take some of those to the van?'

'They'll be too heavy for you,' Victor said. 'Five foot and a feather there – most of those boxes are bigger than you are.'

'You'd be surprised at what I can do,' Zoe said. She wasn't offended by his remark – she was used to people making fun of her stature, and even she had to admit she was a little challenged in the height department.

She took off her coat and hung it on a peg before going over and testing the weight of the nearest box. 'Piece of cake,' she said with a grin, taking it out. Before she'd gone halfway across the yard, she was shaking with exertion, but there was no way she was going to put it down now, not when she absolutely knew that Victor was watching her from the window.

6

Zoe wasn't used to having so much freedom. Freedom to start and finish work according to whatever schedule she set herself, to use the tiny treatment room set up for her at the surgery or to make home visits if she preferred. Freedom to roam the hills, valleys and lakesides of her new home whenever she felt like it, and freedom to clean her house or not. To eat when and what she wanted and to go to bed whenever it suited her, with cold feet or without.

Nobody seemed to mind what she did as long as her days ticked along. There were parts she liked – the trust the partners at the surgery placed in her to get her job done with minimal interference from them was flattering and welcome. The time she spent at home doing as she pleased elicited more mixed feelings.

While she took advantage of the spontaneous urge to go walking to discover more of her new home, the moments after she'd locked the doors of an evening and settled down in her cottage alone sometimes stretched out in a more unwelcome way. She missed Ritchie. Or perhaps she missed simply knowing someone else was there. Whichever it was, she thought often of the times during her marriage when she'd been content, the small moments, like washing the dishes together as they shared anecdotes from their work days, bickering over what TV show they were going to watch first, Ritchie warming her feet whenever she got into bed after him. Zoe was no wearer of rose-coloured spectacles – she knew life hadn't been perfect with Ritchie, and it had been downright difficult towards the end, but it felt like she'd had an ally, someone who had her back. Now she was on her own, and whenever the notion would strike her, she'd feel its full force.

Two weeks had passed like this. They'd flown by, despite Zoe's more melancholy moments. During that time, she'd introduced herself to all the expectant mums on her list, and everyone was taken by surprise at the surgery by how fast it was growing. Fliss wondered aloud one lunchtime – nodding pointedly at Ottilie's growing bump – about what might be in the water locally because she'd never known Thimblebury to be in the grip of such a baby boom.

'You won't hear any complaints from me,' Zoe said in between mouthfuls of the cottage pie brought in by Lavender for her colleagues to share. 'The residents of Thimblebury can rut morning, noon and night and make as many babies as they like – keeps me in a job.'

'So you've already decided you're going to stay for good?' Fliss replied, raising a knowing eyebrow, and Zoe nodded, not realising until that moment that at some point during the previous fortnight she had, indeed, unconsciously decided she was beginning to like life in the Lake District. For good was perhaps a stretch, but for now, she was perfectly content, absorbed by work and gradually getting to know the villagers.

'Good,' Fliss said. 'You'll be here for the quincentenary then?'

'The what?'

'We're celebrating five hundred years of Thimblebury. At

least, we're celebrating five hundred years since it first appeared in the records as an actual village.'

'Oh... What does that entail?' Zoe had no clue about that sort of thing, but she was impressed that the village was so old. 'I mean, if there's a celebration, it's going to be a big deal.'

'I'll say. There's going to be all sorts happening in the village. You know – food, music, silly little plays and readings, local dignitaries plying their trade, historical re-enactments and that sort of thing.'

'And when's this?'

'In a month or so. I'm surprised nobody's mentioned it to you.'

'No, it hasn't come up.'

'And that's the biggest shocker,' Lavender put in from across the table. 'You'd think they were helping to organise the London Olympics the way Magnus and Geoff are going on about it.'

And then she launched into a list of all the other annoying things Magnus and Geoff did, and then the annoying things other villagers did, and the conversation moved along at such a pace that the quincentenary was soon forgotten.

'So...' Fliss said into a gap, 'Zoe, have you manged to see much of the area since you arrived?'

'Not as much as I'd like to, but I've been busy getting the cottage how I like it and sorting out broadband connections and all that sort of thing. You know, all the boring stuff. I keep thinking I'll make time to go and see some of the surrounding towns, but it hasn't happened yet. I suppose a lot of the tourist stuff will be finishing for the season soon?'

'A lot of the tourist stuff barely closes at all these days,' Lavender said. 'My brother-in-law works on the steamers on Ullswater and they've hardly closed at all over the winter the last couple of years. People come for Christmas and New Year breaks, and if they're willing to pay for a boat trip, then why not take their money?'

'It'd be freezing out on the lake at Christmas!' Fliss said. 'No thank you!'

Lavender shrugged. 'They can sit inside, and there's blankets and hot chocolate and that sort of thing. I imagine it's nice enough.'

'I bet it's a great job,' Zoe said.

'He's done it for years and he complains, but I don't think he'd do anything else. His boat is lovely. It's about a hundred years old – maybe more. They're very particular about the upkeep too. You know, if you wanted to take a trip, I'd take you over there – just say the word. I'm sure I could get us a couple of tickets... he owes me enough favours from over the years.'

'Really?' Zoe sipped from a glass of water. 'That would be nice.'

'Forecast is good for this weekend,' Lavender said carelessly. 'If you're not busy, it might be a good time to go. I can phone him to expect us if you like.'

'Oh, I'd love that!' Zoe beamed. 'Are you sure it's no bother?'

'It'd give me an excuse for a couple of hours out of the house, and I haven't been to Ullswater for ages, so I'll sort it. Sunday good for you?'

'Yes, please!'

'Right – it's a date!'

Lavender picked Zoe up from outside the shop. She'd arrived early to get some flowers as a thank you, then indulged in a lazy chat about the Indian summer they appeared to be enjoying. Finally, she had stepped outside as the sun rose above the rooftops to warm her face, watching as a bee bumbled in and out of a hole in a nearby tree. All around was birdsong, and a gentle breeze rustled the trees. On a day like today, it was easy to see why Ottilie had fallen so deeply in love with this village.

'You didn't need to do that!' Lavender said as Zoe offered the flowers.

'I just wanted you to know I appreciate the effort you've made for me today.'

'It's hardly an effort to have a nice day out on a lake. Besides, it's good for us to get to know one another, isn't it? We barely have time to exchange two words at work, and there's usually someone else around when we do.'

'Agreed,' Zoe said. 'I'm looking forward to hearing all about... well, everything, really. And I'm looking forward to the trip. You weren't wrong about the weather – it's glorious.'

They called at Lavender's house so she could pop the flowers in some water, and while Zoe waited in the car, Lavender's husband came out to introduce himself and warn her that his brother was prone to terrible dad jokes, and then Lavender was back in the driver's seat and ready to set off.

They wound their way through scenery that Zoe was getting used to now, but no less breathtaking for all that. Along twisting, steep-sided roads, speckled with leaves that were just beginning to turn into their autumn colours. The place seemed deserted apart from the odd rogue sheep clinging to a heathered hillside, unbothered by a rushing torrent of water pulsing from gaps in the rock, or the occasional red kite or falcon riding the air currents high above as it searched for prey.

Lavender switched the radio on, and while Zoe found it pleasant enough, the soapy pop music seemed lacking in the right kind of drama as she gazed out of the windows at the passing landscape, a landscape that had been millennia in the making, as eternal and old as the earth itself. Whenever they emerged from the shelter of the hills and out onto open road, there were yet more peaks, rising up in the distance, and the odd glint of water from rivers and lakes.

After finding a parking space, Lavender locked the car and led Zoe to the pier where the boat sailed from. By now, the town and nearby lakeside were getting busy, full of people making the most of the last days of warm weather with picnics and ice creams on benches. Every so often, there would be a shriek and someone would be running from a persistent wasp.

Lavender shook her head as a group of teenage girls squealed and ran around in circles, trying to evade a trio of stripey pests. 'All people have to do is stay still and the wasps bugger off eventually.'

'Easy for you to say,' Zoe replied. 'I'm with them – terrible around bees and wasps. I've never been stung, and I don't want to be, so if there's one trying to get into my cheese butty, I'm running.'

'I can't see Pat,' Lavender added as they approached the pier. 'He said he'd meet us, but we're a bit early.'

'I don't mind buying a ticket,' Zoe said. 'I feel as if I ought to, really. It can't be very good business for them to give tickets away.'

Lavender waved an airy hand. 'Ah, they can afford two freebies for family.'

She turned and headed for the ticket office and went to the assistant at the sales window. 'Is Patrick around?'

'Oh, you're Lavender?' the girl asked.

'Yes.'

'He said you'd probably come and ask for him. He's gone to pick up some supplies for the boat. I'll sort your tickets out while you wait for him – he won't be long.'

The girl printed two complimentary tickets and handed them to Lavender, who then took a seat on a bench close to the pier, beckoning Zoe to join her.

They chatted as they looked over the glittering lake, where many other boats were already out – smaller ones with engines zipping up and down, more sedate rowboats going around in small circles closer to the shore, and modern pleasure cruisers.

Zoe thought that *The Lady Susannah*, the steamer they

were due to travel on, was far more beautiful than anything else on the water that day, with a glossy walnut hull and sleek red chimney stack, and brass railings on the deck. It was like something from a glamorous old movie.

As Lavender began to recount what little she knew of the boat's history, she stopped to grin at a man with heavy black brows and a mop of grey hair making his way over.

'All right, trouble?' he said, kissing Lavender on the cheek. 'Only here when you want something... nothing changes.'

'I came because you have no friends and nobody likes you and I didn't want you to be lonely, but if you don't want me here...' Lavender prodded him in the chest, and he chuckled.

'I want you here,' he said, turning to smile at Zoe. 'And you must be the lass from work?'

'Yes,' Lavender said. 'I have friends.'

'Lavender was telling me what a nice trip it is,' Zoe said. 'The boat is gorgeous; I'm looking forward to it.'

'That's not a boat,' Lavender said. 'That's his girlfriend.'

'I can't argue with that,' Patrick said. 'Come on,' he added. 'We've got a few minutes before we're due to let everyone board – I'll let you on first so you can have a sneaky look around.'

Patrick undid a rope that kept the boarding ramp closed off and then led them up it onto the boat, raising a few curious stares from people who were clearly waiting to be shown aboard themselves.

Lavender grinned at Zoe. 'This must be what it's like to be on the VIP list at a swanky party.'

'I wouldn't know – I don't think I've ever been to a swanky party. Unless you count Abigail Ferrier in year eight, who had three bathrooms in her house.'

'Perhaps they weren't posh,' Patrick called behind him. 'Perhaps they all had weak bladders.'

Zoe laughed. 'You might be right. I never thought of that.'

Lavender leaned in. 'Don't encourage him. Before you

know it, the terrible jokes will be out. He loves it when he gets a new audience.'

'I don't mind. I like a dad joke every now and again.'

The deck was furnished in the same gleaming wood as the hull, and there was a cabin with wide windows framed by the same, but the body of it was painted sage green. There were slatted benches running the length of each side of the deck and many more inside, and cheerily striped rubber rings secured along the guardrails. At the stern fluttered a green, white and blue flag on a pole, unfurled every now and again to its full width as the wind lifted the fabric.

Zoe pointed to it. 'What's that, Patrick? I've never seen that flag before.'

'That's Cumbria's flag, that is,' Patrick replied with obvious pride. 'See, all the colours of the lakes on there.'

'Oh,' Zoe said, gazing up at it. 'I didn't know you had one. It's nice.'

There wasn't much time for Patrick's sneaky advanced tour, but it was just as well. Despite the boat being beautiful, it was compact and there wasn't all that much to see.

Five minutes later, Zoe and Lavender found a seat on the deck, and then the boat began to fill with the people who had bought tickets to join them. Everyone seemed so excited and happy to be there that even if she'd wanted to avoid catching the enthusiasm in the air, it would have been impossible. Someone brought an adorable cocker spaniel aboard and sat close to Zoe, sending Lavender into raptures as she fussed it. Zoe listened politely as the woman explained it was an orange roan, and Lavender asked the sorts of questions that told Zoe she knew some facts about the breed already.

When the boat was full, they cast off, and then a sort of hush fell over everyone. There was chatting, but it was mostly in reverent tones about the scenery as they cleaved a graceful path across the water. The lake was like glass, reflecting the hills and valleys crowded along the shore as if a mirror world lay beneath its surface. The sun was mellow and warm on Zoe's face, but the breeze stirred by the boat moving lifted her hair and cooled her neck. As she twisted to lean over the rail, watching and listening as the water rushed along the sides of the boat, she wondered if she'd ever felt so contented in her life. But it wasn't to last because just as she was completely in the moment, Ritchie's text arrived to shatter her peace.

> *My phone reminders say it's five years ago today that we went to Lake Garda. Do you remember that old Italian man in the café who was trying to chat you up? It still makes me laugh. Good times, eh? x*

Zoe recalled the day, vividly now, but it hadn't played in the good-natured way Ritchie was describing. In her version, the old man who'd owned the café they'd wandered into had been a sweet soul, who'd only been interested in Zoe because his first great-grandchild had just been born, and Zoe had gone over to the pram next to the counter to admire the little one and had struck up a faltering conversation – alternating between broken Italian and English – telling him she was a midwife. He'd been so pleased to learn this that he'd offered her a free glass of some local liqueur and an almond cake he'd baked himself.

Ritchie had sat at the table a few feet away, looking at his phone, and when the old man came over to introduce himself, he'd seemed... Zoe had struggled for years to admit what she'd seen in his face that day, and many other times during their marriage. Instead, she'd done her best to ignore his displays of possessive jealousy because to acknowledge it would be to face a painful truth. Ritchie wasn't keen on Zoe having a life outside their marriage, and he didn't like sharing her attention with anyone.

The notion of what he might have been like had their baby

survived and grown into a child who would naturally demand so much of her time had troubled her in a vague way, but it had been overshadowed by the weight of the loss itself. She tried not to think about it now as the boat glided across Ullswater, and wondered, perhaps a little unreasonably, if throwing her phone into the lake would mean she wouldn't have to respond to a text that had gone a long way to ruining her day.

In the end, all she could send as a reply was: *ha ha, yes*, before stuffing her phone firmly into the depths of her handbag and feeling that, if ever a text had been wholly inadequate in addressing a situation, it had to be this one.

7

Zoe's third Monday morning arrived, and as she drove down the steep track that led from her cottage into the village, she recalled that Victor had offered to carry out some repairs to make the journey easier for her. Ottilie had warned when she'd first arrived it was a tricky drive, though she conceded that Zoe was a more confident driver than she was and probably wouldn't break a sweat. While Zoe appreciated the compliment, she had found it trying, especially after rain. This morning she noticed it was easier and assumed that whatever improvements he'd intended to make had been done at some point during the weekend. Zoe had to admit she hadn't noticed much in the way of noise, but her cottage was set a field or more away from the section Victor had worked on, and perhaps that, coupled with the very loud music she'd played as she'd cleaned the house, had been enough to shield her from it.

Close to the junction at the foot of the hill, where the track forked to go up to Hilltop, the neighbouring farm, or to join the road into the village, Zoe was forced to move over to allow a van to squeeze past. It was a good size, and there was just about room for the both of them, but that wasn't what suddenly caught Zoe's full attention. In the driver's seat was the man she'd met on the day she'd first got the keys to her cottage. Next to him was a slight, pale young woman. She had narrow shoulders and long, honey-blonde hair tucked behind her ears. From the brief glimpse Zoe managed to get, she was pretty in a demure, unassuming sort of way, but there was obvious stress in her features. Instantly, Zoe recalled the name of an expectant mum who was due to move into Hilltop. Was this her?

Zoe put her hand up, but the man didn't respond. Either he didn't remember their meeting like she did, or he was preoccupied with the drive up to the farm. Knowing how difficult that road could be, Zoe could hardly blame him.

Later, perhaps, she'd make a point of calling in to say hello. She'd already said hello to... Alex, wasn't it? Yes, that was it. How could his name have slipped her mind for a moment? He'd made an impression on her that had lasted for a couple of days after their first meeting, though the face she'd just seen through the windscreen of the van was a far cry from the relaxed charm of his expression that day. Today he looked... harassed. Yes, that was the word. Not stressed, exactly, or worried, but like someone who was managing, but only just.

'I hear you've got new neighbours.'

Zoe put three packs of biscuits onto the counter. It was her turn to buy for break time at the surgery. Magnus rang them up while she looked for her purse.

'What's that?' she asked, glancing up.

'Someone's moved in at Hilltop, haven't they? Flo saw the van this morning.'

'I'm sure she did,' Zoe replied.

'Yes, she's a one-woman neighbourhood watch,' Magnus replied with a grin, saying what Zoe still felt too much of a new arrival in the village to say. 'One day, she might actually do something useful with her superhuman observation skills. Not that it's anything to do with me, of course, but have you met the new arrivals yet?'

'You're right,' Geoff shouted from a shelf he was restocking. 'Stop being so nosy. We'll all meet them in good time, I'm sure.'

'Sort of,' Zoe said, noting Magnus frown at his husband. The furrows in his brow disappeared as he returned his full attention to her. 'I've met the man in any case. He seems nice enough.'

'A nice family, I expect,' Magnus said. 'I hope so. Hilltop needs a nice family living there. It's not the same without Ann and Darryl.'

'You hardly said two words to them of a week!' Geoff cut in, and this time Magnus rose to the bait.

'How do you know? How do you know who I talk to when you're not around? Are we joined at the hip?'

'Practically,' Geoff said, in such a dry tone that it took all Zoe's effort not to laugh out loud.

'Well,' she replied in an effort to soothe Magnus's ire, 'as soon as I know something I'll report in. Unless you meet them first, of course, and then you can tell me all about it.'

'Have no fear,' Geoff said. 'He'll do that all right.'

'You're giving Zoe a very bad impression of me!' Magnus huffed.

'You're doing that without my help,' Geoff shot back.

'No you're not,' Zoe said, unable to hold back a broad smile. 'We're all curious, and it's only natural for villagers who've lived here a long time to want to know what sort of people are moving in. I mean, first there was me, and now, only a few weeks later, there's someone else. I suppose it makes a big impact in a little village like this.'

'Exactly,' Magnus said, seemingly soothed, exactly as Zoe had hoped he would be. 'One new person arrives and everything changes.'

'For what it's worth, I have no plans to tip anyone's apple cart up. I'm going to be very quiet in my little cottage on the hill. The most trouble I'll be is when I don't have the right change for some biscuits.'

'I'm sure...' Magnus blushed. 'We don't have a problem with newcomers, you know. We only mean—'

'Magnus,' Geoff said. 'Put the shovel down – you're only digging deeper every time you open your mouth. Zoe, what he's trying to say is sorry if it appears we're a couple of outrageous gossips, and sorry if we're coming across as judgy.'

'I've never thought that.' Zoe collected the biscuit packets into her arms. 'I think you're both lovely.'

Magnus beamed.

Geoff turned back to his stock with a broad smile of his own. 'The feeling's mutual. Have a good day.'

'You too.' Zoe headed for the door.

No sooner had she emerged onto the street than she heard Flo's voice. She turned to see the old woman charging towards her at a speed that didn't seem possible for someone of her age. 'Morning!'

'Have you met your new neighbours yet?' Flo asked breathlessly. 'They've moved in, haven't they? I saw a van!'

'I've seen the van too, but I was on my way down the hill, so no, I haven't had a chance to call in yet.' Zoe gave a patient smile and decided not to divulge that she'd met Alex a few weeks before anyone had known he'd be moving in. It would demand more information from Zoe than she had time to give, and even if she had time, she wasn't sure Flo was the best person to share it with.

'Funny couple,' Flo said. 'He looks a lot older than her. Sugar daddy or something, I'll bet. Perhaps he's got a lot of money – though why someone with money would buy Hilltop is beyond me. It's a desperate spot up there – needs plenty of work.'

'Perhaps he likes work,' Zoe said, choosing to ignore Flo's speculation on the relationship between the new arrivals. 'He might be into fixer-uppers.'

'Do you think? He's a builder then?'

'I didn't say...' Zoe held back a sigh and checked her watch. 'Sorry, Flo. I'd love to chat, but I'm going to be late for my first appointment if I don't get a move on.'

'Oh...' Flo looked disappointed but stood back, as if she was somehow blocking Zoe's way. 'Nobody has time to stop these days. That's how the world is now – no time for us old 'uns.'

'Sorry,' Zoe said, and she was sorry. Much as she'd dug deep into her well of patience to listen to Flo's idle gossip, she hated to think she'd offended the old lady, especially as she was practically family to Ottilie now. 'Any other time I'd have stopped for a bit, but, you know... work. I'll have no cottage on the hill if I don't earn enough to pay the rent. I promise if I meet the people at Hilltop before you, I'll make time to tell you all about it.'

'You could call round for a cup of tea,' Flo said, brightening. 'I'm always in.'

'That sounds nice. Thanks. I'll do that.'

'Met your new neighbours yet?'

Zoe halted at the door to the reception with a frown. 'Is there anyone who hasn't seen that van go up the hill? Has GCHQ been informed yet? Do you think we should ask the BBC to send a reporter?'

'OK,' Lavender said with a smirk. 'Someone got out of the wrong side of bed this morning – I only asked.'

'Sorry... it's just you and everyone else I've bumped into on the way here has asked me the same thing.'

'We did warn you nothing much happens around here – it's hardly surprising we get a bit overexcited when someone new moves in. You should have heard the fuss about you when you arrived.'

'I'm glad I didn't,' Zoe said, putting the biscuits she'd bought from the shop onto the counter for Lavender to put away. 'I dread to think what sort of theories everyone had about me.'

'Oh, they weren't too bad,' Lavender said carelessly. She scooped up the biscuits. 'Ottilie got much worse. So you haven't met them yet?'

'Not officially. I did pass them on the road. They looked normal enough, if it helps. I only counted one head on each of them, so that's a good sign.'

Lavender began to laugh as she put the biscuits into the drawer of a filing cabinet. 'Oh, you've got the measure of this place already. *One head each...*' She continued to chuckle as she went back to her desk and began to type. Zoe couldn't help but smile as she went to her own office. On the way through, she popped her head around the door of Ottilie's room to say good morning, and then did the same with Fliss and Simon.

Almost as soon as she'd got her coat off, the office phone rang. Lavender was on the line.

'Your nine thirty is here.'

Zoe looked at the clock. There was twenty minutes to go until the appointment time. She was about to say so when Lavender anticipated it.

'I've told her she's early and you're not ready yet, so don't stress. I'll make her a cup of tea.'

'That's sweet of you, thanks.'

'Well, I'm making one anyway, so... you want one?'

'Of course!' Zoe settled into her chair and switched on her computer. 'What did you think I bought the biscuits for?'

Lavender was chuckling again as she put the phone down. Lavender found almost everything funny. That was one of the first things Zoe had noticed about their receptionist, and it had been confirmed by Ottilie – nothing fazed her, and she could find the humour in almost every situation. It was a nice quality, one that Zoe liked.

She spent some time going through her emails to make sure nothing urgent had come in over the weekend, and then spent some more time prioritising what had come in. Once that was done and she'd formed a plan for the day, she called in her first appointment.

Maisie was tiny – smaller than Zoe herself, which was some feat. She looked far younger than her twenty years too.

Zoe glanced at the notes after they'd had a brief, introductory conversation. 'You're due your first scan next week... I don't see an appointment on the system yet. Have you made one?'

'I was hoping you'd do it.'

'An appointment? I mean, I can, but it's probably easier for you to go online and choose a slot.'

'I meant the scan. Can't you do it here?'

'I don't have the equipment here at the surgery. You'll have to go to the ultrasound department.'

'Oh.'

'Is that a problem?'

'No, it's just... It's OK – I can go on the bus.'

'Do you have someone to go with you?'

'Kyle, my boyfriend... maybe he'll go.'

'Is he baby's dad?'

'No. Does that matter?'

'I'm sure it doesn't, as long as he's happy to go. Can I ask about the baby's father? No judgement, of course, and if you don't want to talk about it, that's completely fine, but it might help me to care for you if I know more about your situation.'

'He's not mad at me or anything. About the baby, I mean.'

'I should think *not*. It takes two to tango.'

'Huh?'

'You know, two to make a baby.'

'We're not together. We were sort of... I was sort of drunk.'

'And how do you feel about it all?'

'Oh, I want the baby if that's what you mean. Kyle says he'll help. We haven't been together long, but he's all right about it. He says Harvey's a dick.'

'Harvey... that's the father?'

'Yeah. I mean, I'm not going to ask Kyle to be the dad or anything.'

'But it's good he's being supportive. Who else do you have in your corner?'

'Huh?'

'Do you have a good support network? Family, friends?'

'I've got Mum and Dad and my sister. They're all right about it too. I mean, Mum says she doesn't want the baby to call her grandma because she's not an old woman, but she's happy about it... I think. Well, I mean, she's not mad. Not too mad. And Dad doesn't say much at all, but I don't think he's too mad either.'

Zoe kept her expression neutral, but there were doubts forming in her mind. It wasn't what Maisie was telling her but what she seemed to be keeping back that worried her. She was doing her best to paint a positive picture of a scenario that – to Zoe – had worrying aspects. But Zoe had to remember her role. First and foremost, she was there to take care of Maisie and the baby in a clinical capacity. As she got to know them better, if she was still convinced there would be other needs, she'd have to talk to Maisie about referring her to the appropriate service, but it was early days yet, too early to say.

'Do you mind if I have a look?' she asked, gesturing to the treatment couch. 'I'll take some initial measurements so we can keep track of baby's growth over the coming months.'

'Um, yeah, I guess so.'

'Don't look so worried,' Zoe said with a reassuring smile. 'It's all pretty straightforward. Have you thought about names yet?' she added as Maisie got comfortable. It was a well-used question, but so often it served to steer an anxious consultation into calmer waters.

'Oh, yes!' Maisie said with a new enthusiasm that Zoe was pleased to see.

Appointments over the next couple of days were far more straightforward and a lot less worrying, unless you counted the complaints from some that they'd had to travel in from a neighbouring village to see her. She'd promised to see what she could do to make it easier for them by travelling out to do home visits, but warned that it would very much depend on her workload over the coming weeks and months.

She hadn't quite got her clinic up to full speed, even though referrals were beginning to arrive with more regularity as word got round she was now in post and ready to go. That day she had only one patient booked for the early afternoon, who didn't show up. She noted with interest that it was Billie Fitzgerald, her new neighbour at Hilltop Farm.

She tried to phone, but there was no answer, and so she decided now would be a good time to pop over to the parent and baby group at the village hall to introduce herself and get to know everyone. Really, her remit finished when the babies were far younger, but she'd probably still have contact with many of them anyway. Not to mention the possibility that some of the mothers would be pregnant again at some point.

She arrived back at the surgery just in time for tea and biscuits, phoned again to see if she could get hold of Billie, but with no success, and then spent an hour or so getting her notes up to date before heading home.

As she left the surgery, she decided to make a detour on her way back to Kestrel Cottage. Not only did she want to drop by to make sure all was well at Hilltop, she couldn't deny that she was mad with curiosity.

8

Zoe knocked at the front door of Hilltop Farm. There had already been changes since her last visit, the day she'd helped to move Ann out. The clutter of the front yard had been cleared away, and the soil was newly turned over. Some of the trees and shrubs still remained on the outskirts, but piled neatly in a corner of the yard were rolls of new turf and a tiny mountain of golden gravel, presumably waiting to be used to landscape the rest of the garden. The new owners of Hilltop hadn't messed around. The windows – which had been noticeably grubby during Ann's time – were now clean, as was the front door and step, and there were modern blinds where there had previously been greying nets and faded curtains. Tugging at the knots in her wind-tangled hair, she idly took in the changes as she waited for someone to answer. From within, she could hear barking, and then a stern voice that made it stop.

'Hello...'

She spun back to the door. There he was: well-worn jeans teamed with a brushed shirt in a blue check, open at the neck, sleeves rolled up to expose muscled forearms. His dark hair was messy from being pushed back from his face, and there were flecks of paint in it. He was clearly in the middle of something, and he ought to have looked scruffy, but the effect was quite the opposite.

'Hi. I don't know if you remember, but we met... briefly, when you were looking around a few weeks back. I'm Zoe. I live over there,' she added, flinging an arm out in the direction of Daffodil Farm.

He showed her a smile that looked like it was draining him of his last reserves. It was nothing like the relaxed and warm one he'd given her during their first meeting. 'I remember. You live in Kestrel Cottage.'

'Yes,' Zoe said, slightly taken aback that he'd recalled quite so much detail. 'I thought, as we're neighbours proper now, I'd come over and introduce myself. And I have another... well, I also thought I might be able to kill two birds with one stone. I understand Billie Fitzgerald lives here?'

The tired smile faded, and his expression was cautious now. 'What do you want her for?'

'I'm the midwife. Billie's new midwife. I mean, she's been referred to me.'

'Oh, right... you make house calls? At this time of day?'

'No, not officially. Like I said, I was planning to say hello anyway, and as Billie didn't show for her appointment today—'

'She had an appointment? She didn't say.'

'Is she in? I only wanted to see if everything was all right.'

'Everything is fine. I'll tell her you called.'

'About her next app—'

'She won't miss the next one – I'll talk to her and make sure.'

'But could I just—'

'Thanks for checking on things, but if you don't mind, I've got to—'

The door closed before he'd finished his excuse. Was it an excuse? It certainly sounded like one.

She paused on the doorstep. She didn't like it, but she wasn't sure why. He'd been pleasant enough, but she'd been in this job long enough to know that not everything could be taken at face value. In a second, her decision was made. She rapped at the door again. There was more barking. A moment later, it opened and he reappeared.

'Was there something...?'

'I really would like to speak to Billie, if it's all right with you. Could you tell her I'm here?'

'I said she wouldn't miss another appointment.'

'Yes, but I really need to make contact sooner rather than later, and I'm here... it's part of my job, you see, a tick-box thing, you know.' She gave a cheerful shrug to make light of the little white lie. 'I have to say I've seen her and all is well, otherwise it's an outstanding thing in the protocols. So if she could come to the door, it would help me out ever so much.'

'I'm sorry, but she's asleep, and I'm not going to wake her for your protocols.'

'Can I come over again tomorrow then?'

'Couldn't you make an appointment to see her tomorrow if you're that desperate?'

'It's not that...' Zoe paused. It wasn't that simple. 'Would she come if I did?'

'I'm not her boss, but I'm sure she would.'

'You'd bring her down to the surgery?'

'She's old enough to bring herself to the surgery.'

'But it's important she attends her appointment... you do understand that?'

His jaw tightened. Zoe could see when someone's patience was wearing thin. 'Make her one and I'll march her down to the surgery myself. There, does that satisfy you?'

Zoe held back a frown. 'Thank you. It won't be tomorrow; it'll probably be next week now because—'

'Sure, great.'

The door closed again. This time, Zoe's brow was etched with deep lines of dissatisfaction. Something was going on here. She couldn't say if it was bad or not, but she was going to get to the bottom of it.

The first thing she did at work the following morning was look for Billie's phone number. But before she could dial it to reschedule their appointment, the phone rang, and it was Billie herself on the line.

'Is that the midwife?'

'Yes.'

'It's Billie Fitzgerald. My dad says you came up to see me yesterday. I'm sorry I didn't come to the clinic. I was...'

The explanation tailed off. Zoe spoke into the gap it left. 'Pregnancy can be a tiring time, can't it? Especially so when you've just moved into a new home. Things aren't as easy or straightforward as they'd usually be, and we all forget things from time to time, even the best of us. Don't worry about it.'

'Yeah. So I guess I need to come down? Like, I definitely need to see you?'

'Nobody can force you, but I'm sure you understand that it would be better for you and baby if I could keep an eye on things. Besides,' Zoe continued, keeping things as light and cheery as possible, 'I'm new here, and I could do with enough work to persuade the partners I'm worth the salary, so you'd be doing me a favour, really.'

'What time?' Billie asked, and Zoe couldn't help but note the flatness of her tone.

'Today? I don't have—'

'When then?'

'Let me see...' Zoe clicked through her appointment slots on the computer. There was no space for that day, but if she skipped lunch, she could make a slot, and she did want to see Billie sooner rather than later. 'Can you come today at one? The surgery would be closed for lunch, but if you phone when you get here, I could let you in.'

'OK.'

'So I'll see you—'

The call was ended before Zoe could say goodbye. There was no point in feeling offended – and Zoe dealt with so many different personalities in her line of work that she rarely did. Instead, she dialled reception to let Lavender know the plan.

'It's a slippery slope,' Lavender tutted as Zoe filled her in. 'You do it once or twice and before you know it everyone's demanding we open at lunchtime. And then it's no breaks and backs to the grindstone, lads.'

'I promise it'll be just this once. I'd hate to be the person who ends your lunchtime get-togethers.'

'And it's moussaka today as well – Simon made it. Well, when I say Simon made it, I expect Stacey did.'

'Stacey? Oh, right, his girlfriend. He's not that hopeless, is he?' Zoe laughed lightly.

'It's more a case of him not having time.'

'Right. So that's OK then? I'd be ever so grateful if you could save me some moussaka and I'll stuff it into my face at some point before the afternoon clinic.'

'See...' Lavender said, 'the slippery slope.'

Zoe grinned as she put the phone down.

No sooner had she gone back to look at the morning schedule than there was a knock on the door and Lavender opened it. 'I'm making coffee, but I can't tell what's a mug and what is you.'

Zoe burst out laughing. 'That's one way of making your opinion of me clear.'

On finishing her morning list, Zoe checked her phone and saw a text from Ritchie. It was no surprise, though part of her wished he'd stop doing it. They'd agreed to remain on good terms as the divorce was going through, but, for her, that didn't mean almost as many messages as he'd sent to her when they'd been happily married.

> *How are you settling in? I've been thinking about you. I'd love to come and see where you're living. I googled the village – it looks tiny. I can't imagine what there is to do, but I guess you're there to work. I'm decorating here, hope you don't mind but I thought it would be all right as you're not coming back, and as soon as we've worked out the details, I'm going to be buying you out anyway. It's mostly grey. You'd hate it, of course. x*

Zoe paused, a vague frown creasing her forehead before she tapped out a reply. She had to get the wording right because Ritchie tended to read into messages what he wanted to see, regardless of whether it was there or not. At least, that was how it used to be, and she had no reason to suppose he'd changed since their split. There had been a time, in the beginning, when she would have been glad to know he was thinking of her during their time apart, but as the months went on, she wished desperately he'd find himself a new partner and move on. She didn't want the constant reminders of what she'd lost, no matter how well intentioned they were.

> *All good here. I'm not quite settled in, but it's nice and I'm sure I'll get there. People are friendly, and the team at the surgery are lovely. If you're worrying about me, you don't*

need to. Ottilie is here too, so help is never far away. Paint whatever you like in the house. You're right, it'll be yours soon anyway.

That's good. You're not angry that I messaged? x

Of course not. There's just nothing much to tell. I'm fine, thanks for asking.

I saw your brother in town. He says he hasn't been over to see your new place either yet. I told him I could come over when he does, kill two birds with one stone. Not that you'd want to kill us, lol! At least I hope not! x

Zoe heaved out a sigh. She'd always be grateful that their divorce was amicable and they could be grown-ups about it, but she didn't want to do this. After considering many replies, she decided to put her phone away. Maybe the right one would come to her later, but she didn't have the time or energy to find it now. Instead, she wiped down the surfaces of her treatment room, her stomach grumbling as the aromas of the lunch she was missing reached her. As she tidied, she half wondered if Billie would fail to show again, but at one on the dot her phone rang.

'I'm here,' was all Billie said, and Zoe went out to meet her at the front door of the surgery, ushered her inside and then locked it again.

Billie was slender, and her features were taut, in the way that someone who lives with constant worry looks, but closer up she was far prettier than Zoe recalled from that brief glimpse of her in the van the day she'd passed it on the road.

'Thanks for coming down,' she said as she led the way to her room. 'How are you settling in at Hilltop? I'm new around here myself, actually. It takes some getting used to – it did me, at any rate.' Zoe closed the door to her room and gestured for Billie to take a seat.

'It's fine,' Billie replied, with that same flat tone she recognised from earlier on the phone. 'It's as good as anywhere. For now.'

'You don't plan to stay long term?'

'If you mean did I plan to be single, pregnant and living with my dad in the back of beyond at twenty-three, then let's just say it wasn't on my life's bingo card.'

'Do you want to talk about it? I mean, say no if you like, but you're lucky – its lunchtime, the surgery is closed and I don't have anyone waiting to come in for a while yet. We wouldn't be disturbed.'

'I'd rather not. Unless I have to.'

'Of course you don't. It might help if I know something of your circumstances, but it's not the law or anything. You say baby's father isn't around? Are you still—'

Zoe froze, her stomach dropping through the floor. The look on Billie's face told her that things were far worse than the father simply skipping town, and she could have cheerfully slapped herself for jumping to silly conclusions. It was unlike her – she was usually so professional and diplomatic about these things. There was something about Billie that flustered her, but for the life of her she couldn't work out what it was.

'All you need to know,' Billie said in a very deliberate tone, 'is that he's not around and he never will be. I don't want to talk about it now.'

'Right.' Zoe went to her desk. 'But you have your dad, you said. That's good. I'm sure he's a big support.'

'I try not to bother him. He's had his own problems since Mum died.'

'Your mum died? Billie, I'm so sorry. When was this?'

'It'll be two years at Christmas.'

'It must have been hard.'

'It was. I had Luis, and he was amazing, so it wasn't so bad for me. Until I lost...'

Billie's shoulders sagged. The whole of her seemed to sag, as if her soul had left her body. Zoe saw in her eyes dullness where there ought to have been life and hope. It worried her. Pregnancy and motherhood was hard enough, harder still when the new mother wasn't able to experience the reward in it.

She paused, studying her for a moment. She wondered whether Ottilie ought to come and talk to her. Something had obviously happened to the baby's father – seemingly the Luis she'd mentioned – and whatever it was, it had been tragic enough to take him from Billie's life forever. Ottilie knew more about that kind of loss than Zoe did. Not that Zoe hadn't suffered her share of tragedy, but if anyone was living proof that things could and would get better, then it was Ottilie.

'So it's just you and your dad up at Hilltop?'

'Does that matter?'

'Of course not. I'm only trying to get a sense of your circumstances so I can help you better. It's nice, actually, to be able to get to know my mums-to-be on a more personal level. When I worked in Manchester, I had so many on my list I barely had time to say hello during the appointment.' She left a gap for some kind of response, but when there was none, Zoe gave a mental shrug. There was plenty of time and no need to rush things – she felt confident she could gain Billie's trust and get her to open up. She decided to stick to business for now. 'Do you have a care plan from your previous midwife?'

'Didn't she send it over?'

'I'm afraid not. I wondered if she'd given you physical paperwork... you know, a little folder or something. We used to use those, years ago. You had to carry them around everywhere.'

Billie shook her head and regarded Zoe as if she was wishing she could find her off switch.

'OK,' Zoe said, choosing to ignore the withering looks, 'I've got some medical records, so we'll have to muddle through as best we can. I'll contact your old midwife to see if I can get more info for next time I see you.'

She went to her computer to pull up the relevant pages. As she did so, she noticed Billie staring out of the window. Absent, looking but not seeing, a hand resting on her belly. Her sadness didn't only fill the room; it threatened to suck the oxygen from it. Zoe was no stranger to sadness, but she'd never experienced it like this, and she hoped, looking at the younger woman now, she'd never have to.

9

Zoe ended up taking her moussaka home with her. By the time she'd seen Billie off, tidied her room and got the afternoon's clinic prepped, it was too late to join the others and she'd gone past being hungry anyway. Lavender had popped her head around the door to say they'd put a doggy bag in the fridge for her and then plied her with extra cake during afternoon coffee break, and by the time Zoe walked into the door at Kestrel Cottage, her mouth was watering at the thought of the meal that everyone had raved about earlier. The fact that she didn't have to cook it herself was a very welcome bonus.

She'd no sooner put the oven on to warm it when there was a knock at the front door. For the briefest moment, she considered ignoring it. The working day had felt like a long one, and all she wanted was a few moments to herself. But she decided it might be something important – perhaps Victor or Corrine, who, she'd discovered, never seemed to phone anyone when they could call to see them instead. In fact, Victor didn't even possess a mobile phone – he'd lost too many around the place, he said, and didn't see the point in continuing to add to the cache already languishing in the fields around Daffodil Farm.

Ottilie confirmed that both Corrine and Victor were stubbornly old-fashioned about communication but that everyone knew they were never going to change at this point in their lives. Zoe had set up a standing order to pay the rent, and there was some due out that week. She hadn't yet seen it leave her account and perhaps there was a problem.

Whatever it might be and no matter how she might want to ignore it, Zoe decided she'd better go and see.

'Oh...!'

'Sorry...' Alex was on the doorstep. He was out of his scruffs today, but still casual in a denim shirt and black jeans, and there were traces of paint in his dark hair, only visible up close. And Zoe found herself looking and wishing she was even closer...

He glanced at her work uniform. 'Is this a bad time?'

'Um, no... I mean, I didn't mean to make it sound as if it was. I wasn't expecting it to be you.'

'Ah. I just wanted to check... Billie says she came to see you today. I mean, she did, right?'

'She did.' Zoe relaxed into a smile.

'And did she tell you...? I mean, what did you talk about? If I'm allowed to ask.'

'Mostly about her pregnancy,' Zoe lied. It was only a little one, and in the name of patient confidentiality, so it was for a good cause. Those sorts of lies didn't bother her one bit.

He held up a carrier bag. 'They said at the shop that you liked these chocolates.'

Zoe frowned. He was bringing her chocolate? He'd asked Magnus and Geoff what she liked? Even more surprising, as she took the bag and peered in, was that Magnus and Geoff had even noticed what brand of chocolate she favoured. The bag was full of it. She'd been given chocolates before, but never like this, and she had no clue what they were for.

'Are they wrong?' Alex asked.

'No, these are my favourites,' Zoe said, smoothing her frown as she looked up. 'And so much of it... I won't have to buy any for the next year. Thank you.'

There was a gap – not long, but long enough to start feeling awkward. With a sudden desperation to fill the silence, Zoe said the first thing that came into her head. 'Would you like to come in?'

'If you're busy, then—'

'I'm not especially. I've got time for a tea or coffee if you'd like one.'

He seemed torn before nodding. 'That sounds good. You were right – if we're neighbours, then we ought to get to know one another a bit better.'

Zoe wondered whether she might get more information about his and Billie's circumstances. Perhaps, once they'd relaxed and started to chat properly over a hot drink, he might open up. She'd felt a strange pull to Billie ever since the appointment over lunch, and her thoughts had turned to the young woman often during the afternoon. Her other expectant mums had been fairly happy, straightforward cases, and so it had left plenty of space for Zoe to mull over her more complicated ones.

It was hard to tell whether Alex was happy to be in Zoe's house or not. He seemed ill at ease as he stepped in, and yet she'd put no pressure on him to accept her offer. She turned off the oven she'd switched on before he'd knocked on her door and then put the bag of chocolate on the kitchen table as he took a seat there.

'Would you like tea or coffee?' she asked. 'I can only do instant coffee, though. I've got chai, or green or chamomile if you'd prefer tea.'

'Am I interrupting your evening meal?' he asked, his gaze going to the oven she'd just switched off.

'Not at all. It only needs reheating, so it won't take long. I'll have it later. What'll it be to drink?'

'Instant coffee is fine, thank you.' He turned his attention to his surroundings. 'You say you haven't been here long?'

'A few weeks now.'

'You seem to have settled quickly. Quicker than we have. You've got it nice... homely.'

'I can't take any of the credit for that – it was furnished when I got here.'

'It's rented?'

'Yes, from Victor and Corrine... Daffodil Farm,' she added in response to his puzzled look.

'So you're not planning a long-term stay?'

'Quite honestly, I don't know yet. I'm on a six-month trial at the surgery. Ottilie – that's my friend who's a nurse there – is fairly certain I'll be kept on. She says the trial's just a formality, but...' Zoe shrugged as she opened a cupboard and got out two mugs. 'Who knows? I'm old enough not to take anything for granted.'

'How are you finding it?'

'The job or the village?'

'Both, I suppose.'

'The job's straightforward enough – I've adapted to new workplaces before, and there's no reason why I won't do it this time. The village... well...' She gave a small smile. 'It's a bit of a culture shock. A nice one, but very different to what I've been used to.'

'Where's that?'

'Manchester. That's where I know Ottilie from. She got me the job here – at least, she nudged it forcefully in my direction. I never would have considered a move like this if not for her doing it first. And it seems to have worked out really well for her, so...' She poured hot water into the mugs. 'Do you take milk and sugar?'

'Both, please. One sugar.'

'What about you?' she asked as she poured milk into his mug.

'Me? There's nothing interesting to tell.'

'Have you moved far from where you were?'

'We've lived here and there. We got back from Spain a few weeks ago.'

'You were living there?'

He nodded.

'Wow, that's a move and a half! Don't you miss the sun?'

'Sometimes,' he said, and while his face was smiling, his eyes were not. 'But circumstances changed, and we couldn't stay.'

'*We?* Billie lived out there with you?'

'She did.'

'Just you and her? Like it is now?'

'This coffee's not bad, for instant,' he said with a brisk nod, and Zoe recognised a segue when she heard one. What he really meant was: don't ask any more about Spain. That didn't mean she wasn't desperate with curiosity, though. She'd wanted to get him to open up about Billie, but right now she was getting very little about either of them. If she opened up herself, would that encourage him?

'I'm going through a divorce,' she said. 'It's all perfectly civil, and we're still friends. I mean, I'd prefer if it hadn't come to this, but it did and we're dealing with it. That's part of the reason I chose to take this job. It seemed like a clean break, a fresh start, you know?'

Opening up about the divorce was one thing, but the baby she'd lost... Zoe decided there was no need to relive that particular pain, and so she kept that factor in the end of her marriage to herself for now.

'I'm sorry to hear that, but if it's amicable and it's what you both want then... I don't know. Am I supposed to say I'm pleased for you? Or is it still a bad thing? I've never been through one, so I don't know. Do you have children?' He looked around the kitchen, as if he expected to find a clue to the answer there.

'No children,' Zoe said with all the strength she could muster to keep her tone even. 'It's all nice and clean... if there can ever be such a thing where divorce is concerned.'

'I see.'

'You've just got Billie?'

'Yes.'

'You're close? I mean, it seems so. To me.'

The look in his eyes softened. Zoe couldn't help but dwell on them for a moment – they really were the warmest, gentlest shade of brown, and when he allowed himself to relax, they became deep wells of open generosity. 'I suppose we are. How was she? When you saw her today?'

'You haven't seen her yourself today?'

'I meant her pregnancy. It's all as it ought to be?'

'Oh.' Zoe smiled as she sat down. 'I see. I'm sure she won't mind me telling you everything is as it ought to be. I can't say anything more than that, of course.'

'Of course. Thanks for telling me what you could.'

She could see how much her brief reassurance had meant to him by the way the tension visibly drained from his expression.

'Are you planning to farm?' she asked. 'I mean, that's what Ann and her husband did with the land at Hilltop. I don't think she did so much after he died; I understand she struggled to run it on her own.'

'Actually, no,' he said, taking a sip of his coffee. 'I'm planning to build pods.'

'Pods?'

'You know, camping pods. Glamping, really.'

'Holiday lets? I didn't realise. Are you building them yourself? Are they difficult to put up? I have no clue how these things work, but I'm sure you'll have no trouble renting them out when they're ready.'

'It's early days yet. That's the plan. As for the logistics, I'm just working those out. I've got some money put aside from the sale of the holiday villa I had in Spain and a bit of inheritance, so I'll manage until it's all up and running. In reality, I don't expect to start making anything for the next six months or so. Who's going to want to stay in a pod on a hillside in the British winter, even if they were ready to go?'

'Not me, that's for sure,' Zoe agreed. 'It sounds like a great idea for summer, though.'

He peered at her, something like curiosity on his face now. 'You're not worried that it'll shatter your peace? Having people coming back and forth to stay?'

'You forget, I've lived in Manchester my whole life. It would take a lot more than a few tourists to be worse than some of the house parties I've had going on next door to me over the years. What makes you worry about that? Has someone complained already?'

'You're the first person I've told, but I've been warned by a friend who did something similar to be ready for local opposition, especially in a small place like this. People tend to be wary of change.'

'I don't expect it'll be all that bad. Victor already has a business geared up for tourists.'

'Oh? What's that?'

'Alpaca trekking. He takes big parties out over the fields all summer. Does well out of it, I think.'

He nodded slowly, as if digesting the information. 'That's worth knowing. I'm sure we could be good for one another.'

'I'm sure he'd agree. He seems like a nice, reasonable guy. You should go over and chat to him.'

'I will, thanks.'

'It really helps to have good neighbours, in our situation, I think.'

'Yes,' he said, turning that warm openness on again. 'I couldn't agree more. Not that we'd be bothering you every hour of the day, but it's reassuring to know you're not far away. For Billie, I mean.'

'I actually meant Victor and Corrine, but I take your point.'

Zoe silently wondered what sort of neighbours Alex and Billie would turn out to be. Something told her she'd like having them around, but they'd come with baggage. Did she want that? She was still dealing with so much of her own, after all.

'Ah,' he said, taking another sip of his drink. 'Of course. We tend to keep ourselves to ourselves, so don't worry about—'

'I didn't mean that at all,' Zoe cut in. 'Anything you need, anything Billie needs, please don't think you can't come over and ask. In fact, I'll give you my phone number before you leave. Billie has the surgery number in her records, but you can have my personal...' Zoe flushed. It was silly, there was nothing in her offer but friendship, but she suddenly worried that it would be taken the wrong way.

'Thank you,' he cut in. 'It's kind of you.'

She relaxed as she realised he'd taken it at face value, just as she'd intended. Or perhaps he'd understood her mortified expression and wanted to put her at ease. Either way, it was a relief.

'I wanted to say,' he continued, his words measured, as if he'd rehearsed them, 'I am sorry about the way I spoke to you yesterday when you came to check on Billie. I'm surprised you didn't throw her out of your clinic.'

'Why on earth would I do that? Even if you had been unforgivably rude to me – which you weren't – it's not Billie's fault, and it's certainly not her baby's!' She shook her head. 'I'd never turn her away!'

He stared at her. Perhaps it had been something of an impassioned outburst, and perhaps it had been a little too dramatic, but since she'd lost her own baby, her motivation to make sure it didn't happen to anyone else was something like a personal religion. She'd never been one to take life seriously until it had happened to her, but losing her own child had changed her. These days she took life, and her job, very seriously indeed. That didn't mean she couldn't enjoy it, and she did, but she was determined to pull out all the stops to care for her expectant mums in the very best way she knew how, no matter what it took, no matter if it encroached on her personal life.

'You really... I'm glad Billie's got you in her corner.'

Zoe flushed again. She suddenly felt silly for the way she'd reacted, quite certain that he hadn't been looking for such a passionate response. The kitchen fell into an embarrassed silence.

Then the moment was punctured by the sound of a phone pinging the arrival of a message.

'I think that's yours,' he said. 'Doesn't sound like mine.'

'I think it might be,' she said. 'I'll get it later.'

'Don't mind me, if you want to see who it is—'

'I'm sure it will wait half an hour or so. If they really need me, they'll phone rather than text.'

'Good point.' He tipped up the mug to drink the last of his coffee.

'Not that I meant you only had half an hour or anything,' Zoe added hastily, realising how that sounded and blushing again.

'I know what you meant,' he said with a warm smile. 'But I think I probably have outstayed my welcome, and you've got an evening meal to heat up.'

The smile that broke free from her now matched his. 'I'd offer you some, but there's not enough.'

'I wouldn't dream of it, and besides, I've got to get back. Billie's cooking, and I'm sure it will be nearly ready.'

'It's good to know she's looking after you as much as you're obviously looking after her.'

'She does,' he said, his smile spreading, warm and mellow as a summer's evening. There was so much pride in it, so much protection, so much subtext that told Zoe that his daughter was everything to him, and if Zoe had ever doubted their relationship, that smile would have swept it all away.

Zoe's phone pinged again, and this time a vague frown creased her forehead. She got up to put it on silent and noted the identity of the messenger, and her frown deepened.

This village of yours is really hard to find. Did you choose it deliberately so I wouldn't be able to visit, lol? x

What did that mean? Surely Ritchie didn't mean literally? He wouldn't be on his way in the car? Would he? They'd made no arrangements, even though he'd mentioned coming over earlier that day.

No, Zoe decided, even Ritchie wasn't that obtuse. He must have been looking on Google Maps or something, trying to find Thimblebury's location online. Even that bothered her, though she couldn't exactly say why.

Despite trying to draw a sensible, reassuring conclusion to what Ritchie's message might mean, Zoe was suddenly gripped by a vague panic and a need to get Alex out of her house. As she scrabbled for an excuse that wouldn't sound rude, he seemed to understand. She looked up from her phone to see him put his mug down and stand up.

'I can see you're busy,' he said. 'I'd better be off anyway. Thanks for the drink – and for seeing Billie earlier today.'

'Oh, that's... thank you for the chocolate. You really didn't have to, but—' Her sentence was cut short by a knock at the door. A wave of dread swept over her. 'Could you wait here for a moment while I see who it is?'

Zoe left Alex in the kitchen without waiting for his reply. If Ritchie was at the door, what did it matter? They weren't together, and she had nothing to hide, so why did she feel guilty for having another man in her house? And what did she hope to achieve by asking Alex to wait? Was he going to cotton on and climb out of the window so he'd be gone by the time she'd shown Ritchie in? And why did the prospect of it being Ritchie make her heart sink like this? They'd agreed to stay friends, and they still got along well, so there was no reason for it.

There was a second knock at the door.

'OK, OK!' Zoe called, and this time she knew for sure. There was nobody else in her life with that kind of impatience.

She threw open the front door and there he was, Ritchie, on the doorstep with a bunch of flowers and a grin that blindly assumed she must be pleased to see him.

'Housewarming,' he said, shoving the bouquet at her. 'This place is a bugger to find. What do you want to go and live up here for? It's like that village out of the *League of Gentleman* – you know, *This is a local shop for local people...*'

Zoe had never regretted a decision quite so much as she did at that moment. What had possessed her to give Ritchie her address when she'd taken possession of Kestrel Cottage? At the time, she'd thought nothing of it – she had nothing to hide, after all – but what kind of idiot had she been not to have seen this coming?

Things were made worse when she heard Alex's voice in the hallway behind her.

'Sorry,' he said, glancing from her to Ritchie and then back again. 'I see you have... I should go. Thanks again for the coffee.'

'Right...' Zoe flattened herself against the wall of the hallway to let him past, flowers right under her nose making her want to sneeze. Ritchie paused and almost seemed to make himself bigger as Alex approached the front door, and then, after a strange, charged moment, he moved aside to let him out.

Nobody said a word as Alex made his way down the path and away from the house.

As soon as he was out of earshot, Ritchie turned back to Zoe. 'Aren't you going to ask me in?'

'Yes, I was ... yes, come in.'

Ritchie followed her inside and closed the door behind him. 'God, this is tiny!'

'There's only me so it's big enough. I wasn't expecting you... I'm sorry, I'm still a bit upside down.'

'I said I was coming.'

'You said you wanted to. I didn't realise that meant immediately.'

He paused as she led him to the kitchen. 'You want me to go? After I drove all this way?'

'I didn't say that. I meant I wasn't expecting company.'

'Except for *him*.'

'What?'

'The bloke who just left. So you had company. Is that why you didn't want me to come over?'

'I never said I didn't want you to come over – you didn't give me a chance!'

'So what was all that about your door always being open? When you moved away, you said you wanted to stay in touch and you wanted us to be friends because you hated to see when couples threw away big piles of memories they'd made with someone because of a divorce.'

Zoe pulled in a long breath to steady herself. She had said all of that and she'd meant it, but she hadn't realised Ritchie would take it quite so literally. She'd always wanted them to be able to speak to one another civilly if their paths were to cross, and she didn't want to taint the good memories from their marriage by turning what they'd once had into hatred. And while she was happy to have a relationship of sorts with him, surely he understood that didn't mean he should have a presence in her life that was almost as big as it had been when they'd been together?

At first, she'd understood they needed one another – they'd both been grieving the loss of their baby even as their marriage had disintegrated, and she'd wanted to be there for him. But there was a time limit – there had to be. She couldn't be there for him forever. She needed to move on, and so did he, and that was hardly likely to happen if he kept turning up every time he was bored or lonely.

'I only wanted to make sure you were all right,' he said as she put the flowers into the sink and searched for a vase. 'Is that so bad? I still care about you, even though we're not together. And is it so wrong to worry about you? You did go a bit crazy for a while after the baby...' He shrugged. 'You know, all that business when we lost it...'

It still stung. It stung that Ritchie could talk about those times as if they were a minor inconvenience instead of the earth-shattering, soul-crushing weeks that they were.

'*Him!*' Zoe snapped. 'When we lost *him*! Because our little boy died!'

'I know,' he said, flushing. 'That's what I meant... Come on, Zo, you know I'm no good at this stuff.'

Zoe folded her arms tight, but the hurt on his face shattered her resolve. 'I know. I still care about you too – you know that. Whatever happens, that won't change. I only meant... well, don't you think we should look outside what we had a bit more now that we're not together. We both need to build new lives.'

'And you seem really keen to build yours. Was that your new boyfriend?'

'What?' Zoe let a cupboard door slam with more force than she'd meant to as she spun back to face him. 'Alex? God no! He's a new neighbour! He only came by to say hello.'

'I bet he did.'

'He did, and even if he hadn't...' Zoe sat down across from Ritchie, who'd taken a seat at the table. 'You're telling me you haven't even started to think about seeing other women?'

'It's too soon for that.' He paused, his expression strangely worried. 'You have?'

'No, but that's not the point. If the right person came along for either of us, it'd be silly to ignore that, wouldn't it? I'm not looking for a second go, but if the opportunity came along, I'd like to think I'd have your blessing. You'd have mine.'

'You would – you know you would, but...'

Zoe suppressed a sigh. How could she make it clear that she didn't want him to keep coming around, without him getting that expression that made him look like a puppy she'd just kicked? It was becoming clear that the staying-friends thing wasn't working. The only way they could move on was to let go.

While she'd been living in Manchester, he'd come round to her flat every week, but she'd written it off as him feeling lost and not having a huge network of friends. The fact was, her place was close by and so she'd forgiven it. She'd even tolerated it with some positivity because she'd been relieved that they'd been able to stay friends, and having him round for the odd meal had reinforced that friendship. But part of her making the decision to move away had been to loosen those ties. It had become too regular and too much, and she'd started to see that it wasn't doing either of them any good. Did she have to keep moving? Was that the answer? Would she have to keep changing her address until he lost track of her? Or did she simply have to take the bull by the horns and tell him?

'I'm sorry for coming,' he said into the gap. 'I only wanted to talk. I've had a redundancy notice.'

'What?'

He nodded. 'Yeah. Last thing today before we went home. It's been coming for a while, but it's still a shock.'

'You never said anything!'

'I didn't want to bother you with it. I mean, we're not together so I didn't think you'd be that interested.'

'Of course I would be, Ritchie. We're still friends. So how long have you got?'

'A couple of months, so I can try to find something else.'

'They really have no other post they can slot you into?'

'They're closing our branch, and they've said we can relocate to another, but I don't want to move, so...'

'What are you going to do?'

'I don't know.' His shoulders slumped as he looked up at her. 'You were always so good in these situations. I feel as if I'm losing everything, bit by bit. You're gone, and now my job...'

'You're *sure* you can't see yourself relocating?'

'Is that what you think I ought to do?'

'It doesn't matter what I think – I'm asking you what you think. Have you really gone through it, or have you made a decision based on your gut reaction? I know you love Manchester, but there's a big world out there, and some of it is almost as good.'

His smile was small and rueful. 'See. This is why I was so much better with you.'

'Ritchie... let's not go down that road again.'

'I know, I know – you're right, like you always are. I didn't mean to...'

Zoe reached to give his hand a brief squeeze. 'You'll be fine, you know. You're going to get another job, or you're going to relocate, and you'll surprise yourself at how well you handle it.'

'I wish I could agree, but thanks. See, I know you didn't want me to come, but when you make me feel so much better, how could I not?'

'I never said I didn't want you to come.' And there it was – the moment had come and gone. This wasn't the time to tell him that they had to stop getting together like this. Ritchie clearly needed her, and how could she refuse him? If not for what they had now, she owed him for what they'd once had.

'Have you eaten yet?'

'No.'

'I've got some moussaka to heat up. It's not much, but I can make it stretch. I mean, we'd have to put some bread with it, and it's only cheap bread, but... well, do you want to stay a while? What there is you're welcome to share.'

'You're sure it's no bother?'

'Not a bit,' she said, even though there was a little voice in her head telling her she would regret it.

10

Ritchie stayed for two hours. Their meal had been pleasant enough – Zoe had listened to him go through his options at work and given cautious opinions. While not wanting to get too involved, she wanted to show her support.

He'd dropped hints about Alex too. He kept asking how well she knew him, when he'd moved to the area, what his plans were, who was living at Hilltop with him. She couldn't see why he was so fixated on a man who'd barely spoken two words to him. Or perhaps she could, but she didn't want to acknowledge it because it would mean facing the fact that Ritchie was struggling to let go, despite the impending finality of their divorce. More than once, she came close to airing her worries, reasoning that if she didn't say something, their amicable relationship might be soured. And yet, she couldn't bring herself to raise the subject. Next time, she told herself, if there was a next time. Perhaps he'd go home and reflect on what she'd said when he'd first arrived and he'd work it out for himself and she wouldn't need to.

She'd seen him off, cleaned her kitchen, showered and then climbed into bed, her mind a whirr of activity, despite her exhaustion. And so, even though she was tired, it had taken over an hour for her to finally sleep.

Most of what had been on her mind popped back up the minute she woke the following morning, and it was still there when she arrived at work. If there had been more time to kill before her first appointment, she might have been tempted to seek Ottilie's opinion, but as they were both busy with full schedules, she decided it would wait. And then, as the morning went by, she decided the situation would resolve itself without having to burden anyone else.

The morning was uneventful. Everyone she saw was fine and healthy and progressing as they ought to be. The last appointment was a home visit, not too far out of the village, to see Sally, who'd given birth to a little girl the week before but while visiting relatives out of the area, and so it was the first time Zoe had managed to call on her since then.

'Can I get you a cup of tea?' Sally asked as she let Zoe in.

'Oh, no, thanks. I'm going to be having my lunch as soon as I've seen you. How have you been? Did you enjoy your time in... Surrey, wasn't it?'

'Yes, I was visiting my parents. I mean, it was a bit eventful...'

She raised her eyebrows, and Zoe laughed. 'Yes, I dare say giving birth could be considered eventful. I bet your parents were thrilled to have you close by, though.'

'My mum was – it meant she could be at the hospital with me. They've been brilliant, actually. Between you and me, I'd been getting a bit nervous as the birth approached, but Mum and Dad were so good and such a huge help, we've all completely forgotten by now that they were dead against the sperm donor business in the beginning.'

'I would imagine one look at baby would fix that,' Zoe said as Sally showed her into the sitting room, where a Moses basket sat on a stand.

Sally went to it and lifted her baby out. 'Here she is. Primrose Honeysuckle.'

'Awww...' Zoe drew closer. 'Hello there, Primrose! Aren't you the most beautiful little thing?'

'I think so,' Sally said. 'But of course, I would.'

'They're all beautiful to me,' Zoe said. 'All perfect. So, any worries? For Primrose or yourself?'

'Not that I can think of. I'm amazed at how relaxed I feel with her already. Mum kept telling me how hard it would be on my own, but I don't feel it yet. I suppose I might do when I go back to work, but I'm not even going to think about that until I have to.'

'You're taking the full year maternity leave?'

'I'm going to play it by ear. I did think six months – the pressure of being sole wage earner and all that – but I might enjoy my time with Primrose too much for that. I'm sure I'll find a way, whatever I decide to do. Mum and Dad will be desperate to help, of course. They're already smitten.'

'I'll bet they are.' Zoe smiled as she got out her scales. She was heartened to see that Sally seemed to have everything under control. She'd prove to be a calm and capable parent, she had no doubts there, and it sounded as if she had a good support network, even if they were a few hours down the motorway. 'Right then,' she added, holding her arms out for the baby, 'shall we see what's what?'

Zoe made it back from Sally's house as the surgery was closing for lunch. They were having Thai massaman curry and rice made by Fliss, which everyone agreed was a delicious surprise because she'd told them the day before it was going to be sausage casserole. And then the afternoon clinic was in full swing, and before she knew it, Zoe was calling in the final appointment.

'Hello, Tegan.' Zoe gestured a seat. 'How are you doing?'

'I'm not too good. I know I'm not due to see you yet, but...' Tegan dropped into the chair.

Zoe would have known things weren't good, even if Tegan hadn't just said so. 'I'm here whenever you need me – that's my job. You don't have to apologise.'

'Thanks for fitting me in anyway.'

'Again, not a problem. So what's worrying you?'

'I don't know. I mean, I'm knackered all the time. All I seem to do is sleep, and I was never this bad with either of my others. I'm older, I suppose. Is that normal?'

'It's not unexpected.'

'I feel different. I can't say what it is. I don't feel well at all. I know it's been eighteen years since my last one, but I don't remember feeling like this. I wasn't exactly bouncing around last time, but I didn't feel this exhausted. All I want to do is stay in bed, but I can't because I have to work and there's stuff to do in the house.'

'Can't you get help with the house? I'm sure if you explain to your family—'

'I have, but I don't think they get it.'

'Perhaps it would do you some good to take time off work? I could see about a note for you, to give you a couple of weeks' rest.'

Tegan nodded. 'That would be good.'

'And while you're here, I'll do some checks to make sure there's nothing going on undetected that we need to deal with. I expect it's all perfectly normal. Perhaps a little bit of it is your age – you're an older mum now, which I know you know all about – but it wouldn't hurt to cover all the bases.' Zoe got out her blood pressure reader. 'Any headaches? Blurred vision? Dizziness or nausea? Anything like that, or are you just tired?'

'Not just tired, absolutely exhausted. All the time. If I could take to my bed now I'd sleep for the rest of my life.'

'But nothing else?'

'I have had some headaches.'

'Do you think you could get a urine sample to me?'

'Already done it.' Tegan got a tiny bottle from her handbag and held it up. 'It's not my first time around the block, you know.'

'I see that,' Zoe said, taking the sample with a smile. 'I'll get it checked. I don't suppose you've managed to take your own blood pressure too?'

'Sorry, I'm not that good.'

'Not to worry; let's do that now. Baby seems all right? Any movement?'

'I haven't felt any kicking yet; it's hard to tell.'

'That's OK. I only ask because it's not your first and so I thought you might have noticed a bit of fluttering, but you're right, it's early. No bleeding?'

Tegan shook her head as Zoe wrapped the cuff around her arm and read her blood pressure. After a moment, she frowned but then immediately smoothed her expression into a bright smile. She didn't want to alarm Tegan, who had already proved to be nervous, despite the fact it was her third pregnancy. 'A bit on the high side,' she said. 'Higher than I'd like. But don't worry,' she added, aware that worrying was likely to drive Tegan's blood pressure higher still. 'I'm sure some rest and calm will bring it down.'

'Are you?' Tegan's eyes were wide.

'Absolutely. I'll want to keep a close eye on things, and so I'm going to ask that you come to see me a bit more often until I'm happy with it. And of course, I'll check your sample to make sure there's nothing else. I want you to take it easy until I see you again. Will you be able to do that if I give you a note for time off work?'

'I think so, as long as I have something official.'

'It will be. I think, to be on the safe side, you should stay at home for the next week at least. I'll see you again after that to check things, but if there's anything bothering you, phone me. Don't hesitate to call, no matter if you think it's silly. But the most important thing – and I can't stress this enough – is try not to worry. I know that's easier said than done, but if you can relax, that will help. Take advantage of some well-earned rest. I'm going to check a few other things while you're here, but I don't want you to think any of it is bad news.'

'OK.' Tegan nodded, her eyes still trained on Zoe as if her life depended on her. Zoe tried not to think about that. Instead, she got on with the task in hand and put her own fears to one side.

After work, Zoe changed quickly out of her uniform and freshened up before heading to Daffodil Farm. At the farmhouse back door, she shook out her umbrella, marvelling at how, only the previous weekend, she'd managed to get sunburned on the boat across Ullswater.

'Here.' Corrine pointed to a bucket with two other umbrellas already in there. 'Pop it in here, my love. It's coming down in stair rods out there, isn't it? Victor picks his moments to go out to the paddock to see to the girls.'

'The girls?' Zoe blinked.

'Oh, you know, his herd.'

'Oh, his alpaca!' Zoe cast a glance around the empty kitchen. 'Am I the first here?'

'Oh no, Ottilie and Stacey were here, but they've gone across with Victor. Ottilie's in love with those animals almost as much as he is – any excuse to go and see them.'

'She must be – she'll get soaked out there.'

'Don't worry, we fixed her and Stacey up with some of our old raincoats – they'll be all right in those. I shouldn't imagine they'll be long.'

'I'm a bit jealous. If I'd known there would be an alpaca visit, I'd have got here earlier myself. Is Victor joining us for our first girly night? He could be an honorary girl, couldn't he?'

'Lord no!' Corrine laughed as she went to the fridge and got out a pot of double cream. 'He wouldn't be able to keep up! He's got a programme to watch, so he'll be as good as gold in the living room. We can gossip about him as much as we like – he'd never know. Now where did I put my...?' Corrine searched the table and then let out a little huff of satisfaction. 'There you are!' she said, picking up an emerald ring. She seemed almost relieved when it was on her finger.

'That's a gorgeous ring,' Zoe said.

'Yes, isn't it? Victor got it for me a couple of years ago. I was poorly, you know. He bought this to celebrate when I got the all-clear from the hospital.'

Zoe nodded. She recalled Ottilie telling her about noticing the worrying signs of skin cancer shortly after she'd first met Corrine, and how she'd acted quickly to help Corrine get it diagnosed.

'I feel so bare these days without it. But, daft old thing that I am, I lost it in some pastry last year, so I take it off now when I'm kneading.' Corrine went to the stove and put on the kettle. 'Tea while we're waiting for the others? Unless you want to go over to the paddock, of course...'

'I think I'll stay here. I'll go over another time. Tea would be lovely.'

'Ottilie tells me you've met your new neighbours at Hilltop,' Corrine said as she lit the stove.

'I did. Alex bought me some chocolate. Which I thought was a nice little present just for me, until Magnus burst my bubble by telling me he'd been buying things for other people too...'

Corrine grinned. 'He did indeed – came over with some wine for us. Even though we don't really drink it, I thanked him for it and fed him. Seems a nice chap. Had a big conflab with us about his posh camping ideas.'

'Oh, his glamping. I imagine that's why he's buying us presents,' Zoe said, still wondering why she'd been disappointed to learn that she hadn't been the only recipient of Alex's gifts. 'He's trying to sweeten up his neighbours.'

'Without a doubt. If you know you might be causing a ruckus, you do what you can to get into people's good graces first. Although, I did say to him if he runs it right, he shouldn't have too much trouble. Not that it would trouble us in any case.'

'Will it trouble anyone? How much disruption can one camping field cause?'

'Around here, people will complain for the sake of hearing their own voices. You'll learn that soon enough.'

'I'm not sure I want to,' Zoe said, and Corrine started to laugh.

'I'm sure they won't be complaining about you. Who could do that?'

'You'd be surprised. Catch me on the right day, I can be annoying enough – ask my ex.'

Corrine shook her head. 'It's such a shame – lovely, pretty girl like you on your own.'

'Hardly a girl, and there are days when I wake up and look in the mirror and I'm anything but pretty. It doesn't bother me. Being on my own isn't where I saw myself at this point in my life, but it's where I am, and there's nothing I can do but get on with it. I intend to. It's good to have a man, and you and Ottilie and Stacey all seem to have struck gold, but I can do all right without one.'

'I'm sure you can,' Corrine said. 'As for gold...' She glanced out of the window and smiled. 'Here they all are now, like a bunch of drowned rats.'

A moment later, the back door of the farmhouse flew open,

and with a flurry of limbs and wet coats and laughter, Victor, Ottilie and Stacey stepped inside.

'I hope you're going to mop that puddle up,' Corrine said. Ottilie went towards a door in the corner of the room, and Corrine stopped her. 'I don't mean you – you're a guest. I mean that oaf of a husband of mine.'

'If it's all right, I'll go and wash my hands,' Ottilie said.

'Me too.' Stacey followed her. They both went through a door that led to a set of dark stairs.

Victor appeared from the broom cupboard a second later with the mop and began to clear up what was really hardly a puddle at all. Zoe thought, as she watched, that if they'd left it for a few minutes, it would have dried up all by itself, as they'd shaken most of the rain from their outdoor clothes into the porch.

'You can go now,' Corrine told Victor once Ottilie and Stacey returned.

'Give me a minute,' Victor said. 'What's the rush? You desperate to talk about me?'

'Pah,' Corrine said. 'We'll find more interesting subjects than that to talk about, no fear.'

'Well,' he replied, trying to hold back a grin. 'Do you want this water mopped up or not?'

Ottilie and Stacey shared a grin of their own as they sat down at the table with Zoe. Victor finished his chore and, with a wink at Corrine, left them to it.

'How were the girls?' Zoe asked.

'Cute as ever,' Ottilie said. 'I wasn't sure how long you'd be, otherwise we'd have waited for you.'

'Don't worry, I was a bit late coming out of clinic. My last appointment took longer than I'd planned, and I had some ringing round to do.'

'Lavender said you needed a last-minute sick note.'

Zoe nodded. 'It's all sorted now.'

'Was that Tegan Forester?' Stacey asked.

Zoe opened her mouth to reply without being quite sure what she was going to say.

'It's all right,' Stacey added. 'I saw her at the shop. She asked how Chloe was getting on and she told me about it.'

'Ah,' Zoe said. 'I'm still not used to how news travels around here and how everyone knows everyone.'

'Pretty much. I also know that your new neighbour is causing a bit of a stir.'

'Which one?'

'Hilltop.'

'No, I mean Alex or Billie?'

'Oh, Alex. I don't think anyone's clapped eyes on Billie since she first arrived, but he's been in and out of places chatting to everyone.'

'Has he?'

Zoe tried not to frown, but the description didn't fit the Alex she'd met. Not the one who'd been so obviously worried about his daughter, at any rate. Perhaps the Alex she'd met in the field on the day she'd moved into Kestrel Cottage was an image he projected to hide what was really going on in his life. Not that she knew a lot about that, only what she'd gleaned from Billie's visit to clinic and what he'd told her when he'd come bearing chocolate.

'I think,' Stacey continued, 'that he's on some sort of charm offensive, and I'm sure he thinks it's how we do things around here, but all he's doing is making people suspicious of what he's up to.'

Ottilie laughed. 'I can imagine. Which one of us is going to give him the bad news?'

'He wants to build... pods,' Corrine said from the stove. 'That's right, isn't it, Zoe? Pods – that's what they're called?'

'Camping pods,' Zoe clarified to Ottilie and Stacey. 'He wants to build them on the land around Hilltop, and he seems to be under the impression the villagers might not like the idea.'

'He might be right,' Stacey said. 'I remember when the council wanted to change the road sign outside the village – it was carnage.'

Ottilie burst out laughing. 'I can imagine!'

'They won't like cars up and down that hill and holiday-makers in the village all summer,' Stacey said.

'But they're all right with Victor's alpaca treks, aren't they?' Zoe asked.

'People tend to come and do their treks and then leave again.' Corrine brought the teapot to the table. 'They hardly bother the village at all, apart from once in a while someone will pop into the shop for some cartons of juice and sandwiches for their journey home. If people are staying here for a week or two at a time, they'll probably be in the village a lot.'

'Surely it won't make that much of a difference?' Zoe took a cup from Corrine with a nod of thanks.

'Depends how many pods he's building. A dozen or so, I daresay we could cope and there wouldn't be too much bother, but if it's more than that...' Corrine poured hot water into the teapot. 'I expect we'll find out soon enough. If he wants to put pods on his land, it's a free country, and nobody here can stop him. Doesn't mean they have to like it, though.'

'Doesn't he have to get planning permission?' Ottilie asked.

'I would have expected him to have done that before he started announcing his plans to everyone,' Corrine said. 'It's a bit daft if he didn't.'

'He doesn't strike me as someone who doesn't know what he's doing,' Zoe said. 'He ran a holiday villa in Spain until a few months ago.'

Stacey sat to attention. 'Did he? How do you know that?'

'He told me.'

'So he knows a thing or two about tourism. That's interesting.'

'Is it?' Ottilie asked.

Stacey turned to her. 'Don't you think so?'

'I don't know what it means. Does it mean he knows how to do this without annoying everyone in the village, or does it mean he knows how to do it sustainably, or does it mean he's out to make a fast buck and will fill Thimblebury full of holiday-makers every summer? We don't know any more than we did a minute ago, other than he's done this sort of thing before.'

Stacey folded her arms. 'You really know how to kill a vibe, don't you?'

'Oh,' Zoe cut in, grinning, 'she's always been like that. Want to indulge a wild theory? Don't worry, Ottilie will shoot it down for you.'

'I don't do that!' Ottilie huffed. 'You make me sound so boring!'

'You're the sensible one – that's all I meant. Even you have to admit you're the first person to inject some sanity into the daftest speculation – always have been. I'm not saying it's a bad thing.'

'So,' Ottilie said, choosing not to address Zoe's dubious compliment, 'he's moved here from Spain? And it's just him and his daughter?'

'As far as I know,' Zoe said. 'Billie's mum died...' As soon as she'd said it, Zoe wished she hadn't. It wasn't exactly confidential information, but it had been shared with her during a clinic appointment. 'Please don't spread that around the village,' she added. 'I'm not sure it's common knowledge.'

'I won't say a word,' Corrine said, though it was clear from the expressions on their faces that all three women wanted Zoe to share more. She wasn't worried about trusting them, but things often slipped out when people didn't mean them to. If information she'd been given at clinic became gossip in the village, Billie might think she was the culprit and never share anything with her again. Zoe couldn't allow that to happen, and so she decided that was all she was going to give out for now. If Billie or Alex wanted people to know their circumstances, then they would let them know, and it wouldn't come from Zoe.

'I have to say' – Corrine lowered her voice – 'that Alex. He's easy on the eye...'

Ottilie's mouth fell open, and Stacey burst out laughing.

'Corrine! You little madam! Better not let Victor hear you say that!'

'Well...' Corrine blushed. 'I'm only human – how could I not notice?'

'I'm surprised at you for looking,' Stacey said.

Ottilie let out a giggle. 'Ignore her, Corrine. I noticed too. Of course, I'm madly in love with Heath so there's no contest, but even I've had a *little* look.'

'Well, I wouldn't kick him out of bed for eating crackers,' Stacey said.

'You're spoken for too!' Corrine replied with a half gasp, half laugh.

'I know, but like Ottilie says, no harm in looking, is there?' She turned to Zoe. 'Looks like it's on you, as the only singleton here. You'll have to take him on.'

'God no!' Zoe said, reaching for her cup. 'Another man is the last thing I need right now. I can't get rid of the one I'm divorcing without taking on anyone else.'

'He's still hassling you?' Ottilie asked, her expression now one of sympathy.

'Not hassling, exactly,' Zoe replied, though she certainly felt hassled. 'But he's around... makes his presence felt...'

'Turns up when he's not wanted,' Ottilie finished for her.

'Does he?' Stacey asked. 'That must be awkward.'

'It's not ideal,' Zoe agreed. 'We always said we'd stay friends, and I know he's only looking out for me, but I wish he wouldn't. Is that a bit mean of me? I mean, we're getting divorced because we don't want to be together as a couple any more, but he's acting like nothing's changed, we're still married and I'm just working away from home. It's...'

Zoe paused. Everyone was hanging on her every word, and despite how much she liked and trusted the women around the table, she suddenly felt like the newest subject of village gossip. She was doing a good job of making herself that. Had she overshared? It wasn't like they could do anything to help.

'I take it you've spoken to him about it?' Stacey said.

'You don't know him. He'd be so upset and offended if I said something like that.'

'Would it matter if he was? You're getting divorced anyway.'

'He's having a tough time of it at the moment, and I don't want to make things worse.'

Stacey picked up her cup. 'Sounds to me like you'll have to say something whether you want to or not. Otherwise you're going to have him coming around all the time, and you just said you didn't want that.'

'I know. It's hard.'

'I don't think it is,' Stacey said, and Corrine nodded her agreement.

'Sometimes,' she said gently, 'you have to be cruel to be kind.'

'She's right,' Ottilie said. 'Would it help if I had a word with him? I could say you—'

'I appreciate the offer,' Zoe said, 'but I don't think it would be a good idea to get anyone else involved. I'll talk to him when I find the right moment.'

There was a brief silence, and Zoe couldn't help but feel it contained some silent judgement of her words. They all doubted she'd pluck up the courage to say what she needed to. She doubted it herself most of the time, though she knew she'd have to.

'Magnus wants to know when you're going to come to film club,' Ottilie said. 'You know it's a rite of passage for all new Thimblebury residents that they have to go to Magnus and Geoff's little cinema.'

Zoe turned to her. 'Really? Must I?'

'Well, you're new, and Magnus loves having new people there. I think you'd make him ever so happy, even if you only go once.'

'Oh, I don't know. I don't really like arty, high-brow films. I don't understand them.'

'Neither does anyone at film club,' Stacey said, and Ottilie let out another giggle.

'That's true! Most weeks you're more likely to get a showing of *Dirty Dancing* than *The Piano*. It's only a bit of fun, an excuse for everyone to get together.'

'I don't know...' Zoe sipped at her tea. 'I don't think so. Besides, it's such a trek down the hill at night – I don't know if I can be bothered. I mean, I know I do sometimes go into the village after dark, of course, but still... the road can be challenging later on...'

'I mentioned that, and Victor's planning to put lighting up,' Corrine said.

Zoe's face fell. 'Oh, I didn't mean... You didn't tell him I was complaining?'

'No, don't worry. Melanie had been saying for years it needed lighting, but then she got so used to driving it, she gave up nagging us. I did say to Victor when you first moved in that we ought to make it a bit safer for you. In fact, I think Victor had a conversation about it with the new fella at Hilltop too. They share some of the road, after all, so they might do it between them.'

'That would make me feel a bit easier,' Zoe admitted.

'And as for film club,' Corrine continued, 'we could do our own up here. I'd be glad of the company of someone who wants to watch something other than *Gardeners' World* and war documentaries of an evening. You'd all be more than welcome to come and have a little film night with me.'

Zoe gave a warm smile. She suspected that what Corrine was really saying was that if Zoe ever felt lonely in her little cottage all that way out of the village, she should seek company at Daffodil Farm.

'Perhaps we could ask that young girl at Hilltop too,' Corrine added thoughtfully. 'She'd likely say no, but there's no harm in making the offer. She seems right lonely, and it must be hard being in a new place where she doesn't know anyone, and pregnant to boot.'

'I get the impression she doesn't mind her own company,' Ottilie said. 'Not that I've spoken much to her.'

'I think there's more to it than that,' Zoe put in, and when the others turned expectantly to her, she simply shrugged. 'Sorry, you know how it is. I can't really say more than that, but I do feel she needs the company more than she'd ever want to admit. I think she'd do a lot worse than come over here to be spoiled by Corrine every once in a while – even if it was only for the cake.'

'She needs feeding all right,' Corrine said. 'It wouldn't hurt to take some good home cooking over to them. I think I'll make a pie and take it over tomorrow.'

'That's me officially jealous.' Ottilie smiled. 'I'd be your instant best friend for life if you were making me a pie.'

Corrine beamed at the compliment. 'You know my guardian angel can have one any time she likes.'

Corrine and Ottilie shared a look of understanding and deep affection, and Zoe felt a pang of real jealousy. Or rather, not so much jealousy but longing. She was envious of how settled Ottilie was here, how much of a shared experience she had with other women in the village, whereas Zoe felt keenly her status as recent arrival. She had work to do before she became a real part of the community. She'd persuaded herself she didn't care, that she had no plans beyond her six-month trial at the surgery, but that wasn't true. She wanted to belong because ever since she'd lost the baby and then Ritchie, she'd felt lost in life too. Reflecting on it now, however, it struck her that was one thing she had in common with Billie. Perhaps, she thought, that was the way to connect. If she could use her outsiderness to some advantage, then perhaps she could turn it into a force for good.

'If you're going over tomorrow, Corrine,' she began slowly as the plan formed in her head, 'I'd like to come with you – if that's all right.'

Stacey laughed. 'Aye, aye! We set her a challenge to take on the new man and she's gone for it!'

'No!' Zoe laughed herself, though it was more self-conscious. 'That's not it at all! I only meant it would be good for me to check in on Billie, and this is a way to do it that won't seem obvious. Like Corrine said, she seems lonely, and that can't be good for a girl of her age, especially one who's pregnant.'

'Yeah, you keep telling yourself that,' Stacey fired back with a grin. And then she looked up at Corrine. 'This cup of tea is all very well, but weren't we promised a girls' night? Shall we open the wine I brought up?'

'I can't drink it,' Ottilie reminded her, but Stacey's grin only spread.

'Aww, shame, we'll have to drink your share, won't we? It's a hardship, but for you, I'm willing to bear it.'

11

It was raining again the following evening when Zoe met Corrine on the path between Kestrel Cottage and Daffodil farmhouse. Corrine was carrying an insulated bag containing a pie dish covered in tinfoil. Zoe could smell the pie as Corrine greeted her.

'That smells gorgeous – what is it?'

'Chicken and leek.'

'I'm kind of hoping Billie and Alex are vegetarian so I get to eat the whole thing,' Zoe said.

Corrine gave her a bright smile. 'Don't worry – I've made one for you too. It's on the side in the kitchen – you can pick it up before you go home. And I know they're not vegetarian because Magnus told me.'

'Of course he did. How does Magnus know?'

'He told me Alex picked up some Quorn from the shop, and when Magnus asked him about it, he said they didn't eat it because they were vegetarian, only that sometimes they liked to cut out meat to be a bit more environmentally friendly.'

Zoe pondered what that might say about Alex and Billie and decided that, whatever it was, she approved.

'I think they'll be all right with a bit of chicken from a local farm, won't they?' Corrine added. 'That's quite environmentally friendly, I'd say.'

'Of course. I'm sure it will go down nicely either way. I wonder if that means their camping pods will be all eco-friendly too?'

'It seems to be something they're interested in, so perhaps they will.' Corrine studied her for a moment. 'How are you settling in? You've been in Kestrel Cottage almost a month already – can you believe it?'

'It's flown by, hasn't it? I like it there. It took some time to get used to the quiet, but now, if you asked me to go back to Manchester, I don't think I could cope.'

'Oh, I couldn't be doing with a big city. When I was a girl, I dreamed of running away to London. It seemed so glamorous but I don't expect it's like on the films. Anyway, I met Victor and that put paid to London.'

'Do you ever regret not giving it a go?'

'Oh no.' Corrine shook her head. 'It was just a silly girl's idea. I'm sure I'd have hated it. You know, when you grow up in a place like this, all you want to do is leave, and some get the chance to leave, and more often than not they realise that yonder hill isn't as golden as it looks. They come back and they tell you what it was like, and then you realise you had all that you wanted all along.'

'And that's you?'

'That's me. I've had a good life at Daffodil, and I wouldn't want to be anywhere else now.'

The path was on the boggy side, and Zoe frequently had to check where she was walking, but Corrine seemed to have no such issues. She was decades older than Zoe, but from a distance she looked like the fitter and stronger of the two women. Zoe wondered vaguely if she might end up like that, if she lived in the hills for long enough.

They continued to chat as they walked, about life in Manchester, about Zoe's divorce and about her work. Corrine was pleasantly interested but not pushy, and when Zoe hinted that a particular topic was off limits, she changed the subject immediately. She told Zoe about the skin cancer Ottilie had spotted very soon after they'd met, but her telling differed from Ottilie's modest version. Corrine couldn't praise their village nurse highly enough, and it was clear she valued her friendship. Zoe had noticed a similar love for Ottilie in everyone she'd met in Thimblebury. She was glad her friend had found a place where she so clearly belonged, and she wondered if she'd ever slot into the village in the same way. While she liked Thimblebury well enough, she couldn't imagine it at all.

Corrine knocked, and they could hear barking inside the house. Alex seemed puzzled as he opened his front door. Today, he was in an old Aran jumper, with a thread loose at the hem and the beginnings of a hole in one of the sleeves. Zoe had never found Aran jumpers – especially ones with holes – particularly sexy before, but as she took in the sight, the notion popped into her head anyway. That was quickly followed by a second thought – that she took far too much notice of what he wore whenever she saw him, and that, no matter what it was, she always decided it looked good on him.

'Can I help you, ladies? Is there a problem?'

'Not at all,' Corrine said. 'We've brought you a little something.' She held out the pie dish. 'It's a chicken and leek pie. You do eat chicken? You'll need to warm it up I'm afraid.'

As he took it, he looked more puzzled than he had before. Zoe supposed that two of them randomly turning up with a pie was rather unexpected. But he pushed a courteous smile across his face. 'Thank you; that's very kind of you. Would you like to come in?'

'We don't want to keep you from your evening,' Corrine said, halfway over the threshold even as she did.

'You wouldn't be.'

Alex stepped back to let them both in. As they followed him to the kitchen, Grizzle made his presence known with more barking, but it wasn't aggressive. He proved this a moment later by jumping up at Corrine, his tail wagging like mad. She let out a chuckle.

'Get down,' Alex commanded. 'Come on now, basket!'

Zoe felt almost sorry for the dog, who'd only been excited to see them, as he sloped off to his bed and settled, shooting doleful looks at Alex.

The last time Zoe had been in this kitchen it had been bare, the décor dowdy and in need of a serious refresh, and Ann had been weeping at the thought of leaving it. Alex had clearly wasted no time making it the way he liked. The walls had been painted a rich cream, some new tiles had been put in around the hob and sink, and his furniture was far more modern than Ann's had been. To Zoe it was somehow sterile, though, lacking in the personality that had said more about Ann and her life than this could ever say about the current owners. It seemed that the mystery of the real Alex was not going to be illuminated by his home – at least, not yet. Perhaps it would in time, when he'd been here longer.

'Oh, you've got it nice,' Corrine said briskly as she pulled off her boots and left them at the door.

'You don't need to do that,' Alex said, watching her, but Corrine shook her head.

'Don't want to tramp a load of mud through your house.'

Zoe then felt obliged to take off her shoes too, and stood in her socks on the stone floor of Hilltop farmhouse, the cold seeping into her feet.

'Would you like to sit down?' he asked.

Corrine and Zoe both took a seat at the table.

'I'm not sure what I've got...'

'Oh, don't worry about that,' Corrine said. 'We didn't come over to drink all your tea, only to drop the pie in.'

'Would you like tea?' he asked, showing her a box of teabags. 'I can do that. I just don't have anything more exciting in.'

'That'd be lovely, if you're making one,' Corrine said.

Zoe's gaze wandered the kitchen for a moment. 'How's Billie?' she asked.

'She's fine. She's upstairs filling in some forms for something or other. She wants to find a job.'

Zoe frowned. 'But she's pregnant.'

'That's what I said. Not that she can't do a job, but I doubt anyone will want to employ her until she's had the baby – they'd have to lose her for maternity leave almost as soon as they'd taken her on. But you can't tell Billie about anything – she does what she wants. Headstrong, like her mum was.'

'I'm not lazy...'

All three of them turned to see Billie at the doorway.

'Were your ears burning?' Corrine asked.

'Yeah.' Billie threw a knowing look at her dad. 'I'm not headstrong; I'm just *not* lazy.'

'But you are pregnant, and that's enough work for anyone,' Zoe said.

'I'm pregnant; I'm not dead.' Billie leaned against the door frame and studied them all. 'I can't sit around here all day and night doing nothing – I'll go mad.'

'But you—' Zoe began.

Corrine cut across her, a shrewd smile on her lips. 'You want something to do?'

'I'm looking for a job, yeah.'

'And I still say nobody will hire you right now,' Alex insisted. 'You've only got about... how many months?'

Billie rolled her eyes. 'I'm nineteen weeks.'

'We could use some help over at Daffodil Farm,' Corrine continued. 'We wouldn't be able to pay much, but you might enjoy it.'

'What would it be?'

'We could do with some help with the alpaca. Grooming, washing, feeding them... that sort of thing.'

Zoe had serious reservations about that plan: not only did it sound strenuous, but she would absolutely advise any woman in her care to be cautious around farm animals. She wondered whether to intervene and say so, but then realised that, based on what she knew of Corrine, her neighbour would already have considered that. She was sure Corrine had made this job up on the spot – because it was the first time she'd said anything about wanting help – and that she'd ensure they only gave Billie easy and safe tasks to do.

'No, thanks,' Billie said. 'Not that I don't appreciate the offer, but I want something more than a bit of Saturday work.'

'Billie...' Alex said, a note of warning in his voice. 'Hear Corrine out. You don't know that it's Saturday work.'

'It's the kind of thing you'd offer a fifteen-year-old after school,' she said and then turned to Corrine. 'No offence.'

'None taken, sweetheart. Think about it,' Corrine said. 'Let us know. Like I said, we'd pay you.'

'It's a kind offer,' Alex said.

'What's that?' Billie nodded at the foil-covered dish on the table.

'Your dinner,' Alex said with a smile. 'Also courtesy of Corrine.'

'Oh.' She glanced at Corrine. 'What is it?'

'Chicken and leek pie.'

'Right. I don't know if I'll eat much, but it sounds nice. Thanks.'

'Billie,' Alex began carefully, 'Corrine has gone to a lot of trouble to—'

'Yeah, I know,' Billie cut in. 'I said thanks. I mean...' She turned back to Corrine. 'What I meant was my appetite is weird right now. It looks good, and I'll try.'

'You don't have to explain to me,' Corrine said with a reassuring smile. 'I'm old, but I still remember what it was like to be pregnant.'

'While I've got you both,' Alex began and went to search through a drawer, 'I wonder if I could ask you about these?'

He came back to the table and let some tiny pieces of metal clatter onto it.

'What are they?' Zoe picked one up and turned it over in her fingers, studying it closely.

'I think they look like they might be arrowheads or something. Old anyway. I found quite a few when I was digging foundations on the fields today. Is there a lot of that kind of thing around here? I hardly think of the Lake District when I think about archaeology. Not that I think about archaeology on the regular or anything.'

'I couldn't say.' Corrine took one into her hands and examined it. 'Quite a few years ago, someone found a great load of Bronze Age bits in a burial mound. I think that was closer to Keswick. It would make sense that if people lived there, then they probably lived hereabouts too. Is this all of them?'

'I don't know. I'm surprised Ann and her husband didn't find anything like this when they were farming the land. These weren't buried all that deep.'

'I doubt they were looking so close,' Corrine said. 'And quite honestly they'd have ignored it – wouldn't want anything disrupting their work. Having a load of archaeologists traipsing up and down would do that, all right.'

Alex nodded and collected the pieces up again. 'I have to say, I'm curious to see if there are more. There's still a kid in me that would love to find something bigger still.'

'Like a woolly mammoth?' Zoe quipped.

'Imagine.' Alex grinned, and the sight of it did something unexpected and yet not unwelcome to her. It was a tiny thing, but it felt like such a significant shared moment that she didn't know what to make of it. 'It would be cool if there were some pots or treasure or something.'

'Dad,' Billie cut in with a withering look. 'There isn't going to be treasure.'

'I know, but I'm still going to have a look. It might be good for business if I do find something else.'

'You won't be able to carry on building if you find a load more,' Billie said.

'I'm no expert,' said Zoe, 'but that sounds about right. They were digging foundations for a new office block in Manchester a few years back and they found old factory workings from the Industrial Revolution. Work was stopped on the building until they'd excavated it all. If that's what they do for the Industrial Revolution, imagine what they'd do for a load of... what did you think it might be?'

'Not a clue.' Alex shook his head. 'Corrine, you said it was a Bronze Age hoard they found in Keswick?'

Corrine gave the tiniest shrug. 'I think so, but it was quite a few years ago, so my memory might be failing me.'

'Well,' Zoe continued. 'I would imagine if you found something interesting enough, someone somewhere would want to dig it up to make sure there wasn't anything more buried deeper down.'

'Unless you don't report it,' Billie said.

'But like you said' – Zoe turned back to Alex – 'a big find like that might be good publicity for your pods. People who are interested in that sort of thing will want to come and stay. You could even make a feature of it, couldn't you? I mean, I'm not trying to tell you how to run—'

'That's actually not a bad idea,' Alex said, giving her

another one of those smiles that were like jolts of pure desire. 'That settles it. I'm going to do some more digging tomorrow.'

'Maybe get those ones checked out first,' Billie said, angling her head towards the tiny slivers of metal in his hand. 'They might be a load of old junk, and there's no point in breaking your back digging up more if they are.'

'They're older than that,' he said, looking at them, his tone giving the impression that he was willing them to be something far more exotic than junk from 1985.

As she looked, Zoe had to agree. She didn't know anything about archaeology, but even she could see they were very old and crudely fashioned, and looked like the sort of thing she'd seen dug up on *Time Team* on the rare occasion she'd caught it while flicking through the TV channels. And his sudden enthusiasm was infectious. This might be the most animated, the most positive she'd ever seen him. She wanted it to be something exciting for his sake because she could see what a wonderful effect the notion had on him. She was suddenly excited for him, and if she'd been in any position to offer help, she'd have been tempted to dig with him.

'I'd imagine you could find out more online,' she said. 'There must be pictures of similar things that have been found. It might help you to figure out if you *might* have something old or not. I bet there are Facebook groups too for that sort of thing – you could upload some photos to see what people think.'

'I wouldn't do that,' Billie put in. 'You'll have every weirdo in the country driving over here to dig around themselves.'

'You wouldn't have to say where you found them,' Zoe said, unable to keep the tone of offence out of her voice.

'People have a way of working it out,' Billie replied flatly. 'You wouldn't have to say where you'd found them. I'd bet there'd be a load of metal detectors up and down that field the day after you'd posted.'

'I think you might be right,' Alex told her. 'But there must be some expert somewhere who can tell me.'

'I can ask Victor,' Corrine said. 'He might remember more about that other find than me, and he might know who to ask.'

'Could you?' Alex dropped the bits back into the drawer and returned to the table. 'That would be amazing.'

'I should warn you,' Corrine added with a wry smile, 'when I do tell him, he might be one of those metal detectorists going up and down your land. He's got one, you know. Hasn't had it out in years, but it's there at the back of the shed, and I don't think he'd need much encouragement to dust it off.'

'Boys and their toys, eh?' Zoe said, and Corrine rolled her eyes.

'Enough to drive a sane woman mad.'

'I'd better put the kettle on again,' Alex said. 'Totally forgot about it.'

Zoe was about to make a joke about it when her phone bleeped a message. She pulled it out to see Ritchie's name. With a frown and a curse under her breath, she switched it to silent and slipped it back into her pocket.

'Everything all right?' Corrine asked.

'Yes,' Zoe said briskly. 'Something and nothing. Someone I can't speak to right now.'

'Ah...' Corrine gave a knowing look.

She glanced up to see Billie still hovering at the doorway. 'How are you feeling?'

'I'm fine.' Billie looked at the table, as if deciding whether to join them. 'All good. I'm bored, mostly, because Dad won't let me do anything around here.'

'Good,' Zoe said. 'Depends what it is you're wanting to do, but if your dad doesn't want you to do it, then it's probably something I wouldn't want you doing either.'

'I think I'm meant to be flattered by your trust,' Alex said from the kettle. 'I'm not sure I deserve it, though.'

'You don't even know what it is,' Billie said.

'It's decorating, Zoe,' Alex said. 'Up ladders. With paint and fumes. Even I know that's not a good idea, and I'm a useless man.'

Corrine laughed. 'I'm sure you're not useless because you're a man!'

'You'd think so, to listen to my daughter. I know nothing about pregnancy, is all I get from her. Like I wasn't there when her mother was carrying her. I might be a man, but I have a good-enough memory.'

Zoe could imagine him being a considerate, solicitous partner. She hadn't known him long, but what she did know had already convinced her that he'd looked out for his pregnant wife and done everything in his power to make things easier for her. When she'd come to see Billie and he'd refused to get her, Zoe had imagined all sorts of bad things, but now she realised it was simply him doing his best to look out for his daughter, even if it was a little misguided.

She glanced at Billie but didn't see the reaction she'd been expecting. Instead of smiling, or even teasing her dad, she looked desperately sad. Without another word, she turned and left the room. Zoe looked up at Alex. He'd seen her go, and now he looked awkward and sad too.

'Is she all right?' Zoe asked quietly.

'Yes,' he said, though he didn't look as if he really believed that. 'She's probably had enough of me going on.'

'Her partner,' Zoe began carefully, at once convinced she shouldn't be asking her next question but too far down the line to take it back, 'the baby's father. Billie told me he'd never be involved.'

'He's not around.' Alex paused as he opened a cupboard, staring into it as if he couldn't see the mugs that were right in front of his face. 'He died just before she found out she was pregnant.'

'Oh, the poor thing.'

Zoe turned to see Corrine tearing up. Lost in the moment, she'd almost forgotten her landlady was there.

'I see,' Zoe said. 'I'm not prying for the sake of it,' she added. 'It helps me to understand what she needs, and she didn't exactly want to tell me at clinic... at least, it didn't seem as if she did.'

'I think there's an element of denial,' Alex said. 'If she doesn't say it, it's not true. It came out of the blue, and then we left Spain so quickly that I don't think she's really processed it yet.'

'I'm sorry.' Zoe forced a bleak smile. The mood in the room had deteriorated in seconds, and she couldn't help but feel it was her fault. And that she ought to have saved a conversation like this for clinic, where Billie could say it for herself. Zoe suddenly felt guilty, as if she'd gone behind Billie's back and betrayed her trust. 'I shouldn't have asked.'

Alex came back to the table. 'It's all right. Like you said, it means you can help her better, now you know. I think she worries about when the time comes. She doesn't even have a birth partner, and I'm sure she doesn't want to ask me. Maybe you could talk to her about that next time you see her in your clinic? She shuts me down when I bring it up, so I'd appreciate your help.'

'Absolutely,' Zoe said. 'We would have covered that when we drew up her birth plan, but I'll mention it next time I see her.' She shot a glance at the doorway, wondering if Billie could hear all of this, and decided that if Alex was comfortable saying it, he was probably fairly certain that she couldn't. And if the past half hour was anything to go by, if Billie could hear them, she wasn't the sort of woman to keep quiet about it.

'Other than bits of old metal,' Corrine began, perhaps in a bid to change the subject to something she felt more comfortable with, 'how is the building going? On your little camping huts, I mean.'

'I haven't done much towards it yet apart from trying to level some of the field and put foundations in. I got sidetracked by my *bits of old metal*. I probably ought to focus. I won't get very far if I stop every time I find something shiny, will I?'

'No,' Corrine agreed. 'Are you getting contractors in? You're surely not planning to build it all by yourself.'

'I'm going to do as much as I can to save money. I don't foresee anything I can't do, to be honest. Like you said, they're only little camping huts at the end of the day. I might need a hand with plumbing for shower blocks and such, but then again, isn't that what YouTube is for? I'm sure if I watched a video or two, I'd be able to do it.'

'I have to admire your confidence,' Zoe said.

'Or stupidity,' Alex replied, and she couldn't help but agree a little with that.

'I'm sure Victor would be able to recommend someone local if you're after a reliable tradesman,' Corrine said.

'I'm sure he could, but the name of the game is keeping the costs down. If I really have to, I will get someone in, but I'd rather not.'

Zoe wondered if money was as big an issue as it was sounding. He'd told her before that he had money put aside, but now it didn't sound as if he was sure it would be enough. Unless he was so confident in his own abilities he'd decided he didn't need the help. She resisted the urge to give her head a wry shake. That was also the sort of thing Ritchie would do. And then she was suddenly annoyed that she kept thinking of Ritchie. She didn't want to, but he was always there. He'd been such a huge part of her life for so long, perhaps that was to be expected, but she had to wonder when it would stop.

As Alex turned his attention to the tea he'd promised them a good half hour before, she peeked at her phone. Since she'd checked it before, a new notification had arrived – this time a missed call from Tegan Forester.

Zoe frowned and got up. 'I'm sorry, I have to make a quick call. Do you mind if I take it outside? It's one of my mums...'

Alex nodded and began to chat to Corrine while Zoe hurried out. But there was no reply when she returned Tegan's call, and so she phoned Ottilie instead.

'Hey, I know what you're going to say, that I'm paranoid and that I should switch off when I'm not on duty – and you're absolutely right – but I need an emergency contact, and it's in my address book at the surgery. I don't suppose you have a key to get in?'

'What's wrong?'

'I have a missed call from Tegan Forester.'

'Oh, she's the worrier, isn't she?'

'Yes, but the last time I saw her I was worried about her blood pressure, so...'

'Right. Well, I don't have a key, but Lavender does. Do you want her number?'

'I have it, I think. I'll phone her. She's going to kill me if I ask her to go and open up, isn't she?'

'I don't imagine she'll be thrilled, but if you explain, I'm sure she'll understand. There's always Fliss or Simon, if you'd rather. They've both got keys too.'

'I think Fliss would be scarier than Lavender.'

'Probably. Simon would come if you asked him – he's good like that.'

Zoe paused for a moment, considering her options. 'Simon, yes, I'll call him. Thanks, Ottilie.'

'Phone if you need me – I'm not doing anything.'

'I will, thanks.'

Zoe had no intentions of phoning Ottilie or anyone else if she could sort this herself. She needn't even drag Simon out if she could go to his house and get the key to open up the surgery herself. She scrolled her contacts and then dialled his number. He answered within three rings, a note of puzzlement in his voice.

'Hello, Zoe. Everything all right?'

'I'm so sorry to phone you out of hours, but I need a favour. Could you let me into the surgery? I need an emergency contact from my office.'

'Are you on call?'

'No, but... Please. It would put my mind at rest if I could see that this lady is all right.'

'Of course; I understand. I can meet you at the surgery in ten minutes.'

'I'm up at Hilltop, so could you make it twenty?'

'Sure, I'll see you then.'

Zoe dashed back in. 'I'm so sorry, but I have to go.'

Corrine spun to face her. 'Is everything all right?'

'Yes, I need to go into the surgery to check on something and it won't wait.'

'Now?' Alex asked.

Zoe nodded.

'You're going to walk down there in the dark?'

'I'll have to go back to Kestrel Cottage to get my car, and I'll drive down.'

'Victor will take you,' Corrine began, but Alex cut in.

'I'll take you – it will be far quicker than you going to get your car.'

'But what about—'

'If all you need is dropping off, then I'll be back in half an hour, if not sooner. Everything here will wait.'

Corrine got up. 'I'll head back and let you both get on then. Phone us if you need us, won't you, Zoe?'

'Of course; thank you.' She turned to Alex. 'Are you sure you don't mind?'

'I wouldn't have offered if I'd minded. Let me tell Billie where we're going and then we'll head off.'

12

'If you take a left, Simon's house is a bit down the road. You can drop me there, if that's all right.'

'I'll wait; I can take you to the surgery afterwards.'

Zoe glanced to her side to see Alex's attention on sweeping beams illuminating the road ahead. The dark came that bit earlier every evening as the year hurtled towards its end, far too quickly for Zoe's liking. Today, dusk had fallen and night had taken hold completely during the short time Zoe had been sitting with Corrine in the kitchen of Hilltop Farm. She would have made the drive down the hill alone willingly, but in her current state of anxiety, she was glad she didn't have to. All would be fine. Everyone had told her what a worrier Tegan was, and the call was probably nothing. But if Zoe really believed any of those possibilities, why was her stomach in knots? She'd tried Tegan's number twice more since, and there had been no answer either time, and that had only made her more desperate to speak to her.

'There's no need,' she said. 'It's a two-minute walk – you've already been kind enough to bring me down.'

'How will you get back?'

'On foot.'

'In the dark?'

'Maybe Simon will take me home.'

'I'll wait. You said it was only a phone call to check on everything, so you won't be long, will you? I don't mind.'

'What if it's...?'

'If it takes longer, then all the more reason for me to wait.'

Zoe couldn't argue with his logic. If it was more than a quick phone call would fix, then she might need his assistance. It wouldn't hurt for him to be on hand.

A couple of minutes later, Zoe was letting herself into the darkened surgery. She'd asked Alex to wait outside. It took a moment to feel along the wall to the light switch, the sudden flood of yellow light forcing her to squint, and then she rushed to her office and switched on her computer. She stomped her feet and blew into her hands as she waited for it to boot up. The office was cold, but she was impatient too.

After what seemed like hours, she managed to open up the file containing Tegan's details and typed the emergency number into her phone. It went straight to voicemail, and she almost squealed with frustration.

'What's the bloody point of an emergency contact who isn't there when there's an emergency?' she huffed under her breath as she switched everything off again. She'd done all she could do for now and could only hope that Tegan or her husband, whose number she'd just called, would phone her back shortly to let her know it had all been a false alarm and everything was fine.

'I think I might be overreacting,' she said to Simon when she took the key back. 'I'm sorry; it's just that I don't know why she'd phone me out of hours if there was nothing wrong.'

Simon gave a reassuring smile as he took the key from her. 'I'm not going anywhere. If you need me again tonight, all you have to do is call. I'll keep my phone close by.'

'Thanks, but I'm sure it will be fine. If I don't hear anything from them tonight, I'll pop—' She slapped her forehead. 'I'm such an idiot! I'll go over to her house! It's on the outskirts of Thimblebury, but that's like, what? It can't be any longer than a fifteen-minute drive.'

'Want me to come?' Simon asked.

Zoe shook her head. 'I'll go and get my car – there's no point in dragging everyone out.'

'Is there any point in you going out at all?' Simon asked pointedly, and though Zoe disagreed, she could see what he was getting at. Driving to an expectant mum's house every time she had a missed call from them or a vague feeling of unease wasn't going to be a sustainable way to do her job in the long term. But she'd only just arrived in Thimblebury, and she wanted to start out on the right foot. Besides, the worrying aspects of Tegan's recent clinic visit were playing on her mind.

'I know... but I'd feel better if I went over there. If I don't get any joy, then it will have to wait until tomorrow. At least I'll know I did my best to be there if I was needed.'

Simon's look of intense sympathy told her he'd do exactly the same thing. She'd been told by Ottilie how dedicated he was to his patients – often to the detriment of his own well-being – and though she'd yet to see it in any extreme form, looking at him now, Zoe fully believed it.

'Again,' he said, 'let me know if I can assist. I'll keep my phone close by.'

'Thanks.'

Zoe walked back to the car, where Alex was waiting to take her back to Hilltop. 'Could you take me home?' she asked as she got in. 'I need to get my car after all.'

'You're going out again?'

'I want to call at someone's house.'

'This is your patient? You want to go there now?'

'I sound crazy, I know, but it would only take half an hour, and if there's someone home, I can get all this sorted out. I'll sleep a lot better for knowing.'

'It's pointless going all the way back up the hill to get your car, and then for you to drive down again when we're right here in the village already. Surely it's better and quicker for me to take you now.'

Again, Zoe wanted to argue, but there was no point. His suggestion made too much sense. And so she relented and typed the address into the map function on her phone so she could direct him. The sooner she could get to the bottom of this and confirm it was all a silly misunderstanding, the better, and she said so at least three times as they drove the short distance to Tegan's house, which lay on the road between their village and the next.

'This is it,' she said, pointing out of the window at a large, double-fronted new build. The garden path leading to the front door was lit by a pair of antique lanterns and flanked by neat beds of flowers. Aside from the outdoor lighting, the house seemed to be in darkness, and Zoe was disappointed to surmise that nobody would be home. Despite this, she knocked anyway, waited for a couple of minutes, knocked again, and then made her way back to the car where Alex was waiting.

'That's that,' she said flatly. 'All I can do now is go home and see if I can get hold of her tomorrow.'

'You're annoyed,' he said.

'Not annoyed, just frustrated. I don't think she would have called for nothing, and I don't see how it was a misdial because she's never phoned my mobile number before, so it's not like it would have been on her list of recent calls or anything.'

'She may only have wanted to ask you about something she wasn't certain of.'

'Yes,' Zoe said, though she wasn't convinced of that. 'I'm sure that was all. I'm sorry I've made you drive round all night for nothing.'

'Not for nothing,' he said. 'It's shown me how much you care for your patients. I'm glad to see how good you are at your job; it makes me glad you're looking after Billie.'

'She'd be fine with any good midwife,' Zoe said, blushing at the praise. 'She's healthy and young.'

'She might be healthy, but I think you and I both know she needs special care all the same. She's healthy, but she's not strong...' He tapped his head and then placed his hands over his heart. 'Not up here or in here. It's been a tough couple of years.'

'She's had you. I think she's grateful for that.'

'Fat lot of good I've been. I did my best, but I had no clue if it was what she needed.'

'I'm sure your best was all she wanted from you.'

'Hmm...' He was silent as he turned the key to start the car.

Zoe, having seen light through the chink in his armour, wanted more of the picture, but something told her she wasn't going to get it – at least, not so easily. Like Billie, he seemed slow to trust, and whenever he came close to letting something meaningful begin, he shut it down again.

'You don't need to go anywhere else tonight?' he asked.

'I don't think...' Zoe paused, watching another car slowly pull to a halt a few yards ahead of them. A man got out and went to the gates of Tegan's house. She tumbled out of the car to follow.

'Hello... Excuse me... Are you... Do you live here?'

The man turned to her with a deep frown. 'What are you here for?'

'I'm Zoe Padbury.' He showed no sign of recognition, and Zoe cast around her memory for the name of Tegan's husband. 'Dennis?' she blurted out after a gap. 'Are you Dennis?'

'Yes, who...?'

'I'm Tegan's midwife.'

His stoic, unreadable expression suddenly collapsed into something far more desperate. 'We tried to phone you.'

'I know. I'm sorry I didn't... Is everything OK?'

He drew a breath, as if trying to prop himself up with it, and then shook his head. 'She's in the hospital. They say she's lost the baby.'

'Are you sure?' Zoe asked, even though she immediately realised it was the most stupid response to a statement she'd ever given. Of course he was sure. Of course it was true because the staff at the hospital didn't say things like that if they didn't know it for certain. She felt sick. She should have seen this coming. She'd been responsible for keeping Tegan and her baby safe. She could barely look Dennis in the eye as he nodded.

'They're keeping her in. I've just come home to get some things for her.'

'Right...' Zoe looked helplessly at the car where Alex seemed to be following their conversation, though she was glad to see he'd understood the need to keep a respectful distance.

She looked back at Dennis. She could offer to go to the hospital to see Tegan, but the team caring for her there would probably see it as an imposition. There were midwives who worked both out in the community and in the hospital, but Zoe wasn't one of those – her remit now was community only. The hospital team would have it under control, and her presence would only complicate things.

But that didn't mean she didn't want to go. She wanted to go more than anything, if only to lend support. Tegan didn't even need that, not really, because she had her husband by her side. Perhaps wanting to go was more about Zoe than Tegan. Perhaps there was guilt that needed to be alleviated. Hard as it was to face, it was almost certainly true. 'Do you need anything from me?'

'I don't think so.'

After a brief hesitation, Zoe gave a short nod. 'I'm really sorry to hear about it. I'll phone Tegan tomorrow to see how she is.'

'Thanks, I think she'd appreciate that.'

'Everything all right?' Alex asked as she got back into the car.

'Yeah.'

When he didn't restart the engine, she turned to see him frowning at her. 'You don't seem sure about that.'

What could she say? She couldn't tell him what had happened – even if it wasn't breaking the rules, it wasn't her place. She'd risked enough getting him this involved and was already beginning to regret her decision to let him drive her around.

'It's all sorted,' she said, finding the effort to make her voice sound calm utterly draining.

'So you want to go home?'

'Yes, please.'

Home, where she could reflect on all her failures and spend a sleepless night worrying about how she could mess up the care for all the other women she was meant to be looking after.

13

Did you get my message the other night? x

Zoe locked her phone with an impatient exhale. Ritchie's message was where all the trouble began. If not for Ritchie's message, Zoe wouldn't have had her phone set to silent and wouldn't have missed Tegan's call. The last thing she wanted to do this morning was read or respond to Ritchie's stupid messages.

There was a light tap at her office door.

'You can come in.'

Ottilie pushed open the door. 'Hey, how are you? Simon told me about Tegan. You mustn't blame yourself.'

'I saw her in clinic.'

'And you put her under surveillance, which was what any of us would have done with any other patient. There was no huge red flag... was there?'

Zoe didn't like the way Ottilie had left the question open-ended. As if there might have been a red flag and that Zoe might have missed it. She'd been over the question herself many times since she'd left Tegan's house. Could she have done more?

Should she have seen the signs? But every time she asked herself, the answer was the same. If time had somehow rewound and she could have done the clinic appointment again, she'd have done the same thing, every time. It was what her training would have told her to do. There were warnings of something, but nobody at that point could have known what.

'Fliss wants you to pop in to see her,' Ottilie added. 'If you can spare five minutes.'

'Did she say what she wanted?'

'No, but I wouldn't worry.'

Zoe got up. 'I might as well go before clinic starts. I'm assuming her first patient isn't in with her yet.'

'I don't think so. Knock and if she tells you to bugger off, you'll have your answer.' Ottilie gave a smile of encouragement, but Zoe couldn't return it.

'This is not like you,' she added as Zoe made her way to the door. 'I know this is a disappointing outcome, but you've dealt with cases like this before. I've never seen you so down.'

Zoe almost flinched. Ottilie had always been compassionate. The Ottilie Zoe knew would have been as cut up about a patient in her care coming to harm as she was. A disappointing outcome? They didn't sound like Ottilie's words, and Zoe wondered whether she was paraphrasing something Fliss had said that morning. Perhaps that was why Fliss wanted to see her, to say: *Chin up. It was a disappointing outcome, but life goes on.* And life would go on – Zoe knew that. Knowing it eased the guilt. Perhaps there had been a time when she would have seen this as part of the job, but that was before she'd lost her own baby. Now, she understood, for the first time, that it was so much more.

'I'll go and see,' Zoe said as Ottilie moved out of her way. 'If she fires me, don't worry – I'll say goodbye before I leave.'

. . .

Fliss did not want to fire Zoe. The expected pep talk was issued. Zoe nodded to everything and answered in the way she thought Fliss might want her to, and at Fliss's prompting agreed to bring any worries to one of the partners rather than fretting. She left the office feeling like she'd been to see the headmistress at school over some minor misdemeanour and then went to get on with her day. Luckily, her morning clinic was a light one, and as she didn't particularly want to socialise, she skipped lunch, taking herself out for a walk to clear her head instead.

As she passed the shop, she saw Magnus outside, putting up a large poster on the village noticeboard.

'Hello,' he called as he spotted her. She'd tried to sneak past, but it seemed she'd have to do better next time. 'Out for a walk?'

'Yes.' Zoe forced a smile. 'I've only got half an hour, though, so I doubt I'll get far.'

'I thought the surgery was closed for the whole hour?'

'Oh, yes, but I've got to eat too,' Zoe said, her ruse to get away from a protracted conversation with Magnus well and truly rumbled.

'I suppose you'll be coming.' He angled his head at the poster. 'Most everyone in Thimblebury will be there.'

Zoe stepped forward to take a closer look. 'Oh, I've heard about that. Fliss said there was going to be an event of some kind, but I hadn't realised it was going to be quite so big.'

He tapped a hand on the page. 'Five hundred years. You can't imagine it, can you? Five hundred years of this little place. I don't know where they've got that number from, but someone's worked it out.'

'Five hundred years of it being an actual village or just people recorded as living here?' Zoe asked, her mind going vaguely to the possibly Bronze Age finds she'd looked at during her visit to Hilltop.

'Oh, I think people have lived around here for thousands of years. It's probably when the king or queen recognised it or something like that. Geoff says it's in the Domesday Book, and that's ancient.'

'I'm sure it would be,' Zoe replied, not a clue whether it might be or not. Though, like most people, she'd heard of it, she barely knew what the Domesday Book was, let alone what was in it.

'We've been given money,' Magnus continued.

'Have we?' Zoe wondered who 'we' might be. Presumably the village, though knowing Magnus it could have been anyone.

'Yes. There's going to be fireworks and music and circus acts.'

'Is there?' She took another look at the poster. 'I'm surprised they're doing it so late in the year... Won't it be a bit cold? Is it all going to be outside, I take it?'

Magnus gave a vague shrug. 'To me, it's not so cold. In Iceland, we'd be wearing our shorts.'

'Would you?'

He laughed. 'No, but I like to tell people that and see if they believe it. We'd wear big coats, like you.'

'Oh, of course.' Zoe made a show of laughing along, though she didn't much feel like it. 'I'm sure it will be a lovely occasion. I expect we can just turn up?'

'Yes, yes. Geoff and I will be helping with the organisation. We're on the committee, you know.'

'That's good of you.'

'There's going to be little films to tell stories of Thimblebury through the ages.' His chest puffed out ever so slightly. 'I've been asked to make one about coming to live here from Iceland. I can't believe people are interested, but they must be.'

'I can imagine you being good at that.'

'Oh, I don't know about that,' Magnus said, clearly flattered anyway. 'Did you enjoy your chocolate, by the way?'

'My... oh, yes, thanks.'

'He's been asking us what so many people like, and he's

spent so much money. A sure sign he's up to something, correct?'

'I couldn't possibly say,' Zoe replied and then began to walk away, the sounds of Magnus chuckling to himself fading with every step. She'd been warned that Flo was the village gossip, but she was beginning to see that Magnus would give Flo a run for her money. Now that she thought of it, so would Lavender. And to an extent, Ottilie's friend Stacey too. Thimblebury, on the whole, seemed to thrive on gossip. Zoe had never lived in such a tight-knit community before, so perhaps it was the same wherever you went.

As she retraced her steps to the surgery, her stomach began to growl. She was hungry, and that was good. She'd had no appetite at all so far that day. She took it as a sign that she was feeling better. After work, she'd drive back out to Tegan's house. The hospital had sent discharge notes, so Zoe knew Tegan had been sent home and that, aside from the obvious, there were no immediate concerns.

Which reminded her that she still had to reply to Ritchie. Not because she was desperate to, but because he'd keep messaging until she did. Or worse, he'd turn up at her house again. She'd get back to work, see if there was any lunch left and then do it before she started the afternoon clinic. She only wished she didn't have to. Why couldn't he leave her alone and move on?

14

'I was too old to do it again anyway.'

Tegan hadn't asked Zoe in, and so they stood at the front door, Tegan hugging herself tightly against the cold. Zoe had said she didn't want to keep her, and that she only wanted to know if she was all right, and it seemed Tegan had taken her at her word.

'Even if you thought that, you're allowed to grieve.'

'I know, but I'm sure in a few months I'll see it as a blessing in disguise. Dennis didn't really want the baby either. I mean, he was coming round to the idea, and so was I, but we were both worried about starting all over again, and then there was the question of whether the baby would even be all right. I mean, everyone said I was old and there were more risks...'

Zoe recognised a brave face when she saw one. What Tegan was telling her might have been true at first, but it had been clear from what little interaction she'd had with the couple that they had grown to want and look forward to their baby, no matter what Tegan was saying now. 'I want you to know that—'

'There's no point. I don't need to see you again, and I don't need any counselling. I've already been offered that. I'm fine; I just want to move on and forget this all happened.'

Zoe wanted to tell her that she understood because she'd been through it, and what a mistake she thought it would be to refuse help because she'd refused it and found out the hard way. She wanted to tell her that it would take time to get better and that she needed people around her, but she couldn't tell her any of that. Tegan didn't want to hear it, and it would be inappropriate for Zoe to talk about her personal experiences, even if she did. And in the end, no matter how over it Zoe felt she was, remembering the time she lost her own baby still hurt.

'You have a follow-up at the hospital?' she asked quietly.

'Yes, it's all taken care of. Thanks for coming anyway.'

Tegan nodded shortly, but she barely made eye contact with Zoe as she went inside and pushed the door closed.

Zoe hesitated on the step for a moment and then made her way back to her car. She'd done as much as she could, and though it hardly made her feel better, there was nothing to keep her here any longer.

It was probably more about company than anything else, but as soon as she got back from Tegan's house, Zoe washed the dish that had housed Corrine's chicken pie and walked across the fields with her torch to take it back.

'You didn't have to come over with that so quickly!' Corrine said, ushering her in.

'If I don't bring it over when I think of it, I'll forget.'

'I've got plenty of dishes; I wouldn't have missed it.' Corrine took it from her with a broad smile. It was so warm, so welcoming and free of judgement, it was exactly what Zoe needed right now. She almost burst into tears at the kindness in it. Corrine, she was beginning to see, had a warm smile and generous words and deeds for everyone. Zoe couldn't imagine her being angry or unkind about anything or anyone. 'You'll stay for an hour?'

'I wouldn't want to be in the way.'

'You wouldn't be. We're expecting company anyway, so as long as you don't mind another set of feet under the table...' She pulled out a chair. 'Sit yourself down, my love. What can I get you to drink?'

'I don't mind – whatever you're making is fine. Who's coming over? Anyone I know?'

'Alex is coming to see Victor. They *were* arrowheads, you know, the bits he found. Victor's like a little boy – can't wait to go out onto the fields at Hilltop with him to see if they can find more.'

'It sounds as if they're becoming good friends.' Zoe glanced around the kitchen. 'Victor's out?'

'Only in the sheds, cleaning some equipment.'

'At this time of night?'

Corrine came back to the table with a tin and opened it to reveal two slabs of different cakes – one fruit and one chocolate. 'When there's only the two of us doing what needs to be done around here, you get round to it when you can.'

'Hmm...' Zoe watched as Corrine got out some plates. 'Is that why you offered Billie work?'

'Well...' Corrine looked awkward now. 'In a fashion. To be completely honest, it was more what you said.'

'Me?'

'She needs something to take her mind off her troubles, and it must be lonely up there, a young woman in her condition with no friends in the village. I know we're old folks, but I thought even old folks are better than nothing, and we'd only have her petting the girls a bit, really. We wouldn't have had her mucking out or anything too hard. Perhaps she could do a bit of paperwork, computer stuff – that would help Victor out no end; he hates all that online business.'

'I bet she'll be doing all that for Alex when he gets his holiday site up and running.'

'I'm sure, and there's no pressure on her to do it for us. It was only a thought to tide her over.'

Zoe was silent for a moment as she pondered Corrine's words and wondered if Corrine saw her living in Kestrel Cottage and discussed with Victor if they thought she was lonely there. Did she feel lonely? She certainly felt cut off at times, and sometimes the house felt too big and too silent for her, but there was also peace and the loveliest neighbours not so far away.

'Which one do you want?' Corrine asked as she hovered over the cake tin with a knife. 'Or have a bit of both if you like.'

'Your kitchen must be like Mr Kipling's factory when there's nobody here.' Zoe looked up with a smile. 'A big old assembly line of cakes. Every time I come over, you've got a full tin.'

'I do bake a lot of cake,' Corrine agreed with a laugh, 'because I'm married to a big child who has a sweet tooth. He'd go on strike if there was no cake after tea. Or before tea. Or with tea, come to think of it.'

Zoe laughed. 'If it's not depriving him of his favourite, I'll have some of the chocolate one, please. Will you be getting involved in the celebrations?' she asked.

'What celebrations?' Corrine cut into the chocolate cake and placed a slice on Zoe's plate.

'The five-hundred-year celebrations. Magnus was telling me about them.'

'Oh, those! Yes, I'll probably be doing a stall with Penny – my youngest. Cake, of course... We'll give the money we make to a charity – haven't decided on one yet. I suppose you'd know one or two. Something to do with babies.'

'I know a few, yes, and they'd be glad of the money. That's a lovely idea.'

'Well, it's not costing us anything other than a few raisins and some flour.'

Zoe suspected there was a lot more to it than that, but it was nothing less than what she'd come to expect from Corrine.

'It all seems to be moving fast, this... what is it again? The word, I mean.'

'Oh, the quincentenary. I don't know why we can't just call it a five-hundredth birthday and have done. I think it's been rushed through, to be honest. Someone realised at the last moment that this year was a big date, and then it was a race to see someone at the council. They must have made a fuss about it because here we are. It'll be nice to celebrate something – not much happens around here in general.'

'Magnus says there'll be fireworks and circus acts.'

'And that's only Magnus and Geoff having one of their tiffs,' Corrine said with a laugh.

She was still laughing as the back door flew open, blowing Victor in on a gust.

'Someone's having far too much fun!' he said as he took in the scene. He turned to Zoe. 'Hello, love. Come to cause mischief?'

'I came to bring your dish back. I think Corrine is causing the mischief!'

'That'll be about right,' he said, giving his wife a wry glance. 'I see I'm just in time for elevenses.'

Zoe checked the clock, wondering if she'd fallen into some crack through time, but no, as she'd thought, it was early evening. Then she felt quite dim as she got the joke.

'It's always elevenses where you're concerned,' Corrine said. 'Get those boots off before you come and steal all the cake.'

'All right, all right. Already doing it – see?' He kicked off one wellington and then the other and stood in his socks for her approval. 'That satisfy you?'

'You'll do,' she said. 'Your trousers aren't muddy, are they?'

'No, don't think they're too bad,' Victor said, coming to the table without bothering to check.

They looked a bit muddy to Zoe, but she didn't say anything, sharing a grin with him that made him look like a naughty young boy.

'What time did Alex say he was coming?' Corrine asked as she poured Victor some tea.

'I thought he'd be here about now, to be honest. Must have got held up.'

'Speak of the devil...' Corrine went to the window. 'He's on his way over.'

Zoe wiped imaginary crumbs from her mouth and smoothed her hair down, her gaze on the door. A moment later, it opened, and as Alex greeted everyone in the kitchen, his eyes settled on her.

'Hello,' he said. 'I wasn't expecting to see you here. How are you doing? Only the other night...'

Zoe's stomach dropped as she was reminded of Tegan. 'It's resolved,' is all she said and hoped nobody would ask her anything else about it.

'Good,' he said, and it was clear that he wasn't sure whether it was good or not. 'Billie didn't feel like coming out,' he said to Corrine and Victor. 'She sends her apologies.'

Zoe was sure Billie had done no such thing. She believed Alex's daughter probably didn't feel like going out on a blustery night across darkened fields to visit elderly neighbours, but not that she'd sent her apologies. She doubted Billie thought she owed anyone those, and it was clear from their last interaction that although she tolerated Victor and Corrine, she wasn't interested in getting to know them.

'That's a shame,' Corrine said. 'But I expect she gets tired. Did she say anything more about our little job offer?'

'Not yet,' Alex said, taking a seat at the table. 'I'm not sure it's really her, though, so...'

Corrine nodded and then went to get more plates and cups

from the cupboard while Victor, his eyes suddenly keen, leaned across the table to Alex.

'What did your expert say then?'

'More or less what I told you on the phone,' Alex replied. 'Almost certainly Bronze Age. He only looked at them over Zoom, of course, so I think he was being cagey and wouldn't be pinned down. To be honest, I'd expected him to be more excited than he was. He said there would be bits and pieces spread all over these hills, so he wasn't surprised these had turned up.'

'He doesn't want them?' Victor asked, the disappointment evident in his tone.

'I told him we were going to look for more, and he said if we found anything significant to let him know.'

'Significant how?' Zoe asked.

Alex shrugged. 'He wasn't very clear on that. I don't know whether he meant a lot more items, or more important or rare items.' He looked up at Victor. 'You're still game to go hunting?'

'I am!' Victor grinned. 'If he wants more significant, we'll give him significant! I've a mind to search my own land too. If there are things on yours, there's bound to be some on mine as well.'

'Imagine if you found a load of treasure,' Zoe said. 'What would you do? You could retire on the profit.'

At that suggestion, Victor looked mildly horrified, and Zoe had to laugh. 'Retire? Why would I do that? Who'd look after this place?'

'You could give it to Penny, like you've been saying for years,' Corrine put in.

'Penny doesn't want it,' Victor said. 'Her and Leon would take it on if I asked, but they don't really want it.'

'You don't know that for sure. They don't say anything because they know you'll be in your grave before you give it up, and even then you'd be bossing them around from the afterlife.'

Zoe and Alex shared a private grin. She'd had a horrible

day, but an hour here in the kitchen of Daffodil farmhouse was making her feel better. She loved Victor and Corrine already, as Ottilie had promised she would.

'Away with yer,' Victor huffed. 'I'll give it up when I'm good and ready, but there's plenty of work in me yet.'

'If you don't want the money,' Alex said with a mischievous gleam in his eye, 'I'll take the treasure off your hands when we find it.'

'Ah, I never said I didn't want the money!' Victor replied, matching his mischief. 'I only said I wouldn't use it to retire. Nobody's going to see me complaining about a nice new car and some decent boots.'

'A new car!' Corrine scoffed. 'You'd never get rid of Old Banger either! You love that thing more than me!'

'You're right, I wouldn't. I'd have another one for posh drives out.'

'It'd rot in the garage,' Corrine fired back. 'When do we go for posh drives out?'

'What's all this for?' Victor reached for his cup, shaking his head. 'We haven't even found a scrap of treasure yet!'

'But we might,' Alex said.

'It'll be more arrows, I expect,' Victor replied with the confidence of a man who was never less than pragmatic about his fortunes. 'Not that I won't enjoy the looking, mind.'

'I'll be digging again this weekend, I expect,' Alex said. 'I can't get to it before then; I've got too much on.'

'Suits me. I'll walk over with my detector.'

'I noticed that was out,' Corrine said. 'You didn't waste any time, did you?'

'Billie's got a scan at the hospital tomorrow,' Alex said to Zoe.

Zoe nodded. 'You'll be taking her?'

'Yes. Is there anything I should know? Anything she needs to do beforehand?'

'I expect the hospital have sent her a letter with the details. Does she have it?'

'I don't know – she hasn't said. I'll ask. Sorry...' He seemed awkward now. 'I don't suppose you want to talk shop every time you're out.'

'I don't mind it as much as everyone seems to think. I love my job, and nothing makes me happier than helping mums and babies. Anything you need to ask, just ask. I might not always have the answer, but I'll always try to help.'

'Aww...' Corrine gave a warm smile. 'Thimblebury is lucky to have people like you and Ottilie looking after us.'

'We are,' Alex agreed, his glance lingering on Zoe long enough to make her suddenly flustered.

'We're only doing our jobs. So...' she added in a bid to take off the heat. 'We were just talking about the five-hundred-year celebrations. What do you think? Should be fun, eh?'

'I didn't even know there were any celebrations,' Alex said. 'When's this?'

'It was Michaelmas,' Victor said. 'But I think they've had to move it because there wasn't enough time.'

Alex frowned. 'I probably ought to know, but when's Michaelmas?'

'September. It's been and gone,' Victor said.

'Magnus was putting up a poster,' Zoe said. 'It's happening at the end of the month now. Seems too cold for that sort of thing, but I'm guessing they've got it in hand.'

'Much better, if you ask me. Always more than enough going on in September as it is. For us at any rate.'

'I'm surprised nobody realised the anniversary was coming up,' Zoe said. 'Everyone around here seems really hot on things like that.'

'Oh, they make a show of saying it,' Victor said. 'But they're all too busy with their own things. Still, I expect it'll go all right, and if it doesn't, what's to be done? You ought to get involved,' he added, looking at Alex. 'It'd make you some friends in the village.'

'I don't know... I've got a lot going on up here, and I'm not sure anyone in the village wants to be my friend.'

'You'll need them onside if you're going to get your camping field up and running.'

'You might be right. Who would I go and see? I mean, I don't have a clue what I can offer, but I could have a think about it and see what I can come up with.'

'Magnus would be a safe bet, wouldn't he?' Zoe asked Victor.

'Him and Geoff are usually at the centre of things,' Corrine said. 'If it's not them you need, they'll know who else to talk to.'

'Sounds like a good place to start then,' Alex said thoughtfully. 'I'll go and see them when I can.'

The conversation turned back to the finds on the fields of Hilltop, and it was clear that Victor was more excited about them than Alex was. And while Zoe enjoyed listening to them for a while, half an hour later she found herself surprised by a violent yawn.

She laughed. 'God, I'm sorry! I'm not bored, honest!'

'That's all right,' Corrine said. 'You must be tired.'

'It's been a long day, to be honest,' she said. 'I think I might go home.'

'Would you like Victor to walk you back across?' Corrine asked.

'I'll be all right – I have my torch.'

'I'll go as far as the path with you,' Alex said. 'I need to get back anyway.'

'So soon?' Corrine asked and then glanced between the two of them, a knowing look suddenly appearing as she backed down. 'I dare say being outside all day does take it out of you.'

'And I've got an early start tomorrow for Billie's appointment,' he said. 'If you want, Victor, I'll pop over again once we're back from the hospital; otherwise we can arrange to meet up at the weekend.'

'Don't come away on my account,' Zoe began, but he got up from his seat.

'It's no bother. Like I said, I was thinking I ought to get home anyway. It makes sense for us to walk together.'

Zoe could have put up more of a fight, but she didn't want to. Against her better judgement – which was the way she seemed to be operating all the time these days – she wanted his company and him to herself, if only for a few minutes, and the temptation of his offer was too much to resist.

After thanking Corrine and Victor and bundling up in coats, Zoe and Alex followed the beam of his torch and headed towards Kestrel Cottage. Victor had put sporadic lighting along parts of the path from Daffodil farmhouse to Zoe's home, but it still never felt like enough – not that she'd ever utter a word of complaint because she knew if she did, they'd end up overcompensating, and by the week's end there'd be a row of motorway-worthy lampposts spanning the entirety of their land.

'They're so lovely, aren't they?' Zoe said as they walked, buffeted by winds that seemed to be blowing from every angle.

'Victor and Corrine? They're great. I don't think I could have asked for better neighbours.'

'I think he might be more excited about your arrowheads than you are.'

'You might be right,' Alex said, and though she couldn't see it in the gloom, she could hear the smile in his voice. 'He's been telling me about some of the other finds around here from over the years.'

'I had no idea he was such an archaeology buff.'

'Me neither. Just goes to show.'

They were silent for a moment, and when it started to feel too heavy, Zoe began again. 'How's Billie feeling? In herself, I mean? Is she looking forward to the scan? I always think it makes such a difference when you see your baby on the screen – it reminds you that they're really in there.'

'I think so,' he said, but she could hear caution there. 'It's a strange time for her. This wasn't how...'

'How she expected things to be?'

'Exactly. I think she's torn. She wants the baby, of course, because it's all she has left of Luis. She doesn't say it to me because... well, I'm sure she would have found it easier to share with her mum, if we still had her, but I think she's terrified. Sometimes I get the feeling she doesn't want to admit the baby is there because she's scared of doing it alone.'

'But she's not alone – she has you.'

'It's not really the same, is it?'

'Probably not.' She regarded him thoughtfully, wishing she could see his face in the darkness. 'She told me that you lost your wife. Christmas, wasn't it?'

'Around then.'

'I can't imagine it. Ottilie – you've met her, I imagine – she lost her husband, you know. She never stops thinking of him, even though she's with Heath now and she's happy. I suppose that's how it is for most. For you...?'

'God, yes, but even I've started to recognise that life goes on. I know for sure that if Jennifer were here, she'd tell me the same. I try to convince myself that helps, but some days are harder than others...'

'It sounds like she was a smart woman. Is Billie very like her?'

'You noticed she doesn't look much like me? Yes, she's the image of her mum. Lucky for her, eh?'

'She's beautiful. I thought how pretty she is the first time I saw her. Your wife must have been too.'

'Thank you,' he said. 'I think so, but I might be biased. I wish I could help her through this, but sometimes, when I look at her pain, I feel as if I'm drowning under the weight of it. I know I lost Jennifer, but we had twenty-four brilliant years, enough memories for me to dig into when I'm down. In fact, we met when we were teenagers, and when I think of it that way, I had more of my life with Jennifer than without and I feel really lucky. But Billie has none of that. Her life with Luis was only just beginning. And then... it was over.'

'How did he die?'

'Motorbike crash on a mountain road. Hairpin bend that he took that bit too fast. The worst of it is, the road was so deserted nobody found him for hours, but if they had, he might have survived. I always think that now we're back home, if he'd had the same accident on a busy road here, it wouldn't have been the same at all.'

'God, that must have been so hard for Billie.'

'It was. Still is.'

The low walls around Kestrel Cottage began to appear in the distance. 'I'm all right from here,' she said.

'I might as well go the whole way with you now. It's no bother, and I'd feel happier knowing I'd seen you home.'

She let out a sigh. 'I don't suppose it's that far. All right then.' She wondered whether he was expecting to be invited in.

Just as she thought about how she might word that invitation without giving him the wrong idea, he spoke into the gap.

'The man who came over when I was last at your house. That was your...?'

'Ex. Ritchie. We're on good terms still, and he was only coming to see how I was settling in.'

'Ah. It's good that you can be friends.'

Thoughts of Ritchie had suddenly clouded her judgement. Or perhaps they cleared it. While he was still in her life, in whatever capacity, was she able to get involved with another man? And why was she thinking that way? Nobody had said anything about romance – certainly not Alex – and a new relationship would complicate her life in ways she didn't need.

Right now, even inviting him in without any romantic subtext seemed like a bad idea.

'I didn't mean to pry,' he said. 'Tell me to keep my nose out if it's something you don't want to talk about.'

'It's not that. There's nothing to tell, really.'

'If you're still such good friends, there's no possibility that you and him will...'

'Get back together? No, none at all.'

'Right. Not that it matters; I was only wondering. Making conversation, you know... Ignore me; none of my business.'

There was a text message from Ritchie still unanswered on her phone, and she was reminded with more force than she'd like that she needed to do something about that. She hadn't known what to say, and she hadn't wanted to think about it, not when she had Alex beside her and she was fighting the urge to invite him inside. Not when his tone was telling her that he wanted the same. Was it in her head? She could imagine a flush, a hopefulness in his face that she couldn't see in the gloom, and she wanted it to be true.

As they arrived at the gate, Zoe smiled up at him. 'Thanks for seeing me home. I'll get a report at the surgery, of course, but if Billie wants to talk to me about anything at all after her scan, she's more than welcome to come over. Of course, ask her to message me first to make sure I'm in – no point in her having a wasted journey.'

'I'll do that. Thank you. You've been... well, thank you.'

She made her way up to the front door of Kestrel Cottage, and by the time she'd turned back to see where he was, he'd already been swallowed by the darkness of the hills.

15

The panic in Lavender's voice set Zoe's nerves on edge. She'd just packed her bag to head out on a home visit when the call came through from reception.

'Zoe... can you go up to Ottilie's room?'

'Is everything all right?'

'I'm not sure. Fliss is in there with her and says she's had a funny turn. She wants you to come and check her over.'

'Yes, of course... I'll go up now.'

If Fliss was asking for her, then it had to be something to do with Ottilie's pregnancy. Zoe was well trained to deal with problems, but she always hoped she'd never have to, and she couldn't deny the heightened sense of urgency rushing over her. Ottilie was a good friend and a colleague, after all. Not only that, but she'd been on high alert ever since the incident with Tegan, despite the logical part of her knowing it had never really been anyone's fault.

She picked up the bag she'd packed to go out and took it with her as she hurried to Ottilie's room. If she needed any equipment, it was already in there and ready to go.

She knocked lightly at the door but didn't wait to be called in, assuming Ottilie and Fliss were in there alone.

She was right. Ottilie was sitting in a chair looking ghostly white, and Fliss was taking her pulse.

'She's all right, I think,' Fliss said in her usual brisk manner.

Zoe wasn't so sure.

'It's only a bit of dizziness,' Ottilie said. 'I got up too fast or something.'

'I've checked her over for the obvious,' Fliss said, already making her way towards the door. 'I'll leave her in your capable hands, Zoe. If you think she needs to go home, let Lavender know.'

'But I have a full clinic—' Ottilie began, to be shot down immediately by Fliss.

'I doubt you'll be much use here if you're not fit, full clinic or not. If the worst comes to the worst, Simon and I will share your patients out and try to get them seen somehow. I would imagine that Lavender may be able to reschedule some of them too. We'd manage, and I'd rather you act early in aid of a speedy recovery than soldier on and end up having to take twice as long off because you've overdone things.'

'She's got a point,' Zoe said as she bent to feel Ottilie's cheeks.

Fliss left, probably to stop Ottilie from arguing.

'Have you had enough to eat and drink today?' Zoe asked.

'Yes.'

Zoe raised her eyebrows. 'Honestly?'

'Yes, honestly. Heath wouldn't let me leave the house if he hadn't watched me demolish a full breakfast first.'

'Hmm. I'll check your blood pressure... and I know you've probably already done it, but I'm going to check again.'

'Are you going to be like this with everyone now? Because I don't think I can take it.'

'What does that mean?'

'Checking and rechecking every time I have a little dizzy spell.'

'You mean because of... Ottilie, if you weren't poorly right now, I'd tell you that's below the belt. You'd know it too, so I'm going to let you off.'

'I'm sorry,' Ottilie replied in a weak voice. 'I just can't stand the fuss.'

'You're pregnant – take advantage of the fuss now because when the baby comes, everyone's attention will soon switch. You'll long for the days when people fussed over you.'

Ottilie offered her arm without further argument, and Zoe checked her blood pressure.

'Not too much to worry about there,' she said. 'A bit on the low side, but it's all right. If I phoned Heath, would you let him take you to the hospital for a check-up?'

'No.'

'Good. I'll phone him anyway.'

'Zoe—'

'Humour me,' Zoe cut in. 'If the tables were turned, you'd be doing the same.'

'I'll be there for hours. What about clinic?'

'Are you well enough to see patients right now?'

'Not right at this minute, but—'

'So there's no point in you being here anyway. You heard Fliss – she's happy to work with Lavender to get the rest of your patients seen. Depending on what the hospital says, I'm sure you'll be back in tomorrow, and you can catch up then.'

'Fine.' Ottilie rested her hands on the desk and laid her head on them. 'Phone Heath. I don't know how close to home he'll be, though.'

'If he's too far out, I'll get an ambulance.'

'No!' Ottilie's head shot up again, and she grimaced, clutching at it. 'Don't do that to me.'

'We'll find some way to get you there. I'd rather be safe than sorry. I've got a home visit this afternoon, but I could always put her off and take you myself.'

The fact that Ottilie didn't argue with this plan was proof enough to Zoe that she felt worse than she'd admit to. On a more positive note, the ghastly shade she'd been when Zoe had first come in was definitely clearing to a healthier colour. Pregnancy was a funny thing, and events that would have signalled serious illness to anyone else would often turn out to be a blip in a pregnant woman. The flipside of that was it paid to take everything seriously anyway – there was the well-being of more than one person at risk.

'Have you got Heath's number to hand?' she asked.

Ottilie reached for her phone and unlocked it before handing it to Zoe. 'It'll likely be on my most recent calls. I'll let you break the good news to him.'

Zoe dialled and was relieved to hear him answer within a few rings.

'Hey, gorgeous, what did you want?'

'Heath, it's Zoe.'

His tone was immediately sharper. 'Zoe... what's wrong?'

'There's no need to panic, but are you free right now?'

'I can be.'

'How close by are you?'

'I'm close enough. What's happened?'

'Ottilie's not well, and I'd rather she got a full check-up at the hospital. Can you take her?'

'To the maternity unit?'

'Yes, I'll phone ahead and let them know you're coming.'

'I'm on my way.'

'I still say it's a fuss about nothing.' Ottilie took her phone back.

'But you don't really think that, otherwise you wouldn't have let me call Heath.'

'Only because...' Ottilie's voice shrank. 'Only because I've never done this before and I don't know what to expect. And I know you're looking out for me because...'

'You know I don't want what happened to me to happen to you. It's all right – you can say it. I don't want anyone to go through that. I'm not so stupid that I think it will never happen to any of my expectant mums, but it's still so hard to see when it does.'

'That's why you took Tegan's loss so hard?'

'It never gets easier. I remember one of the old midwives when I was training saying it didn't get easier, but you learned to shut it out. I think I'd got to that point before I lost my own, and then... well, it became harder because I knew what it was like. When I hadn't known I could treat it as part of the job, but after... Anyway...' Zoe took a deep breath and pushed a smile across her face. 'You're going to be fine, so I don't want you to worry.'

An hour before the working day was due to end, Zoe received two messages. One was from Ottilie telling her everything was OK and she'd be coming to work the following day as normal. Apparently, Fliss hadn't been happy with the plan and had ordered Ottilie to take the rest of the week off and rest, an order which Ottilie fully intended to ignore, now that she'd been given the all-clear.

The second was a general notification from the ultrasound clinic at the hospital.

'Oh, Billie...' Zoe murmured as she read it. She dialled Billie's number but got no answer. Then she tried Alex, who picked up after a few rings and pre-empted her question.

'Yes, she's here,' he began with a tone of desperation. 'And I know why you want to talk to her because I know she didn't go to her ultrasound. She told me she had a headache and didn't want to leave the house. I said she needed to reschedule her appointment... Didn't she do that?'

'She didn't,' Zoe said patiently. 'I'm happy to do it for her if she's not feeling up to it.'

'Thanks – we'd really appreciate that. I mean, I could, but I don't think I'm allowed... am I?'

'Listen, don't worry, I'll do it. But could you do me a favour? If the same happens again with the new appointment, and she gives a reason not to go, could you give me a call?'

'Yes, but—'

'I know it's probably me sticking my nose in a bit too far, but I'd like to know. I might be able to help, and she does really need to attend for the scan.'

'I didn't mean that. I just don't know what you can do.'

'I can come and talk to her, to find out if there's something more than a headache going on.'

Alex sighed deeply. 'Good luck with that because she won't even talk to me these days.'

'You're a man and her dad – she might feel you won't be able to understand. It might be easier for her to talk to me.'

'I could ask her to phone you now. She's watching television.'

'I tried to call a minute ago and she didn't pick up. I'll try her again.'

'That's OK. Let me go and tell her you'll be phoning so she knows to look out for the call.'

'Thanks, Alex. I'll give it a couple of minutes – it'll give me time to get another appointment for her – and then I'll try her again.'

Zoe did exactly that. She managed to find another slot on the system for Billie's new appointment, one that had been made vacant by a last-minute cancellation for the following day. In the hopes that it would be all right, she snagged it and then tried to call Billie's number to let her know. Once again, Billie didn't answer. She decided to text Billie the details, and then wondered whether she ought to send them to Alex too, so that he could make sure to get her there. Was that crossing a line? Professionally, it was a very grey area, and she wasn't meant to share details in that way, but she reasoned that if a letter had gone to the house, he may well have intercepted it anyway. Wasn't this sort of the same? And if it meant Billie going to the appointment, perhaps it was worth a little bending of the rules. Without further consideration, she did just that.

She'd dealt with women who weren't exactly over the moon about their pregnancies before, of course. Not all were planned, and not every pregnancy was enjoyed, but Billie's case still bothered her. She had a feeling that Billie wanted her baby, but she was afraid of her future and she was still wedded to the past, and a possible future that had once existed but that she could now never have. As far as Zoe could tell, Billie was not only mourning the death of her boyfriend – the baby's father – but the death of the future they could have had as a family. And now she had to face that future alone, with the child who was a constant reminder of what she'd lost. She'd love the baby – Zoe felt certain of that – but it was easy to see why her love would be more complicated than it might be for other new mums.

A minute later, Alex replied to say he'd ensure Billie attended the ultrasound.

Happy she'd done as much as she could, Zoe put it out of her mind as she cleared down for the day and got ready to go home.

16

One of the parts Zoe enjoyed most about her job was when she got to visit newborns to see how baby and mum were doing. She didn't have a lot of contact with them, but she was always there in the first few weeks to keep tabs on the little one's development and make sure mum was recovering well from the birth. It was so rewarding when all was well, and Zoe liked to think her small contribution during the pregnancy had made a difference.

The weather was damp, the verges becoming littered with leaves of fading golds and ambers, and what was still on the trees was ochre and scarlet in the morning sun. Zoe hummed softly along to a tune on the radio as she drove out of Thimblebury towards a neighbouring village where she was scheduled to meet Nadya and baby Musa. Nadya hadn't been in her care for the entire pregnancy, having been looked after before Zoe's arrival by a rotating team that were based with the area's health authority. When Zoe had taken over, the young mum expecting her first child had been delighted to finally get consistent care from one person, even if it was a little late in the day, and Zoe had loved seeing her. The pregnancy had progressed like a dream, and baby had been born without complications at a healthy nine pounds during the early hours of the previous Saturday.

Twenty minutes later, she pulled up outside a modest, newly built cottage and gathered her things before going to the front door. She knocked softly in case baby Musa was asleep, though with enough force to hopefully alert Nadya to her arrival.

During her training, Zoe had worked with an old midwife who'd insisted on hammering at every front door, stating that the baby had to get used to noise and learn to sleep through it, otherwise it would be a restless sleeper for the remainder of his or her life. While Zoe had swallowed every bit of advice and logic from the more experienced woman, she'd come to her own conclusions over the years that her theory was a bit rubbish. In Zoe's opinion, motherhood with a newborn was exhausting enough without waking the poor woman's baby when she'd finally got it off to sleep. She might have to, of course, to do her checks, but even then, there was a chance the little one would sleep through being picked up and weighed and measured if they were tired enough, and Zoe could sneak away and leave mum to enjoy a few more precious moments of peace.

Nadya opened the door looking tired and dishevelled, but broke into a broad smile at the sight of her midwife.

'Hello, mummy,' Zoe said brightly. 'How are you doing?'

'Not too bad,' Nadya said, ushering her in. 'My mother-in-law has been here for a couple of days, so she's been helping with Musa.

'So that's a gold star for mother-in-law,' Zoe said. She followed Nadya into the living room where an older lady was cradling the baby as his eyes drooped for sleep. Zoe went over to take a look. 'Aww, he's a little cutie, isn't he? Look at all that hair already! Is he being good for you?'

'Very,' Nadya's mother-in-law said. 'He's our little prince, isn't he, Nadya?'

Nadya's warm smile spread. Zoe was glad to see that Nadya had plenty of support from someone she clearly liked. As she understood it, Nadya's mother lived abroad and was ill at that time, and so it seemed her mother-in-law had taken up the responsibility of helping out the new parents.

'I hate to deprive you,' Zoe said, taking out her scales, 'but I'm afraid I do need to take him from you for a few moments.'

Nadya's mother-in-law gently handed him to Zoe, who scooped him into her arms. No matter how many babies she held like this, she never tired of the feeling, of the happiness, the unique and wonderful smell of a newborn, the little faces they pulled as they gazed up at her or sought sleep. She smiled down at him, all that warmth flooding back, as it always did.

'Sorry about this, poppet,' she said, placing him on the scales. He grumbled, but he didn't cry, and after recording his weight and then giving him a brief once-over, she looked up. 'Don't fight – who wants him?'

'I'll take him,' Nadya's mother-in-law said, and Nadya simply grinned.

'I can barely get a look in.'

'Take advantage of the help while it's here,' Zoe said. 'How are you feeling? Recovering from the birth OK? Nothing worrying you?'

'I think I'm all right,' Nadya said. 'Tired all the time, but that's it.'

'That's to be expected. Like I said, take advantage of the help when it's here, rest when Musa rests; even if you look around the house and think things need cleaning, resist the urge. There's plenty of time to have a neat house, but this isn't it. All that will wait; enjoy getting to know your son.'

'I will,' Nadya said.

'I'll make sure she doesn't overdo things,' her mother-in-law said.

Zoe gave a nod of approval. 'I'm glad to see it.'

Zoe was packing up her equipment, chatting to Nadya and her mother-in-law, when she became dimly aware of her phone pinging the arrival of a text message. But it slipped her mind, only coming to her attention again as she drove the road back to Thimblebury and started to run through a mental list of all that she had left on her to-do list for the day.

Back in the office, she completed her notes for the home visits she'd made and then checked her phone to see that the message was from Alex. Even if he hadn't told her about Billie's refusal to go to her scan, she would have seen the second notification from the hospital before the end of the day anyway. She let out a sigh, though this time it wasn't sympathy for the young woman but exasperation. There was only so much Zoe could do for her. If Billie wanted the best care for her baby, then she had to make the effort.

Despite knowing all this, there was no way Zoe could ignore what was going on. Aside from concern for the baby, she was worried about the impact Billie's neglect might have on her own health, so she certainly wasn't going to leave Billie to decide whether she took care of herself or not.

She was about to phone when she realised that phoning was no good. Billie hadn't wanted to talk to her the last time she'd failed to attend her hospital appointment, and there was no reason to suppose this time would be any different. It was out of her remit, yes, above and beyond the call of duty, and some might even say meddling further than was polite, but Zoe was going to go up there and see Billie face to face. One way or another, she needed to make her understand how important these appointments were. If anything happened to Billie or the baby and Zoe had done nothing, she wouldn't be able to live with herself, and so whether it was beyond her professional remit or not, the first place she was going after she packed up for the day was Hilltop Farm.

She messaged Alex to check that someone would be home, wrapped up the day's loose ends and then headed out.

'Hi.' Alex seemed tense as he opened the door to her. He managed a courteous smile and nod, but his movements as he stepped back to let her in were taut and anxious. 'I haven't told her you're coming. Should I have done? I thought she might make an excuse to go out so she wouldn't have to see you, so...'

'That's your call,' Zoe said. 'I do think it's important I see her, but it's a free country, and if she'd wanted to go out, then it would have been her prerogative. But if she's in, that's good. Hopefully, she won't try to climb out of a window when she sees me.'

Zoe had kept her uniform on, partly because she'd come straight from work, and partly because this felt like work and it seemed a good idea to clearly mark that this was a professional visit.

Alex gestured to the closed living-room door. Zoe could hear the sounds of the television coming from the other side. It sounded like a quiz show or something, and Zoe suspected that Billie wasn't really watching it, only distracting herself from having to acknowledge her current situation. She knew this because she'd done it often enough herself during tough times, and the last year or so hadn't been short of those.

Knocking softly, she waited for a second and then went in.

Billie was curled up under a blanket on the sofa. As Zoe suspected, she didn't appear to be watching the television because she had her phone in her hand.

She looked up from it as Zoe walked in. 'Oh,' she said in a dull voice.

'You can guess why I'm here,' Zoe said.

'Not really,' Billie replied, going back to her phone, but Zoe knew better than to believe that.

Zoe took a seat on an armchair and took off her coat. 'Do you mind if we turn the telly off for a minute?'

'If you want.'

Zoe looked for the remote control but couldn't see it. Billie watched her for a moment before turning her attention back to her phone.

'Could you help me out here?' Zoe asked. Then Billie rummaged in the folds of her blanket and offered up the remote. 'Thanks,' Zoe said before switching it off, the room suddenly quiet.

'Where's Dad?' Billie asked.

'I don't know. He let me in, but I don't know where he is now. Would you be happier if he was here with us?'

'It doesn't really matter. I wasn't very well.'

'I'm guessing that must have been the case, otherwise you'd have gone to your ultrasound, right?'

'Yeah. But I wasn't up to going.'

Zoe put the remote to one side and leaned in. 'Not up to it here?' she asked gently, pointing to her head. 'Or here?' She pointed to her heart. 'Or were you really just sick? Whichever one it is, it's all right to say so. We can work with any of them.'

'I don't know what you mean.'

'Billie, I can't tell you what to do, but you realise it's important to go to these appointments? If there's a problem with you or baby, these are good opportunities to pick it up. I'm not trying to scare you, but I'd hate for there to be something wrong and we didn't know about it until it was too late to do anything. Unless being scared is the reason you don't want to go?'

'I told you, I wasn't feeling great.'

'OK...' Zoe said slowly. 'So that's twice you weren't well enough to go. Should I be worried about that? It seems a lot, doesn't it?'

'You've never been ill more than once?'

'But it's a coincidence that both times you were ill were the days of your scans. Billie, you no-showed at one of my clinic appointments too. I only want to know that there isn't something deeper going on. I can't help you if you keep it to yourself.'

Billie gripped her phone as she rounded on Zoe. 'There's nothing wrong! Stop saying it! Stop talking to me like I'm going mental!'

'I never said that.'

'It sounds like it to me.'

'I'm sorry, I didn't mean it to sound that way. I'm only trying to understand what's going on.'

'Nothing's going on – I was ill.'

'Will you do me a favour?' Zoe asked after a pause. 'When the next appointment comes through from the hospital, if you're not up to going, will you phone and tell me? Even if you don't want to call the ultrasound department, please tell me. Or your dad so he can tell me. It's important, as your midwife, that I know. And I realise this sounds patronising, and I'm afraid it has to, because I need to get through to you how important this stuff is. I have to know, and I have to somehow find a way to make sure you go to these appointments, and I have to be sure that when the baby comes, you're going to be in the right place, mentally, to cope. Because if not—'

'You can't take my baby away!'

'Nobody wants to, but you have to understand that, even though we're friends—'

'We're not friends.'

'—even though we're *sort of* friends because we're neighbours, my first duty is to the protection of you and the baby. I have to do what's right no matter how I might personally feel about it. So believe me, Billie, if I have any doubts, any at all, I will act on them.'

Billie stared at her. It was hard to tell what was going on behind her eyes. 'Is that a threat?' she asked finally.

'No; it's a promise.'

'Dad!' Billie yelled.

Alex appeared at the door almost immediately, and Zoe motioned for him to leave them again.

'It's all right,' she said. 'Give us another minute.'

'We don't need another minute,' Billie said, but when Zoe asked him again to leave, he did.

Zoe took a deep breath and did the thing she hadn't wanted to do. But her hand was being forced, and she couldn't see any other way to get through.

'I don't have children,' she began. 'I'd love one, but I've never been lucky enough to carry a baby to term. I haven't even had much luck getting pregnant in the first place.'

'I'm sorry,' Billie said, though she sounded as if she didn't want to be sorry but couldn't help herself. 'I didn't know.'

'It's nobody's fault – certainly not yours. For a while, I thought it was mine. I was pregnant, not so long ago, but I lost the baby in my second term. That was hard. I thought if I'd done more, looked after myself better, worked less, eaten healthier... all that stuff. Even though I know this job inside out, and if it were any other mother I'd be telling them they weren't to blame, I couldn't tell myself that.'

'You want me to take care because you think you didn't?'

'Sort of. I want you to take care because I want you to enjoy what I couldn't have. I want all my mums-to-be to have what I couldn't. I want them to do it for me because then at least I feel as if I mean something to someone. Does that make sense? And I'm sure you're finding it hard doing this alone, and I can imagine you're scared, but the alternative is worse – take it from me.'

Zoe drew a breath. Had she crossed a line? Sharing something so personal with a woman in her care, laying it on the line like this – was it professional? Probably not, but if it worked, Zoe would consider it had been a risk worth taking. 'I don't usually tell people... well, not the women I look after anyway.

I'm not even sure I should be telling you, but I have. I only hope it somehow helps.'

Billie was silent for a short while. Zoe looked towards the window, recognising that the younger woman needed time to process what she'd been told. She had things to process of her own. It was true that she had her own rules about not sharing the loss of her baby, and the reasons were complicated. This was the first time – other than having to explain to people who'd already known she was pregnant – that she'd told someone in her care about it. Did she feel better for sharing? Had it lifted a weight? She didn't think so, because she didn't think anything would ever do that, but she hoped some good might come from it. If it helped change the way Billie felt about her own pregnancy, then that had to be good.

'I *am* scared,' Billie said finally. 'I never asked to do this on my own. I didn't even plan to get pregnant. I can't do it without Luis.'

'I know,' Zoe said. 'Nobody expects you to. Your dad wants to be there for you. I want to be there for you.'

'It's your job,' Billie said with a dismissive waft of her hand.

'Yes, it is, but there's nothing in my job description that says I owe you anything once the baby is born. Even then, I'm only a field away, and you can call on me any time for anything. Yes, you will be bringing up baby as a single parent, but you don't ever have to do it alone.' Zoe smiled, encouraged by the sense that Billie's walls were lowering, ever so slightly. 'There are other women locally who will be single mothers, and there are parent and baby groups in the village too. I know they probably sound boring, but would it hurt to give one a try? You might make a friend or two with people who understand what you're going through.'

Billie shook her head. 'I don't think so.'

'Billie... I need you to be honest with me, no matter how painful it is. Do you want to keep your baby? When he or she is born, do you want to keep them? Because if you feel it's going to be too much, nobody would judge you. It's not a decision to be taken lightly – I'm not suggesting for a minute it is – but it is a decision that you are allowed to make.'

'I couldn't do... It wouldn't be right. It's not fair.'

'What's not fair? Who wouldn't it be fair to? At the end of the day, you might not be as alone as you think, but you will be a mother, and that comes with responsibilities that you can't get away from. There's no shame in admitting that you can't face them – sometimes it shows the greatest love for your child to know that you can't care for them and to give them a better chance with someone else who can.'

Billie's eyes were wide. She suddenly looked so much younger than her twenty-three years. 'Do you think I should give the baby up?'

'That's not what I'm saying, and it's not for me to say even if I had an opinion – which I don't. I'm not entitled to one. I'm simply saying that if you think there's only one way to go here, that's not true.'

'But Dad says—'

'It's nobody's choice but yours. Forget what anyone else has to say on the matter. But I will ask you for one favour – whatever you decide, that little one growing inside you needs to be cared for, and that's one responsibility only you can take on. Please go to your appointments and let people help you to do that. Your baby deserves the best start, even if that's as far as your part in their life goes.'

Billie nodded. 'I'll go to the next one, I promise.'

Zoe got up. 'Thank you. I'll ask the hospital to send one through... unless you'd rather phone the department and reschedule yourself?'

'You can do it... if you don't mind, I mean.'

Zoe watched her carefully. The act had been dropped. She looked as scared as she'd admitted to – and ashamed. It hadn't been Zoe's intention to do that, but if it was the only way to make her see that she had a duty to the baby she was carrying, then she'd have to deal with her part in that outcome. She was only glad she didn't have a colleague looking over her shoulder right now because she wasn't entirely sure what she'd just done was professional.

As she left the living room, Alex came from the kitchen to meet her.

'How did it go?' he asked.

Zoe shrugged. 'She's promised to go to her next one,' she said in a low voice as she glanced back to the closed living-room door. 'I can't really do a lot more than that, so fingers crossed I've managed to get through.' She paused for a moment. 'Do you talk to her much?'

He frowned. 'What do you mean?'

'About the future? About what it's going to be like, your part in her life once the baby is born?'

'She knows I'll always be there for her. She's my daughter – of course I will be.'

'But do you say it? Because I don't think she does know that. It seems obvious to you, but I don't think it would hurt to make it crystal clear to her.'

Alex seemed offended, but he nodded anyway. Zoe had definitely crossed a line this time, but she was tired, stressed and almost past caring. Whatever she had to do to get this family on the right track, she would do. They were far from dysfunctional – and she'd certainly come across a lot worse – but she could see that their relationship was strained in a way it didn't need to be, if only they'd communicate better.

'I'll get the ultrasound department to send another appointment,' she added, realising they were way past the point of worrying about confidentiality. 'If you could look out for it and make sure Billie doesn't forget she promised she'd go this time...'

'I will. Thanks for coming over.'

Zoe left, emotionally drained. The truths of her own experiences she'd told Billie felt like truths she'd barely shared with anyone. She'd never before admitted that so much of what she did as a midwife was coloured by the loss of her own baby, and yet it was. She cared more than was good for her, and she panicked when she ought to have been calm. She knew her job inside out, but there were things that worried her, even if more often than not they worked out.

It wasn't only that. Billie's plight had touched her in an unexpected way. She couldn't say what it was that felt so personal about it, but there was something. Perhaps it was simply because she was a neighbour as well as a client, someone new to the area in the same way she was and so there was some sense of camaraderie, of shared experience. Maybe, but it seemed too simple an explanation for something that felt so much more complicated.

As she marched towards her own cottage, the path marked out by the soft yellow lanterns Victor had installed for her, she tried not to work it out. Because she was certain that there was no answer to be found.

17

In the end, Zoe had been so tired, she'd opened the first tin of soup she'd laid her hand on and tipped it into a saucepan to heat for her evening meal. She stared into the pan as it began to warm, momentarily blank, until the sound of her phone ringing jerked her back to reality.

She took the pan from the flame and went to see who was calling. If it was Billie – or any other of her mums for that matter – she wanted to be available. So she was disappointed, even vexed, to see Ritchie's name on the screen. She wanted to ignore it, but he'd been texting and she hadn't replied, and if she didn't pick up, there was a distinct possibility that he'd jump in his car and drive over.

'Hey...' he said. 'How's things?'

'Hi, Ritchie. Fine. How are you?'

'I'm good. I just thought... well, I was worried because you didn't reply to my messages. Thought I might have pissed you off or something.'

'Of course not. Why would you do that?'

'I don't know. But it was weird that you didn't text back. I know you read them...'

'I did. I'm sorry, I got busy and forgot to reply.'

'You forgot to reply to *all* of them?'

'Yes, Ritchie,' she replied, struggling to keep the irritation from her voice. 'I meant to do it, but then things kept getting in the way. I have a lot on, you know. I have a full-time job that often spills over work hours and a house to run by myself.'

'Ouch. Got it.'

'Sorry...' Zoe let out a sigh. 'I didn't mean... I've had a tough day, that's all. How are you doing?'

'If you need help there, you only have to ask. I can come over and do bits and pieces for you... Last time I was there, I noticed there was a dent in the plaster on the stairs. And one of your kitchen cupboard doors is loose when you open it. And—'

'Victor will sort all those things out.'

'Victor?'

'My landlord.'

'I suppose it's his job. Even so...'

'You really don't need to worry about it. I have to learn to do things without you sometime, don't I?'

'Do you? We're still friends, and I'd never leave you in a bind.'

'I'm not in a bind, Ritchie. Those are little things that I can live with. I can't even see the point in getting Victor to look at them, quite honestly, because they're not exactly impacting my life. They're niggles, like all houses have, like ours used to have.'

'I fixed things in our house.'

'Yes, but then there'd be more things. That's the nature of living in a house, isn't it? There's always something to repair.'

'You said you had a tough day. Want to talk about it?'

'Not especially. I feel as if that would be a bit of a slap in the face for you – because at least I have a job, right? How's the job-hunting going? Having any luck?'

'It's so hard,' he began, and then there was such a heavy pause that Zoe braced herself for the onslaught she knew was coming. 'I'm either overqualified or too old, or not qualified enough... it's so frustrating. There's so much competition, like a hundred people going for every job...'

Zoe's attention drifted to the window as she listened. The moon was peeking out from a low bank of cloud, hazy in the damp night air. It was beautiful, like an impressionist painting, like the ghost of a moon, half there, half not. She could see the warm glow of the windows of Daffodil farmhouse, and she could picture Victor and Corrine, sitting across from one another on matching, well-loved armchairs, laughing together at something on the television as they munched on one of Corrine's incredible cakes and drank tea so strong you could stand a spoon up in it.

She wouldn't have minded a life like that. Perhaps she might even have had one if things had panned out differently. Not exactly like that, of course, because she would never have bought a farm or worked the land – that wasn't her. But the cosy domesticity – that would have been nice. Victor and Corrine were more than a loving couple; they were a team, pulling through life together, both striving for the same goals, holding one another up when it was needed, celebrating success together and comforting each other when times were tough. They were two halves of a whole like no other couple Zoe had ever met. She'd loved Ritchie, but it had never felt like that. She had to wonder if what she'd had was real love at all, but how could she compare? If she'd never had real love, she wouldn't know what the difference was.

'Zo...'

She shook herself. 'Sorry, I missed that last bit.'

'I'm boring you.'

'Of course you're not. I'm tired. Tell me again.'

'I don't want to now; I feel stupid having to repeat it.'

'Don't be...'

'Stupid?'

'I didn't mean...' She sighed. She felt guilty, and feeling guilty often made her do things she'd later regret. Like now. 'Look, if you want to come over and talk properly, then how about the weekend? Come for a few hours on Sunday if you're free; I'll do a roast.'

'I do miss your roasts but there's an away match this weekend and we're staying over in Tyneside. I can come next weekend.'

'Well then, you're welcome to come next weekend if you're free.'

'I'm always free these days.'

It was a loaded comment, but Zoe resisted the urge to remark on it. The same could be said for both of them, but they'd both agreed that a divorce was the best way to preserve any kind of relationship at all and prevent it from souring beyond redemption. 'There's no pressure, but if you want to come, let me know so I can get extra food.'

'That sounds good; I'd like to, thanks. Do you want me to bring anything?'

'I don't think so. I'll let you know if I think of anything,' Zoe said, already regretting an offer she didn't feel she could take back, not when he sounded so happy about it. 'It'll be good to catch up.'

'I'm really glad we can do this, Zo. Stay friends like this and it not be weird. Loads of my mates can't even be in the same room as their exes, let alone phone them up or go to lunch. It's good; it says a lot about what we had, doesn't it? I miss having you around, just to talk to, I mean. I know we agreed on this, but—'

'I still think it's for the best, but I'm glad we didn't have to be weird about it. So I'll see you next Sunday maybe?'

'Definitely. Thanks, Zoe.'

'Don't mention it.'

After a few more false starts, Zoe managed to get him off the phone and leaned on the sink, staring out of the window. The moon had disappeared behind the clouds again, and now the lights in the windows of Daffodil farmhouse were down to one, upstairs, muted by closed curtains. Zoe knew Victor and Corinne often went to bed early because they had to be up at the crack of dawn, so it was no surprise to see. She wondered if she ought to invite someone else to lunch on Sunday. It wasn't that she didn't trust herself around Ritchie – but she wondered if he was getting mixed signals, and perhaps having someone else there would help to clarify things. Ottilie and Heath might come. Ritchie knew Ottilie, and he knew she and Zoe were old friends, so he wouldn't be surprised to see her there.

Yes, that could work. She'd invite Ottilie and Heath too; it might just save her from the most awkward lunch of her life.

18

'I'm so sorry, we've got plans already. We're taking Flo to Kendal, and if we cancel, she'll never forgive us.'

Ottilie picked up a teacloth and began to dry the mugs on the draining board, while Lavender swept the floor of the surgery kitchen. The air was still heavy with the spices of the Goan curry they'd shared for lunch, Zoe pleasantly full but slightly concerned about the effect that breathing on anyone during clinic might have on them. She suspected she might smell very garlicky about now, though she'd eat it all over again if she had the chance.

'It's OK.' Zoe's smile was perhaps more forlorn than she'd meant it to be because Ottilie grimaced at the sight of it.

'Honestly, I would if I could. Can't you ask Ritchie to come another day, one we can do?'

'I don't know why you're having him over at all,' Lavender cut in. 'Tell him you can't do it and leave it at that – you're not married now, so you don't owe him anything.'

'I know, but I want to stay civil,' Zoe said.

'What for? It's not like you have kids or anything, so there's no reason you have to stay in touch. Move on – that's what everyone else does.'

Zoe tried not to let the sting of Lavender's careless comment bother her. It wasn't her fault – Zoe hadn't told her about the baby she'd lost. 'It's what we agreed,' she said. 'He wanted to stay friends, and he's in a tough place right now.'

'Aren't we all?' Lavender pushed the broom around the floor, oblivious to the look of warning coming from Ottilie. But Zoe saw it and then caught Ottilie's eye. She mouthed an apology, and Zoe shook her head to let her know it wasn't a problem.

'I'm sure it'll be fine anyway. I'll make some lunch, we'll have a quick chat over it and then I'll send him on his way.'

'Watch he doesn't try to move in,' Lavender called from the far side of the kitchen. 'Sounds to me like that's what he's after.'

'It's not like that,' Zoe said. 'He needs a bit of support right now, that's all.'

'I'd better get back to my room,' Ottilie said. 'Sorry I couldn't help you out, Zoe.'

'It's really fine; forget about it.'

'Want me to come?' Zoe turned to see Lavender wearing an expression of mischief. 'I can put him off coming for lunch ever again – say the word.'

Zoe smiled, a more genuine one now. 'Tempting as that is, I'm going to say no thanks.'

'Your loss.' Lavender started to sweep the little pile of dust into the pan. 'Just saying.'

Zoe's smile grew. 'I'd better get to clinic myself. See you later.'

'Think about it!' Lavender called as Zoe left the kitchen. 'If you change your mind, I work for reasonable fees!'

'Hello, Maisie.'

Zoe held open the door for the young woman to come

through to her room and then closed it again. 'Is everything all right? I'm not due to see you for a little while, am I? Unless I've got my dates mixed up...'

'I don't think so, but I... well, I couldn't feel the baby moving so I wanted to ask. Someone told me it was supposed to move, but I haven't felt anything.'

Zoe briefly checked her notes. 'You won't – it's a bit early yet. You might get a little feeling almost like trapped wind, but you wouldn't be able to tell what it is. I can have a listen to baby's heart and give you the once-over if you like. You're here anyway, so it wouldn't be a problem.'

'So it doesn't kick yet?'

'He'll be moving about, but too small for you to feel it yet. Don't worry, it won't be long before you'll have little feet and elbows bothering you all night.'

'Oh, because my nana said...'

'I'm sure it's a while since your nana had her babies, and we tend to forget the details. It might be best if you take advice with a pinch of salt, however well meant it is. You did the right thing coming to see me. Why don't you get comfy on the couch and I'll have a look at you?'

'Mum says I'm eating too much.' Maisie settled on the examination table and looked up at the ceiling while Zoe warmed her hands to feel at her tiny bump. 'She says they say you should eat for two, but it's not true. She says everyone will start to notice I'm pregnant if I get fat.'

'You're far from fat.' Zoe frowned as she moved her hands gently across Maisie's belly. 'Are you eating healthy food?'

'I think so. Sometimes it's hard because we don't have vegetables in.'

'You don't even have a bag of peas in the freezer?'

'I don't like peas.'

'What do you like?'

'Um... I don't really like vegetables.'

'Nothing at all?'

'I don't know.'

'How about something like guacamole? Or salsa? Do you like things like that?'

Maisie nodded. 'I have those sometimes when we go to Nando's.'

'Eat things like that then, as long as you can get them fresh. It's as good as plain veg.'

'Fresh?'

'Can you make them from scratch?'

'I don't think so. I don't know how.'

'I could give you some recipes.'

'I don't know if Mum would buy the stuff.'

'But you could.' Zoe went to get her stethoscope. 'It's not hard. It'll be good practice for if you decide to make your own baby food too. Do you cook at all?'

'I can do pizza. And chips and burgers and nuggets.'

'I suppose those are the things your mum buys in?'

Maisie nodded. 'Shouldn't I eat them? I know I was told about eggs, but...'

'In moderation those things are fine. But if you're finding you're hungry a lot more often, it might help to eat things that are a bit more nutritious. Doing that will mean you keep your weight healthy without going hungry. Do you see?'

'So what should I tell Mum to buy?'

'I'm not going to tell you how to do your shopping – that's up to you and your mum.'

'But what should I eat so I don't get fat?'

'Maisie...' Zoe folded the stethoscope back into its case. 'You're pregnant. Your body is going to change no matter what you do, and that's all right – that's part of nature's way. Your mum will know this because hers will have changed when she had you.'

'She always says it's my fault she lost her figure.'

'I wouldn't go that far, but some women do find it hard to get back to their old shape. And then some women snap back as if they never had a baby in the first place. But whether you can see them or not, there will be changes. You've got to accept that because trying to fight it will drive you mad.'

'Mum says I'll be sorry if I let myself go.'

Zoe tried not to show her disapproval. 'Sit up; we're all done. Everything is absolutely fine as far as I can see. Hang on...' She went to her filing cabinet and took out some pamphlets. 'These have lots of advice around eating and some easy things for you to cook. No matter what your mum says, you need to feed your baby well, and you can only do that if you're eating well. So eat what and when your body tells you to and you won't go far wrong. However... I would try to lay off the ultra-processed food a bit. I know it's hard if that's what comes in with the shopping, but perhaps you might want to go out and do a bit of shopping of your own, just for you, if you can manage it.'

'I don't know if Mum will like that.' Maisie looked at the pamphlets and then back at Zoe. 'Thanks. So if I eat these things, I won't get fat?'

Zoe gave a taut smile. 'You won't get *unhealthy*. Getting a little fat while you're pregnant isn't a bad thing. You really shouldn't worry about it. If you eat well, you'll lose any weight you gain when the baby is born.'

'OK.' Maisie got off the treatment table and pushed her feet back into trainers she hadn't undone. 'I'll tell Mum what you said.'

Zoe wondered whether what she'd said would reach Maisie's mum exactly how she'd said it, or how much would be lost in translation. And Maisie was quite old enough to make her own decisions about her pregnancy. At times like these, Zoe wished she could have a quiet word with mums and nanas and aunts and all the other women who were queuing up to give outdated or unhelpful advice and tell them to butt out. In fact, it was becoming a regular little fantasy, one that she'd sadly never be able to indulge.

'You're happy now?' Zoe asked. 'Nothing else is worrying you?'

'I don't think so.'

'You know where I am if you think of anything you want to ask.'

She saw Maisie out and straightened up before calling the last appointment of the day through.

Saturday was mild but gusty. Zoe had been down to the shop to get a few last-minute things for lunch with Ritchie the following day and had been quizzed by Magnus on her social life. What he really wanted to know was why she didn't attend film club; it was clear that he could see no reason why she wouldn't.

She was passing by Daffodil Farm when she saw Victor coming out of the gate.

'Morning!' he called. 'You're up and about early – your bed on fire?'

'It's not that early!' Zoe replied, laughing as she went over to have a proper word. 'And you're up.'

'But I'm a farmer. If I wasn't, I'd sleep the clock round.'

Zoe glanced down to see Victor had what looked like his metal detector with him. 'Are you going over to Hilltop with that?'

Victor beamed. 'I am. Hope it's worth my while.'

'It'll be fun even if you don't find anything.'

'He's a nice fella, that Alex. I used to get on all right with Ann's other half before he died, but he could be a bit up and down. I think Alex will be a good neighbour. How are you doing over there in Kestrel Cottage? Does it feel like home now?'

'It's getting there,' Zoe said. 'I mean, it's a lovely little house and I'm grateful...'

'Of course, but it's all new for you here.'

'Not so much now, thank goodness. I'm getting used to the pace, but it seemed ridiculously quiet at first. So are you going over to do your detecting now?'

'I've got to go and see to the girls first. Come over with me if you like – say hello. They love visitors.'

'I've got my shopping to take home—'

'I'll wait if you want to drop it in and come back. No bother.'

Zoe thought about saying no thank you and going about her day. But what would she be doing with it? Cleaning, ready for her visitor, and really, what would Ritchie care if her house was clean? What did she care, even if he did have an opinion? It was her home, not his, and she didn't have to answer to anyone these days. If she wanted to live in five feet of filth, she could and nobody could tell her not to. It would be fun to go and see Victor's alpaca, and maybe she'd even get an invite to watch him and Alex do their detecting. It wasn't the conventional way to spend a Saturday, but perhaps convention was overrated.

'I'll dash over and get my wellies on,' she said. 'And then I'd love to come and see the girls.'

'You go and do that,' Victor said cheerfully. 'I'll be here when you get back, don't worry.'

A few minutes later, Zoe was trying to keep up with Victor as he strode across his land.

'Five foot and a feather, remember?' she panted. 'Could you slow it down a bit for my little legs?'

Victor turned to her with a chuckle. 'Sorry, flower, I forget. I'm so used to marching up and down these fields on my own.'

'And I'm sure it's kept you very fit over the years, but I'm not fit; I'm a lazy millennial with no stamina and a very short stride, so if you could just take your foot off the gas...'

'Understood!'

Despite his promise, it didn't seem to Zoe that they'd slowed the pace much at all. She was still out of breath by the time they reached the paddock where he kept his alpaca herd, wondering if she ought to join Stacey, Ottilie's friend, on her current fitness kick.

'Here we are...' Victor started to undo the gate, and before he'd managed it, had already been noticed by at least four of his herd, who had started coming over.

'See, they know it's treat time,' Victor said with a laugh. 'All right there, Alice, Ottilie... calm down; I'll be with you as soon as I can.'

'It still makes me laugh that you called one of them Ottilie,' Zoe said. She reached a tentative hand out to pat one of them on the nose. She didn't think she'd ever be as comfortable around them as Victor was, and on first meeting she'd been a little nervous, but she was getting more used to them now.

'Suits her,' Victor said. 'Next one we come by we'll call Zoe – how's that?'

'I'm not sure. Obviously she'd be rubbish at trekking, and she'd be the one that kept going in the wrong direction all the time. Probably have short legs too.'

More of the alpaca came over, and Victor greeted them all. 'Morning Daisy, Dorothy, Kitty.' And then they followed him to the stables, Pied Piper style, because, as he pointed out to Zoe, they all knew where he kept the treats, locked up so they couldn't break in and take them all while he wasn't there.

While Zoe handed them out, he took the brief opportunity to check them all over. 'Alice... look at the state of you,' he grumbled. 'What have you been rolling in? You're going to need a bath, and I wasn't planning on doing it this month.'

'I could do it,' Zoe said.

Victor gave her a patient smile. 'I think you'd regret offering. Likely get a kick in the face if you don't know what you're doing. She wouldn't mean it, mind, but might do it by accident. Better if I do it.'

'Right. Well, is there anything else I can do?'

'Not really, unless you fancy shovelling up some dung.'

'I don't mind doing that. Once you've been present at a birth or two, you can cope with any kind of bodily waste.'

Victor threw his head back in laughter. 'I'll have to remember that! No, I think I'll fasten them in for now and come back up later. There's nothing really urgent that needs doing.'

'Ah, I see. You're excited to start detecting?'

'I don't know what you mean,' he replied with mock innocence, and it was now Zoe's turn to laugh. 'Do you mind if I walk to Hilltop with you?'

'Want to join in, eh?'

'I thought I might call in to see Billie – take the opportunity to see how she is.'

'Just like young Ottilie – you never stop working, do you?'

'I don't know about that, but it doesn't really feel like work to me. It's only visiting one of my expectant mums for a chat. I'd call that a nice morning rather than work.'

'Either way, you're more than welcome to walk over with me.' Victor locked up the box where he kept his treats and put it on a high shelf, and the minute he did, his herd started to wander off. 'It's a fickle kind of love,' he said with a wry smile, 'but I'll take it over none.'

'I don't blame you.' Zoe followed him out of the field and waited for a moment while he fastened the gate, her gaze on the dew-soaked hills rolling away towards the horizon. Below, somewhere in a hollow but unseen from this vantage, lay the village of Thimblebury.

'Have you always lived here?' she asked.

'Man and boy,' he said briskly. 'Wouldn't be anywhere else.'

'I'm not surprised.'

'What do you think?' he asked her with a shrewd look. 'Can you see yourself staying?'

'I'm not sure yet. My head says to wait and see, but my heart...'

He gave a sage nod. 'Fair enough. Come on – let's get going. It'll take us twice the time if we have to walk at half the speed for your little legs. If we're not careful, we'll be losing the daylight before we've started anything.'

'Oi!' Zoe squeaked with a grin. 'I'm not having leg slander like that!'

'Should have eaten your crusts as a girl then.'

'I thought that gave you curly hair?'

'Does it?' Victor chuckled. 'That's put me right...'

It took them a good fifteen minutes to negotiate the fields and paths that led to Hilltop. By the time they got to the neighbouring farm, Alex was already out at the front gate, scraping the mud from a shovel that was propped up against the garden wall. Grizzle had his nose stuck around the base of a tree, presumably on the scent of something interesting. The minute he sensed new arrivals, however, his head whipped up and he bounded towards the garden wall, tail wagging.

'You been out already?' Victor called, nodding at the shovel as he reached to fuss Grizzle.

'I had an hour to kill so I had a poke around,' Alex said, his attention diverting to Zoe with an unspoken question.

'Find anything?' Victor asked.

'No. But there's plenty of time, right? Morning, Zoe...'

'I've come to see how Billie is,' she said. 'Don't worry, I won't be crashing your party over on the fields.'

'She's still in bed. If I'd known you were coming, I'd have got her up.'

'But she's all right?' Zoe asked pointedly and was satisfied that his response was relaxed enough.

'Better, actually. Whatever you said to her seems to have had some effect. She said she was tired last night and went to bed early, but she wasn't ill or anything, so I thought better to let her sleep as long as she needs.'

'I think that's probably the best idea.' Zoe smiled up at Victor, patting Grizzle, who'd diverted his attention to her, absently. 'I reckon I'll get back then. Thanks for taking me to visit the girls.'

'Girls?' Alex looked from one to the other with interest.

'My herd,' Victor said. 'They're all girls, see.'

'Ah, right. You know, I think I must be the only person around here not to have met them yet.'

'That's easily remedied,' Victor said. 'Say the word and I'll happily take you over. Your lass too.'

'Oh, I don't think Billie should go,' Zoe cut in. 'Sorry,' she added at Victor's look of vague confusion. 'It's a germ thing... She's pregnant, and she needs to be careful around livestock.'

'Fair enough,' he said with a shrug. 'In a few months then.'

'Sorry,' Zoe said again, but Victor simply shrugged off the apology.

'Not to worry. So what are you going to do with your morning now? Corrine's home if you want some company.'

'I don't want to keep bothering her; I'm sure she's got lots to do. I expect I'll clean the house or something. I was meant to do that anyway.'

Alex glanced at Victor with raised eyebrows. 'Couldn't we use an assistant? If you wanted to come over to the pod site with us,' he added, turning to Zoe. 'It might not be very exciting if we don't find anything, but you seemed interested the other day, and I don't mind you tagging along if Victor doesn't.'

'Of course not – you're more than welcome,' Victor said with a smile that Zoe could have sworn was a bit too knowing.

'All right,' she said after running every alternative scenario rapidly through her head and deciding that poking about on Alex's land looking for treasure sounded far more fun. 'I've already got my wellies on, so I'm ready to go when you are. If you're sure I won't be in the way.'

Alex called Grizzle over, opened the front door, ushered him inside and then shut it again. 'He'd end up eating whatever we found, daft dog,' he said before going over to a collection of tools standing next to his shovel and pulling a mud-splattered metal detector out. 'There you go – you can be in charge of this.'

Zoe grinned as she took it. 'You mean I get to do the beep-beeping?'

'Why not? You've probably got more patience than me with it, if I'm honest. I think most people would have.'

'I don't know about that, but I'll have a go.'

'Right then. You take that and I'll grab the other tools.'

'Can you manage everything?' Victor asked. 'I can get the Land Rover if we need it.'

'I've got it,' Alex said, collecting his equipment. 'No need to go all that way.'

'I can carry something else,' Zoe said, which made Alex grin and hand her a trowel.

'There you go.'

'Why does everyone think I'm a weakling?' Zoe huffed but only pretending to be annoyed.

'Because you're... and I realise this might not be a very feminist thing to say, but I think the word is *petite*,' Alex said, making Victor laugh again.

'I think the word you want is *Borrower*,' Victor said, still laughing, and then Zoe had to laugh too. She'd heard all the jokes before, but told in the right way by the right person, they were still funny, even to her.

. . .

As they walked towards the site of Alex's intended camping field, Victor whistled so loudly it seemed to bounce from the hillsides. Alex was in a good mood – Zoe considered that it might be the most cheerful she'd ever seen him. Perhaps the fresh air made him happy too, or perhaps it was a sense of anticipation at what they might find. Or maybe it was the company, which was certainly doing a lot to improve Zoe's mood too. Digging about in a muddy field looking for ancient odds and ends wasn't what she'd imagined she'd be doing with her Saturday off, but it had come as a welcome surprise. And wasn't life full of little moments like this: unexpected, totally out-of-the-blue pleasures? Wasn't that how it ought to be?

'So Billie seems good?' she asked Alex as they followed in the wake of Victor's longer strides.

'It's hard to say for sure, but I think so. She's opening up a bit more. I thought about what you said,' he continued, his gaze trained on the path ahead. 'You know, about talking to her, telling her I'm there for her no matter what. She was a bit... Well, I feel as if we were both a bit embarrassed, to be honest – we don't talk like that. But I'm glad I said something because she didn't really answer it, but I think she understood. Thanks.'

'No need to thank me. It was your doing.'

'But I needed that kick up the backside to make me see that I had to do something. Are you always right about everything like that?' he added, giving her a sideways look.

She smiled up at him. 'Annoying, isn't it?'

'Infuriating.'

'Keep up, you two!' Victor called behind him, laughing as he did. 'It'll be dark at this rate.'

'It's barely eleven!' Zoe shouted back. 'Don't be so bossy!'

'If I'd known you were going to be such a slave driver, I wouldn't have invited you!' Alex added.

'Too late now,' Victor shouted back. 'You're stuck with me.'

Zoe lowered her voice. 'Bless. He's excited. Like a little kid. He was the same at the paddock – couldn't wait to get done and come over here. Isn't it cute?'

'I have to admit, I've been looking forward to more searching myself. I've got no patience for the task, and I will be complaining if I don't find a chest full of gold in the first ten minutes, but I'm still up for it.'

'So that's why I'm here, is it? To keep you both in line.'

'I was hoping you wouldn't notice.'

Victor stopped for a moment and scanned the landscape. 'Where did you say it was?' he asked, turning to watch Alex and Zoe catch up.

'Over on that plateau.' Alex pointed to a spot that was perhaps another two or three minutes' walk away. 'You can just about see where I've been digging there.'

'Your eyes are better than mine,' Victor said, 'so I'll take your word for it. At least I know where I'm going now.'

He started to walk again, and Zoe and Alex followed. Before too long she could see the beginnings of some foundations, which Alex had clearly intended to create many more of before he'd got distracted by his first find. A meandering trench of different depths spilled out from that original section. It was hardly precision engineering, and Alex said as much as he noticed her looking.

'I probably ought to try and make it more methodical. I expect if we had professionals up here, they'd do that and get better results.'

'Will there be any professional digging?' Zoe asked.

'I don't know. The expert I've been speaking to says there's nothing of enough significance yet for that, though he's happy to take what I do find off my hands for cataloguing, and if the department decides there might be a reason to come up, they'll get in touch with me.'

'But you still want to dig?'

He turned to her with a smile. 'How could I resist? I wouldn't be able to rest knowing there might be something amazing under the soil here and I'd never tried to find it.'

Zoe had to smile; his enthusiasm was infectious. She'd never been interested in this sort of thing before but found herself fascinated now. 'What do you think you'll find?'

'I don't know. I have no clue what sort of things might be there. It would be incredible to find something of value, like jewellery or something, but I doubt that's going to happen. It's more likely to be everyday stuff.'

Victor was already walking the length of haphazard trench when Zoe and Alex got there.

'What do you reckon?' Alex asked.

'I reckon you've made a lovely mess,' Victor replied.

'I know, and it'll get a lot messier by the time I've finished. Shall we get cracking?'

Victor flicked a switch on his detector while Alex meddled with his own, trying to remind himself how it worked. After a minute or so, he had it set and handed it to Zoe. 'You're chief detector today.'

'What are you going to do now I have your metal detector?'

'I'm going to prod about with my big stick to see what I hit.'

'Well, that sounds technical.'

'You're impressed, right? You must be.'

'Oh yes.' Zoe raised her eyebrows and nodded very deliberately. '*Very* impressed...'

'You know, you gave me that same look Billie gives me when she thinks I'm being a total spanner. I don't know what it is that all the women I know seem to think I'm an idiot.'

'I'm sure she doesn't,' Zoe said with a smile.

'If that's the case, she has a funny way of showing it.' He rubbed his hands together, surveying the ground he'd already dug. 'I'll start here. You go and pick a spot – I don't think it matters where. Give it a sweep and see what you can find.'

'How will I know if I've found something?'

'Oh, you'll know,' he said with a grin. 'You'll be able to hear the alarm on that thing in Windermere when it goes off.'

Zoe wandered to a spot a few feet away that was still covered by wild grasses and began to move the detector back and forth, slowly and methodically. She had no clue what she was doing, but she suspected none of them really did so that was all right. In fact, it was funny.

She looked up to see Victor doing the same as her with his detector, a look of concentration on his face so serious and absorbed that it seemed faintly ridiculous. Alex wasn't faring much better. He'd told her he'd poke about in the mud, and that was exactly what he was doing. He had a large rod and was prodding it into the soil at random intervals, waiting for a moment to see if he hit anything and then trying again in a different place when he didn't. After ten minutes, despite working in silence, none of them had hit anything at all.

'Well, this is a thrill a minute, isn't it?' Alex said, looking up.

'You said you had no patience, but I thought you'd last a bit longer,' Zoe said, taking off one of her earphones to listen to him.

'Did I say that?'

Victor looked up and noticed them talking and then took off his headphones too. 'Who's got the flask?'

'Not me,' Zoe said. 'I was a last-minute addition, and I didn't know I needed to bring a flask.'

'Neither did I,' Alex said.

'Hopeless,' Victor said and then took one from his bag. 'Only two cups, I'm afraid, because I didn't know I'd need more, but if someone doesn't mind sharing...'

'You have a drink first,' Alex said to Zoe. 'I don't mind wiping out the cup and using it again afterwards.'

'Is there some of Corrine's cake?' Zoe asked, taking a drink from Victor.

'Of course there is – what do you take me for? Ginger or lemon drizzle?'

'Oooh, lemon, please!' Zoe held out her hand, and Victor put a small parcel in it. 'Thank you! And thank you, Corrine. How do you stay so slim, married to the world's best baker?'

'I must walk it off. Corrine says it's black magic, the amount I eat in a day.'

'I think she's right.'

'Cake?' Victor asked Alex.

'I'm getting some too? I'll take whatever's going – don't want to deprive anyone of their favourite.'

'There's plenty to go round,' Victor said, handing another wrapped slice to Alex before digging in the bag for his own and sitting on a mound of earth to unwrap it.

The mug was hot but comforting in Zoe's hands as she sipped at her tea and munched on her cake, gazing out over the landscape.

'I could do this every day,' Alex said as he stood at her side and followed her gaze. 'It's funny, when I bought Hilltop, it was a pure business decision. It was the right place for the right price at the right time. But since I arrived here, I've started to get attached to it in a way I never expected.'

'You didn't move here because you were drawn by some mystical force?' she asked wryly.

'Were you?'

'Oh yes, it was called a job offer.'

He grinned. 'Money then. I think mine might have been a very similar motivation.'

'Disappointingly cynical, eh?'

'I prefer not to think of it as cynical, but I'll admit there was more logic than emotion involved. I thought it was the sort of place people would want to come on holiday, so of course it's a lovely part of the world. But there are lots of lovely parts of the world and... I don't know, but I can't imagine them feeling so...'

He shrugged as he bit into his cake. 'Healing, I think that's it. Standing here, looking at all this' – he nodded at a majestic panorama of rolling fields, valleys and hilltops crowned by cloud – 'it's so peaceful, so much bigger than us, it sort of puts your life in perspective, doesn't it? And I think that's good, knowing that your problems can be shrunk down like that. Because our place in the bigger picture is tiny.'

'I'm not sure if that makes me feel better or not. I do think you're right, though. Feeling small... makes me feel lost.'

'It makes me feel free. Any mistakes I make are a blip – they don't really matter in the grand scheme of things.'

'That sounds a bit like shrugging off responsibility to me.'

'I don't mean it like that. Obviously I'm still going to take seriously what I have to do for Billie. I want to provide for her, and I want to make her life good, but in the end, how much of what I do really matters? I'll be here for a moment, and then poof, I'm gone. Just like the people who left those arrowheads I found.'

'I get it, but I prefer to think what I do matters a lot.'

'Ah, well, that's probably true. It probably matters more. After all, you're bringing the next generation into the world, and without them, there is no future me trying to make one of your descendants understand what they're saying... very badly, I might add.'

It had been a wholly unexpected foray into philosophy that Zoe didn't fully comprehend and hadn't seen coming, but she appreciated the sentiment behind it. As she turned back to the hills and valleys laid out before them, she agreed on one point – being here was sort of healing. In the peace of this landscape, it was hard to believe there were struggles going on beyond it. It was also easy to imagine a simpler life, one where eating and sleeping and working hard and loving the people around you were all that mattered, the sort of life the people who'd left the arrowheads behind must have had.

'More cake?' Victor asked as he scrunched up a bit of greaseproof paper and dropped it into his bag.

'I'm full up for now,' Zoe said.

'I'll take some more.' Alex wandered over to Victor's seat.

'Have my cup now too,' Victor added. 'I'm done. I've got some water here to give it a rinse...'

As they worked out how best to clean the cup and then filled it for Alex, Zoe watched. The day she'd first met Alex she'd been struck by his looks. Now that she knew him better, his looks seemed to matter less. She still liked them, but it wasn't his warm smile that made her think of him when he wasn't there. It wasn't his patient and soulful dark eyes that made her want to watch him when he wasn't aware of her gaze. There was an aura, an indefinable something that she simply found magnetic, a feeling that grew stronger every time their paths crossed. She hadn't yet worked out what it meant, but she couldn't deny that it was becoming worryingly addictive. He was complicated, but she wanted to figure him out. He came with problems that she wanted to solve.

As these thoughts ran through her head, he turned and caught her eye, and she blushed, tearing her gaze away and taking a gulp of her tea. 'This is a perfect cuppa. Is Corrine good at everything?'

'I'll have you know I made the tea,' Victor said. 'But yes, she is good at everything. Why do you think I snapped her up all those years ago?'

'Because you thought she was beautiful and funny and intelligent.'

'Oh, that too, but mostly I tasted one of her dinners and then never looked at another woman again.'

Alex and Zoe both laughed.

Victor poured a tea for Alex, offered Zoe a top-up, which she took, and then screwed the lid back onto the flask. They chatted about what they might find that day, what they hoped to find and revisited their earlier conversation about what they'd do with the money if they struck gold. Alex was adamant that Zoe would have a cut of the spoils, leading to Victor weaving a pretend scenario of treachery which involved him taking Zoe's cut and denying she was ever there, and by the end of it they were all laughing so hard, she could barely sip her tea without snorting it back down her nose. Then they picked up their tools and began work in earnest, buoyed by a warm drink and a sugary snack and a sense of camaraderie Zoe had never expected to find with her two neighbours.

19

Victor had invited Zoe and Alex back to Daffodil Farm to eat with him and Corrine. He'd promised that there would be enough food, and a surprise doubling of their number wouldn't put her out one bit. Zoe wasn't sure Corrine would agree, and Alex wanted to get back to Billie, and so they left Victor to make his way back to Daffodil Farm alone. Zoe decided to detour to Hilltop to see if Billie was up so she could have a brief word. She wanted to see for herself that things were improving. She and Alex had mostly chatted about the day; they'd found disappointingly little, apart from some old bottle tops and a bit of what looked like it might be pottery, though nobody knew what period it might have come from. They also spoke of Billie and her pregnancy, about their lives before Thimblebury, and Alex was noticeably more open about that than he had been before.

Back at Kestrel Cottage, Zoe's muddy wellington boots were standing on a sheet of newspaper by the back door while she ran a bath, her mind very much on that conversation as she watched the bubbles swirl and bloom as the tub filled. He hadn't said much about Jennifer, the wife he'd lost, but Zoe sensed he wanted to. Perhaps he didn't think it was the right time or the right company to talk more honestly about her and how her loss had affected him. It needed time, she decided, just like it had needed time for Billie to open up to her. As far as both were concerned, it was a work in progress and would be for a while yet, but if Zoe had one thing to offer them, it was time. She could wait, and when they were ready, she could give them all the time they needed to talk their feelings through. In fact, in a strange way, she looked forward to that day. She'd never admit it to herself, but fixing other people was a welcome distraction from trying to fix her own problems. She didn't always succeed, but she liked to try.

She'd left her phone on the bed, and as she went to fetch her towelling robe, she noticed a text had come through. Ritchie. Her day had been so enjoyable that she couldn't even bring herself to be annoyed about it. In fact, she was looking forward to seeing him the following day for lunch too, despite knowing she oughtn't. He was more than her ex, after all; he was an old friend too, someone who knew her as well as anyone. Everyone in Thimblebury had been lovely since her arrival, but only Ottilie really knew her, and she missed having people she could truly be herself with.

Looking forward to tomorrow. What time should I be there? x

Zoe tapped out a brief reply and then left the phone on the bed as she went to have her bath.

Corrine had threatened to send the cute little apron Zoe was currently wearing to charity, but Zoe had been in the kitchen of Daffodil farmhouse when she'd mentioned it to Victor and had snapped it up. It was printed with lemons on a white background with frills at the hems. Corrine had received it as a Christmas gift and although she liked it complained that it covered her so inadequately she might as well not bother wearing one at all. Zoe, on the other hand, thought it was perfectly serviceable and very pretty, and was only too happy to take it off her hands.

She wiped her hands down it and set the pan onto the stove, and then was annoyed at herself for dirtying it because she liked it almost as much as the top she had on underneath. There was chicken roasting in the oven, and the kitchen was glorious with the scent of the lemon and thyme she'd stuffed it with. The potatoes were parboiling, and she'd just peeled the accompanying carrots and parsnips, while broccoli waited on the worktop to cook last. She was bang on schedule and stopped for a mouthful of wine. Dutch courage, perhaps, but it slipped down nicely all the same.

She wanted this meal to go well, to mark a new phase in their relationship – the start of a proper platonic friendship – and she planned to use the occasion to make that clear. They could do this every once in a while, have a nice time, catch up, but this was also a way of setting a boundary, a time and a place they could agree on for contact that meant dipping in and out when it wasn't wanted was off the table. She was going to make that bit especially clear – no constant messages, no turning up unannounced, no wanting more than she was willing to give. She would be there for Ritchie as a friend, but there would be rules.

There was a knock at the door. Putting the wine down, she frowned at the clock. Ritchie was half an hour early and she wasn't yet ready, and this was exactly the sort of thing she meant. It was a small matter to anyone else, but they didn't know Ritchie.

But she opened the door, and her frown turned into a look of consternation as she found not Ritchie but Alex in the porch.

'Have I come at a bad time?' he asked, looking her up and

down. She wondered how flushed her face was – she certainly felt hot.

'I, um…'

'I'm sorry, I should have messaged first. I only came to give you these…' He produced a posy of autumnal flowers. 'To say thank you. For sticking by Billie and me when I know we're not the easiest of projects.'

'It really wasn't like that at all… I like spending time with you and Billie…' Zoe took the flowers. The polite thing to do would be invite him in, but Ritchie was due, and she was up to her elbows in goose fat and herbs. 'Thank you, but there was no need to go to all this trouble.'

'I was wondering…' he continued, seemingly unaware of her snub. 'I might do some more detecting up on the field later… did you want to come? I mean, say no if you're busy, but I felt like we had fun yesterday and…' He took a step back from the porch. 'I can see it's not a good time. Forget I said anything.'

'It's not that… I'd love to ordinarily, but I've got someone coming over for lunch.'

'Right, of course, that's why there's such a good smell coming from your house. Well, I hope you enjoy it, I'm sure you will.'

He looked so crushed that she wasn't sure what to think, but she hated the way it made her feel. What was this? Flowers to thank her for helping them out was one thing, but the look on his face was saying more than that. Why had he come? Was there something more he wanted to say? A minute before, she'd been only too happy to welcome Ritchie in, but now she wished he wasn't coming. Now, she wanted nothing more than to invite Alex in and have him sit at her dining table to eat the food she was cooking, to be in his company and to hear what he had to say.

'Maybe another day?' she said.

'Another day, yes. That would be good.'

'Will you go up there later anyway? I mean, if I finish here and it's not too late, maybe I'll come and find you.'

'I think so. The sooner I feel I've searched everywhere, the sooner I can go back to getting the foundations for the pods in.'

'And maybe I can come in to see Billie too.'

'I think she'd like that.'

Zoe was about to make a tentative date, already running through excuses in her head to get rid of Ritchie straight after lunch, when his car stopped at the end of the path. She let out an involuntary groan as he got out with flowers of his own and a look at Alex that was rife with distrust. Without thinking, she tossed the flowers Alex had just given her behind the front door and painted on an innocent smile for Ritchie, but her heart sank behind it as she realised Alex had seen what she'd done.

Ritchie strode up to the door and gave her the bouquet, all the time staring at Alex. 'Afternoon... You're Zoe's neighbour, right?'

'Yes...' Alex stuck out a hand and Ritchie gripped it so hard as he shook that Zoe noticed his knuckles whiten. Ritchie was slightly taller than Alex, with darker hair than Alex's chestnut and broader shouldered too. But if his actions bothered Alex, he didn't show it. Despite being at a slight physical disadvantage, Alex still held his own. He simply returned the handshake with a courteous nod. 'Alex Fitzgerald.'

'I'm Ritchie, Zoe's husband.'

'Soon to be ex,' Zoe reminded him with a sudden rush of vexation. She didn't have a clue what was going through his mind, but he had no right to go around making it look as if they were still together. At least Alex knew the truth, and he gave a strange, knowing smile, as if he had the measure of the other man from that short interaction.

'But we're good friends,' Ritchie added, still staring Alex down. 'We're still close.'

'I'd better go,' Alex said, turning back to Zoe. 'I only wanted to tell you about Billie's ultrasound.'

'Oh, right, yeah, thanks.' Zoe gave a taut smile, all at once grateful for his accurate reading of the situation and his quick excuse, but mortified that he'd been forced to do that. And as she ushered Ritchie inside and caught sight of Alex's discarded flowers, she felt sick with shame. How had she been so unforgivably rude? No matter what the sight of them might have stirred up between her and Ritchie, she should never have done that.

She told Ritchie to go through to the kitchen and sit at the table, retrieved them and then opened the front door again to see if Alex was still within hailing distance. But he'd been too quick. Wherever he was heading for, he'd gone there fast and she couldn't see him. With regret like a stone in her gut, she closed the door again. Before she went back to the kitchen, she hurried upstairs and put Alex's flowers into the little vanity sink in her bedroom before taking Ritchie's downstairs to a vase in the kitchen.

'This looks amazing,' Ritchie gushed as Zoe finished putting the food out.

'It's only Sunday roast.'

'Yeah, but you know I love your Sunday roast. I've missed them. Microwave lasagne just isn't the same.'

'You *can* cook.' Zoe took a seat and poured herself some more wine.

'I can't be bothered. There doesn't seem like much point when it's only me. All that work and cleaning up and nobody to share it with.'

'I think it's important to keep some standards, and looking after yourself with good food is one of them. Cut corners where you like, but not with what you eat.'

'I appreciated how you used to make sure I ate well, like

when I'd come home tired and go for a pack of instant noodles from the cupboard and you'd be like, "Even if you want to eat those, at least stir-fry some vegetables or chicken to go with them!" You were right, of course. I was definitely healthier when I lived with you.'

'You look fine.' Zoe reached for the potatoes and spooned some onto her plate.

'You look amazing. This place must suit you.'

'I suppose it must. Thanks.'

'I mean it.'

Zoe looked up and gave a tight smile. 'OK. Thank you.'

'So your neighbour...' Ritchie said as he grabbed the bowl of carrots. 'His wife's preggers?'

'Billie's his daughter.'

'Right. How old is she?'

'Twenty-three... I think. It's hard to keep track of all my mums, but she's about that.'

'He doesn't look old enough to have a girl that age.'

'I'll tell him you said that – I'm sure it'll make his day.'

'So he pops over now and again to let you know about her?'

'More or less. I mean, he's a neighbour, so sometimes there are things happening locally that he tells me about. He's friends with my landlord as well, so there's the odd occasion where I bump into him at Daffodil Farm too.' Sensing an inquisition and determined to head it off, Zoe changed the subject to one she knew Ritchie would be keen to discuss. 'How's the job hunt going? Any progress since I last spoke to you?'

Zoe mentally buckled in. She knew from experience this was going to be a lengthy conversation, but while Ritchie was occupied on this, he wouldn't be quizzing her about areas of her life she wanted to keep to herself. As she poured gravy over her meal, he began.

'Not really. I mean, there's this guy... you remember Blakey from the pub? He knows a man who knows someone who works for the engineers on Fawcett Street. They want someone for turning or cutting or something. I dunno. I'm way overqualified for it. I might apply anyway and take it if nothing else comes up. I've got my name down with all the employment agencies, but they keep finding things that are miles out, and I don't see why I should spend hours driving every day. My redundancy package will be all right, though I did want to go to Bali, you know, and there'd be enough in there. Foster, who goes to the footie, buys and sells on that clothes website, makes a bit on the side – he reckons I ought to do that. But can I be bothered with that? I ought to do a couple of years on the dole. I mean, I've paid my dues over the years, and I've never claimed, and there's people who've never done a day of work in their lives scrounging off my tax ...'

Zoe had stopped listening. She hadn't meant to, but she was finding it hard to concentrate because Alex's face at the front door as she'd thrown his flowers to one side kept swimming in front of her eyes. She would have to go and apologise, as soon as Ritchie was gone.

She chewed slowly, running the conversation through her mind. Should she try to explain why she'd done it? But how could she when she barely understood it herself? She could pretend it was an accident, a slip, but she didn't see that washing either because it was a very deliberate action, and he wouldn't buy that excuse for a minute. Perhaps the wisest course of action was to gloss over it, pretend it hadn't happened and never mention it. Perhaps he'd forget and they'd simply move on. She supposed in time he might, but the look on his face told her otherwise. And she'd know what she'd done, and she wasn't sure she'd be able to forget it. She knew she'd feel guilty every time she saw him for a long time yet.

Maybe she'd misread the situation. What if he hadn't even noticed? Zoe only thought he had.

She suddenly became aware of a gap in Ritchie's conversation and smiled vaguely at him. 'How's the chicken? I put half a lemon in it.'

'It's great,' Ritchie said through a mouthful. 'I saw Ellen from the newsagent's at the end of the road where our first house was, and she said another factory near us was laying off as well. It's bad. You know what it is, don't you? It's all this stuff being made in the Philippines and Taiwan and China and all these other places where people are earning pennies. There's no way we can compete with that. No wonder this country is on its arse. What do they want? Do they want us to work for pennies? Is that the only way around it? You know, if I lived somewhere like that, I'd be a high-up manager with my qualifications. It's an insult, the jobs I'm expected to take. I wouldn't get out of bed for the wages of some of them...'

Zoe nodded, but she'd stopped listening again. She glanced towards the window to see that the weather was dry and the sky promised that it would stay that way. She might be able to catch Alex at his excavation site if Ritchie didn't stay too late.

'It's hard for you to understand,' he continued, Zoe doing her best to pay attention again. 'Because you've got a job that will never get rid of you. People will always have babies, so you'll never be out of work. This redundancy has made me think – imagine how we'd have been up shit creek if we had—'

He stopped dead, suddenly silent and awkward. 'Like, I don't want to say it, but you know what I mean. I'd never wish for what happened, but I'm relieved, in a way... Oh, shit, Zoe. I didn't mean it like that.'

Zoe reached for her wine and knocked the remaining half of the glass back in one go. 'I know what you mean. I suppose it would have been hard if we'd had a child and you'd lost your job, but we'd have found a way to manage.'

'I didn't mean that to sound the way it did.'

'I know you didn't,' she replied stiffly, pouring some more wine into her glass. 'You're right, silver linings and all that. I was devastated at the time, but hey, at least we don't have to feed our son on end-of-day bargains from the market because you lost your job, right?'

'Zoe,' he said quietly. 'I always said we could try again. For another baby, I mean.'

There it was. Zoe was forcibly reminded of the very reason why their marriage had fallen apart after she'd lost her baby. Because he didn't understand what she was going through. He didn't understand that you didn't just make another baby to replace the one you'd lost. He'd never seen their unborn child as a complete person as she had. To him, the baby had been an abstract bump, one day there, the next gone. Zoe had since realised that, in a way, neither of them were wrong or right in the way they'd viewed it, only different. She couldn't see it from his perspective, and he couldn't see it from hers. In the end, the two views had been so incompatible, so utterly beyond reconciliation that they'd both agreed the only thing to do was split.

'But you didn't want one,' he added. 'You said you didn't want that.'

'There's no point in going over this again,' she said. 'Not now. What's past is past.'

'I had thought...' he said, moving to take her hand across the table. She slipped it from his grasp and put it in her lap. 'I always thought we might get around what happened and we might try again.'

'I know you did, but I always told you that wasn't going to happen.'

'But you were happy to see me. Like today. You invited me.'

'Because I thought you might need a friend. Because I care about you.'

'I care about you—'

'I'm not sure it's the same. I'm not sure you understand what I've been saying this whole time. We're almost divorced and I'm not going to turn back now. We agreed it wouldn't work.'

'We said it wasn't working, but we didn't say it never would.'

'I did. I thought the divorce was saying that too. You agreed to it.'

'I know.'

She got up and brought the roasting tin to the table. 'Do you want some more chicken? There's loads here.'

'Yeah,' he said in a dull voice. 'I'll have some.'

He looked up at her as she scooped up a leg and put it onto his plate. 'Why did you ask me to come here today?'

'I told you why.'

'That's not it. I thought...'

'You thought wrong. Sorry, Ritchie. It was only friendship.'

'Are you seeing someone else?'

'You think just because I say no to us getting back together there must be someone else?'

'I don't know. You tell me.'

'There isn't.'

She went to put the roasting tin back on the worktop, and when she returned to the table, he was smiling. She stared at him, not daring to ask why. He'd been so resentful, almost angry only a moment ago, and now he looked as if he didn't have a care in the world.

'I'm sorry,' he said. 'I've been totally out of order. It means a lot to me that we're still friends and we can still do stuff like this, and I don't want to ruin it. Please scrub the last ten minutes and let's start again.'

'I can do that,' Zoe said. At least, she wanted to.

'Tell me about the village,' he said. 'What's it like? Are there any village weirdos? There must be, right? Anyone with six fingers married to their sister?'

Zoe rolled her eyes and tried not to let his comments rile

her. It was the kind of flippant stereotype he'd always made jokes about. He could only change so far, and as she didn't have the energy to fight him on everything, she had to pick her battles. 'Sorry to disappoint you, but everyone is perfectly normal and very nice.'

'You're telling me there's nothing strange going on? These tiny places are always a bit backward, aren't they?'

'Only on TV.'

He paused, studying her for a moment. 'You've changed.'

'Of course I have. I was married and living in Manchester, and now I'm single living out in the countryside. I'm bound to have changed.'

'I haven't.'

Zoe considered his remark before she nodded. 'I think you might be right.'

'I don't mean it as an insult,' he said. 'You're different. I wonder...' He shook his head. 'Never mind.'

Zoe was beginning to see what a mistake it had been, inviting him over for lunch. Perhaps she was giving him hope for something more, and that hadn't been her intention at all. And as always when they were together, she wasn't comfortable with the direction their conversation kept taking. What was worse, there was a part of her that still cared for him more than she ought to. One or two moments of weakness...

She shook herself. She wasn't a teenager; she was a grown woman with common sense and self-control. She picked up the wine, stared at it for a moment, before putting the bottle down again and reaching for her glass of water. Better to be safe than sorry.

20

Disappointing as it was, Zoe was forced to admit as the sun went down and Ritchie showed no signs of leaving that she wasn't going to make it to Alex's fields to help him search for his treasure.

What was worse, as lunch wore on and spilled out across the afternoon, she realised she wasn't going to get much else done either. She'd been prepared for that to an extent – she hadn't invited her ex over with a strict time slot in mind, after all – but she still marvelled at how little awareness he had for etiquette.

Like all their interactions these days, he behaved as if he was still entitled to her time in the same way he'd been before they'd split. He couldn't seem to see that things were different, that the way they were had to change. And every conversational topic she opened up left her wishing she hadn't. His redundancy, his job hunt, the new couple who'd moved in next door, the potential struggle with his buy-out of the house they'd once shared (though she'd reassured him that she could wait as long as it took for him to get back on his feet), his parents, her parents, people at the pub... no subject was too insignificant to provoke an opinion, usually a negative one.

It brought back complicated emotions for Zoe, reminded her of feelings she'd had when they'd first started to drift apart, feelings she'd somehow forced herself to forget. Was she clinging on to a friendship based on wanting to keep a man who no longer existed in her life? It made her remember how changed she'd found him during that time. Though she'd always put that down to their loss, she had to wonder now if he'd been changing all along. Even without the death of their baby, would their marriage have ended just the same?

By the time Ritchie had sloped off at around nine, Zoe had been so exhausted from his company she'd watched some television and then gone to bed. And then Monday morning came around once again with alarming speed.

Magnus was wiping down the counter as Zoe walked in. The sound of the bell at the door made him look up, a broad smile on his face as he saw who was coming in.

'Here she is!'

'Oh,' Zoe said, trying her best to be wittier than she felt. 'That sounds ominous. What have I done?'

'You're only guilty of loveliness,' Magnus said. He balled up his cloth and put it to one side. 'What can we do for you this morning?'

'Just milk and biscuits for the surgery. Oh, and I'd better get teabags; I think we might be low.' Zoe went to the shelf. 'Have you got those ones in the gold pack? Ah, here...'

After collecting what she needed, she went to the counter and gazed absently around the shop as Magnus scanned her shopping.

'Good weekend?' he asked.

'Yes, it was nice.'

'What did you get up to?'

'This and that.'

Magnus gave a knowing look that threw her momentarily. What did he know? There wasn't even anything to know, so why was she concerned?

'This and that,' he said. 'This and that always makes for the best kind of weekend, don't you think?'

As he bagged up her goods, the door opened and Alex came in. His gaze went straight to her, and then he seemed to jump, as if someone had pinched him, before collecting himself and greeting them both.

'Morning.'

'Hello,' Magnus said. 'Come for more chocolate?'

At this comment, Alex seemed even more awkward. 'No, just milk and bread. And do you have lemons? Billie wants to suck on lemons...' He shrugged at Zoe. 'You have to get her what she's craving, right?'

'You do,' Zoe said, offering him a warm smile that he didn't return. The memory of his face as she'd tossed his flowers to one side came back to her, and she felt as awkward as he seemed to be. He was annoyed by it. Offended. Hurt.

'There you go.' Magnus pushed a bag across the counter at Zoe. 'By the way, there's a film club on Thursday. You're more than welcome to join us. We're watching *Wicked* – have you seen it? If not, it'll be worth coming down for. It's ever so good. We have food and drinks afterwards' – he wafted his arm towards the rear of the shop – 'in our private cinema. It's a good night. If you've got nothing else to do, of course...'

'I'm not sure if I'm free yet, but I'll keep it in mind, thank you.'

Magnus looked as if he didn't believe her, but then he turned to where Alex was pulling a bottle of milk from the fridge. 'You're welcome too, of course,' he said.

'Sorry?' Alex turned with a vague look.

'Film night on Thursday. We're going to watch *Wicked*.'

'Oh, I don't think so; it's not really my sort of thing...' Alex glanced at Zoe. 'Billie might want to come down. She might if you were there.'

Zoe couldn't imagine Billie wanting to go to Magnus and Geoff's film club, even if she were to go, but she simply nodded. 'If she wants to, tell her to message me and I'll go with her.'

'Thanks,' Alex said, but although his words expressed gratitude, he still seemed off.

Zoe picked up her bag. 'I'd better go.'

'Have a good day!' Magnus called after as she left the shop, though afterwards she couldn't say whether she'd replied or not. Her mind was full of Alex and how angry she was at herself for being the cause of that look on his face. She couldn't exactly name it; she only knew it made her feel bad.

The last appointment of Zoe's morning clinic was Petra, who waddled into her room with such effort that Zoe promptly decided she'd make a home visit for the next one.

'Seven months and look at the size of me!' Petra grumbled as she dropped into a seat. 'People keep asking me if I have my bags packed for the hospital. I tell them I've got two months yet and they're in shock. I'd be in shock too.'

'You are having twins,' Zoe said with a smile. 'Do you tell them that bit?'

'Of course, but I'm still massive even with twins, aren't I?'

'I'm sorry to break it to you, but I think you're about right. You're quite tall, and you said your husband is tall too, so I expect your babies will be a good size. Which isn't a bad thing, considering they're twins, because the last thing we want is for one or both of them to be underweight. Now then, let me have a look at you. Apart from feeling massive, how are you doing?'

Petra launched into a litany of complaints from swollen feet to constant overheating to the smell of melted chocolate making her feel sick to how she was going to cope when the twins arrived because she already had a toddler at home, while Zoe took measurements and made notes. Despite the outward appearance of health, Petra was one of Zoe's worries. Twins were often complicated, and those challenges sometimes cropped up in unexpected ways. She was relieved to see that, on this occasion, all seemed to be progressing as it ought to.

'Who's looking after your other little one today?' Zoe asked as she took Petra's sample bottle from her.

'Jason. He's got the day off. Good thing too because that little monster's into everything at the moment. She's like the Tasmanian devil – if I'd brought her with me, you'd have had nothing left that wasn't broken. And she keeps slapping my belly. It's like she knows what's in there and she's not happy about it.'

'I'm sure she'll be made up when her sisters arrive.'

'I'm glad it's more girls so I don't have to buy a load more clothes. I saved Isabel's just in case. Jason said it was taking up too much room in the loft, but I think he was secretly hoping for a boy and he didn't want to tempt fate by saving girls' stuff.'

'It's always a good move if you're planning to have more,' Zoe agreed. 'I'm sure Jason is happy whatever you have.'

'He's all right now. He says if we have two more, he can start a girls five-a-side team.'

'Next time I see you, I'll come to the house,' Zoe said. 'Save you the journey out here. Will that be better? I can say hello to Isabel at the same time.'

'Next time you see me, I don't think I'll be able to walk under all this weight so a home visit would be great.'

Petra pushed herself out of the chair, and Zoe could see it was taking some effort.

'Anything else you want to ask me before you go?'

'Don't think so. Unless you know a way of hurrying this all up? I've had just about enough of being pregnant now.'

'I'm sorry, I'm good but not that good. I wouldn't wish it

along too much – from what you've said about Isabel, it sounds as if you'll have your hands full.'

'Ah well, it was worth a try.'

Zoe showed her to the door, and as she left noticed that Ottilie had returned from a home visit of her own.

'All good?' she asked.

'I was about to ask you the same thing. I didn't have a chance this morning to ask you how it went with Ritchie.'

Zoe's face must have given away more than she'd intended because Ottilie gave a sympathetic grimace. 'Oh dear. Want to talk about it over lunch?'

'I don't think it's that deep. Anyway, there'll be too much else going on at lunch – at least, there usually is.'

'I'm going over to Stacey's later if you want to come. We can talk about it on the way. And Stacey's a good listener if you want to share with her.'

She didn't have much else going on and decided it would be nice to have some female company, and so she nodded. 'Thanks, that sounds lovely. Let me know what time you're going, and if you're sure you don't mind me tagging along, I'll come.'

'Of course we don't. I'll warn you that Chloe might be in, but you can cope with her, can't you?'

'I doubt she'll have much interest in talking to me anyway,' Zoe said wryly. 'She doesn't have the time of day for me as her midwife, so I'm sure she won't want to socialise with me. At appointments she'll ask for my opinion or advice on something and when I'm giving the answer, she looks as if she's not listening at all.'

'She doesn't have the time of day for anyone,' Ottilie replied. 'And she does exactly the same with me. I think she is listening, really; it's only the way her face looks. I wouldn't take it personally – it's just her way.'

'I don't,' Zoe said. 'So I suppose that's lucky for me, isn't it?'

. . .

Zoe dropped her phone into her bag before heading out to meet Ottilie. There was a text message from Ritchie on there, thanking her again for lunch, telling her how much he enjoyed seeing her and then something about some job interview he had the following day. She hadn't yet replied because she was thinking carefully about what to say and how to say it. Every interaction with him these days seemed to cause her more confusion than it ought to. To a point, she'd enjoyed his company at lunch too, but it had also been fraught with mixed signals and possible misunderstandings, none of which she wanted to repeat if they did it again.

She'd also thought about visiting Hilltop. In the end, her afternoon clinic had run over, and the decision had been taken out of her hands. If she'd gone up to Hilltop, she'd have been late for Ottilie. That didn't mean that it wasn't still on her mind. She would have made it about Billie, but in reality it was about Alex too. She couldn't stop thinking about how awkward the meeting in the shop that morning had been. Alex had been courteous, but the warmth she'd felt from him when they'd been detecting on the fields of Hilltop had gone. Ottilie had promised to be a friendly ear, but was that what Zoe needed? Thinking about how complicated the situation seemed anyway, perhaps neighbourly courtesy was the best way to deal with Alex, especially when she added in her professional obligations to Billie, which she knew she ought to keep very separate from anything else. The way things stood, her friendship with Alex and Billie and her professional relationship with the latter were getting horribly muddled, and that wasn't how she did things.

She was still turning it all over in her mind when she arrived at Ottilie's house. Her friend was waiting outside on the path. She waved at the window, where Heath stood, waving back, and then she fell into step beside Zoe.

In anticipation of the quincentenary celebrations, there was a team in hard hats on a cherry picker putting up support structures for what Zoe guessed might be some kind of light display. Someone shouted for them to give the workers a wide berth, and Ottilie rolled her eyes at Zoe.

'As if we couldn't figure that out for ourselves.'

'Let them feel important,' Zoe said with a light laugh. 'I'm surprised they're out in this weather doing anything at all.'

'And it's dark,' Ottilie said. 'Someone said it was all being rushed along, and it looks as if that's true. Either way it should be fun. Fliss mentioned us having a fundraiser on the day – raffle tickets and that sort of thing. You'll be able to lend a hand, won't you?'

'Corrine's doing something similar and donating the money to the neonatal unit. Do you think Fliss might want to add to that?'

'I doubt she'll mind. She'll have had some ideas of her own, I imagine, but you could have a word with her tomorrow.'

Zoe pulled her coat tighter. It wasn't cold, but the air was damp, making the temperature seem lower than it was.

'So, Ritchie...' Ottilie began. 'Is he still the prize whinger I remember?'

Zoe's mouth fell open as she turned to her friend.

Ottilie laughed. 'Oh, come on! Don't look so shocked. You have to admit he thinks the world revolves around him. He definitely thinks it owes him a living. Unless he's had a miraculous personality transplant.'

'Have you always thought this?'

'Yes, but you were married to him, so it wasn't my place to say. But now you're almost divorced. I didn't say anything even then because there's always that chance that you'd get back together after I slated him, and then it would be really weird. But since he came over for lunch and you haven't told me you've called the divorce off, I'm assuming this is the point where I can finally tell you what I think.'

'We had a nice lunch, to be honest. We're not getting back together...'

'I sense a but. Please tell me there's no but coming.'

'I think he wants to.'

'What makes you say that? Was it something he said to you?'

'Yes. Not directly but... well, you get a feeling for these things, don't you?'

'What about Alex?'

'What about him?'

'A little bird tells me you spent the day with him on Saturday.'

'I spent the day with him *and* Victor. And it wasn't the whole day, only some of it.'

'I heard you and Alex got on well. Very well.'

Zoe turned to her. 'I'm guessing this little bird has a name beginning with C? Ends in E, is married to a man who keeps alpaca and loves to bake?'

'I'd never reveal my sources.'

'It wasn't anything. I went to see the alpaca with Victor, and we ran into Alex, and it seemed like a fun thing to do. I hadn't got anything else on, and the alternative was cleaning the house.'

'I bet you cleaned the house anyway.'

'Well, yeah, of course. I did it later on.'

'It wouldn't be the worst idea in the world if you did get with Alex.'

'How do you work that out?'

'For one, it would make sure you're not tempted to give it another go with Ritchie.'

'Nobody said I was going to.'

'You didn't sound very convincing when you ruled it out just now. Which makes me think it's crossed your mind.'

'It hasn't, honestly.'

'Because I get that it could be tempting. You know him, you feel comfortable with him, you already know what he's like to live with.'

'I'm not going to go back to Ritchie!'

'Good. That's all I wanted to hear. But you do need a plus one for my wedding next year, don't forget.'

'Why can't I come on my own?'

'You could, but then I'd have to get you fixed up with Heath's best man, and, trust me, you don't want that.'

'I'll find someone then. What's Flo doing? Can she be my plus one?'

Ottilie laughed lightly. They kept their banter up until they got within sight of Stacey's house. Zoe still couldn't get used to how close everything was in Thimblebury after living in Manchester her whole life, and it took her quite by surprise to see that within minutes they'd reached their destination. When Stacey opened the front door, she was followed by the aroma of fried chicken and coriander.

'I've made nibbles,' she said. 'I wasn't sure if you'd have eaten or not, but I'm starving anyway so they won't go to waste.'

'You don't have to try very hard to persuade me to have nibbles these days.' Ottilie patted a gentle hand on her tummy. 'This one loves his food, just like his dad.'

Stacey let them in and then took their coats before opening non-alcoholic wine for Ottilie and something stronger for her and Zoe.

'How's Chloe doing?' Zoe asked. 'I thought she might be home.'

'She's staying over at Ollie's house tonight. Taken Mackenzie with her. I think his parents are driving them to get furniture for the flat tomorrow or something.'

'I thought she wasn't going to move out until she'd had the baby?' Zoe asked.

'That was the plan, but you know Chloe. She's seen the

place she wants and doesn't see any point in waiting. It makes sense.' Stacey took a quick gulp of her drink before going to check what was in the oven. 'I try not to think about it.'

'Why?' Zoe asked, and Ottilie turned to her with the answer.

'She's gutted that Chloe's leaving. Aren't you, Stacey?'

'I never thought I'd say it, but yes. She's a royal pain in the arse, miserable, moody, difficult and secretive, but I bloody love her to death. Mackenzie too. The house is going to feel massive and empty without them.' Her eyes filled with tears that she sniffed back. 'Stupid cow, aren't I? It's not like this day was never going to come.'

'You're allowed to be sad about it,' Ottilie said.

'Don't get me wrong,' Stacey continued. 'I'm sure it'll be lovely having the place to myself when I get used to it. Life will certainly be easier.'

'Won't Simon be moving in?' Zoe asked.

Stacey shrugged. 'I don't want to ask.'

'Why not?'

Stacey turned and leaned back against the kitchen counter. 'If he wanted to, he'd already have said so. He knows Chloe is leaving and I'll have the space, and he's renting from Fliss so it's not like he can't give up his house. But he hasn't said a word, so...' She shrugged. 'I reckon that's my answer, and I'm not going to beg.'

'Maybe he's waiting for you to ask because he doesn't want to be pushy?' Zoe replied.

'That's what I keep saying,' Ottilie agreed. 'I wish you two would talk more.'

'We do talk. Things have been good the way they are over the past few months, and I don't know if I want to push it somewhere more intense. If I put pressure on him, then that's what I'm doing, isn't it?'

'It's hardly putting pressure on him to ask if he wants to

move in,' Ottilie said. 'You'll have space, and he can give up a place that's costing him a lot of money. If anything, it's common sense. Simon would see that.'

'Easy for you to say. I don't want him to feel I'm pushing him into it, that's all.'

'What *do* you want?' Zoe asked.

Stacey gave a half-smile. 'Now we're getting to it. I mean, I'm *so* into him it's ridiculous, and that ought to be enough for me to know what I want. But I don't. If I'm being honest, it might be about more than pushing Simon. I've never been on my own. I was young when I met Chloe's dad and we moved in together, and then I had Chloe when he left, and she's been here ever since, and then Mackenzie came. I don't know how to be on my own, and I'm nervous about it, but I think it might be good for me to try. I've spent so much of my life being something to someone else that I don't even think I know who I truly am. I think, as well as not knowing what Simon wants, I wonder if I ought to give it six months to find out what I really want.'

'There's nothing wrong with that,' Zoe said. 'I have to admit I'm a bit the same. Even when I feel isolated up on the hill, I sense it's good for me.'

Stacey nodded and then turned to get some pakora out of the oven.

'Make sure you remember that next time you're tempted to invite Ritchie over,' Ottilie said, and Zoe frowned.

'It's not like that.'

'Is that why you're resisting Alex too?'

Stacey spun to face them. 'Alex?' she squeaked. 'What's this? You and Alex? Oh, come on, spill it!'

'There's no me and Alex,' Zoe said, shooting Ottilie a withering look. 'But some people seem to think it's only a matter of time.'

'I mean, he is single, and so are you.'

Zoe had to laugh now. 'What was all that about spending

time on your own so you can find out who you are without the influence of other people? It applies to you but not to me, apparently?'

'I never said you couldn't have a bit of casual sex while you find out who you are,' Stacey said coyly.

'That's the last thing on my mind!' Zoe replied, but flushed anyway and wondered if either of the other women believed her for a second. She hadn't exactly thought about it, but she couldn't honestly say that the notion hadn't briefly crossed her mind on more than one occasion. There was an intensity in the way Alex looked at her whenever they met. It was respectful, generous and open, affectionate even. And yet there was something thrilling beneath all that, something hungry and a little bit dangerous. Zoe was finding it increasingly difficult to ignore the attraction, and she was only human.

'Of course it is,' Stacey said, turning back to tip her nibbles onto a plate before taking them to the table. 'There's more coming, but dig in if you're hungry.'

'So have you got a date for Chloe moving out?' Ottilie asked.

Zoe reached for a pakora, juggling it between her fingers because it was so hot.

'She's waiting for references to clear for the landlord and then we'll know. I would think next month is likely. She wants to be in by Christmas.'

'But she'll come home for Christmas Day, won't she?'

Stacey pulled a second tray from the oven. 'I think so. At least, I hope so.' She turned to Zoe. 'It's good she can still stay under your care when she moves. I don't think she'd cope with having to get used to another midwife. Thanks for doing that.'

'I have warned Chloe that I might not be able to get to her if there's anything urgent, and I probably won't be able to attend the birth, but in the meantime, if things go smoothly, there's no reason why I can't do her routine checks.'

'She'll be a better patient than she was last time,' Stacey said.

'I hope so!' Ottilie said. 'I don't fancy doing that again!'

'Of course!' Zoe said. 'I totally forgot you helped Chloe deliver Mackenzie!'

'Not out of choice. And let me tell you, I wouldn't want to swap jobs with you!' Ottilie replied with such feeling that Zoe had to laugh.

'Don't worry, I wouldn't want to swap with you either.'

Stacey put another tray of nibbles out and turned to Ottilie. 'Those all right for you? Not into weird food yet? Because I'm sure I can fix up some tuna and banana sandwiches for you.'

'No, thank you.' Ottilie grinned as she reached for a second pakora. 'Another plate of this will do just fine, so keep 'em coming.'

21

Zoe was surprised to see Victor in the shop when she walked in to pick up some biscuits on her way home from work the following Monday. He and Corrine didn't often come down to the village – though they were friendly with everyone when they did – and it was even rarer he had the need to buy from the shop. That being said, it didn't seem as if he was buying anything now, as he was having an animated conversation with Magnus and Geoff. At the sound of the door opening, all three turned to Zoe.

Victor's face lit up. 'You'll never guess what we found!'

'You and Alex?' Zoe asked, the only people she could think of who'd been actively searching for something.

'Jet beads! What do you think of that? It's a crying shame we didn't find them on the day you were with us, but still. Didn't even show on the metal detector, of course, but the man Alex has been talking to is excited now all right. He says it's a safe bet there'll be more jewellery. He's wondering if we might uncover some stones.'

'Stones?'

'Like up at Cockpit.'

Zoe was still confused.

'A stone circle,' Geoff clarified. 'Like Stonehenge, except obviously not Stonehenge because if they were that big, I'm fairly sure we would have noticed them by now.'

'Wouldn't we have noticed a stone circle anyway?' Zoe asked.

'Not if most of it had been taken away to build and what's left fell down and got buried,' Victor said.

Zoe thought that sounded quite a stretch, but she didn't want to dampen Victor's enthusiasm so kept quiet.

'Of course,' he continued, 'you'd have thought when Ann and Jim were farming up there they'd have noticed something.'

'Perhaps they did and didn't realise what it was,' she offered.

'I expect that's it,' Victor agreed. 'Would you like to see the beads?'

'Have you got a photo of them?'

'Not with me. No phone. But if you call up at the house later, I've got them. I found them, see, so Alex said for me to keep them until his man decides what he wants to do.'

'Do you think they'll send people up to excavate?' Geoff asked.

'They might,' Victor said thoughtfully.

'Oh.' Magnus grinned. 'That will put the cat with the pigeons.'

'*Among* the pigeons,' Geoff corrected him playfully. 'And you're right. Some round here love a good moan – they'll have something to say about teams of archaeologists driving up and down.'

'Will it affect Alex's plans?' Zoe asked, and when she saw the looks on both Geoff's and Magnus's faces realised immediately that she shouldn't have done.

'What plans are those?' Geoff asked with an air of disinterest that couldn't have done a worse job of masking his obvious curiosity. 'Is he building something up at Hilltop? Is that what the digging is about? We had thought...'

'No point in beating about the bush now,' Victor said in a practical tone. 'Folks will find out soon enough. He's putting camping pods up there. Going to open them in the spring if he can get done in time, though he might be delayed in light of current events.'

'*A lot* of camping pods?' Geoff asked.

'I should have thought so. The man's got to make a living. No point in messing around with one, is there?'

'I don't think people will like that,' Magnus said doubtfully. 'Not me, of course,' he added quickly. 'I wouldn't stand in the way, but some won't like it.'

'Some don't like anything,' Victor said. 'My memory's long enough to recall the fuss they made about my treks when I first started them, and they hardly bother the village at all.'

'It wasn't that bad,' Geoff began, but the look on Victor's face instantly reduced him to a sheepish grin.

'It's lucky I don't hold grudges,' Victor said cheerily, which made Zoe think that Geoff, or Magnus, or both of them had been at least a little opposed to Victor's plans in the beginning.

'I suppose the camping pods would be good for us,' Magnus said. 'They would bring business to the shop.'

'I dare say.' Victor took off his cap and scratched his head. 'Well, I'd better be off...'

As Victor bid them one last good day and headed for the door, Flo was coming from the other direction, and the two almost collided. 'Sorry about that, Flo,' he said with a smile. 'Nearly had you.'

'You did!' Flo snapped. 'You don't change, charging about the place.'

'Well, you don't like change,' Victor said, 'so I do it for you. Cheerio!'

Zoe glanced to see Magnus and Geoff both trying not to

laugh at the altercation. Flo stomped in and slammed her basket down.

'Someone got out of bed on the wrong side today,' Geoff said. 'What's the matter, Flo? Lost a fiver and found fifty pence?'

'Nothing's the matter.'

'Are you sure about that?'

'Oh, it's that Prue Barrett!' she huffed.

'Who?'

'The organiser of this blasted celebration! Asks for suggestions and when I give them doesn't want to know! Four times I've phoned that office and she won't talk to me!'

'Has she spoken to you at all?' Geoff asked.

'Once, last week.'

'That'll be why,' Geoff said to Magnus in a low voice, and Flo's head snapped up.

'What was that?'

'I was only saying what a shame it is. I mean, because you've lived in Thimblebury so long and have so much local knowledge, it seems a waste not to take advantage of your offer.'

As Geoff did his best to soothe Flo, Magnus shot a conspiratorial grin at Zoe.

'I've got some good ideas,' Flo continued. 'Better than some of the rubbish they're putting on.'

'Oh, I don't know,' Magnus said. 'I think some of it's very good.'

'You would,' Flo huffed. 'Because they're showing that film of yours.'

'Prue was very interested in that, actually,' he replied with obvious pride. 'She said it was a lovely document of what it was to come to Thimblebury as a foreigner and how the village welcomed me in.'

Flo sniffed loudly. 'You're not the only outsider, but nobody else is making a fuss about it.'

'I don't think I'd know where to start if I wanted to make a film,' Zoe said. 'And I'm sure Ottilie hasn't got time.'

'Nobody asked my Heath,' Flo said.

'He's not exactly an outsider, is he?' Geoff said.

'He moved here from Manchester only this year!'

'But he came back from Manchester. Technically this was home for him already.'

'Ooh, you've always got an answer for everything, haven't you, Geoff?' Flo replied, tottering over to the fridges. 'I ought to take my business elsewhere.'

'Good luck with that,' Geoff said mildly. 'As we're the only grocer's in the village.'

'Look...' Magnus tutted and pointed to the counter. 'Victor forgot his magazine in all the excitement.'

'What excitement?' Flo asked, to be ignored by everyone.

'So he did,' Geoff said. He looked up at Zoe. 'You said you'd be going up there to look at his beads. Would you mind taking it with you?'

'Beads?' Flo came back to the counter empty-handed, clearly having decided that what was going on there was more important than whatever she'd gone to the fridge for. 'What beads are these?'

'Never you mind,' Geoff said.

'What's the big secret?' Flo demanded.

'It's not that big a deal,' Zoe said. 'Victor and Alex found them while they were searching for more Bronze Age stuff on Hilltop Farm.'

'What Bronze Age stuff?'

Magnus looked at Geoff. 'She'll find out eventually.' And then he turned to Flo. 'They found some arrowheads and other bits up there, and they think there might have been a Bronze Age settlement. It would make sense, wouldn't it? There are others dotted around the lakes.'

'And the beads might be jet,' Zoe said. 'But they're going to have them checked by an expert. But if they are, I think that might be a big deal.'

'Oh,' Flo said. 'Is that all?'

'Don't you think it's exciting?' Magnus asked.

'Not especially. If they'd found a big pile of gold, I'd be interested. Some beads... pah! Who cares about some old beads?'

'Plenty of archaeologists would.' Zoe reached for the magazine, and Magnus nodded at her. 'Thank you for doing that.'

'Not a problem. Like you said, I was going up to see them anyway, and it's not like it's a million miles out of my way, even if I wasn't. I'm only a field away.'

Half an hour later, Zoe knocked at the door of Daffodil farmhouse. She could hear laughter coming from within, and when Corrine opened up, she saw Alex was sitting at the table with Victor. The smile he greeted her with was easier than last time they'd bumped into one another. Perhaps the excitement of their recent find had wiped the memory of her rudeness from his mind.

'Hello, flower!' Victor said. 'Come to see our treasure?'

'And also to give you this.' Zoe took the magazine from her bag and handed it to him.

'Ah yes, I phoned the shop and Magnus said you had it. Thank you!'

Corrine looked over his shoulder and rolled her eyes. 'Like you need any more magazines about tractors! You'll never buy any of them, so I don't know why you sit drooling over them for hours on end.'

'They're not just about tractors,' Victor said with a note of offence in his voice. 'There's all sorts of farm machinery in here. I have to keep up.'

'Keep up with what? You certainly don't need a combine

harvester, and I doubt you need anything else in there.' She turned to Zoe with a smile. 'Now then, what can I get you? Tea? A slice of Bakewell tart? Or I think I have some flapjacks left from the other day...'

'Bakewell tart sounds lovely.' Zoe took a seat and was suddenly aware of Alex's eyes on her. As soon as she met his gaze, he tore his away and to something black on the table. Taking a closer look, Zoe let out an exclamation of surprise. She hadn't expected them to be in quite such good condition. 'Are these the beads? Wow! They're lovely! How are they even still in one piece?'

'They're beautiful, aren't they?' Victor beamed. 'Like they were made yesterday.'

'Probably were,' Corrine called in a dry tone from the kettle.

'They're definitely old,' Alex said. 'We don't know how old until we get them examined properly.'

'When will you do that?' Zoe asked.

'Victor's going to take them tomorrow.'

'You're not going?'

Alex shook his head. 'They're Victor's find. Besides, I've got to take Billie shopping.'

'What are you going to buy?'

'A cot, actually.' He paused, as if uncertain whether to ask his next question, and as soon as he did, he seemed to wonder if it had been the wrong call. 'You could come with us. If you're not busy. If anyone knows about what cot to buy, it would be you, right?'

'I'd love to say yes, but I've got to work, sorry.'

'After work? The shop will be open late.'

'I doubt Billie will want me there—'

'I bet she will. I won't have a clue – I'm just the wallet. I think she'd appreciate your advice.'

Zoe smiled. While she was warmed by his insistence, she didn't think that would be the case at all. She didn't think Billie would want her there. 'The shop will give her great advice. They'll know all about the products they sell, more than I would.'

'*I'd* appreciate your advice,' he said. 'Billie looks to me for help, and I do my best, but my best isn't always that useful. Sometimes it's downright useless.'

'Why don't you ask Billie what she wants?' Zoe said. 'If she wants my help, of course I'll come, but she might be happier if it's just you and her. But let me know and I'll make time if she does want me.'

'There you go...' Corrine put a plate down in front of Zoe. On it was a large slab of golden-crusted, almond-topped cake, with a generous seam of jam running through it. And then a jug of cream.

'Wow!' Zoe picked up the plate and marvelled at the cake on it. 'You've outdone yourself – this looks amazing!'

'It is,' Alex said. 'I've already had some.'

'You can have another slice if you like,' Corrine said. 'There's plenty.'

'I would, but I don't think I'd ever want to eat again they're so big.'

'I can make it a smaller one.'

Alex smiled. 'Go on then. Just a small one. Nobody tell Billie because she says I eat too much as it is!'

Corrine laughed. 'Strapping lad like you? I don't know how you could eat too much!'

The sun had slipped below the horizon, but as yet, there were no stars in the sky, only the moon, low and huge peeking from behind the distant hills, and a bank of ochre cloud spanning their length as Zoe and Alex left the kitchen of Daffodil farmhouse.

'I'll walk with you,' he said.

'OK. I'd like the company. I know it's safe and everything out here, but sometimes it still spooks me in the dark. Like you don't know what's out there. Rabbits, I suppose. The odd sparrow.'

'Or the ghost of a Bronze Age chieftain, come to take revenge on the people trespassing on his land,' he said in a mysterious voice, and she laughed.

'Or ghosts who want revenge on me for living here. Thanks – that made me feel better.'

'Sorry. Let's go with rabbits then.'

'Let's. Did you want me to regret letting you walk me home?'

'I'd never want that.' He sank his hands into his pockets as they began to follow the path. 'Corrine and Victor are great, aren't they?'

'I love them both already. I'm so lucky to have them as landlords.'

'So the house you're in... it was their daughter's, wasn't it? Victor gifted her and her husband the land? I heard something about it. He had an affair with some girl who was staying in the village and they both ended up leaving. Do I have that right?'

'Pretty much, apart from Melanie – their daughter – had an affair first, and the marriage was on the rocks before Fion arrived.'

He threw her a sideways glance. 'You seem to know a lot about it. Is that what Corrine told you?'

'Ottilie... I work with her at the surgery. Fion's her sister. Well, half-sister. In the end, it was all amicable. Victor and Corrine didn't blame Melanie's husband. I think they're sad she moved away, but they get that she needed a fresh start, and living in Kestrel Cottage had too many memories for her. Lucky for me, eh?'

'Lucky for me too,' he said, and it was her turn to throw him a puzzled look, one that he didn't see in the gloom. 'I mean,' he added quickly, 'you're a perfect neighbour for someone who has a very pregnant daughter who worries him to death all the time.'

'You really worry that much?'

'Of course I do! I don't know what to do for her from one minute to the next. I thought we were doing all right until you pointed out that we don't talk, and then I realised that I'm actually hopeless. It's at times like these I miss Jennifer. Billie needs her mum.'

'For what it's worth, I think you're doing a pretty decent job. The main thing is you're trying. You want to be there for her, and you're doing your best. Nobody can ask anything more than that.'

'It doesn't ever feel like enough.'

'Trust me, if you asked Billie, I'm sure she'd say it is.'

'You seem to be able to get through to her.'

'I doubt that. As a midwife, perhaps. I'm not sure about anything else.'

'I know you said it would be better for us to go shopping tomorrow without you, but I could really do with your help. It's not about the cot, not really. I wish she'd open up. I'm a bloke, I get that, and she probably thinks I can't handle pregnancy stuff, but I think she needs someone. She'd talk to you. She already does, more than she's ever opened up to me, about Luis and about bringing up the baby by herself.'

Zoe let out a sigh. 'Right, I'll come then. But please mention it to Billie, and if she doesn't seem keen, tell me. I'd rather not be there if she doesn't want me to be.'

'I will. Thanks. I won't forget I owe you. I owe you about fifty favours, in fact, for all the times you've had my back since I got here.' He paused before beginning again. 'When I came over to your house and your ex was there... I didn't make it awkward, did I?'

'Why would you think that?'

'I don't know... a feeling. I got a weird vibe from him.'

'That's not unique to you – he gives that vibe to everyone.' Zoe affected a careless laugh for him that she didn't quite feel.

'But I didn't cause you any trouble?'

'Of course you didn't. We're not together now, so who visits me has nothing to do with him.'

'It's not my place to say so, but I'm not sure he got that memo.'

'It's not,' she said and then immediately regretted it. 'Sorry, I didn't mean that. It's just... with Ritchie it's complicated. We have a lot of history that sort of keeps us together. Not as a couple, but we... we're kind of bound together.'

She paused. As well as she felt she was beginning to know Alex now, there was no doubt of his reaction to her next sentence. She already trusted him, but she felt the enormity of saying it out loud to someone new, someone who was beginning to mean a great deal to her.

'We lost our baby earlier this year, and after that things fell apart. I didn't deal with it well, he couldn't work out how to handle me and... here we are. I still care about him. It wasn't so much a case of falling out of love, more like we stopped understanding each other.'

'I'm so sorry to hear that. God, it must take every ounce of what you have to carry on caring for other pregnant women having lost your own baby. I have so much respect for you right now.'

'I don't see it that way. If I can help one other woman so she doesn't have to go through what I went through, then I have to do that. It's not a choice; it's... I'm not sure what it is, but it's why I signed up to be a midwife in the first place.'

'I bet you don't even know how amazing that is.'

'That's because it's not.'

'No, but it is. You are...'

'There's the gate,' she cut in, half thankful, half disappointed that they'd reached her house, desperate to hear what he might have been about to say but scared of it at the same time. She wanted to invite him in, but there was something brewing in the air between them, something that had escalated over the past fifteen minutes, and she was afraid of what might happen, what she might do, if he came inside. 'Thanks for walking me home.'

'It was my pleasure,' he said, leaving her feeling as if there had never been a truer phrase spoken. 'So I hope to see you tomorrow.'

'Don't forget to check with Billie, please.'

'I will, but I'm sure she'll be happy to have you along.'

They paused, the lanterns along her path and the pearly moon the only lights illuminating his face. Even then, she could see the affection in it. Not only affection, something so much more. Hope? Longing? She knew it because she felt it too. Amidst the chaos of the emotions that whirled around inside her at that moment, those shone bright. She didn't know how it could happen, but she was certain that if it did, it could be wonderful. And as he gazed at her, she almost wondered if he'd ask the question. And if he did, she knew she'd say yes.

But after a pause and a small smile, he took a pace back. 'I'll watch you in. Goodnight, Zoe.'

'Goodnight,' she said, barely able to keep the disappointment from her voice.

True to his word, he watched until she'd unlocked the front door and pushed it open, and then he turned and went.

22

Zoe tried not to let the baby store bother her, but it did, and she realised now she ought to have seen this coming. Fortunately, Alex and Billie didn't seem to have noticed.

It was more of a large warehouse than a shop, decorated in pastels and bright, bold murals, and everywhere she looked there were soft furnishings, honeyed and whitewashed pine, and baby toys. She glanced at Billie, who was silent at Alex's side as they walked in. There wasn't a flicker of a smile. Not a hint of any excitement, or anticipation, or any sign to indicate she might be pleased to be there at all. If anything, Billie looked even more depressed by the shop than Zoe.

'Hello...' A young sales assistant bounded up to them. 'Are you looking for anything in particular?' She glanced from Zoe to Billie, as if not quite sure who she was supposed to be addressing, and then Alex spoke for both of them.

'We want to buy a cot. For a newborn.'

'Ah, right this way...' The woman led them to a section towards the rear of the store. 'Did you have anything particular in mind? We've got more traditional ones there... and then some with more modern features. They're all tested for safety, so you don't have to worry about that whichever you choose. What's your budget?'

'I don't think we really have one,' Alex said.

'He means we haven't talked about it,' Billie put in, speaking for the first time since they got there. 'What's your cheapest?'

The young woman looked faintly confused as she glanced between the three of them again, and Zoe inwardly smiled. She wondered if she looked old enough to be Billie's mum, as if she and Alex were the grandparents, which might have been a little bit funny if it hadn't also felt a bit insulting. *Did* she look old enough to be Billie's mum? She hoped not.

'We have some sale ones,' the assistant continued, pointing to a row that included one painted sage green, one buttermilk and a couple of varnished shades. 'There's nothing wrong with them, just end of lines. You could start there if you like.'

'Could you leave us to have a look?' Alex asked. 'We'll call you over if we need to ask about anything.'

'Of course. I'll be over by the counter if you want me.'

'So...' Alex looked at Billie as the assistant left them. 'There's no reason why we can't spend whatever the one you want costs. I've got a bigger budget than the sales ones.'

'There's no point. The baby's only going to sleep in there, and I don't care what it looks like.'

Alex threw a pleading glance at Zoe, but she couldn't help him. There was an undeniable logic in Billie's argument.

'All right.' He turned back to Billie. 'What do you think? Anything catching your eye in the discount section?'

Billie shrugged as she looked over the sale models.

'This one's nice,' Zoe said, going over to the one with the buttermilk lacquer, hoping to encourage some sort of reaction from Alex's daughter.

'It's fine,' Billie said. She wandered over and stared at it for a moment.

'It's a good price,' Zoe added. 'They've knocked a lot off.'

'Yeah.' Alex rubbed at his chin as he looked it over. 'I know she said end of line and there's nothing wrong with them, but this is an important buy, and I'd rather pay a bit more and know that we're getting something without faults.'

'It looks fine to me,' Zoe said with an encouraging smile, trying to facilitate some middle ground between him and his daughter.

Alex glanced up at her. 'You think so? I mean, if you say it looks all right...'

'But Billie is the one who has to decide,' Zoe added. 'Like you say, it's important to pick the right one.'

'They're only going to sleep in it,' Billie reiterated. 'It doesn't really matter.'

'They sleep a lot,' Zoe reminded her. 'And as they grow, they'll wriggle about, and then they'll be messing with bits, and then they'll learn how to stand up and they'll be trying to climb out. You have to have a lot of confidence in your cot – it's not just a place to sleep; it's like a little containment unit when you can't watch them.'

Alex smiled. 'I never thought of it that way. See, it's good that you came with us.'

'The girl said they're all safe,' Billie put in. 'So it still doesn't matter which one we have because they'll all protect the baby.'

'So choose one,' Alex said with the faintest hint of impatience in his voice now.

'I am,' Billie fired back. 'I'm saying it doesn't matter – they're all the same.'

'Then pick the one you like?' Zoe said. 'You must have some sort of preference.'

Alex smoothed his expression and turned back to Zoe. 'Which one would you buy if it was for you?'

Zoe steeled herself. She walked the row of reductions, not wanting to lead him to something he might feel was out of his price range, considering each one. But then her eye was drawn to something that she knew most would consider old-fashioned, varnished in mahogany and dressed in floral cot bumpers. She went over and ran a hand over the fabric. 'We had one like this,' she said quietly. 'Second-hand, given to us by Ritchie's cousin. He wanted to take it to the tip and buy a new one and not tell her, but I liked it. I thought it was perfect.'

When she looked up, both Alex and Billie were staring at her with very different expressions. Billie looked sorry and sad while Alex looked as if he wanted the ground to swallow him.

'Not that it matters,' she added quickly. 'We're choosing for you, aren't we, Billie?' She hurried to another, far brighter and more modern cot and stood over it. 'This is nice and sturdy. A good price too.'

Billie came over to look. 'It's all right.' She undid the section that slid up and down to access the baby and pushed and pulled at it. And then she flicked at the bumpers. 'Do you have to buy all this other stuff as well?'

'I would,' Zoe said. 'You don't have to get any of it now, but at some point, you might want to. When baby starts to move more, they might bump their head on the bars.'

'We should get everything today,' Alex said. 'Then we've got it when we need it. Plus, it will save us another drive out – we might be a lot busier than we are now in a few months.'

'OK,' Billie said. 'I'll have this one then.'

'You don't want to look at any of the others?'

She shook her head. 'Zoe says this one is good.'

'But if you want to choose something—' Zoe began, but Billie was already walking away to look at soft furnishings.

Zoe glanced at Alex. He watched his daughter for a moment and then turned back to Zoe.

'I'm so sorry.'

'For what?'

'For bringing you here. I never thought... I shouldn't have pushed you to come.'

'I didn't mind.'

'You should. It was insensitive of me when I knew about your baby. And then you were looking at that cot and you seemed...'

'I can't go around pretending other women aren't having babies,' Zoe said. She pushed a bright smile across her face for him. 'I mean, that would be daft when it's my job to help look after them.'

'That's your job, but this...' He shook his head. 'I'm an idiot.'

Zoe was about to speak again when she noticed Billie coming back to them.

'I thought you wanted to look at this stuff.'

'We're coming,' Zoe said, giving one last look to Alex to tell him she was OK. She was – she had to be. She didn't want to be the person who sucked the joy from the room, and she was learning to cope with her loss, slowly but surely. There would be moments when she'd think about it, when she'd be too tempted to imagine how her life would be now if her baby had arrived in the world safe and sound, of course there would, but she couldn't let those moments define her.

As Billie and Alex pored over mattresses with the sales assistant, Zoe took the opportunity to sneak off and look at the toys. Alex glanced up once or twice to see where she was, but when she got a moment or two unnoticed, she picked up a colourful rattle and teething ring and took them to the counter to pay. Slipping them into her bag, she went to join the others.

'Are you OK?' Alex mouthed when Billie wasn't looking. She nodded, and he turned back to the assistant as she worked out costs on a calculator.

A few minutes later, he went to settle the bill and arrange for delivery of the things they'd bought. Billie watched him in silence from a seat near the entrance doors, Zoe at her side.

'I think your dad's relieved to have this sorted out,' Zoe said.

'I don't know why – it's not his problem.'

'It's nobody's *problem*,' Zoe said. 'He only wants the best for you and the baby.'

'Maybe…' Billie replied. Then she was silent again.

Zoe felt she ought to say something more but didn't know what, and then Alex was on his way back over.

'They can deliver next week,' he said, rubbing his hands together and offering Billie a smile that was full of hope, desperate for validation. He wanted her to say he'd done a good thing, that he was being what she needed, but Billie only nodded and then got up from her seat.

'One step closer to being all set,' Zoe said, wanting to give him what Billie couldn't. 'That's good. It'll be a lot less stressful when the time comes if you have everything ready.'

Shoving his hands in his pockets, he hesitated and then spoke again. 'I don't suppose anyone fancies stopping somewhere on the way back for a bite to eat? Or a drink or something… it seems a shame to go straight home when we're close to a decent-sized town.'

'I'm tired,' Billie said before heading to the doors.

Alex looked at Zoe. 'Maybe you could come to Hilltop for a drink before you go home? I'd walk you back afterwards.'

'That does sound nice, but if Billie's tired… you could come to mine.'

'I would, but…' He let his gaze wander to the car park beyond the glass doors of the shop, where Billie was waiting.

'Of course,' Zoe said. 'Maybe another time.'

'I'm really grateful, you know,' he added. 'It must have taken a lot for you to come here. I wish you'd said something when I asked—'

'I told you – it's fine. I wanted to come. I'm not sure how much help I've been, but if it's been any help at all, then I'm glad.'

'Billie probably wouldn't say so, but I think you have. She needs a few more women in her life, especially women like you.'

'Like me?' Zoe raised her eyebrows. 'I'm assuming you mean that in a good way?'

'In the best way,' he said, his voice suddenly warm and fervent. 'We're so lucky to have you living so close by.'

'I think so too,' Zoe said, fighting a blush that spread up from her neck. 'Not that you're lucky to have me, but I'm lucky to have you. I mean, you two... both of you.'

He looked to where Billie was pacing up and down next to their car and then offered Zoe a look of apology. 'I suppose we'd better go.'

She hadn't really wanted to come shopping with them, for all sorts of reasons that boiled down to her professional boundaries, but now, as she watched him walk back to his daughter, professional boundaries were the last thing on her mind. She was already way past that, in deep, and she was glad she'd come. She wanted to be a part of their lives – not just Alex's, but Billie's too.

23

Thanks again for helping us to choose a cot. I'm sorry we didn't get to stop for supper afterwards. Another time, I hope. If you're free at the weekend and you fancy doing some more detecting, let me know. You're welcome to join us again. A

Zoe reread the text, imagining all the notes in the margin. There were notes, right? He was sorry they didn't get to stop for supper – translate to: *I wish we'd been able to have more time together.* "Another time, I hope." Surely that meant: *I'm going to ask you again, and I hope you'll say yes.* "If you're free at the weekend and you fancy doing some more detecting..." *Please come over and spend the day with me.*

Perhaps she was reading a bit too much into it, but the text brightened her mood all the same. They were only words, and yet there was so much warmth in them. She liked him. She didn't just fancy him, though it was impossible to ignore the effect those dark eyes had on her, but she liked him as a person. He was decent, good, considerate. A bit stiff at times, but he carried more tragedy with him than anyone ought to, so perhaps that was to be expected. Besides, she could work on that. She shook her head to banish such thoughts.

Was it too soon after Ritchie to be thinking of someone else? Almost certainly – and complicated by the fact that Ritchie was still very much a part of her life. Whoever came next, they would have to work around that.

But there was chemistry between her and Alex, and she knew he saw it too. She couldn't be mistaken about that, could she? The only thing that worried her was what she was meant to do about it.

The heating in the village hall was turned up to maximum, and while Zoe was all for keeping the little ones in the parent and baby group warm, she did wonder if it was overkill. As she walked in, it was like a blast from a furnace blowing into her face.

Pulling off her coat and scarf, she searched the room for Ottilie's friend Stacey. It wasn't hard to find her. Stacey was a striking woman, older than Zoe by seven or eight years at a guess, but she had an amazing figure, a punky hairdo and sex appeal that could fell a man from twenty paces. In any room, she stood out, and it was no different here. She wore simple fitted jeans and knee-high boots and a tailored checked shirt, which would have looked ordinary on anyone else but was elevated to the pinnacle of style by her.

As Zoe's eyes came to rest on her, Stacey looked up and waved. With her grandson Mackenzie on her hip, she came across to greet her.

'I'm so glad you're here,' she said. 'Takes the heat off me for a bit.'

'Are you sure about that?' Zoe wafted a hand next to her face. 'I don't think anything could take the heat out of this room – it's like an oven!'

Stacey nodded. 'I've told the caretaker, and he says he'll pop over in the next half hour to turn it down. Said the forecast was for colder weather than we've ended up getting. I've opened the windows and that's helped.'

'It does explain why all the kids are in their vests and nappies,' Zoe said, her gaze sweeping the room. Some of the mums she knew vaguely from her time in Thimblebury and some she didn't. There were two dads that she didn't recognise at all – and she presumed they were dads but could have been any caregiver, she supposed. 'So where do you want me?'

'Oh, set up anywhere you can find a space. It's only a small room so everyone will be able to hear you. It's good of you to come.'

'I had a spare couple of hours with no examinations today so it's no bother. I might as well be doing something useful with my time.'

'This will be really useful. I get asked about weaning and milk all the time, and I'm no expert. I fed Chloe, of course, and help with this little man' – she jogged Mackenzie on her hip, and he let out a gorgeous giggle – 'but I'm sure you'll give better advice than I ever could. To be honest, I'm hoping to learn something today too.'

'I'll do my best then. Hopefully it won't be too boring, but I'll try to keep it short because the little ones don't stay quiet for long.'

'They're never quiet in here. I love doing this, but I always go home thankful for the peace of my house. While I have you – when you've finished your presentation, of course – I wanted to pick your brains.'

'Oh? About Chloe?'

'No, about me.'

'You're not...?'

'Oh, no!' Stacey started to laugh. 'God no! My childbearing days are over! No, I've been thinking of setting up as a childminder. I love doing the parent and baby group, and I think I do all right. With Chloe and Mackenzie leaving, I could do with some work, but I don't want to drive out of Thimblebury every day, and it's not like there's loads of work here, so childminding seemed like a good solution. But I don't know where to start – I'm guessing there are rules and such. I've done a bit of googling—'

'That's a brilliant idea!' Zoe beamed. 'I don't know how much help I can be, but I'll do my best to answer any questions you have. I also know one or two registered childminders, and I can put you in touch with them so you can pick their, probably more knowledgeable, brains. But I'm sure there are a lot of people who would be glad of a childminder in Thimblebury.'

'That's what I'm hoping.'

'Ottilie would definitely be your first customer. You've mentioned it to her?'

'Oh, yes, and she said the same. She says it's perfect for her to have me. I can't wait, actually. I bet Ottilie's baby will be a dream – if they're anything like her.'

'Well, you and I know you can't always guarantee that, but I'm sure she'll be a chilled mum, and that will help. You know Billie, up at Hilltop?'

'I've seen her once or twice but not really spoken to her.'

'I think she'd be glad of a few hours of your time too. I'll talk to her and let her know your plans. When are you thinking you might be up and running?'

'It depends on what I need to do first. As soon as possible, really – at least, as soon as Chloe has moved out.'

Zoe felt a little hand tugging at her skirt and looked down to see a toddler grinning up at her. 'You're an extrovert in training if ever I saw one!' She smiled. 'Hello!'

'Sorry!' The child's mother came dashing over. 'He's at that age where he thinks everyone wants to play.'

'They go one way or the other, don't they?' Zoe said. 'Very

shy or the life and soul of the party.' She crouched down to talk to the child. 'What's your name?'

He simply grinned, exposing two tiny teeth and a stream of drool that oozed down his chin.

'You're Carlton, aren't you?' his mum said, scooping him up. 'Say hello, Carlton.'

Carlton didn't say hello; instead, he wriggled to get free of his mother's arms.

'Carlton,' Zoe said. 'Haven't met a Carlton before. How do you do, Carlton?'

He grinned again then started to pull a face of desperate concentration that slowly turned puce, and then he settled into a look of deepest satisfaction.

His mum sniffed the air. 'You little... I've just changed your nappy!'

Stacey and Zoe both laughed as Carlton's mum threw an exasperated look their way and then took him off to the changing station. A moment later, Mackenzie started to wriggle to be free of Stacey's arms.

'Go on then.' She put him down, and he toddled off in the direction of the toy box.

'Where's Chloe today?' Zoe asked.

'It's a study day.'

'She's still doing her course then?'

'She wants to keep on with it as long as she can. The plan is to get as many credits as possible, and then she can pick it up and finish the course after the baby is born.'

'It's a good idea.'

'It's not often she has them, but I think so too. I would imagine Ollie has had a hand in the decision. He seems to have his head screwed on. Lucky she dropped on such a good one – things could have been worse. She could have stayed with Mackenzie's dad, for a start. Although, I'd have driven her to a convent myself if she'd told me she was doing that.'

'Ollie's the new baby's father? Forgive me, I lose track.'

'Of Chloe's baby daddies or everyone in general?'

Zoe's face fell. 'Oh God! I didn't mean—'

Stacey laughed. 'I know you didn't! Your face! Sorry, I didn't mean to make you freak out; I was only joking. I forgot you're not tuned into my humour yet – it takes most people a while. That's why I love Ottilie so much – she got me straight away. Come on – the natives are getting restless so you might want to get your talk started.'

While Stacey began to clear a space for her to sit, surrounded by her displays of baby foods and information leaflets, Zoe watched, smiling to herself. She could see why Ottilie had become such firm friends with her, and she wondered if Stacey might be the perfect, no-nonsense woman to help Billie out when the baby arrived. Even if Alex could only afford a few hours a week, having Stacey take the baby off their hands might relieve a lot of the pressure from both him and Billie. She decided she'd call over to see them later and mention it.

In the end, she didn't make it to Hilltop. In fact, she didn't get back to Kestrel Cottage until gone midnight, and by that time all she wanted to do was fall into bed. Earlier that evening, one of her expectant mums, Helena, had called after clinic hours in a blind panic because she'd gone into premature labour, and it was progressing so rapidly she didn't think she'd make it to the hospital. Zoe always trusted the mother's instincts, and so she'd raced over, ready to take on an unplanned home birth.

It was lucky she'd made such haste because Helena's instincts had been right, and labour had progressed to the point where it might have made it unsafe to transport her, and so she'd jumped into a routine she knew well, ordering members of Helena's family to fetch cushions and glasses of water and whatever else she needed, and shortly before 11 p.m., just as the rest of the medical team arrived and with her three other children crowded around, she'd given birth to a healthy little girl.

The following morning, Zoe got ready for work and planned again to go over to Hilltop to tell them about Stacey's childminding plans. But once again, the day wasn't to go the way she'd anticipated. Morning clinic was uneventful, but lunch brought big news. As they all tucked into their tuna pasta bake, Fliss dropped the bombshell with the nonchalance of someone who had simply decided hers needed more salt.

'While I've got you all here, I might as well tell you I've decided to retire. I'd like to be gone by the end of the year.' She glanced at Simon, who was so unmoved that it was obvious he'd already been told. But Lavender looked horrified and then burst into tears.

Fliss shook her head impatiently. 'Now, now, Lavender. You must have known this was coming.'

'Not this soon!' Lavender sniffed, getting a grip again.

'It's a bit sudden, isn't it?' Zoe asked.

'Not really. I've been thinking about it for some time, and I have Charles to think about. He's recovered from his heart attack last year, but he still gives me the odd sleepless night worrying about it happening again. We both need to slow down, and so this is the decision we've come to.' She glanced at her watch. 'Look, there isn't time to go into details now, but I'd be happy to do that later when surgery is done for the day.'

'Of course,' Zoe said. She'd made plans, but they hadn't been solid ones and only really in her own head. She was tired, too, from her late night at the home birth, but this was important, and she'd have to muddle through somehow.

Despite Fliss's insistence that there wasn't time to discuss the details over lunch, Zoe, Ottilie and Lavender were full of questions for Fliss that simply wouldn't wait until the planned after-work meeting. Most of them revolved around timing.

Fliss laughed. 'There's really nothing sinister at play here. As you well know, it's been on my mind for some time, but I've kept putting off the decision for one reason or another. I didn't say anything before, but Charles had another minor scare and that settled things. We have both come to realise that life is too short to spend it working, and there are many things we'd like to do before we shuffle off. We're comfortably off, have one another and a long-held but unrealised thirst for travel. In fact, we decided over a bottle of red last night that we'd quite like to rectify that last bit. Charles said I'd change my mind once I sobered up, but I woke this morning feeling it was still the right decision, and there we are. It's done.'

'When?' Ottilie asked. 'When is all this going to happen?'

Fliss looked at Simon, who took up the baton. 'We haven't worked out the details yet, but as soon as we can find a replacement for Fliss, she can begin her countdown.'

'So you *are* going to get a replacement?' Zoe asked.

Simon nodded. 'I'd like to say I can manage this place alone, but it's impossible when you take on-call and emergencies into account. I can only do so much.'

'Of course,' Zoe said. 'Where... I'm not trying to make this about me, but where does all this leave me?'

Fliss gave her a blank look. 'What do you mean?'

'I've only just arrived, and at your request. Will the new doctor still want me?'

'I don't see why not. And in any case, Simon is going to take over my role, so the new doctor will be junior to him. Not in skills, of course, but as far as the running and staffing of the surgery is concerned.' She turned to him. 'And you have no plans to change any of that, have you?'

'It's a big-enough transition as it is without disrupting a good existing team into the bargain. I wouldn't want to change anything. And I hope' – he glanced at Lavender – 'you'll all be happy to stay. But that's something we can talk over later at the meeting. Inevitably, some things will change.'

'We're not going to get rid of our lunches?' Lavender asked with real horror in her face.

Simon paused and it was clear he realised he was on shaky ground. 'Nowhere else has them,' he said.

Lavender opened her mouth to reply, but Fliss got in first. 'I'm sure you'll all be able to work something out. Let's think about some solutions and talk them over later.'

'Do you want me to get food in, if we're staying behind?' Ottilie asked. 'How long do you think the meeting will be?'

'I was thinking I'd take you all out for food,' Fliss said. 'What about that pub you and Heath go to? They do good food, don't they? That's if everyone is free. If not, we can make it another night.'

'I'm not doing anything,' Zoe said, noting with a pull of regret that she *had* planned to be doing something, and the others all nodded their agreement.

'Good,' Fliss said, going back to her tuna pasta bake. 'I think we should save any more discussion on the topic until then, otherwise our lunch will be cold and the break will be over before we've finished it.'

The surgery meeting more or less reiterated what they all already knew about Fliss's retirement, and once again she stressed that she wanted to go before the year was out. They reminisced about old times over a pub supper at a place new to Zoe called the Happy Greyhound. It was all warm stone and heavy woods inside, with small casement windows and low ceilings hung with dried flowers and brass pots. Around the walls were paintings of Lakeland scenes during various seasons, the artwork styles ranging from very traditional to modern, Some of them had price tags in the corners, so that people who took a particular fancy to them could buy them.

At the top of the meeting, Lavender complained that life at the surgery would never be the same and then mooted the idea that she might also quit her job, leaving Simon looking so hurt that she immediately took it back. Not to mention the loud complaints from Ottilie and Zoe, who reminded her that as the surgery mum, it was her duty to stay and look after them, even if it took her beyond her own retirement. It went on longer than anyone had intended, especially when Fliss got stuck into a bottle of red and they all had to stay until she'd finished it. As a result, once again, Zoe was too late to go over to Hilltop.

As soon as she got home, she sent Alex a quick message.

Are you by any chance free tomorrow night?

Sorry, but Billie needs me to take her to antenatal class. You could come over when we're home, but it might be a little late for you.

It sounded as if he'd rather she didn't come after antenatal class. Perhaps he wanted to dedicate that evening to Billie – Zoe could hardly be mad about that. And she didn't want to be so needy that she'd be trying to tie him down to a time and day, so she played it cool, while feeling anything but, replying that she'd maybe see him at the quincentenary celebrations, assuming he would be there.

As she put her phone down, her eyes fell on the little gift bag sitting on her kitchen table containing the rattle she'd secretly bought for Billie at the baby store. She'd planned to take it over with her, but she wondered now whether it was a good idea or not.

Her phone buzzed another text message. She smiled as she read it.

You have no idea how sorry I am about tomorrow.

It's all right. You're busy; I get it.

Still gutted. I hope we can do something soon.

What did that mean? It meant he wanted to see her, didn't it? Did it mean more than just those words? He was gutted that he couldn't see her. Clasping her phone to her chest, she went to the window. She'd wondered how she'd feel if he asked her out, and now she knew. She'd love it. She only hoped she wouldn't have to wait too long for it to happen.

24

She was leaving for work the following morning when she heard barking. As she fastened the gate, she looked up to see Grizzle bounding towards her, Alex running after and calling him back.

'Griz! Here, boy!'

The dog's tail was wagging madly. Zoe was pleased to see him, but she hoped he wasn't going to jump up at her while she was wearing her uniform. Quickly, she went back behind the gate and fastened it again, but this time to keep her in and Grizzle out.

'Hey...' Alex smiled at her as he grabbed his dog and put the lead on. 'You're off to work?'

'Yeah. But I'm not running late or anything. In fact, I'm probably early. How are you? I see you're getting your exercise.'

'Can't do anything else with this one.' He ruffled Grizzle's head, and the dog sat to enjoy it. 'I'm sorry we're busy tonight.'

'I know. It's not a problem; it was a last-minute thing anyway. I suppose Billie and your farm plans are taking up a lot of time.'

'The digging too. I might be meeting the expert tonight as

well now. I mean, you could come, if you're not too tired – of course you're welcome to sit in – but Victor will be there, and it might be kind of boring. That's not to say I don't want you there.'

'I wouldn't want to get in the way. I doubt I'd get a word in anyway with Victor being there, even if I had something to say. Those finds are yours and Victor's, nothing to do with me.'

'But you helped to look.'

Zoe smiled. 'Fat lot of good I was.'

'Your hair looks nice this morning,' he said and then seemed immediately mortified by his compliment. 'I mean... shiny. Like you just washed it...'

Zoe grinned. 'Thanks. I mean, yesterday was the first anniversary of my last hair wash so I thought I'd make the effort.'

'Oh God... I've come to realise that I don't know how to do this.' He took a breath. 'It'd be stupid to pretend I'm not over here with Grizzle for any reason other than I really wanted to see you. I've been thinking about it all night. And then I got up this morning and thought, *What am I waiting for? Why am I putting it off?* And so I've come to ask – and you can say no; I won't be offended – but I wondered if you wanted to go for a drink. Not in my kitchen or talking about the baby or anything. Like a proper drink. You and me.'

It seemed he'd run out of air long before he'd finished his sentence because as he waited for her answer, he seemed to suck in his next breath with enough force to fetch tiles from her roof.

'Yes,' she said without hesitation, and the doubt in those huge brown eyes of his cleared.

'Yeah? Really?'

'Of course. I thought you'd never ask.'

'Wow... I mean, that's great! When are you free? Next week?'

'Why don't I meet you at the celebrations tomorrow? We're both going to be there anyway... we could do something afterwards?'

'Sounds good! Perfect! Thank you.'

'For what?' Zoe asked, her smile growing.

'I don't know... for saying yes.'

'You're daft,' she said, and then he laughed.

'Probably. In that case, thanks for saying yes even though you think I'm daft. God, I'm supposed to play it cool now, aren't I?'

'I like that you're not.'

She wanted to kiss him, but it would have to wait. They hadn't even had their first official date yet and she needed to get to work. Not to mention that she didn't trust Grizzle to behave because Alex's excitable dog was already getting restless.

'Actually,' she said, something occurring to her. 'Wait there.' She dashed back to the house, opened up, ran to get the gift bag from her kitchen table and went back out to him. 'This is for Billie. For the baby, actually. It's not much, but I thought... well, you've been lovely neighbours, and I saw it in the shop the other day, and...' She shrugged. 'I hope she likes it.'

She suddenly wondered if it was entirely professional of her to be buying gifts for one of the mums-to-be in her care, but it was done now. He beamed at her as he took the bag. 'I'm sure she will. Thank you. So... I'd better let you get to work.'

'I probably should. So I'll see you tomorrow at the quincentenary?'

'Tomorrow. Looking forward to it.'

He shot her a warm, lingering smile before he led Grizzle away. She watched him walk. He turned back once, smiled again and then she finally allowed herself to stop looking so she could head off to the surgery. But not before taking a moment to address herself in stern tones.

'Yes, it's exciting, and yes, you can't wait, but you've got work to do, Zoe Padbury, so get your head screwed back on!'

She was aware she was going to be out in the cold all day and that the quincentenary event – for her at least – was going to be as much work as it was fun. With that in mind, her clothes had to be practical, but she also wanted to look nice. More than nice, she wanted to look irresistible. So she'd set her alarm to go off an hour earlier than she needed, taking extra care showering and styling her hair, and then went to study what was in her wardrobe.

The outfit she'd settled on the night before was laid out on the bed, but somehow it didn't seem right when she looked at it now. It looked too try-hard. She wanted to look as if she'd made an effort but not like she'd made an effort at all. She wanted to be able to say, *This old thing? I threw it on*, which was code for *I always look this good*. It wasn't a problem she often had to grapple with these days, and it was proving to be trickier than she'd imagined.

Casual and cute or straight-up sexy? How sexy could someone be at what was essentially a glorified village fete selling raffle tickets for the village surgery? She tried to reason that Alex would like her anyway – after all, he'd seen her in her uniform and still wanted to take her out. She knew it didn't matter, but that didn't stop her from fretting over the decision far longer than necessary.

Finally, and not entirely happy with her choice, she looked at herself in the mirror and didn't want to immediately take off what she was wearing, and so reached the conclusion that it must be the one. It was a calf-length, needlecord dress, fitted around her neat torso and flaring out over a pair of boots. Then she turned her attention to her hair, which was normally no bother at all but today would not do what she wanted, and then smudged her eyeliner three times trying to apply it, and finally threw her hands into the air and declared to an empty room that it would have to do.

As she approached the village, she realised that for this one day, the population of Thimblebury had grown so big that the streets could barely contain it. Cars and vans lined the grass verges for a good mile on the road into the village, and streams of people were already making their way in, even though the official opening of the quincentenary event wasn't for another hour. Zoe couldn't understand why so many would travel to such an insignificant place, and when she said so to anyone who'd listen, most of them were forced to admit that they didn't understand it either.

The displays she'd seen the workers putting up when she'd walked through the village with Ottilie were now in their full glory. Some were lit signs proudly declaring *500 Years of Thimblebury*, some were banners depicting all sorts of hand-painted (mostly by children, from what Zoe could tell) scenes from the past and village locations, and some were floral displays. She noticed people walking around in costumes from various historical periods who were presumably meant to represent previous residents of the area, though some of them were so laughably fancy dress that Zoe wondered if they'd simply had them left over from Halloween.

'It's hardly the centre of the universe,' Geoff said as he set up their coffee and light refreshments outside the shop. Later, they planned to open their little home cinema (and Zoe had discovered, despite never getting round to film club, it *was* an actual cinema and they hadn't just been saying that) to show the film Magnus had made documenting his arrival in Thimblebury from Iceland during the nineties. They hoped for a good attendance, and Zoe had promised to be there. 'It goes to show, people will turn up for anything if it's free.'

'I'm sure it can't be that,' Zoe said. She hugged a bucket to her chest as she watched Magnus and Geoff race about their stall putting out stacks of disposable cups, stirrers, sugar packs and anything else needed to serve hot drinks.

'What's the bucket for?' Magnus asked as he tore open a trade box of biscotti.

'I couldn't find anything else to put the raffle tickets in. I wasn't sure how big it would have to be, so...'

Magnus grinned. 'I see you've been... what is the word?' he called to Geoff.

'Press-ganged,' Geoff called back.

'That's it.' Magnus turned back to Zoe. 'Couldn't you think of an excuse to get out of it?'

'I don't mind one bit. I've only got to sell a few strips this morning – they're calling the numbers at lunch.'

'Who gets the money? That's what I want to know,' Geoff said, pulling a large silver urn from a box.

'The neonatal unit,' Zoe said. 'They let me choose.'

'Ah well...' Geoff huffed. 'That's all right then.'

Zoe smiled. 'That's why I wanted to do it.' She looked towards the main street, which was rapidly filling with similar stalls to the one Geoff and Magnus were setting up. Some had colourful striped awnings, some had calico canopies and some had solid roofs. There was food prepared by the local pub, slushies, ice cream and mini-donuts from a company outside the village, a cake stall being manned by Corrine and her daughter Penny, a stall where one could play various games being set up by the ladies of the WI – and that was only who'd already arrived. Magnus had told Zoe they were expecting a lot more.

'As if we don't have enough already,' Magnus said, looking around with some disgruntlement.

'Surely that's a good thing? It'll bring more people, and you'll make more money.'

'You'd think,' Geoff said, 'but apparently nobody talks to

one another. We said we were doing hot drinks and snacks, and look – Corrine is doing the same.'

'Well, Corrine's snacks are different from yours,' Zoe said.

'I'll give you the cakes, but she's doing tea and coffee too. What's the point in both of us doing them? And then there are at least two other stalls from out of town doing hot drinks, and then there's the donut van and the one doing pancakes. There's only so much sweet stuff people can eat.'

'I think it will be fine.' Zoe offered an encouraging smile. 'You might be glad there's more than one place to get food and drinks when the queues start.'

'I suppose you might be right,' Geoff conceded, though he looked far from convinced.

'At least it should stay dry,' she said. 'The forecast looks good for the day.'

'I had a look this morning, and I think the weather should hold,' Geoff agreed. 'Aww...' he added, his gaze going to a spot beyond Zoe. 'Look...'

Zoe turned to see Victor leading two of his alpaca. He'd tied colourful ribbons around their necks with name tags hanging from them. 'Got my dates!' he said with a grin. 'What do you think? They scrub up well, don't they?'

'They look lovely!' Zoe went over to give them a fuss and noted their tags. 'Alice and Daisy Are they your favourites or just the best behaved?'

'I don't have favourites – God forbid! But...' He leaned in and lowered his voice. 'If I did, it'd be these two.' He turned to them. 'Don't tell the others, eh, girls?'

'What have you brought them down for? Don't tell me... they wanted to come and see the oompah band.'

'They're going to earn their keep,' Victor said. 'Thought we could raise a bit more money for your cause by walking them around for a couple of pounds a time and at the same time people will get to know about my treks. Everyone's happy.'

'That's a brilliant idea. Thank you for helping with the fundraising!'

'It was Corrine's idea, really,' he said, though Zoe realised he was being far too modest. The initial idea might have been Corrine's, but she knew Victor well enough by now to imagine he'd have jumped at it.

'Well, I'm going to get them settled.'

He led both alpaca away. Zoe had wondered what the enclosure lined with straw was for when she'd first arrived, but now it was clear that it was going to be home for his girls for the next few hours.

'I'd better go and sort out this raffle stuff,' Zoe said. 'I can see Fliss and Ottilie over there setting up the prize table – my name will be mud if they think I'm skiving over here.'

As she wandered over, she noticed two more vans arrive. One of them contained miniature sheep, and as the driver unloaded them into an enclosure next to Victor's, the passenger went to have a word with him. They seemed to know one another well, Victor clapping him on the back and laughing loudly at something he'd said. The other contained what looked like a sound system. Zoe was too busy to take much more notice than that.

'Morning,' Ottilie greeted. 'You look nice.'

'Oh...' Zoe looked down to remind herself of what she was wearing, though it had taken her so long to choose, she really oughtn't have needed to. She flicked back her hair and grinned. 'This old thing...'

'You also look like the cat who got the cream,' Fliss said. 'What's gone so well for you this morning that you're so full of beans?'

'Or maybe it was last night that went well...'

Zoe turned around to see Lavender carrying a crate full of bric-a-brac over. She dumped it on the table and gave Zoe a pointed look.

'Nothing like that,' Zoe said, and Lavender gave a low whistle.

'Although… if I lived next door to that hunk of meat, I'd arrive at work every day full of beans too. I mean, look at him!'

Alex had just turned into the main street. He wore a heavy, tailored coat and boots and had a leather overnight bag at his side as he made his way over to Victor. Zoe watched, hoping to catch his eye, but he didn't look her way once. It was strange because she'd become used to him looking for her in every situation where they might meet.

When she turned back, Ottilie, Fliss and Lavender were watching her. Fliss folded her arms and raised her eyebrows, while the other two simply grinned.

'What?'

Fliss shook her head. 'Is that for the raffle?' she asked, nodding at the bucket in Zoe's arms.

'It's the best I can do, I'm afraid.'

'Really? The very best a woman of your resources and talents could do?' Fliss rolled her eyes and held out her hands. 'Come on then – hand it over. As long as it's clean it will have to do.'

As they set out their table, Zoe noted in a quiet voice to Ottilie that she was surprised to see Fliss so enthusiastic about the event. It was a running joke that she'd heard often since her arrival in Thimblebury that Fliss really didn't care for her patients much on a personal level. At least, while she went above and beyond in her duty to care for their health, the thought of having to interact with them socially was a fate worse than death.

'It's probably because she's about to get rid of them all,' Ottilie replied in an equally hushed tone and then grinned. 'I'm sure she's thinking about that lovely retirement and how she can tell every one of them to bog off the minute they come up to her with a question about whatever rash on whatever unmentionable bit of their anatomy they currently have.'

Zoe was distracted by Alex, who was talking to Victor and the man with the sheep. Why wasn't he looking for her? She'd been at the surgery stand for ages now, and he had to know she was there. She didn't expect a dramatic race into her arms, but a wave and a smile would have done. It was strange too – it suddenly occurred to her that there was no sign of Billie. Perhaps she'd simply decided this sort of event wasn't for her, but Zoe couldn't help worrying that all wasn't well. It might also explain why Alex was being so evasive, though she didn't see what being distant towards her would achieve.

'Earth to Zoe...' Ottilie's voice brought her back to the conversation.

'Sorry? What was it you wanted?'

'Nothing, only to know why you keep staring at your neighbour like you're trying to work out some massive long division sum.'

'I'm not; I merely happened to be looking in that direction.'

Ottilie raised her eyebrows.

'OK, maybe I am. It's just that he's barely even noticed me today. Like deliberately not looked at me.'

'Should he have done?'

'Well, no, but... he kind of asked me out yesterday. And I kind of said yes. And we said we'd get together after all this was done.'

'You little madam! And when were you going to tell me this?'

'I meant to, but... well, I felt like I would jinx it if I told anyone.' Her gaze went back to the alpaca enclosure. 'Although, I think I already have.'

'You said you'd get together after the event is done, and it's only just started. And he's trying to make inroads with the locals to get them onside so nobody makes a fuss about his pods. So maybe it only looks that way because he's focusing on that. If you think about it, he's sort of working.'

'He can't even say a quick "hello" and "I'll catch you later"?'

Ottilie gave a vague shrug. 'I know, but it's the best I've got.'

'What are you two whispering about?' Lavender called over from a plastic seat where she'd settled to devour a breakfast sandwich from one of the vans.

'You,' Ottilie fired back with a grin.

'Oh, of course, you're discussing how amazing I am.'

'Exactly.'

Lavender went back to her sandwich. 'Ask a silly question...'

An hour later, from a stage set up at the far end of the main street, a man with the most boring voice Zoe had ever heard gave a speech about the history of Thimblebury, its mention in the Domesday Book, how important it was to the surrounding area (not very, Fliss whispered in Zoe's ear) and how proud he was to be celebrating with them. Nobody actually knew who he was, which led Fliss to ponder that he was some regional council nobody who happened to draw the short straw for the gig. As she tried to absorb at least some of the information, Zoe munched on a donut from the slushie van, which wasn't on a par with the rustic, home-cooked fare that was available on offer elsewhere, but the bag Ottilie had purchased smelled so good she'd been unable to resist. And as Ottilie reminded her, they could take the girls out of Manchester, but they couldn't take the funfair-and-junk-food-loving Manchester out of the girls.

Fliss and Lavender had both gone into the bag too, and the only person at their NHS-themed stand who wasn't eating one was Simon, who, said Lavender, was far too virtuous for his own good. He had a grain salad under the table for his lunch, and when he'd added this information, Fliss had simply laughed out loud.

Most of the crowd were facing in the direction of the stage where the random council official was holding forth, but it seemed a lot of them were having equally as hard a time paying attention as Zoe was. They looked at him every so often, and some even offered lukewarm applause, but most seemed preoccupied with scanning the displays and planning what to do the moment he was done and it was socially acceptable to move away. Judging by the reactions of the youngsters present, they all wanted to go and see the miniature sheep and Victor's alpaca, which was understandable. Their parents, however, were more interested in the food, and the flavoured ciders and gins at the pub stall – which was also understandable. More than once, Zoe glanced over to where Victor and Alex stood together watching the speech, but Alex never looked her way once.

She'd guessed that his leather bag contained his finds, and she was yet more convinced of this as a man with a bow tie and a flat cap made his way through the crowds and shook hands with both him and Victor. The man opened out what looked like a miniature landscape on a display board. It was hard to see from this distance, but it looked like it might represent the hills around Thimblebury, and it had little huts on it. Alex studied it with him for a couple of minutes while the man pointed out features as he spoke, and then Alex opened his leather bag to show him what was inside. Was this their archaeology expert? Zoe thought it must be. Perhaps he'd expressed interest in the quincentenary celebrations and they'd rescheduled their meeting from the previous evening so he could kill two birds with one stone. She resolved to go and find out as soon as she had a spare moment.

There was a ripple of polite applause, and then it seemed the man with the boring voice was done, and then someone else got up and started to talk about the importance of community and how Thimblebury typified those values. While he was slightly less boring than the first man, nobody had a clue who this was either.

And then Mrs Icke, who currently held the honour of being Thimblebury's oldest (and most cantankerous, Ottilie said) resident was helped onto the stage and told a rambling story that nobody could really follow, but it was something to do with evacuees who'd come during the war to stay with her family and who'd never seen sheep before. From what Zoe could gather, Mrs Icke took a very dim view of children from the East End who'd never seen sheep.

Last but not least was a representative from the tiny German town that was twinned with Thimblebury (nobody seemed to have a clue about this either, and nobody could pronounce its name) who wished them all well and hoped they'd enjoy the oompah band who'd come over with him, and that got the biggest applause of the day so far.

'Right...' Fliss wiped sugar from her hands and surveyed her team. 'Now that's all done with, let's con some locals out of their pocket money, shall we?'

'I'm on it.' Zoe said, collecting the satchel she'd brought with her for money and the book of raffle tickets. 'I'll have a wander, see if I can guilt some of them into buying a ticket.'

'That's the spirit,' Fliss said. 'Make sure you lay it on thick. And if they don't buy one, threaten them with me – that ought to do it.'

Zoe gave a salute while Ottilie grinned and Lavender simply nodded.

'It would work for me,' she said.

Zoe left the table. The day was bright – thankfully – but already she was getting cold. Pleased as she'd been with her outfit that day, it wasn't the warmest or most practical thing she owned. Before long, she'd be colder still. Perhaps regular visits to the hot drinks being dished out by Magnus and Geoff or Corrine and Penny would do the trick. And perhaps she could persuade Alex to go with her when he'd finished whatever it was he was up to, though she still wasn't entirely sure what was going on there.

She looked across to where he remained deep in conversation with his bow-tied, cap-wearing guest. Victor was now busy with a group of children who were crowding around his alpaca. Zoe supposed she could have gone over and struck up a conversation with Alex and his visitor – after all, she knew something of the finds too – but she had her own work to do, and she didn't feel she could interrupt. So she started to scan the crowds for likely targets, feeling like a Victorian conman choosing his mark, before settling on a trio of older ladies who were peering at a board of discoloured maps and sepia photos of the area.

An hour in and Zoe had almost sold her first book of tickets. People had been only too happy to take them when she'd told them what cause they would be supporting, and on her way back to her own table to get more, she stopped off at Corrine's stall to see how her sales were going.

'I'd sell more if people weren't buying those donuts,' she said, balefully eyeing the slushie van, and Zoe decided she'd never tell her that just over an hour before, she'd been eating those donuts too. 'But we're not doing too badly. How about yourself?'

'Actually,' Zoe began, but then she noticed Corrine break into a broad smile at someone behind her, and turned to see Ann, the previous owner of Hilltop, making her way towards the stall. She looked a lot healthier and happier than the last time Zoe had seen her, the day they'd been helping her to move out of the farm.

Corrine rushed from behind her table and threw her arms around her old neighbour. 'Look at you! You look so well!'

'So do you,' Ann said.

'Where's your Darryl?'

'At home. He's good as gold now he's settled into the new house. I've only popped out for an hour to come and see what the fuss was about here, left him with a new DVD about the train works at Crewe. Well, when I say new, he's only watched it two dozen times or so, so it's new to him. I thought I'd come over and see these finds I keep hearing about. The things the new owners found at Hilltop. I can't believe it. All those years we lived there and we never knew.'

Corrine smiled. 'I said the same thing. Have you had something to eat? Here... take a slice of anything you like. And take one home for Darryl too. I've got one there suitable for diabetics...'

'You've thought of everything,' Ann said as she pored over the cakes on display. As she did, she glanced up briefly and noticed Zoe. 'Oh, hello... how are you? You came to help me move, didn't you?'

'I wasn't sure you'd remember,' Zoe said. 'It sounds as if you're settling into your new house with no problems.'

'I love it,' Ann gushed. 'I don't know why I didn't make the move years ago. Of course, I loved the farm, but it made me miserable more often than it made me happy. So much work to do – far too much for me. What's the new fella like? Do you have much to do with him?'

'He's very nice,' Corrine cut in before Zoe had the chance. 'Comes round now and again – mostly asking if Victor can come out to play...' She winked at Ann, who laughed. 'Thick as thieves the pair of them these days, ever since they started all that detecting nonsense. Still, they've had a bit of luck, can't deny that.'

'Sounds like they've had a lot of luck,' Ann said.

'Well, it wasn't all luck – they had to do an awful lot of digging,' Corrine said. 'You should go and have a word. I'm sure he'd be happy to show you what he's found. Say hello to Victor too while you're at it – he'll be pleased to see you.'

Zoe had wanted to catch Alex all morning, but every time she'd spied an opportunity, someone else had stolen it from her. Either he was with someone or she was, and it looked as if Ann was going to thwart her again now.

Corrine watched Ann walk towards Alex and then turned to Zoe. 'Poor thing. Putting a brave face on it.'

'She sounds happy.'

'I'm sure she's convinced herself she is, but I can't imagine swapping Daffodil Farm for some poky little new build out of Thimblebury. It'd be awful, so cramped and airless. No, give me my high ceilings and the hills and fresh air any day.'

'Well, I don't know her like you do, but she looks a lot better than last time I saw her. In fact, she looks about ten years younger, so living in her new house must be doing something for her.'

'Do you think?' Corrine asked thoughtfully as she followed Ann's figure up the high street. 'Happen you could be right. Anyway...' She shook herself and started to rearrange her trays, filling gaps where people had taken slices of cake with yet more cake. Zoe half wondered where it was all coming from and how she'd had the time to bake so many, but then she remembered who she was dealing with and the puzzle solved itself.

Then Zoe noticed a woman in the crowd who noticed her at the same time and changed direction to come over. She was smiling warmly enough, though Zoe didn't feel she deserved it.

'Hello, Tegan,' she said, suddenly tense. 'How are you doing?'

'I'm fine, much better,' she said. 'They said at your table you were selling raffle tickets for the neonatal unit. I thought I might buy some.'

'I, um... well, yes, of course, but I've sold out, and I need to get some more, so...'

'Oh, OK. I'll come with you.'

Zoe half wished she wouldn't. Her colleagues had told her more than once that she'd done her job and that what had happened to Tegan was not her fault, and yet she still felt it was.

'Have you come with the family?' she asked, grasping for something to say that wouldn't leave them with an awkward silence, where her guilt could grow to fill in the gap.

'Yes. They're at the cider stand. Dennis is buying Laurel her first alcoholic drink – she's eighteen today. Not that she's never had alcohol, of course. I mean, what eighteen-year-old having their first official drink has actually never drunk alcohol before?'

'And she wanted to come here on her birthday? Not that it's not fun, but it's a bit...' Zoe couldn't think of a word that would convey her meaning without it being an insult, so she gave up.

'She's going out with her friends later for the proper, cool celebration. She's always been a home bird really, loves being with her family, though she'd never admit it. I wanted to say...' Tegan continued. 'It's OK. What happened... it happened for a reason – I really believe that. I don't blame you or anyone else. I'm too old to start again. I was upset at the time, of course, and I'm still sad about it now, but when I sit down and think about it, life would have changed so much for me and Dennis and the kids, and I don't know if it would have been a good thing. Maybe, but I'll never know, and I think I'm happy to leave it at that. Dennis is going to get a vasectomy. He doesn't want this to happen again, and I'm with him on that.'

From nowhere, Zoe's eyes misted with tears. She tried not to get emotionally involved with the mums in her care. She wanted to do her best by them, of course, and she felt that befriending them was always the way to do that, but she firmly believed there had to be a barrier so she didn't let them get too close. Tegan, right now, was crossing that barrier with far too much ease. Talking to her brought back memories of her own loss, memories she always tried to push down when she was a midwife. And though she was off duty, she considered herself to be a midwife right now. Despite this, she'd needed to hear what Tegan had to say; she just hadn't realised it until this moment.

'How many tickets would you like?' she asked, sniffing hard as they reached the surgery table. It was lucky the others were all busy in other conversations or they'd have wanted to know why Zoe looked so upset. Tegan noticed, however, and put a hand on her arm.

'I never blamed you.'

Zoe nodded, tears squeezing out against her will, and she sniffed harder still in a desperate attempt to stem the tidal wave of emotion she could feel building. This was not the time or place, and yet it felt like it could be such a welcome release. 'Thank you,' she managed to squeak before pulling a fresh book of raffle tickets from a box and holding them up.

'I'll take a couple of pages,' Tegan said, saving Zoe the trouble of trying to speak, which was lucky because she didn't think she was able.

Once the transaction was complete, Tegan went back to her family, and Zoe wondered whether she'd ever have cause to see her again.

25

Despite indulging in more than one slice of cake from Corrine's stall, plus her rogue donut and two lattes, Zoe was still hungry as lunchtime arrived. She packed away her raffle tickets and announced her intentions at the surgery fundraising table, shouting over the sounds of the brass band who had now launched into a medley of soundtracks from eighties blockbuster films.

'I'm going to get some lunch, and then I'll draw the raffle numbers. Anyone want me to get them anything?'

'I've eaten,' Fliss said.

'I'm all good too,' Simon chipped in before being distracted by old Mrs Icke, who wanted to complain about something or other.

'What are you having?' Lavender asked.

'Not sure. I like the look of that van selling Nepalese food.'

'No, thanks,' Lavender said. 'I'll probably grab a pasty later.'

'I'll come with you,' Ottilie said.

Zoe waited while she got herself organised, and then they walked together to the van.

'Oh my gosh!' Ottilie pointed to a line of around twenty

small children, ranging from perhaps four or five to ten, walking in pairs and dressed in Tudor clothes. Not exactly Tudor, of course, but clearly as close as their parents or teachers had been able to find. What they might lack in historical accuracy was more than made up for in cuteness. They were all waving at a crowd that was rapidly distracted from whatever else they'd been doing to watch them.

Zoe smiled. 'They're so adorable!'

'I wonder if they're going to put on a little show or something.'

A few feet away, Zoe noticed Stacey with Mackenzie in a pushchair. She waved and then grinned, pointing at the children. Zoe and Ottilie both grinned back, Ottilie nodding with enthusiasm.

'I'm going to have a quick word with Stacey; shall I catch you up?'

Zoe wondered whether to take this opportunity to speak to Alex. But as her gaze found him, watching the children in their period costumes, he seemed far from warmed by the sight. In fact, he looked as if he felt nothing. Zoe couldn't help a deep frown.

'What's wrong?' Ottilie said.

Zoe turned to her. 'I don't know. Something weird is going on.'

'With him?' Ottilie angled her head at Alex, and Zoe nodded. 'Want to go and see what it is?'

'I'm not sure he wants to talk to me.'

'Why? What have you done?'

'Nothing. At least, I don't think so. Will you get me some dinner when you go? I think I do need to get to the bottom of...'

Zoe's sentence tailed off as she noticed Alex leave his spot with the miniature sheep man. They went to the cider stand together and seemed deep in conversation. For now, Zoe decided she'd have to wait. 'Never mind,' she said. 'I'll come with you and catch him later.'

The food carton warmed her hands as they walked back to their colleagues. But then Zoe noticed that Alex had returned from the cider vendor and was now standing alone staring into space.

'Ott...' Zoe gave her carton to her friend. 'Would you take that for me? I want to have a quick word with Alex.'

'No problem. It'll be all right, you know. You'll probably find it's something and nothing and there wasn't any need to worry at all.'

Zoe gave her a grateful smile, but she wasn't so sure. Something was off. He'd been so keen, so interested only a day before and now he was acting like he didn't even know who she was.

'Don't take too long,' Ottilie said. 'Only I can't promise I won't eat yours as well.'

'I won't,' Zoe said, striding off.

As she approached, she painted on a bright smile. 'Hey... how's it going? It's crazy here, isn't it? I never imagined it would be so busy. Where's Billie? Has she come down to join in?'

'No,' he said with such a lack of emotion that Zoe's heart sank. Something was very wrong, and the vibes she was getting told her she was at the root of it. But though she frantically went through scenarios in her head, she couldn't imagine what it was she'd done to upset him like this. She was mistaken; she had to be. He was distracted with other things. Perhaps Billie was causing him stress again and he didn't feel he could keep taking those problems to Zoe. She decided to ignore the frostiness and see if she couldn't lure him out of it.

'So what's been happening with your archaeologist expert? What's he said about your beads? Is it good?'

'Nothing much.'

'But they're genuine? They're—'

'I can't talk to you now.'

Zoe stared at him. 'What?'

'I can't talk. There's too much going on here.'

'Not even... I'm not asking you to debate the meaning of life; I'm only trying to make small talk. You know, like friends do.'

He rounded on her now, like a spring that had been wound as tight as it would go but had suddenly been set free. 'Would a friend go behind my back to ruin my life?'

'I don't understand... What have I done?'

He glanced at the crowds around them. 'Look where we are. I can't go into it here.'

'But I can't spend the rest of the day not knowing what I'm supposed to have done. If I've upset you, I'd rather you tell me now.'

He glanced around once more and then lowered his voice so that it was almost a growl. 'Billie is giving up the baby. She wants to have it adopted. She says you told her to.'

The ground beneath her tilted. For a moment, she had no words in her head, no thoughts, only a chasm of silence. Eventually, she stuttered a reply, though it hardly seemed adequate. 'I said she had that option, but I never said—'

'You had no right!'

'I had every right!' Zoe fired back with a rush of anger. 'She told me she was struggling, and I gave her options! I wouldn't have had to if you'd taken the time to talk to her yourself!'

'I did talk to her!'

'After we'd talked about you needing to! If she's saying it now, then she's given it a lot of thought and decided it's the best thing. What do you want me to say? I haven't made her do it.'

'You put the idea in her head.'

'Don't be stupid. She would have been well aware that adoption services exist and that nobody has to keep their baby.'

'If she goes ahead with this...' he said in a deliberate tone that scared her more than if he'd been shouting, 'it will ruin her life. She'll regret it forever. That's your doing. I hope you're happy.'

'How do you know?'

'Because I know her! She's my daughter, and I know her better than some woman who has been in her life for all of ten minutes!'

'Alex, I'm sorry, but I did what I thought was best for her.'

'And what about me? What if I lose the only chance I'll ever have to be a grandparent? Bad enough that I lost my wife, that she'll never get the opportunity to be a grandmother, but then you want to take my grandchild away?'

'I'm not taking—'

'I thought you were our friend. I thought you were *my* friend. I thought...' He paused, staring at her like he didn't know what he was looking at. 'I hoped for more, that's all. You're right, I'm stupid. I was stupid to hope for anything at all. I should have known it was too good to be true.'

She had no response. What could she say? She could go and talk to Billie, to try to change her mind, but she refused to do that simply to save whatever she might have had with Alex. It had to be Billie's choice, no matter how hurt or angry it made anyone else. Zoe had believed that from the start, and she still believed it now, though there were doubts all the same. Billie had been worried, scared for her future, and even though Zoe had reassured her that there were options, she'd never seen any sign that Billie might want to go down this route. Perhaps there had been disinterest when they'd gone shopping for the cot, perhaps that should have been a clue, but it hadn't been enough for Zoe to consider she might be getting ready to give her baby up.

He turned away.

'Alex, please... talk to me about this.'

'What good will that do?' he asked, without turning back to face her. 'You'll convince me that you were right and it's all for the best? And then we can pick up where we left off? I'm sorry but that's not going to happen.'

'Of course not.'

'Do you intend to fix what you've done?'

'There's nothing to fix; I haven't done anything wrong.'

He spun back. 'What?'

'I get that you're in shock—'

'In shock?' he yelped before lowering his voice to a harsh whisper. 'I'd say that's an understatement! What do you want from me? It's bad enough having to face the prospect of losing my grandchild forever, but the fact that it was instigated by you makes it an even bigger kick in the guts. I'm trying really hard not to be angry with you, but I can't deny I'm struggling. Maybe, one day, I might be able to look at you and not think about that, but it's not today.'

She was consumed by a terrifying mix of emotions. She'd been left fragile by the encounter with Tegan, and now this. She was hurt, upset, devastated by his anger, and yet she was defiant and angry with him in return. She'd done what she felt was right for Billie, as she always did. She hadn't forced Billie to do anything. Surely he could see that? It seemed not. She could only hope that, in time, he would understand. She was so overwhelmed that she didn't trust what she might say next. Deciding it was better to say nothing, she shook her head. Her pulse racing and gravity dragging at her as if it might pull her to the centre of the earth, she then turned to go.

'You're not even sorry, are you?'

She heard him as she left, and she felt as if she was staggering as she walked away. She could go up to Hilltop to see Billie, but that might only make things worse. In the face of all that had happened here today, it was going to be a struggle to continue as Billie's midwife. She wasn't sure she could. Her involvement with father and daughter was too personal now, and she realised what an idiot she'd been. She'd have to talk to Fliss about handing Billie's care to someone else, and Fliss would want to know why. The thought of explaining it to her made Zoe feel foolish and ashamed, as if she didn't have enough to contend with.

Though Alex had kept his voice low and controlled, that had somehow been worse than if he'd raged and shouted. She'd never seen hurt and betrayal run so deep through someone's soul before, and she couldn't believe that she'd caused it.

She pushed through the crowds, making her way back to the table where Ottilie had her lunch waiting, barely noticing what was going on around her. As for her lunch, the last thing she wanted right now was food. She simply wanted to go to her little cottage on the hill and hide and pray that all this awfulness would go away.

'Oi...'

She was dimly aware of the demand for her attention, but it didn't register. And then it came again, louder, more insistent, followed by a loud whistle from between someone's fingers.

Zoe turned this time to see a woman, hardly taller than her but somehow so much bigger, marching towards her. Her face was almost as red as her pillar-box hair, and there was something familiar about it that Zoe couldn't place, though she was certain she'd never met her. The only other thing Zoe knew for certain was that she didn't look happy.

'You're the midwife!'

'Yes.' Zoe frowned. 'What's...?'

'What have you been saying to our Maisie? Telling her our food's no good? What's that mean? Just because you're all la-di-da living up on your farm on the hill, you think that makes you better than us?'

'I didn't say—'

'She pulls her face at everything in the cupboard since you

stuck your nose in. I can't eat this, midwife says... I can't eat that, midwife says... I've got to have vegetables; you've got to make me some crap with an avocado!' The woman prodded Zoe in the chest. 'How I run my house is nothing to do with you! Your job is to make sure she's all right with that baby, and nothing more, so I'll thank you to keep your nose out!'

'Listen,' Zoe began, but the woman cut in.

'Don't you *listen* me with your condescending tone!'

'If you'll let me get a word in—'

'So you can tell me more things I do wrong? I've had a baby, you know. How do you think Maisie got here? So don't tell me how things are done because I know!'

'I'm not trying to tell you—'

'I won't be judged by the likes of you!'

'I'm not judging you!'

'Oh...' The woman swung her hands to her hips and glared at Zoe. 'Raise your voice, will you? Shout at me, will you? How dare you! I could have you sacked!'

Zoe was done. She raised herself to her full height. 'Then Maisie wouldn't have a midwife, would she?'

'Is that a threat?'

'It's a promise,' a voice said behind her.

Zoe spun round to see Ottilie at her back. She'd never been so glad to see her old friend.

The woman rounded on Ottilie now. 'You can't take Maisie's midwife away!' the woman yelled. 'She's got rights, you know!'

'Yes, and so has Miss Padbury. Right now, she's off duty, for one, so you shouldn't even be having this conversation with her. And secondly, even if she were on duty, she could deny Maisie access to care on the grounds of your aggressive attitude. She wouldn't, but she'd be perfectly within her rights to refuse to see her. So I would suggest you think very carefully about what you say or do next. There is no way she is getting fired, but there is every danger you might have to find your daughter a new midwife, and you'd have to drive quite a few miles out of Thimblebury to do it.'

The woman stared Ottilie and Zoe down for a moment and then seemed to think better of whatever retort she had. She was still puce as she stalked away, muttering something about suing and reporting people to the authorities. When she'd gone, Zoe's shoulders slumped and her eyes filled with tears.

Ottilie gave her a sharp look. 'Surely you didn't let that idiot get to you?'

'She wouldn't even let me get a word in to defend myself!'

'I know, but it's not like you to get upset. I've seen you bat off worse than that.'

Zoe sniffed hard. 'I know, but she caught me at a bad time. I didn't even say anything bad about her. All I did was give Maisie some dietary advice.'

'I know that. Everyone knows her around here – she looks for trouble, loves it. She'd take any excuse to come and have a go at you.'

'Do you think I got Maisie in trouble at home?'

'What is this? Zoe, you did your job. Why are you letting this get to you?'

'I'm not. I told you – she caught me off guard, that's all. I'm fine. I'll go and find Maisie and talk to her.'

'You'll do no such thing! We'll go and see Fliss and tell her what Bridget has done and see what she has to say about it. She doesn't stand for her staff being assaulted.'

'But she didn't assault—'

'Of course she did, and you know that too. Verbal assault is still assault, and we don't have to take it.' Ottilie took her arm. 'Come on... Your lunch is going cold anyway.'

As Zoe followed Ottilie, not wanting to see Fliss at all, she caught sight of Alex standing at the table with the miniature landscape and the little houses, and she felt sick. He glanced up, caught her eye and then looked away again with such disdain that she could barely stand it. It seemed like all she could do today was mess up.

She'd been so hopeful as she'd dressed that morning, choosing the outfit that she thought might please him, that might make him notice, but now he hated her. If Billie went ahead with the adoption, he'd never forgive Zoe. She'd stand by her advice before she'd admit she was wrong because she'd given it with the best of intentions. But what if she had been wrong? What if her advice resulted in something terrible, something that Billie would regret when it was too late?

Fliss was halfway through a pint of cider when they found her. She was chatting to Simon and Stacey and her husband, Charles, but she turned and stopped mid-sentence at the sight of both women.

'What on earth is wrong?'

'Bridget bloody Jenkins, that's what,' Ottilie said.

'Ott, I don't want to—' Zoe began, but Ottilie put a hand up and then launched into a summary of the whole sorry encounter.

In a few short seconds, Fliss had caught the gist of it and slammed down her cider. 'Where is she?'

'Fliss...' Simon said steadily. 'You can't tackle her.'

'Can't I?'

'No, not here. I know you're angry – I don't like it any more than you do – but there's a right way to do this. If we don't follow protocol, we'll end up on a disciplinary too.'

'Zoe's not going to end up on a disciplinary!' Fliss raged. 'She didn't do anything wrong! I won't have my colleagues being spoken to in that manner!'

'I'd really rather forget it,' Zoe said in such a small voice that nobody seemed to hear it.

'Bridget Jenkins doesn't have a leg to stand on!' Fliss continued. 'She wouldn't dare start anything with me because she knows I could have her—'

'Fliss...' Simon warned, glancing around to see who was listening. 'You can't say stuff like that.'

'I can say what I bloody well like! And if Bridget Jenkins doesn't like what I have to say, she can jolly well get herself a new GP!'

'You're retiring, remember? You don't want to get into a battle with a patient at this stage, surely.'

Zoe rubbed at her temples and closed her eyes. While she appreciated the support, she just wanted to forget about the whole incident. 'I think I'll go home. I've got a headache coming.'

'Zoe...' Ottilie's voice was gentler now. 'Are you all right? Do you want me to come with you? I can get Heath to drive—'

'No, thanks; there's no point in making you leave the party. I'll be fine.'

'But—'

'Please, Ott, I'd rather go. I'll have a lie-down, and I'll be better in an hour or two.'

Ottilie looked unconvinced but she nodded. 'You're sure you're all right? I know you spoke to Tegan earlier too... Seems like it's ended up being a tough day.'

Ottilie didn't know the half of it, and Zoe wished she had the strength to tell her, but it would have to wait.

26

As she made her way through the crowds, it took every ounce of fortitude she had not to start crying. It wasn't like her to react like this – Ottilie had that right. But it wasn't every day that she managed to make almost everyone she knew angry in some way. She'd been forced to stop and exchange pleasantries with villagers on her way out, and it had been torture. She'd just heaved a sigh of relief on having made it to the end when she felt a hand on her shoulder and turned around to see Ritchie there.

'What...?' Her mouth dropped open, and he grinned.

'Surprise!'

'What are you doing here?'

'Can't I visit? I thought we were OK with that.'

'Of course,' Zoe said. She'd meant to set some boundaries about him visiting when they'd last talked, and for some reason she hadn't. Now she was very much wishing she had. 'It's just *here*... I didn't expect to find you at this. How did you even know?'

'Facebook. I follow the village news page. It's not that hard.'

Of course he followed Thimblebury's Facebook page. Why

wouldn't he? Zoe held in a groan. As if her day wasn't complicated enough. But then she noticed him studying her.

'You're upset,' he said.

'I'm fine.'

'Don't give me that. You think I don't know you well enough by now to see when you've been crying? What's wrong?'

'Nothing's wrong.'

'Come on...' He took her by the elbow and started to lead her away from the crowds. 'Let's go somewhere quieter.'

'That's what I was trying to do when I bumped into you.'

'Didn't look as if you were managing. I've been trying to get your attention for ten minutes, and you kept talking to people.'

She turned to him with a frown. 'How long have you been here?'

He pointed to a road off the main street. 'Is that the right way to your house?'

'Not as such, but you could go that way.'

'It looks less busy; let's go that way.'

'Ritchie, why didn't you tell me you were coming?'

'I only just decided to come and check it out.'

'On your own?'

'I was interested. Anyway, I wouldn't have been on my own – you're here.'

'You didn't know I'd be here. I might have decided to stay away.'

'You?' He gave a short laugh. 'Stay away from a celebration? Anyway, I thought even if you weren't here, I thought I'd have a look and then come up to your house.'

He hadn't really answered her question, but she gave up on it because it was clear he wasn't going to.

She stopped on the narrow pavement. 'I don't want to go home.'

'Why not?'

'Because I don't. If I go home now...'

She *had* wanted to go home, but now she didn't. If she let Ritchie take her home, it would send the wrong kind of signal; it would tell him that she needed him. And she did – at least, she needed someone – and that was even more dangerous.

'If I go home now,' she continued, 'it means they've won.'

'Who's won?'

'People. Problems... I don't know, just *they*. That's what you say, isn't it? When it's all vague and just life. You don't let *them* win.'

'Don't let the bastards grind you down?'

'Yes, exactly.'

'You want to go back to the carnival or whatever it is?'

'Not yet. Maybe in a bit. I might find somewhere to sit and collect my thoughts. You can go back to Manchester.'

'Why would I do that? I came to see you.'

'I thought you'd come because you were interested in Thimblebury.'

'Well, yeah... but I was still counting on you being here. And I was right. It's a good job I know you so well. So where do you want to go?'

Zoe thought for a moment. 'There's a bit of the riverbank where you can sit. It's nice.'

'Lead the way then.'

His hand brushed hers as they began to walk, and though there was something comforting in the contact, she moved out of range. It was a bit too comforting in her present state of mind.

Fallen leaves were mulched into the pathways that led to the riverbank, and the air smelled like the beginning of winter, where the promise of freezing rain and heavy snows were still only that, a promise, but one that would be delivered. Crows cawed in the trees above and circled distant fields, and the sun was already past its zenith.

'Is that a new dress?' he asked.

'You've seen me in this tons of times before.'

'Have I? Well, it looks good. Cute. I always thought that cute was a word that suited you. I mean, it still is, obviously.'

'Thanks.'

'You're meant to tell me I look good now.'

'You do,' she replied vacantly.

'You didn't even look.'

'Ritchie... can we not do this right now?'

'Oh, yeah... sorry.'

'You don't have to be sorry, but I can't.'

'Of course... I'll shut up.'

'I didn't mean that...' Zoe let out a sigh. 'You don't have to shut up.'

'I'm annoying you.'

'You're not annoying me. I don't have a lot of patience to spare today. I don't want to tell you about it; I only need you to know that's how it is. And I do appreciate you being here, but I can't cope with your...'

She paused. She'd offended enough people today, and she didn't really want to add Ritchie to the list, even though his presence was already causing her problems.

'I get it,' he said. 'Not another word.'

'I didn't mean that. Tell me what's going on with you? What about your job hunt? Found anything yet?'

He soon forgot he was meant to be comforting Zoe and launched into a well-worn rant about the state of the job market and how little his worth was recognised in any quarter. She didn't mind. She wasn't really listening, but the sound of his voice was so familiar it took her back to a place and time where she'd been so certain of everything and everyone, she'd barely ever questioned her life.

The sound of running water reached them before they saw the river, shielded by a wall of trees and a high bank, but eventually, through branches pockmarked by the dense remains of old bird nests and the last leaves of the year, they saw it.

The old bench that Zoe had known would be there was covered in soggy leaves and had moss growing in the corners. Ritchie did his best to clear it, but she still perched on the edge to prevent her dress being ruined. He took a seat next to her, leaning forward as she was. Aware of his knee resting against hers, Zoe gazed at the river as it swept past and took a cleansing breath.

'Better?' he asked.

'Yes.'

'It's nice here.'

'I don't come down here that often, to be honest. I never seem to have the time. I ought to try and make time.'

'So you want to tell me what's got you so upset?'

'It's nothing—'

'Zo, I thought we were friends. It's me, Ritchie. *Your* Ritchie; I'll always be that, no matter what. I'm here for you.'

'It's...' Zoe's shoulders slumped. 'Do you ever feel as if nothing you do will ever be right?'

'My whole bloody life. But not you – you're not like that. I always thought, of the two of us, you were the one with a plan, the doer. I only drifted along at your side, but you...'

'I must have been good at faking then.'

'Something's happened today to make you feel like this, I take it?' he asked, and for once she was taken aback by his astute appraisal of the situation.

'More than one thing. And not only today. Ever since... ever since I lost our baby, I haven't felt like anything has been right, and it only seems to be getting worse. That happened, and then we started to break apart, and then... I always had my job. I had faith that whatever else was wrong in my life, I had that, and I was important and what I did mattered, and I was good at it.'

'This is just about your job?'

'No, that's only part of it, but that's the part I always

trusted, and so if that's going wrong, then what chance do I have with any of it?'

'I'm not sure I'm following.'

'I'm not surprised. I wouldn't be following either.'

Zoe stopped and stared out over the river. A tangled clump of twigs and leaves sailed by. She watched its path downstream before shrugging. 'I upset someone. A really good friend. And I don't know if I can fix it.'

'Ottilie?'

'No, not Ottilie.'

'You don't have to tell me.' He reached to loop an arm around her shoulders and pulled her close. She allowed her head to lean on his chest. His smell was so warm and familiar; if she closed her eyes, she could imagine herself in the past, before she'd lost her baby, before they'd fallen apart, when he was all she needed. It felt like a safe place to be, uncomplicated and lovely. As he rubbed at her arm, she closed her eyes and a tear squeezed from the corner of one of them.

'This is nice,' he said after a pause that seemed to stretch for hours, filled only with the sound of the water rushing by and birds in the trees, and muffled music in the distance.

Zoe couldn't deny that it was nice. She took deep breaths, in and out, and with every inhale he was a little more in her head, the memory of him, of what they'd once been when life had been so much simpler. She tilted to look up at him. 'Thanks.'

He smiled – and in the next instant kissed her.

It was so sudden, so quick, that at first she could barely process it. It felt obvious and good, like a favourite pair of comfortable shoes, something she could trust in. Then came the guilt and a realisation that was like a thunderbolt. She didn't want this. She didn't want Ritchie. She wanted...

She tore her lips from his and stared at him. 'What are you doing?'

'I thought... I thought we were having a moment. I thought that was what you wanted.'

'My fault...' Zoe gathered herself and stood up. 'God, I'm so *stupid*!'

'Wait... what's wrong?'

Zoe threw her hands in the air. 'Everything!'

'Even me?'

'Yes, you! Ritchie, I don't want to hurt you, but we can't go back – surely you understand that?'

'Why can't we? We're not divorced yet; we can stop it.'

She stared at him. She understood. Maybe she'd always understood, but she hadn't wanted to admit it. 'That's the only reason you've been coming here.'

'Of course it's not—'

'Oh, Ritchie, why? Why did you have to do that? I thought we'd got it worked out; I thought we'd found a way to split and stay friends. I was so smug about it to everyone who said you can't be both, and I was like, yes, me and Ritchie can. But we can't – today has proved that. I don't want us to go through the rest of our lives hating one another, but we can't have contact, not like this, not like we've been doing. It won't work.'

'There's someone else? That guy, your neighbour...'

Zoe narrowed her eyes. Ritchie had admitted to being at the celebrations for longer than she'd been aware of. Had he seen her argument with Alex?

'If there was, it has nothing to do with us,' she said. She started to walk.

'Where are you going?'

'Home.'

'Don't you want to talk?'

She stopped and turned back. 'There's nothing to talk about.'

'There's loads to talk about!'

'You came for the celebrations, so go and enjoy them.'

'We have to sort this out.'

'We *have* sorted it out. We sorted it out months ago. Nothing has changed since then.'

'You could have fooled me,' he said in a voice heavy with hurt. 'We were getting somewhere, just then.'

'No, you thought you were. You caught me at a vulnerable moment and you took advantage, and that's not fair. You haven't been honest with me this whole time you've been coming to Thimblebury. I didn't want to believe it, but I see it now. It was always your plan to lure me into coming back to you.'

'Would it be so bad?' he asked with outstretched arms, exasperation in his voice. 'Am I that bad?'

'Of course you're not,' she said. 'But we're not the same people we were before. I can't love you like I did before because that Zoe isn't this Zoe.'

'You're making no sense.'

'Probably not to you, but it makes perfect sense to me.'

'What about everything going wrong all the time? I thought you were miserable.'

'I am,' she said, turning once again to leave. 'But that's something I'm going to have to work out for myself.'

27

Ritchie followed her. She tried to ignore him, speeding up in the hope he'd get the message, but after five minutes, still sensing him following her, she spun round.

'What are you doing?'

'We need to talk.'

'We don't need to talk. Go back to the celebrations.'

'I don't want to go to the stupid celebrations.'

'I know you don't. That was never your reason for coming, was it?'

'So stop and talk to me.'

'I don't want to.'

She faced forward again and picked up the pace. She didn't look back, and after a while she thought he might not be there. But when she turned to check, she saw that he was walking a few paces behind in complete silence. She gave a loud click of her tongue and carried on walking. By now she was breathless from the pace she was setting, but she couldn't be bothered to argue. She'd make it to Kestrel Cottage before him, and if he thought he'd be following her inside, he was very much mistaken. She'd lock the doors, and he could sit out there all night if he wanted because she wasn't going to let him in.

But as they carried on and he showed no sign of giving up, her courage started to fail her. She'd never been afraid of Ritchie in all the time she'd known him, but she had to admit to an emotion now that wasn't exactly fear but had the shape of it. Apprehension? Anxiety, perhaps? He could catch up if he really wanted to. He could try to stop her from going home. He could even decide to watch her house and wait until the next time she went out to accost her. He'd never do something so extreme, would he?

She shook the thought. That was crazy. Things were heated now, blown out of proportion and not helped by the fact that she'd already been emotionally on the edge. This was Ritchie; she knew him. He'd never do anything as creepy as that.

The steep path that led to Daffodil Farm came into view. She didn't dare glance behind, but she knew he was there. She considered phoning someone to come to her aid. Who? What would she say? It was funny because now that she thought about it, the only person she wanted to come to her aid was the one person without a phone. It wasn't Alex or Heath or Simon or any of the men she could get hold of; it was Victor. Lovely, dependable, old-fashioned gentleman Victor, the closest thing she had to a grandfather or an uncle here in Thimblebury. She'd only have to say the word and he'd come to her rescue. He'd know how to deal with Ritchie too – not in an alpha-male way but with a friendly, reassuring persuasion that would disarm anyone.

But Victor, like everyone else, was at the quincentenary. Nobody was going to help her, and so she'd have to deal with this mess herself. She had, after all, made it in the first place.

She marched harder still, up the hillside track that led to her home. All the while, she knew Ritchie was still there, and by the time she was at the crossroads between the path that led to

Hilltop and the path that went to Daffodil Farm, she'd had enough.

She stopped and turned, planting her hands on her hips. 'This is ridiculous! I told you I wanted to go home to get some peace, and that means from you as well.'

'I want to look after you. You need someone, even if you don't think you do.'

'I don't need *you*, Ritchie. I'm sorry. It's hard to hear and it's hard to say, but it's the truth. If I did need someone, it wouldn't be you.'

'It'd be *him*?'

'Who? Who are you talking about? And what business is it of yours, even if there was a *him*?'

'None; I'm just asking. I want to know if we're meant to be going out with new people—'

'I've been telling you for months to find a new girlfriend!'

'I didn't think you *meant* it.'

Zoe let out a breath of impatience. 'Of course you didn't,' she said as she started to walk again. 'I only said it because I like wasting my breath.'

'Why are you being like this?'

'Like what?'

'Awkward.'

'There's nothing awkward about reminding you of our boundaries.'

'Zo...' He lunged forward to grab her by the arm and halted her progress. She snatched away from his grasp. And then a loud, low bark echoed across the hillside, and she saw Grizzle bounding towards them, Billie following from the direction of Hilltop.

'Griz!' Zoe went to meet him. She'd never been so pleased to see a dog and couldn't have cared less as he leaped up, licking at her face and pawing at her dress. 'Good boy! Are you out for a walk?' she asked, glancing to see Billie on her way down to them. She didn't seem concerned that her dog had run ahead or that he was currently doing his best to get as much mud as he could onto Zoe's clothes.

Ritchie watched, seemingly uncertain of his next move, even more so when he inched forward and Grizzle noticed, a low growl rumbling in his throat. Zoe had heard it said many times that dogs sensed when a situation was off, and apparently Grizzle was doing that right now.

'Hey, Griz!' Billie called, glancing from Zoe to Ritchie and then back again, her cool expression seeming to ask a question. *Are you all right?* 'I thought you'd be at the five-hundred-year thing in the village,' she said to Zoe.

'I was, but I'd had enough.'

Billie looked at Ritchie. 'This your husband?'

'Yes,' he said.

'Soon to be ex,' Zoe corrected. 'When the paperwork has gone through. He was about to leave.'

Ritchie hesitated. It was obvious he hadn't been ready to give up yet but perhaps was starting to realise his efforts weren't going to get him anywhere.

'Right then,' Billie said. She put a hand up to Ritchie and raised her eyebrows. 'Ta-ta...'

It was so full of sarcasm that if Zoe hadn't been feeling so delicate, she'd have laughed.

'I'll call you,' Ritchie said to Zoe, but she didn't reply; she simply bent to fuss Grizzle, who'd now calmed down and was sitting at her feet. When she looked up again, Ritchie was walking towards the track that would take him down the hill to the village.

'You were married to him?' Billie asked, her tone taking Zoe by surprise. 'Wow.'

'Is that a good wow or a bad one?'

'I don't know. I'm surprised. Did you have to put up with a lot of that bullshit, or is it a new thing?'

Zoe gave a strained smile. 'Now that I think back, I probably put up with more of it than I realised. I know one thing: I was so glad to see you and Grizzle.'

'He was going mad for his walk. I nearly didn't take him; thought Dad could do it later. Luckily, he was a pain in the arse and I got fed up of his whining by the door.'

'Lucky for me.'

'Was your ex bothering you? Do you think you ought to phone the police or something?'

'He'll go home and cool off and realise he was out of order. Ritchie's harmless, all bark and no bite.'

'Like Griz.'

'Like Griz.' Zoe's smile was brighter now. 'Griz has a decent growl on him though. That might be the answer: I should get a dog.'

Billie folded her arms, as if she was looking for an escape from their conversation. And though she didn't want to be annoyingly insistent, especially after the way Ritchie had been with her, Zoe did wonder if this would be her best opportunity to talk to Billie about the adoption.

'Your dad told me about your plans for the baby.'

'He was pissed at you.'

'Yes, I got that. Both barrels, as it happens.'

'Sorry.'

Zoe had to wonder if Billie had been more calculating than she was letting on. Had Alex told her about his date with Zoe and she'd somehow sought to put a spanner in the works? She decided to give her the benefit of the doubt. 'You've made up your mind? You don't want to talk it over?'

'You told me I could do it if I wanted to.'

'I did, and you can. I also said it was one of many choices.'

'Like what?'

'Do you want to come to Kestrel Cottage for a drink and a chat?'

'Not really. I have to take Griz for his walk.'

'He could wait half an hour? I'd make a fuss of him at my place, and I'm sure he'd be fine for a bit. I'd really appreciate the company, if I'm being honest. And if you're there, Ritchie won't be tempted to come back.'

Billie seemed torn, but then she nodded. 'Only for a bit. I think you should do something about him,' she continued as they started in the direction of Kestrel Cottage.

'I think you're right. It's my fault he's like this, really. I think I let him believe we might at some point get back together. I don't know why he'd want to, but...'

'So you're not going out with my dad?'

'No,' Zoe said, which pained her to admit. She wondered whether the news was welcome to Billie or not.

'Only he asked you.'

'He told you about that?'

'Of course.'

'You didn't mind?'

'It's none of my business.'

Zoe didn't think that was true at all, and there was a lot in Billie's manner that suggested she didn't believe what she'd said either.

'It was only a date, to see how things went.'

'Yeah, I know. But now it's not happening.'

'Not at the moment. At least, I don't think so. I don't think I'm your dad's favourite person right now. He blames me for your decision to give up the baby.'

'Oh. What should I do?'

'Do? What do you mean?'

'Should I tell him it's not your fault?'

'No. It's not your job to put him straight. But he does know you're an adult, right?'

'I think sometimes he does forget. He feels like he has to be both my parents and that I still need protecting like a little girl. I think sometimes he wishes I was still little.'

'Because that would mean he'd have his old life back? Like going back in time? So he'd have you and your mum and you'd all be together again?'

'I don't know. I didn't think of that.'

'Do you think that's why he's so upset about the adoption? Because he feels as if he's lost enough already and now he's going to lose someone else?'

'Is that what he said to you?'

'No, but I feel as if I ought to have thought to ask him at the time. To be honest, I was a bit overwhelmed. He was pretty angry. He told me that you'd told him it was my idea. I can't help feeling I've been thrown under the bus here. I said it was an option, but I never said that's what you ought to do.'

'I thought he might roast you. Sorry about that.'

Zoe shot her a sideways glance and was encouraged to see that, although there weren't any huge indications, she did look a tiny bit more remorseful than she had so far today. 'If you thought he was going to roast me, why say it?'

'I didn't know he was going to roast you when I first told him. Obviously. I wouldn't have mentioned you at all if I'd known. I thought you and him were all into each other, so it would be all right.'

They arrived at the gate of Kestrel Cottage. Zoe pushed it open, watching Billie's face as she did. There was more to all this, she was sure of it, but Billie was playing her cards close to her chest and doing a fine job of it.

'Hang on, I need to grab an old towel to dry Grizzle's feet before you come in, if that's all right.'

'Want me to take my shoes off?'

'If you don't mind.'

Zoe kicked off her own boots in the hallway before dashing to the airing cupboard, digging into the bottom layer of her linens to get the oldest towel she had. She half expected to find Billie had gone and taken Grizzle with her when she got back to the front door, but they were both still there, Billie in her socks in the hallway and Grizzle sitting patiently on the step. Zoe bent down to give his paws a wipe. He thought she was playing and started to jump about so that in the end there was yet more mud on her dress and not very much on the towel. She gave it up as a bad job and let him dart into the house.

'He doesn't jump on furniture,' Billie said, only for them both to walk into the living room and find him standing to attention with what looked like a proud grin on Zoe's sofa. 'Not at our house,' Billie corrected.

At this point, Zoe had given up, so she ignored him and went to the kitchen, beckoning Billie to follow.

'When did you decide about the adoption?' she asked as she opened the fridge.

'This morning.'

'This morning?' Zoe took out a bottle of orange juice and held it up.

Billie nodded. 'Yeah, I'll have orange juice.'

'Just like that?' Zoe continued, shaking the juice. 'You thought it and you said it straight out? No wonder it came as a shock to your dad.'

'I couldn't see the point in messing around. Dad would have only said "Why didn't you say something before?" if I hadn't said anything right away. He usually does.'

'Is that usually when you don't have something quite this big to tell him?'

Billie took the glass of juice Zoe offered her. 'He started the serious conversation, so I thought I might as well, as we were being all deep anyway.'

Zoe sat at the table and invited Billie to do the same. Grizzle padded into the kitchen and settled at her feet. 'Oh? What were you being all deep about?'

'Stuff about Mum and how Dad wasn't looking to replace her and...' Billie shrugged. 'That kind of thing.'

Zoe was silent for a moment as she pondered what Billie had told her. It sounded as if he was trying to reassure Billie about his date. It was the only conclusion she could come to that made sense. 'Has he been with anyone since your mum died?'

'No. He was never interested. He always said he'd never find anyone like her.'

Zoe wasn't sure how to answer that so she changed tack to something that felt like safer ground. 'This decision to give your baby up. You said you made it this morning and thought you ought to tell your dad sooner rather than later. Was it really that quick? Had you given it any thought before then?'

'Yeah, of course I did. I couldn't make up my mind before, and then this morning I did. I've thought about it loads.'

'So you're sure? Like really, really sure? There's no chance you might not be sure? That you might change your mind?'

'If I change my mind, then I won't do it.'

'I'm not sure it's that simple. There's an emotional cost to announcing things like this off the cuff.'

'What does that mean?'

Zoe reached for her glass. 'Never mind; it doesn't matter. I know you've already told your dad, but I think you ought to give it a few days before you lock the decision in your own mind. Sleep on it, see how it feels to know that's coming. Try to imagine giving birth and then giving your baby to someone to take away, knowing you'll never see them again.'

'I have. I won't be any good at looking after the baby anyway, even if I wanted to keep it.'

Zoe nodded slowly. 'OK, fine. As long as you've thought it through and you're certain, that's all I wanted to know.'

'You're not going to try to change my mind?'

'No. The only person who can do that is you. If it's what you want, then I'll support you the whole way.'

Billie seemed content with that. She sipped at her juice and then stood up. 'If you're OK, I think I'm going to go. Thanks for the drink.'

'Thanks for being there when I needed you.'

'A girl's got to have a girl's back.'

'Well, you had mine, and I'm glad.'

Billie studied her briefly. 'Want me to talk to my dad for you?'

'About what?'

'You and him? I could if you wanted me to.'

'I don't know how I'd feel about that. It might come across as a bit spineless, if you see what I mean? I think if anyone's going to talk to him about it, that's got to be me. But quite honestly, I don't see him wanting to listen.'

It was strange, but whatever was going on with her and Alex, Zoe had the sense that things had suddenly developed in a far more positive way with Billie. And while she was glad of that, the irony was not lost on her.

28

The only person who asked to come over that evening was Ottilie. Ritchie didn't bother her again, and if Billie had told Alex about him hassling Zoe, he didn't do anything about it. Not that Zoe wanted or expected him to. But Ottilie phoned as she was running a bath to try to unwind.

'What's been happening?' she asked. 'After you left, Alex had a face like thunder. It didn't exactly help when some people started to hassle him about his camping pod plans.'

'What kind of hassle?'

'The usual: complaining about trucks driving through the village and workmen and more visitors and that sort of thing. That's not important. What happened between you and him?'

'Let's just say we won't be going on a date after all. It's fine; I don't care.'

'Sounds like it.'

'I don't. He's unreasonable and quick to jump to conclusions – why would I want to date someone like that? In fact, I've had it with men in general. You'll never guess who turned up at the quincentenary.'

'Ritchie.'

'You saw him?'

'I saw him leave. What did he want?'

'To make my life a misery. You know, pretending to be mister sensitive super-supportive, no strings attached, and no I don't want anything in return because I care about you and that's why. Except there were strings attached and he did want something in return. Don't worry, he didn't get it. He had a bloody good go, though.'

'You should have come to find me.'

'You were all busy. Anyway, weirdly I was rescued by Billie and her dog. That thing's as soft as anything, but he must look scary, because Ritchie scarpered when he started to growl.'

'But you're all right now? You know you can come and stay at mine if you need to.'

'I'd rather be here. No offence, but I want to be on my own.'

'Fair enough, but you know where I am if you change your mind.'

'Thanks, Ottilie. You're a star.'

'You missed all the drama today.'

'So you said: people getting upset about Alex's camping pods.'

'That, and Fliss announced her retirement and the pensioners nearly rioted. The way Flo reacted, you'd think the end of days was coming – and she doesn't even like Fliss! Then Victor lost it with someone – actually shouted! I've never seen him angry before. It was impressive.'

'What was Victor angry about?'

'Mostly people getting on Alex's case. It was Flo who drove the final nail in. I mean, it would be, wouldn't it? She was already having kittens about Fliss leaving, and then she had a rant about the village being ruined. I mean, when I say it was Flo, it wasn't only her. Her and Mrs Icke formed a pincer movement and tried to take Alex down together, but Victor wasn't having any of it. You should have seen Flo's face when he blew up. I had to deal with the fallout, of course, but it was worth it. I only wish I'd had my phone handy to capture it on video for you.'

Zoe smiled. No matter what else was happening, Ottilie could always make her feel better. She hadn't appreciated how much her life had lacked a good supply of Ottilie until she'd been reunited with her in Thimblebury.

'Was it OK in the end?'

'I think so. Everyone got the message not to mess with Victor in any case. From what people said after, it sounds like he must have been a bit of a livewire in his youth. He's such a gentle soul now, I can't imagine it, but if this afternoon was anything to go by, I can definitely believe it.'

'I suppose everyone has a limit.' Zoe reached to swish the water in the bath.

'Even Victor,' Ottilie agreed.

'What was Corrine doing when all this was going on?'

'Looking at him with pure lust in her eyes,' Ottilie said, and Zoe burst out laughing. She didn't stop for a full thirty seconds.

'Thanks, Ottilie, I needed that! I feel better already for talking to you, you know.'

'That was my aim. Glad I could help.'

'Listen, not that I don't appreciate your cheerleading, but I'm going to have my bath now.'

'Got it. I'll leave you to it. See you on Monday.'

Zoe was wrapped in her towelling robe and ready to settle down with a book before bed when she noticed there was an unread message on her phone.

I can't get a job and I can't afford to buy you out now, so you'll have to sell the house after all.

No kiss at the end of the message? Presumably he was smarting at her rejection, but even so, his sudden demand was a petty way to lash out. She wasn't in the mood to mess around with him and so she typed her reply.

I don't have time to sell it. If you need the money so badly, you'll have to do it.

I'm busy looking for work and a new flat, so no. If you don't want to sell it, you'll have to move back in and buy me out.

Nice try, Zoe thought. She wasn't going to give him the satisfaction of knowing it, but she'd been counting on the money she'd make selling her half of their old house to him. She wasn't destitute, but she was using a large chunk of her wages on rent, and after other essentials, there wasn't a huge amount left to simply enjoy life with. And while to some extent she had sympathy with his plight, she wasn't about to do everything for him. If he needed to sell the house, then he'd have to do it. Zoe was staying put in Thimblebury, so moving back wasn't an option. It was time he grew up and took some responsibility.

Zoe locked her phone and tossed it onto the bed. So much for staying friends. Right now, he was her least favourite person in the world.

Trying to put the day's events from her mind, she went to find her book, knowing that she probably wouldn't be able to concentrate on it but desperate to try all the same.

Zoe hadn't been expecting much from her Monday morning, but she surrendered herself to whatever might be coming and started her working day with as much stoicism as she could muster. Before the first appointment of her day was due to arrive, she made coffee for everyone, calling into Fliss's room with her cup last of all.

'Ah, Zoe...' Fliss greeted her briskly. 'Over the weekend's trauma?'

'I think so,' Zoe said carefully.

'You only think so?' Fliss took the drink Zoe had made with a grateful nod. 'You're not still smarting about Bridget Jenkins, are you?'

'Maisie's mum? No, I'm not. What's the point? I've had worse than that; she just caught me off guard.'

'Good, but I can still have a word with her if you like.'

Zoe shook her head vehemently. 'What about you? Did you enjoy the rest of the event? I hear some people were a bit upset about you announcing your retirement.'

Fliss gave a short bark of a laugh. 'Things don't change much around here, and that's the way most like it, so I wouldn't have expected anything less. But like I said to Ottilie when she first arrived and everyone was complaining that she wasn't Gwen – the nurse we had before Ottilie – they have shorter memories than they think. Ottilie's been here, what...? Two years or so, and it's as if Gwen never existed. It'll be the same when my replacement settles in.'

'I don't know about that.'

'They can take it or leave it either way because it's not a choice; it's a fact. Don't you worry – my wine tour of Europe is already in the planning stage as we speak. I intend to be away for a very long time and drink an inordinate amount of wine along the way.'

Zoe smiled. 'That sounds nice. Can I come with you?'

'You'd never keep up.'

'Probably not.'

'Right then. Onwards and upwards, eh?'

Fliss turned to her monitor, and Zoe took that to mean she wanted to get on.

When she finally sat at her own desk, Lavender phoned from reception.

'Have you got time to see someone who isn't booked in?' she asked in a mysterious voice that all at once hinted at mischief but also at some attempt to remain professional in the face of whoever was standing in front of her asking to see Zoe.

'Is it urgent?' Zoe asked. 'I've got a full clinic today.'

'I wouldn't say urgent...' She held the phone away, and Zoe could hear her ask whoever it was in muffled tones whether it *was* urgent, but couldn't hear their reply.

'She feels bad,' Lavender reported back, and now there was definite humour in her tone.

'Bad like she's ill or just bad?' Zoe paused and then shook her head. 'Never mind; I'll come through.'

She didn't know who to expect, but she realised it should have been obvious. Maisie Jenkins was nervously twisting her fingers around one another as she stood waiting at the reception desk.

'Hello,' Zoe said, offering a reassuring smile. 'Everything OK?'

Zoe had a few ideas about why Maisie might have come, and most of them were connected in some way with the altercation between her and Maisie's mum, Bridget.

'You're still going to look after me?' Maisie asked.

'Of course...' Zoe glanced around the waiting room and saw that there were already three patients seated in there. 'Do you want to come to talk in my room for a minute?'

Maisie nodded. 'Yes, please. I thought my mum might have upset you,' she continued as they walked.

Zoe let her in the treatment room before following her in and shutting the door.

'It takes more than that to upset me,' Zoe said. 'I didn't take it personally.'

She'd taken it very personally, but Maisie didn't need to know that, and it was hardly her fault.

'Only, someone told her in the pub that Dr Cheadle said she was going to take us all off the books, like. I mean, you wouldn't look after anyone in my family. Dad needs his diabetes meds.'

'I don't know where they heard that, but it couldn't be further from the truth,' Zoe said.

'It would be my fault if he got ill because he had no doctor.'

'It wouldn't be, even if it happened, which it won't. So you really don't need to worry. Other than that, everything is all right?'

'I think so. I've been trying to eat good food, like you said.'

'I know,' Zoe said wryly, recalling Bridget's complaints only too well. 'It's good to hear.'

'I've started to pee all the time.'

'That's normal in pregnancy; I wouldn't worry about that either.'

'Yeah, my mate said that. Are you allowed to pee in a policeman's helmet?'

Zoe tried not to laugh, all tension leaving her. 'Is this a bucket-list thing for you?'

'Huh?'

'I mean, do you have some burning desire to pee in a policeman's helmet?'

'No, but my mate says it's legal to pee wherever you want if you're pregnant, like even if you were stopped by the police and you wanted to go, you could just ask for his helmet and he'd have to give it to you.'

Zoe smiled. 'Well, as much as I enjoy that particular urban myth, I'd say try not to. I don't think it goes down well. Anything else?'

'No. I'm sorry about my mum.'

'Don't give it another thought. But if you have any worries, or you need extra help with something, you know you can come and see me or phone me any time, don't you?'

'Yeah, thanks. I'll tell Dad his meds will be all right as well.'

As Zoe walked Maisie back to reception, she saw that Ottilie was in there. She waited until the young woman had gone and then turned to Zoe, keeping her voice low.

'What did she want?'

'She wanted to know if she could pee in a policeman's hat.'

'What?'

Zoe smiled. 'She came to apologise for her mum. It was good of her, actually – took some guts. Not sure I would have been able to do that at her age. Maybe she'll be all right when the baby comes after all.'

'Let's hope so. Goes to show, sometimes the apple manages to roll away from the tree.'

'Yes.' Zoe nodded. 'Thank goodness, eh?'

'Are you all right? How was the rest of your weekend? I thought you might call me, but I didn't want to hassle you in case you wanted some alone time.'

'I did, to be honest, and I feel better for it. I had a message from Ritchie. I'll tell you about it later, see what your take is, but I have a feeling our efforts to stay friends might be scuppered.'

'Well,' Ottilie said, turning to go back to her own room, 'I hate to say it, but I think that was always going to happen. Some men can be grown-up about these things, and then there's Ritchie.'

Ottilie had invited Zoe to eat with her and Heath that evening. So had Fliss, and Stacey had sent her a text saying she was available to talk should Zoe need it. But all Zoe needed was her own company. Much as she appreciated everyone's efforts, she was tired and she wanted time to think. She also realised that, no matter how much she wanted to avoid the issue, Ritchie's threat to walk away from his end of the bargain over their old house was real, and she'd have to make plans for that eventuality. There was no time like the present to start doing that. If it came to pass, she wanted to be ready.

And so she headed home, rifled in her freezer for some minestrone soup Corrine had given her the previous week, and ate it with thick sliced bread, sitting at the table in silence as she scrolled through details for financial advisers on her phone. Ottilie had been right – Zoe should have seen this coming. If anyone was going to let her down, it was Ritchie.

After her meal, she emailed a couple of promising-looking candidates to query her circumstances and ask what they'd charge to sort out her affairs, and then she made a hot drink and settled in front of the television.

Half an hour into a medical thriller, her phone began to ring.

'Hi, Billie,' she said, reaching for the remote to turn the TV off. 'Everything OK?'

'I don't know,' Billie said. 'I fell on the stairs. Do you think the baby will be all right?'

Zoe straightened up. 'Want me to come over?'

'Do you want to? Because if you don't, I could come—'

'Absolutely not. I'm sure it's all fine, but I'll come to you anyway. Sit down, have a warm drink… get your dad to make it. Is he there?'

'Yes, he's here. Is that all right?'

'Not a problem,' Zoe said tightly. Every cell in her was screaming that it was a problem. Alex was the last person she wanted to see, but if he could be bigger than what happened between them over the weekend for Billie's sake, then so could she. 'Give me ten minutes and I'll be with you.'

29

Alex opened the front door looking awkward. 'I'm sorry we had to call you.'

'Don't be sorry – I told Billie to phone any time.'

'But it's late and you're off duty,' he continued as she followed him inside. I would have driven her to the hospital myself, but some joker has let down all my tyres.'

'What?'

He didn't look only nodded, his gaze on his feet. 'Yes. Every one of them is flat, so it's no accident.'

'Who would do that?'

'Not a clue. Maybe it's someone in the village who isn't very happy about my plans for Hilltop.'

'Even so, it's a bit childish. What did they think letting your tyres down was going to achieve? It's a minor inconvenience, sure, but it's hardly going to drive you away.'

'It's literally not going to drive me away,' he said, and she thought she might have detected the merest whisper of a smile at a joke that was obviously too good to resist, even for him in the current circumstances. 'Perhaps it's the start of a whole campaign of terror. This week flat tyres, next week horses' heads.'

'Ugh. Perhaps it's the ghost of your Bronze Age chieftain telling you he doesn't want you here.'

'Again, you'd hope even a Bronze Age ghost had seen enough of the world by now to know that letting my tyres down is literally going to prevent me from going anywhere.'

Was this an attempt at some sort of reset? Zoe wondered. He seemed tense and slightly embarrassed by the situation they were now in, but she couldn't help feeling he was trying to reconcile a little. Did he feel ashamed of his outburst at the quincentenary? Had it been a fit of anger that he'd since had time to reflect on and regret? Whatever the reason for his change of attitude, he needed her now – or rather, Billie did – and he knew he had to behave.

Billie was propped up on some pillows, her feet up on the sofa with a blanket. She looked as sheepish as Alex had done.

'Sorry,' she said. 'I feel stupid.'

'Don't. You wouldn't believe how often I get phone calls about my mums falling over. Pregnancy makes you a bit wobblier in all sorts of ways, and you do tend to be a bit less stable than normal. But... you also have an amazing built-in defence system. It takes more than you'd think to do harm. Did you fall forward onto your belly or backwards?'

'Down the stairs. I sort of slid down the last few steps and scraped my spine. I was carrying my laptop though, and it flew in the air and then that hit my belly.'

'Hmm. When did it happen?'

'About two hours ago.'

'And how have you been since then?' Zoe took off her coat and perched on the sofa next to Billie. She removed the blanket and looked up for permission to lift her top. Billie nodded, and Zoe began to gently feel around her bump.

'My back hurts. I felt a bit sick at first.'

'That might well have been the shock. How about now? Better or still sick?'

'You *were* sick,' Alex reminded her from the doorway, where he leaned against the frame, hands in his pockets, watching them. He looked at Zoe. 'She threw up.'

'Shook you a bit, eh?' Zoe turned back to Billie. 'No bleeding, no other kind of discharge.'

'From down there?' She pointed.

'Yes,' Zoe said. 'You haven't been to the toilet since and noticed anything untoward?'

'I don't think so. I might have peed myself a bit.'

'Hardly surprising.' Zoe smiled. 'Sounds like quite a knock.'

Then, to her shock, Billie burst into tears. Zoe stroked her hair and murmured soothing phrases, but there was little else she could do. She glanced up to see Alex looking desperate, but he kept his distance, perhaps deciding that Zoe was dealing with the situation and his interference might only hinder her progress. But Billie's state told Zoe something more important. Whatever she might say, she cared about this baby.

She dug into her bag and pulled out a pack of paper handkerchiefs, offering one to Billie, who took it and did her best to regain control.

'It's a normal reaction,' Zoe said. 'Do baby's movements feel normal to you? About what you usually get?'

'I don't know,' Billie sniffed. 'I don't always notice how much he moves. I mean, I don't think I've felt anything, but I'm not sure.'

Zoe sat back and eyed her thoughtfully. 'I can't see anything to worry about...'

Alex spoke again. 'Should I phone for an ambulance to take her to the hospital anyway? Wouldn't it be better to have scans and heart monitors and whatever else?'

'You might be up there a long time,' Zoe said. 'Most falls don't do any real damage – a pregnant woman's body grows its own safeguards, and you'd be surprised how much it can withstand.'

'But there are times when they fail, right? It's not always OK?'

'True.' Zoe got up. 'If it helps to ease your mind, then I'll drive Billie over. I'll have a word with the on-call team there and see if they'll take a look.'

'Can you get my coat and shoes, Dad?' Billie asked.

Alex left them to do as she'd asked while Zoe helped Billie off the sofa. But as she stood, Zoe's eye caught a tiny patch of scarlet on the throw that had been beneath her.

Shit.

She turned to Billie and forced a bright smile. 'Don't panic, but you might notice there's a bit of spotting on the sofa where you've been sitting.'

Billie looked down, her eyes widening. 'Dad!' she cried. 'Hurry up! We've got to go!'

'It'll be fine,' Zoe said, hoping she sounded more confident than she felt. She couldn't lose another baby in her care, not this soon after Tegan.

Zoe had never been gladder to have her car with her. They were in luck with the roads too, which were empty and dry, and meant they reached the emergency team in a short-enough time to keep Billie calm. Alex sat with her on the back seat. Whenever Zoe caught a glimpse in the rear-view mirror, she could see Billie leaning into him, his arm wrapped around her shoulders. Every so often, he'd give her head a tiny kiss. They didn't often show it in front of Zoe – in front of anyone, really – but they were devoted to one another. It was hardly surprising, Zoe reflected as the beams of her headlights swept the silent road ahead; they were all each other had in the world. And when she thought about it that way, she understood more than ever

Alex's reaction to the news that Billie planned to give up her baby.

Zoe had given Alex the number of the team at the hospital, told him who he needed to speak to and to mention her name and why they were bringing Billie over, so that when they arrived, someone was standing by to examine Billie.

'Hi, Grace,' Zoe said as one of the on-call midwives came to speak to her. 'Do you need an extra pair of hands? I'm here; feel free to use me.'

'We've got it, Zoe. I've pulled her notes up from the system. So what exactly happened here?'

Zoe briefly went over the events since her arrival at Hilltop, and then the hospital midwife went to question Billie, who was now in a wheelchair, ready to go to a treatment room.

Alex stood at Zoe's side and watched. 'Be honest with me,' he said quietly. 'Is it bad?'

'I don't think so. There might be some placental abruption, but if it's small enough at this stage, they can fix it.'

'I have no clue what that means, but if you say it's going to be all right, then that's enough. And that's the truth?'

'That's all I can tell you, but I'm not glossing anything over, if that's what you mean. I'm not going to say nothing can go wrong, but I do think she and the baby are going to be fine.'

Grace came back to them. 'We're going to take Billie down,' she said. 'We might be a while. Are you going to wait?'

'Yes,' Alex said. He turned to Zoe. 'But we can find a way to get home when we're done, if you want to go.'

'I drove here,' Zoe clarified to Grace. 'But I'm going to stay for a while too. You might need me.'

'I don't think we will—' Grace began, but Zoe cut in.

'I'm going to stay anyway. I'd be happier here keeping an eye on things...' She gave her head the tiniest nod to indicate that she meant she intended to keep an eye on Alex specifically, and Grace's expression indicated that she understood.

'You might as well go to the canteen and get a drink then. I've got both your phone numbers, so I'll call when we have news. But don't worry,' she said to Alex. 'She's in the best place. If there's a problem, we'll sort it.'

'Thank you. I appreciate that.'

Grace left them and followed as a porter wheeled Billie away. She cast one last look at her dad that said so much more than words could. She trusted him, she loved him, he was the most important person in her life – that much was obvious. And she was scared too.

'I'll show you where the canteen is,' Zoe said. 'At least it'll be nice and quiet at this hour, but I think it might have to be vending-machine coffee.'

'You didn't have to do all this,' Alex said as he brought two plastic cups to the table where Zoe was waiting for him.

'I'd do the same for any of my mums.'

'Even when their dad has been unforgivably rude and unreasonable to you?' he asked.

Zoe gave him a half-smile. 'None of that is important now. Besides, it wasn't Billie's fault. Why would I take it out on her? Or the baby, for that matter.'

'For what it's worth,' he said, 'and I don't suppose it's much, I'm sorry for the way I spoke to you at the quincentenary. I had no right to blame you. You were right – you had Billie's interests at heart, and, in the end, she's the only person who matters. I'm not going to try and excuse it, but I wanted you to know it was never about you. I reacted badly, it was a shock and I couldn't stop thinking about what I'd already lost. The thought of losing my grandchild as well when we didn't even have to... It got to me, that's all. I can't explain, and I don't expect you to understand.'

'I think I do.' Zoe sipped at her coffee, wincing as it burned her lip. She put it down again. 'Have there been any more discussions about it since she told you?'

'The adoption, you mean?'

Zoe nodded.

'She won't talk about it. She says her mind's made up.'

Zoe wanted to say there was time for Billie to change her mind, but she didn't want to sow that hope into his heart. There was every chance she wouldn't change her mind, and she couldn't bear to be the person responsible for destroying him all over again. At least this way, if he thought it was always coming and Billie did change her mind later on, it would make him happy.

'You're a good person,' he said into the gap. 'I don't know if I could have been as big as you over all this, not after the way I treated you.'

'I told you – it's my job.'

'No, it's more than that. You could have told Billie to call these guys and they'd have sent an ambulance for her. But you came with us because you knew Billie needed a familiar face.'

'I think you might have done too,' Zoe said with a half-smile, one that he returned.

'OK, I think I did too. Probably more than Billie did. I won't forget this.' He paused, staring into his cup. 'The day before the quincentenary, when I asked you if you wanted to go for a drink... I suppose I've blown that now.'

'I wouldn't exactly put it like that, but in the circumstances, do you really think we can date?'

'No, I realise that. I didn't mean it that way. I know it's not the time to talk about it, but I hope it doesn't mean we can't still be friendly. We live next door, after all.'

'Next door and a few fields?'

'Exactly.'

'I was never planning on holding a grudge anyway.' Zoe's phone began to ring. She took the call and listened for a minute, nodding and agreeing every so often. And then she put her phone down and looked at an expectant Alex. 'They're going to keep Billie in for a couple of days. She's fine; they want to keep her under observation. There was a minor abruption – really minor – and if she rests, it should seal back up. You can go down to see her now if you want to.'

He heaved a deep sigh. 'Thank God! Yes, I'll go. Are you coming?'

'I'll only get in the way. I can wait here and give you a lift back to Hilltop if you like.'

'You don't want to see her?'

'Of course I do. But I don't think me being there is going to help right now. And I think you two might have a lot to talk about. If you want to be close at hand, you can stay for the night. They'd be able to sort that out for you.'

'I think I will,' he said, grasping both her hands in his and squeezing them. 'Thank you for everything. I don't know what we would have done without you.'

Zoe showed him the way to the ward where Billie was being kept. She watched him hurry in, wondering whether to go with him after all, but she decided that her initial reaction was the right one: this was a moment for just the two of them.

Deep in thought, she turned away and left them to it.

30

'You look shattered!' Ottilie cast a critical eye over Zoe as she walked into the surgery kitchen to put the bottle of milk she'd fetched in the fridge. Ottilie was making a tray of coffees. 'Here,' she said, handing one over. 'Better have yours black.'

'I'm fine, just had a late one.'

'Oh...?' Ottilie paused.

Zoe looked at her. 'What? What does that mean?'

'Nothing.'

'I wasn't partying, if that's what you mean. Billie Fitzgerald had a fall last night. I went over to see if she was all right and ended up having to drive her to the hospital.'

'Of course you had to go,' Ottilie said wryly. 'Couldn't possibly leave it to the people who were actually on shift.'

'A bit like you then,' Zoe fired back with a tired grin.

'Rumbled. Is she all right?'

'She's fine. They're keeping her in for a couple of days, but it will be all right. Alex stayed up there with her, so I came straight home, but it was still early hours by the time I got to sleep.'

'At least it wasn't anything to do with Ritchie. I thought he might have been hassling you again.'

'No, it wasn't. I haven't heard from him since he texted me about the house. Which reminds me, I still have that mess to sort out at some point, as if I don't have enough to do.'

'Just like Flo to get it wrong,' Ottilie continued as she stirred milk into the drinks. 'She came rushing round last night saying she'd seen his car going through the village. I don't know how she was so sure it was Ritchie's, but she was adamant. She said she'd seen him get back into it when he left the village celebrations. Said there was some sticker or other in the window she recognised. Honestly, that woman's life is an unrealised police career.'

'It's funny Flo should say that,' Zoe said slowly as she began to piece things together. 'Alex couldn't take Billie to the hospital last night because all his tyres had been let down. Deliberately. He thought it was something to do with a pissed-off villager, but...'

'You think it might have been Ritchie?'

'It's such a stupid, pointless, childish thing to do...'

'Sounds like him then.' Zoe frowned, and Ottilie shrugged. 'Come on – you're not still trying to pretend he's ever been anything but a spoiled kid in a man's body, surely? After the way he behaved last weekend? What are you going to do?'

'He'd only deny it if I spoke to him.'

'I'd scare him. Ask him if he did it and then go along with his answer, and lay it on thick that, because Alex's car was out of action, something really bad happened up there.'

'I couldn't do that.'

'Or tell him Alex is getting the police involved. Or setting up cameras or something.'

'I do need to talk to him,' Zoe said, wishing it weren't true. 'I've got to persuade him that he needs to be a grown-up about all this.'

Even as she tried to forget it, back in her room as she prepared for the first appointment of the day, her mind was constantly pulled back to Flo's report. The more she thought about it, the more she was convinced that Ritchie was responsible for the damage to Alex's tyres. She hated to admit it, but it was exactly the sort of thing he'd do.

To think she'd once loved him. Whatever affection she'd still had, even after their split, was fast draining away, and it was mostly down to his recent actions. Perhaps it was better to confront him. He'd deny it, of course, but he'd know she was on to him, and perhaps that would be enough to make him think twice the next time he felt like causing mischief.

She checked the clock. She had a couple of minutes until her first mum. And so she sent him a text.

I know what you're up to, and it's out of order. Stop it.

And then she put her phone into the desk drawer and left it at that.

She didn't check her phone again until lunchtime. As predicted, there was a reply from Ritchie denying everything. There was also a text message from Alex, updating her on Billie's progress, though Zoe already knew about that because she'd spoken to a member of the hospital team during a gap in her clinic. It was hard to read emotions from the words of a brief text, but he seemed much happier. Things were going well and they hoped to have her home the following day. She sent him a reply saying she was glad and that she'd visit Billie as soon as she was back at Hilltop. Then she cleared down and made her way to the kitchen to join the rest of the surgery staff for their communal lunch.

'Well?' Ottilie asked as Zoe sat next to her. 'Any developments?'

'You mean Ritchie?'

Lavender turned from the worktop where she was slicing bread. 'Your ex? Has something happened? Is this to do with him turning up at the quincentenary? Are you back together? What happened after you went home?'

'Steady on, Lavender,' Fliss said mildly as she ladled out chicken stew. 'I'm sure if Zoe has something to tell us, she'll tell us.' She turned to Zoe. 'You'd better tell us, or she'll blow a fuse!'

Zoe couldn't help but laugh. 'There's nothing to tell. I've come to the conclusion that it will be a cold day in hell before we get back together, so that's something. Other than that, nothing much.'

'How disappointing,' Fliss huffed and went back to serving up.

'I don't know how you're going to cope with retirement,' Simon said. He handed a glass of water to Zoe and Ottilie in turn. 'You'll die of boredom without a dose of daily drama in here.'

'I'll cope – you watch me. Anyway, I'm expecting detailed reports. Don't forget, I'll still have sway around here, even if I've finished working. If I don't get my fix, I'll get you all fired.'

'How's Billie?' Ottilie asked as the rest of them continued to banter about the probabilities of Fliss retaining enough influence once she'd retired to get them all sacked.

'Good. The bed rest is doing the trick. I knew it would.'

'Did you?' Ottilie raised her eyebrows, and Zoe smiled.

'I hoped so. We all get a confidence knock once in a while, don't we? I hope Tegan Forrester will be the only one for this year because one is more than enough. Though I can't help thinking that I almost missed Billie as well. It was only when

Alex told me he'd feel better if we took her in that I saw the blood...'

'You'd have caught it one way or another,' Ottilie said. 'If I know anything about you, I know that. And you did take her in, and all's well.'

'I suppose so,' Zoe said quietly. 'I suppose so.'

After three days in hospital, during which time Zoe had received regular updates, Billie was allowed home. Corrine called at Kestrel Cottage that evening with two casserole dishes in a covered basket and a tin of cake.

'I made you some stew,' she said, handing one of the dishes to Zoe. It was still warm.

'Smells lovely, thank you.'

'Steak with a drop of Guinness. I made some for Billie and Alex too. Billie will be able to eat it, won't she? There's not much Guinness in there.'

'I'm sure it'll be fine. They'll be glad of the help – I bet they don't feel like cooking after the few days they've had.'

'And I made coconut sponge,' Corrine said, getting out another package. 'This is yours.'

'Thank you – that smells amazing! Do you want to come in?'

'I'll dash up there and then dash home, if it's all the same to you. We've got the vet coming.'

'Oh... everything's all right?'

'Alice is a bit under the weather. I don't think it's anything serious, but Victor might need my help. You could come over to Hilltop with me, if you like.'

Zoe shook her head. Much as she might like to, she still didn't really know where she stood with them. Alex had spoken warmly about how good she was, how they didn't deserve her, how he wanted to go back to them being good neighbours, but that was all in the heat of the moment. There was still a huge shadow hanging over their friendship – and she was resigned to the fact that friendship was all they could ever have now – and that was Billie's adoption plan. Alex had said he didn't blame Zoe for it now, but she wasn't convinced of that. As the pregnancy progressed and the day drew closer, would his attitude harden again, looking for someone to blame, a way to vent his frustration? She didn't want that person to be her.

'I'm a bit tired. I'll go up over the weekend. Thanks again for the goodies.'

'You're more than welcome, my love.'

Once Zoe had seen her off, she took her food into the kitchen. While the oven warmed to reheat her casserole, she went through the emails on her phone. There was one from a financial adviser she'd reached out to, detailing some ways she might be able to sort her affairs, and she pored over that for a while, doing some sums of her own as she went through it. It was encouraging that things might not be as complicated as she'd feared. If Ritchie wanted to do this, then perhaps the best thing now was get on with it and cut ties after all. Having him in her life was causing more problems than it fixed, and was she really better off for it?

Are you busy this evening?

Zoe was loading the dishwasher when the text came through.

Not especially. Everything all right?

All fine, yes. A bit out of the blue, I know, but do you mind if I come over for an hour?

Of course not!

Wondering what Alex might want, and with her tummy doing odd little flips, she went to freshen up and change into something nicer. It might have occurred to her to wonder why she felt the need to do that, but it didn't, and when he arrived on her doorstep with a large bouquet, she was glad she'd made the effort.

'More flowers, I'm afraid,' he said. 'Sorry, a bit unimaginative.'

'They're lovely,' Zoe said. 'Thank you. What are they for?'

'For being there when we needed you,' he said. 'And if you feel the urge to toss them onto the floor behind your front door, I won't watch.'

Zoe paused and then laughed, flushing as she did. 'Oh God! I forgot about... I'm sorry about that. I felt terrible, but I wasn't sure you'd seen... I have absolutely no intention of throwing these anywhere. Do you want to come in for a minute? How's Billie?'

'She's taking a nap, but she's fine, a lot better. I've left Griz on guard duty. How are you?'

'Me?' Zoe stepped back to let him in. 'I'm fine. Same as always. Do you want a drink of anything?'

'I'm good, thanks. I won't stay too long; I know it's late.'

'It's not that bad. I wouldn't be going to bed for ages yet,' she said, and it was a lie, but only a little one to make him feel better.

'Even so. I wasn't sure I'd be welcome here,' he said as she led him to the living room and offered him a seat.

'Why not? I thought we'd sorted all that out.'

'I know, but smoothing it over is one thing, being in your home is another. I wouldn't have blamed you for not inviting me in. I wanted to say again how sorry I am. You must think I'm an absolute tool.'

'That's one way of putting it,' Zoe said as she took a seat on the sofa.

'So you do? That's fair enough.'

'I did, but only for about ten minutes. I realised you acted the way you did because you really care about Billie.'

'I do – she's everything to me. But I'm beginning to care almost as much about what you think of me.' He dragged in a deep breath and seemed to steel himself. 'Zoe...' he continued after a pause that seemed to last a lifetime, 'is there any way we can start over? Can you forget that I was that man and give me another chance?'

'To do what? We're fine now, aren't we?'

'No,' he said, and there was a sudden intensity in his eyes that sent her heart rate soaring. 'I mean, yes, we're fine, but we're not what I hoped we could be. You must know how much I like you.'

'I'll admit,' she said, her heart still thumping despite her efforts to play it cool. 'You were giving mixed signals not so long ago.'

'Not in the beginning. I think you might have felt the same. I hoped you did.'

'We can't, Alex. Not after all that was said. What about Billie? Nothing has changed there. She's still going to have the baby adopted, and you still think that's my fault.'

'I don't! I lashed out, I know, but I don't think that. Of course you'd talk about it because she asked you to.'

Zoe shook her head. 'I'll always feel as if that's there, in the background. And when the day comes and she gives her baby up—'

'*If*...'

'Right now, we have to assume it's a when. *When* the day comes, how will you feel about me then? When the thing you hate most in the world happens, what then? Will you look at me and think I'm the cause?'

'I can't deny that I don't want it to happen. But the last few days have made me realise that it's about Billie, not me. She's my daughter, and I have to support her whatever she does, however I feel about it, because she's my priority. I know that in the end you were doing the same. That night when you took us to the hospital and you were so kind and so patient with us both, even though we didn't deserve it, it made me realise what I'd done to you, and that I'd love to have a person like you in my life – in our lives, mine and Billie's. You have every right to say no, and you probably will, but if you still, on any level, want to go for that drink, I'd love it.'

He ran a hand through his thick hair as he watched her closely, waiting for her answer.

'I don't know,' she said. 'I want to, but...'

He nodded, seemingly shrinking before her eyes. 'Of course. I'd probably say the same. But we can still be friends, I hope. That would mean a lot to me.'

She paused, her mind racing. She wanted to say yes, but she was afraid.

The sound of a text notification broke the silence.

'I think that's your phone,' she said.

'It can wait—'

'It might be Billie,' she reminded him. 'Maybe get it now. At least that way, if there's a problem, I can come over to Hilltop with you.'

He nodded and then gave a wan smile as he read the message. 'It is Billie,' he said, 'but it's nothing to worry about.' He tapped out a one-word reply.

A second later, Zoe's phone sounded the arrival of a message.

'It'll be Billie,' he said, 'Don't worry about getting it now.'

Zoe frowned. 'Why not? If it's Billie, then I ought to...' She got up and went to fetch her phone from the kitchen. On the way back, she opened up the message.

Why won't you say yes?

Alex was texting when she walked into the living room, and Zoe wondered if he was trying to intercept whatever Billie was up to.

'I take it Billie knew you were going to ask me out again?'

'I'm sorry, she asked me where we were at, and I might have said something about wanting to, and she's been waiting to hear.'

'Hmm.' Zoe studied him for a moment. 'You two really are a package deal, aren't you?' she said with a wry smile. 'Do you tell one another everything?'

'Not everything. I'm sorry. I didn't know what to do, and I ended up blabbing it all out to her.'

'And she said you should come over?'

'She said I was an idiot if I didn't. I mean, I can't argue with that, can I? And I wanted to anyway, before you think this is all Billie's doing. I wanted to come and see you, but I wasn't sure how I'd be received.'

He looked up at her with those sweet brown eyes that were like a warm embrace, and that thick hair, messed up from where his hands had pushed through it. Those lips that she'd thought about kissing so many times since she'd met him. He was a good man – she knew that. Everything he did was to make those around him happy, and even when he got it wrong, his intentions had been right. And the way he cared for Billie... would it be so bad to have someone like him care for her even half of that? It was more than Ritchie had ever done, and didn't she deserve it? She could take a chance, and she could do worse than taking a chance on a man like Alex Fitzgerald.

She unlocked her phone and began to type, a quiet smile lighting her face.

'What are you doing?' he asked.

'I'm messaging your daughter.'

'Oh God, don't blame her for this. It wasn't her fault; she was only trying to—'

'I'm telling her that the answer is yes because she seems more invested than we are.'

Zoe pressed send and looked up to see him frowning slightly.

'You are?'

'I am. Yes, I will go out for a drink with you. And maybe there will be more drinks after that, and even some kissing.'

'I can do kissing. I'm a bit rusty, but...'

'Me too. We can brush up our kissing together.'

'I'd love that,' he said, breaking into a lopsided grin that was at once nervous and sexy. 'When? When do you want to go for our drink? I'm free the rest of this week.'

'Have you got time now? You could stay for an hour after all – I think we've waited long enough, don't you?'

'I do,' he said. 'I haven't brought anything with me, though.'

'I don't have anything in either. I suppose that's the drink bit scuppered then. We'll have to go straight to the kissing instead.'

He laughed loudly, and then stopped and stared at her when she didn't laugh but sat close to him. 'Oh God, you meant it!'

'Yeah, I meant it,' she said before leaning in to touch her lips to his, her pulse suddenly racing and every nerve end on fire. And as they drew one another in, she decided that his kissing technique was really rather good after all.

EPILOGUE

Two weeks later...

To spare everyone's blushes, they did most of their kissing at Zoe's house. Though it had spilled out, on occasion, to a local pub or a lakeside vantage point, in his car, in her car... and even the fields where Alex was excavating.

While they'd been upfront and honest with Billie – whose pregnancy was now back on track, her scare becoming an unpleasant memory – about their new relationship, Zoe and Alex hadn't wanted to announce it to the rest of Thimblebury until they'd been sure about it themselves. Which was odd, when Zoe reflected on that decision, because if the amount of kissing was anything to go by, there had never been a more certain thing than their new relationship. She'd felt like a teenager again, sneaking around and revelling in the mischief.

People had their own suspicions, of course, and it was hard for Zoe to hide her new joy in every morning. Ottilie had worked it out, and Zoe had asked her to keep it quiet for the time being, and while Fliss and Lavender hadn't come to such a solid conclusion, they'd dropped enough hints for Zoe to know they'd figure it out soon enough. Simon, of course, was oblivious, caught up in plans for Fliss's replacement and for the surgery as a whole once she left them.

They finally decided to let the secret out when their hand had been forced anyway. In the end, Zoe hadn't cared that Victor had seen them kissing at her gate one morning – the morning after the night Alex had first stayed over. He'd only grinned and called a cheery greeting, but must have rushed off to tell Corrine because that night after work, Corrine was waiting at her front door with a tin full of cake and a head full of questions.

Zoe pretended not to suspect anything as she opened the gate. 'I suppose this visit has nothing to do with Victor seeing me and Alex this morning?'

'Whatever do you mean?' Corrine asked with almost cartoon innocence. 'I only came to chat. I can come back if you're tired, of course...'

'No, I'm not too tired.' Zoe nodded at the floral tin in Corrine's arms. 'I take it that's cake?'

'Victoria sponge. Fresh cream, of course, home-made jam...'

'As if I could say no to that, even if I was tired! Come on.' Zoe unlocked the front door. 'I'll get the kettle on.'

Zoe filled the kettle and switched it on to boil, and then ran upstairs to quickly change out of her uniform, leaving Corrine in the kitchen to fetch cups and plates. And when she came back down, the table was already laid out and the tea was brewing and Corrine was waiting expectantly on a chair.

She was about to speak when there was a knock at the door. Zoe frowned slightly. She'd arranged to meet Alex but not until much later that evening. They'd met almost every evening since they'd got together, neither able to stay away for long.

'I'm so sorry, love,' Corrine said. 'I should have realised you might be expecting company. You should have said; I'd have come back another time.'

'I'm not,' Zoe said. 'Hang on. I'll just go and...'

She went to get the door and found a sheepish-looking Victor on the doorstep.

'All right there, flower? I thought I'd come and have a look at the hinges on your back door. Squeaking, aren't they?'

'Are they?' Zoe asked with a wry smile. 'I'm sure I haven't noticed.'

'I'd best come in and have a look, while I'm here...'

Zoe ushered him in, her smile spreading as she gestured for him to go into the kitchen and then heard the utter surprise in the exchange between him and Corrine.

'What are you doing here?' she asked sharply.

'I could ask you the same thing,' Victor grumbled. 'Didn't we say...' He glanced at Zoe and lowered his voice. 'Didn't we say we ought to leave it be?'

'So what have you come over for?' Corrine asked.

'To look at the back door. Hinges are squeaking.'

'I've never heard such a flimsy excuse in my life!' Corrine exclaimed.

'All right then,' Victor fired back. 'What have you come over for?'

'Bringing a cake, aren't I?'

Zoe burst out laughing as she followed him in. It was obvious now why they'd both come, and they'd clearly had a discussion where they'd both agreed to stay away. So much for love, honour and obey... it was more like love, honour and ignore.

'Is this to do with what you saw this morning, Victor?' she asked once she'd managed to stop laughing, the sight of them both staring at her in confusion almost enough to set her off again.

'I didn't see anything,' Victor said, though what she could see of his face beneath his bushy beard and hair was bright red.

'Yes,' Zoe said. 'You can stop denying it because I might as well come clean: Alex and I are seeing each other.'

Corrine clapped her hands to her chest and almost leaped from her chair. 'How lovely! We said so, Victor, didn't we? We said what a good match it would be! And then you saw them this morning and—'

'I thought you said you hadn't seen anything this morning...' Zoe said to Victor with mock suspicion, and if it was possible for him to get any redder, she was sure that he did.

'I didn't want to... well, I didn't want you to be embarrassed.'

'Don't worry, I'm not.' Zoe went to get another cup and plate from the cupboard. 'Never mind the back door and your fictitious squeak for now,' she said. 'Come and join us for tea and cake.'

Victor took off his hat and shuffled to take a seat while Zoe poured the tea.

'When did this all start?' Corrine asked, all pretence at disinterest abandoned.

'We've been dating for about two weeks.'

'And it's going well?'

'I think so.'

'He's lovely,' Corrine gushed. 'I'm so happy for your both.'

'Well,' Zoe said as she handed some tea to Victor, 'it's early days yet, so...'

'You can just tell with some people,' Corrine insisted. 'Can't you, Victor? We said so, didn't we? We said what a good match from the minute we saw you talking to one another. I always get a feeling for these things, you know. Don't worry, we'll keep your secret if you don't want anyone in the village knowing about it.'

'I'll see what Alex says, but I think we've both realised we're not going to be able to keep it to ourselves for much longer. And if I'm honest...' She paused, her mind on Alex for a moment. She thought about those soft brown eyes, that mop of hair that never seemed to behave itself, about his broad shoulders and dependable arms, where she felt safer than she'd ever felt. About his gentle concern and his silly jokes, and she wondered why she'd felt the need to keep what they had secret at all. It was early days, but she was beginning to see she'd never felt surer of anyone in her life. Not only did she feel certain of what they had, but she was proud. She was proud of him, of the man he was, and proud to be with him. Why wouldn't she want to shout that from the rooftops? What was more amazing was that, instinctively, she knew he felt the same, a certainty she'd never had with any other man.

'I *really* like him,' she said, unable to stop the huge soppy smile from spreading across her face as if it might burst free. 'He makes me feel like...' She shook herself. 'See, listen to me. You don't need to know this.'

'We do!' Victor said, folding his arms and leaning forward with such eagerness that he looked more like Corrine waiting for a titbit of gossip than Corrine did.

'No, we don't!' Corrine chastised him. 'I'm sure we'll hear all about it when Zoe and Alex are ready. Drink your tea, you great hairy idiot!'

Zoe started to laugh again. Until very recently, she'd never been quite convinced that the move to Kestrel Cottage had been the right one. She'd loved the area and she'd settled in to her job, but there had always been something missing. And even when she'd got together with Alex it still wasn't quite clear. But sitting here now, with the two loveliest neighbours a woman could have, with good strong tea in the pot and a mouth-watering cake, surrounded by the rolling hills and open fields of their land, knowing how they and everyone else was on her side, cheering her on, willing her happiness, she suddenly saw it. Of course it had been the right move. It was almost as if everything in her life, the good, the bad, even the difficult and devastating moments, had led her here, to where she was meant to be.

The past year had been hard, but Zoe had high hopes that things were about to change for the better.

A LETTER FROM TILLY

I want to say a huge thank you for choosing to read *The Village Midwife*. If you did enjoy it, and want to keep up to date with all my latest releases, just sign up at the following link. Your email address will never be shared, and you can unsubscribe at any time.

www.bookouture.com/tilly-tennant

I hope you enjoyed *The Village Midwife,* and if you did I would be very grateful if you could write a review. I'd love to hear what you think, and it makes such a difference helping new readers to discover one of my books for the first time.

I love hearing from my readers – you can get in touch on my Facebook page or my website.

Thank you!

Tilly

https://tillytennant.com

facebook.com/TillyTennant

ACKNOWLEDGEMENTS

I say this every time I come to write acknowledgements for a new book, but it's true: the list of people who have offered help and encouragement on my writing journey so far really is endless, and it would take a novel in itself to mention them all. I'd try to list everyone here, regardless, but I know that I'd fail miserably and miss out someone who is really very important. I just want to say that my heartfelt gratitude goes out to each and every one of you, whose involvement, whether small or large, has been invaluable and appreciated more than I can express.

I don't usually go into the specifics of how I write my books at this point. I rightly or wrongly assume that most people are more interested in the end result than the process, but this time I'd like to say a few things about the research for *The Village Midwife*. Having worked alongside nurses, healthcare workers, midwives and many other amazing health professionals during my ten years as an NHS employee, I'm forced to acknowledge here that there is a lot more protocol and many more rules and regulations than my stories might have you believe. I know that many things are not as straightforward in real life as they are in my books, but I also ask for a little forgiveness for my creative licence. My aim is to tell a tale unhindered by such boring things as paperwork, public health directives, shift patterns, uniform complexities, recruitment processes and a million other issues. So, while I know these things exist, sometimes I choose to gloss over them for the sake of the plot. For anyone well acquainted with the workings of our healthcare system, I hope you won't be too cross with me!

With that out of the way, back to the thank yous! It goes without saying that I have to highlight the remarkable team at Bookouture for their continued support, patience and amazing publishing flair, particularly Lydia Vassar-Smith – my incredible and long-suffering editor – Kim Nash, Noelle Holten, Sarah Hardy, Peta Nightingale, Mandy Kullar, Lizzie Brien, Alex Crow, Occy Carr and Alba Proko. A special thanks also goes to Ruth Jones, who came onboard for this book with a brilliant raft of editing suggestions and was an absolute joy to work with. I know I'll have forgotten many others at Bookouture who I ought to be thanking, but I hope they'll forgive me. Their belief, able assistance and encouragement mean the world to me. I truly believe I have the best team an author could ask for. Signing with them changed my life, and I don't think I'll ever be able to thank them enough for taking a chance on a daft little woman from Staffordshire.

My friend, Kath Hickton, always gets an honourable mention for putting up with me since primary school, and Louise Coquio deserves a medal for getting me through university and suffering me ever since, likewise her lovely family.

I also have to thank Mel Sherratt, who is as generous with her time and advice as she is talented, someone who is always there to cheer on her fellow authors. She did so much to help me in the early days of my career that I don't think I'll ever be able to thank her as much as she deserves.

My fellow Bookouture authors are all incredible, of course, unfailing and generous in their support of colleagues – life would be a lot duller without the gang!

I'd also like to give a special shout-out to Jaimie Admans, who is not only a brilliant author but is a brilliant friend. There's also an honourable mention for my retreat gang: Debbie, Jo, Tracy, Helen and Julie. I live for our weeks locked away in some remote house, writing, chatting, drinking and generally being daft. You are the most brilliant women, and my life is better for knowing you all.

I have to thank all the incredible and dedicated book bloggers (there are so many of you, but you know who you are!) and readers, and anyone else who has championed my work, reviewed it, shared it or simply told me that they liked it. Every one of those actions is priceless, and you are all very special people. Some of you I am even proud to call friends now – and I'm looking at you in particular, Kerry Ann Parsons and Steph Lawrence!

Last but not least, I'd like to give a special mention to my lovely agent Hannah Todd and the team at Janklow and Nesbit. I'm so lucky to have an agent who not only champions my books but is also hard-working and absolutely brilliant fun!

I have to admit I have a love-hate relationship with my writing. It can be frustrating at times, isolating and thankless, but at the same time I feel like the luckiest woman alive to be doing what I do, and I can't imagine earning my living any other way. It also goes without saying that my family and friends understand better than anyone how much I need space to write, and they love me enough to enable it, even when it puts them out. I have no words to express fully how grateful and blessed that makes me feel.

And before I go, thank you, dear reader. Without you, I wouldn't be writing this, and you have no idea how happy it makes me that I am.

PUBLISHING TEAM

Turning a manuscript into a book requires the efforts of many people. The publishing team at Bookouture would like to acknowledge everyone who contributed to this publication.

Audio
Alba Proko
Sinead O'Connor
Melissa Tran

Commercial
Lauren Morrissette
Hannah Richmond
Imogen Allport

Contracts
Peta Nightingale

Cover design
Debbie Clement

Data and analysis
Mark Alder
Mohamed Bussuri

Editorial
Lydia Vassar-Smith
Imogen Allport

Copyeditor
Anne O'Brien

Proofreader
Laura Kincaid

Marketing
Alex Crow
Melanie Price
Occy Carr
Cíara Rosney
Martyna Młynarska

Operations and distribution
Marina Valles
Stephanie Straub
Joe Morris

Production
Hannah Snetsinger
Mandy Kullar
Ria Clare
Nadia Michael

Publicity
Kim Nash
Noelle Holten
Jess Readett
Sarah Hardy

RAISING READERS
Books Build Bright Futures

Dear Reader,

We'd love your attention for one more page to tell you about the crisis in children's reading, and what we can all do.

Studies have shown that reading for fun is the **single biggest predictor of a child's future success** – more than family circumstance, parents' educational background or income. It improves academic results, mental health, wealth, communication skills, and ambition.

The number of children reading for fun is in rapid decline. Young people have a lot of competition for their time, and a worryingly high number do not have a single book at home.

Our business works extensively with schools, libraries and literacy charities, but here are some ways we can all raise more readers:

- Reading to children for just 10 minutes a day makes a difference
- Don't give up if children aren't regular readers – there will be books for them!

- Visit bookshops and libraries to get recommendations
- Encourage them to listen to audiobooks
- Support school libraries
- Give books as gifts

Thank you for reading: there's a lot more information about how to encourage children to read on our website.

www.JoinRaisingReaders.com

www.ingramcontent.com/pod-product-compliance
Ingram Content Group UK Ltd.
Pitfield, Milton Keynes, MK11 3LW, UK
UKHW041434070725
6768UKWH00004B/183